The Magic of Pemberley

A PRIDE & PREJUDICE VARIATION

ABIGAIL REYNOLDS

WHITE SOUP PRESS

Contents

Cast of Characters

At Pemberley

Fitzwilliam Darcy – A landed Talent and mage, preparing for a dangerous mission to France

Elizabeth Darcy – his wife, dragon companion to Cerridwen

Lady Amelia Morgan (Granny) – Elizabeth's great-grandmother from Wales, a mage and dragon companion to Sycamore

Mr. Roderick (Roderick ap Rhodri) – a mage from Wales, Elizabeth's childhood friend, descended from ancient Welsh princes

Lady Frederica Fitzwilliam – Darcy's cousin and daughter of the Earl of Matlock, apprentice to the King's Mage

Georgiana Darcy – Darcy's sister, age sixteen

Belinda Lowrie – Georgiana's friend and companion

Chandrika – Elizabeth's maid from India, previously in service to Rana Akshaya

Mrs. Reynolds – the housekeeper

Hobbes – the butler

Mrs. Charlotte Sanford – midwife and Darcy's illegitimate half-sister

Jack Darcy (deceased) – Darcy's beloved younger brother who was killed in a dragon attack

Cerridwen – Elizabeth's young dragon, with the gift of far-sight, who frequently takes the shape of a kestrel

Sycamore – Granny's dragon

At the Dark Peak Nest

Rowan – a young dragon who has been helpful to Elizabeth and Roderick

Quickthorn – an irritable young dragon

The Eldest – a mature dragon who is responsible for the Nest

Juniper – a dragon poet

Hawthorn – a dragon sculptor

Agate – a young dragon nestling

Elsewhere in England

Lady Anne Darcy – Darcy's mother and the King's Mage

Rana Akshaya – a mage from India

Colonel Richard Fitzwilliam – Darcy's cousin, son of the Earl of Matlock and Lady Frederica's brother

Jasper Fitzwilliam – the youngest son of the Earl of Matlock

Lady Catherine de Bourgh – Lady Anne's sister

Anne de Bourgh (deceased) – Lady Catherine's daughter and Darcy's first wife

Mary and Kitty Bennet – Elizabeth's sisters, in London studying with Lady Anne Darcy

Jane Bingley – Elizabeth's eldest sister, married to Mr. Bingley

Charles Bingley – former librarian to the King's Mage, Darcy's friend, married to Jane Bennet

Mr. Bennet – Elizabeth's father, secretly a mage

Mrs. Bennet – Elizabeth's mother

Lydia Bennet – Elizabeth's youngest sister, still living at home

In France

The Duc de Velaudin – a former close ally of Napoleon who planned the assassination

Napoleon, Emperor of the French

Mme. Hartung, a Prussian exile

Mme. Laurent, her cook

Kapitan Kupillas, her cousin, a Prussian soldier

Coquelicot, a healer dragon in the Vosges Nest

Chapter 1

T HE LAKE REFLECTED PEMBERLEY's manor house perfectly. It was a serene sight, at least until a dozen riderless horses came racing around it, headed directly towards their small party.

Elizabeth Darcy caught her breath, but not in fear. What a vast improvement this illusion was over her husband's early attempts at horses! Roderick was right; something had fundamentally changed in Darcy's ability to cast. And just in time, since all too soon everything would depend upon his illusions – including his life.

Granny eyed the horses critically. "Not bad," she said. "Still, they could be better. Come here, young man."

Darcy pursed his lips to dismiss the illusion, and the horses vanished. His clenched jaw hinted at his displeasure over Granny's reaction, but he approached her chair. "As you wish, Lady Amelia."

"Someday I will convince you to call me Granny," the old lady grumbled, which elicited a small smile from Darcy. "But not today. Lean down, so I can speak in your ear." When he obeyed, she cupped her hand so Elizabeth could not even see her lips move.

What was she telling Darcy that was such a secret?

Darcy straightened abruptly, his cheeks staining with red. "Madam!" His exclamation was a reproach.

Now Elizabeth's curiosity was racing faster than the horses. Her husband almost never blushed.

"Oh, hush," Granny said irritably. "Half a million English soldiers dead in Europe, and you are worried about your fine manners? This will help you stop Napoleon. And for some reason, my great-grand-daughter wants you to come back to her alive afterwards, so pray do as I say."

His color still high, Darcy glared at her, but then he closed his eyes in an obvious attempt to master himself. "Kindly give me a moment," he said in a clipped voice.

"Take as much time as you need," said Granny expansively, her lips twitching.

What in the world was going on? But then Darcy turned to her, his expression unreadable. No, not unreadable – she would know perfectly well how to interpret it if they were alone in a bedroom, but what did it mean here when his eyes turned smoky and his gaze burrowed deep within her? Now it was her cheeks that were growing hot.

Then he flicked his wrist, the way he always did when casting an illusion, but without looking away from her. And she was just as caught as he was, desire rising in a hot current and prickling at her skin.

"Much better!" crowed Granny. "Look at that!"

Her words broke into the odd tension between them, and then Elizabeth gasped. The horses were back, but this time they were charging uncontrollably, not merely running. One tossed its head as if maddened, and steam rose from the nostrils of another. The very sight of them made her heart pound.

Darcy's mouth hung open, as if stunned by the illusion he had created. He moved his hand again, and the rampaging herd veered off to circle the lake. "Roderick never mentioned that technique." His voice was half-strangled, half-accusatory.

Granny sniffed. "It is useless to anyone who cannot entwine their magic with a dragon companion, which means almost everyone. My late husband chose not to share with others that small detail of how he re-learned to use his Talent after marrying me. At least Roderick knew to teach you the basic method."

It was a good reminder for Elizabeth. Darcy would be the one facing the desperate dangers in France, but her abilities as a dragon companion could help him succeed. And perhaps even survive.

He frowned. "This is not a good time for me to start my training anew, but I cannot deny it is effective." He looked at Elizabeth, his eyes drifting down her body in a way that hardly seemed appropriate in public, and then he cast again.

There were no horses this time. He must have created some sort of illusion, though. Elizabeth searched the scene before her. A kestrel circled above them, but that had to be real, since she could feel Cerridwen's unmistakable presence in the back of her mind. Had those two swans on the lake been there before? Elizabeth could make out their wake rippling through the water, and an illusion of moving water was far beyond Darcy's abilities – or so she had thought.

"Surely those swans are not yours?" she asked hesitantly.

Darcy rubbed his hand over his mouth. "I thought it would not work."

Whatever this new technique was, Elizabeth wanted to learn it. But then Cerridwen stole her attention away, plummeting towards her in a steep dive. A moment later the bird landed in front of her and transformed into her beloved dragon.

It still hardly seemed possible, that her magical falcon had turned out to be a dragon! It was good to see her, too. Since Granny had lifted the years-long Silence that barred Cerridwen from the company of other dragons, Cerridwen had spent every waking moment among her fellows at the nearby Nest.

Elizabeth laid her hand on Cerridwen's chest, letting the heat and powerful magic in the lustrous blue and bronze scales warm her, and spoke to her silently. *I had not expected to see you so early, dearest.*

Cerridwen's aura spilled grumpiness. *All the dragons are upset about something, and they will not tell me what. They say I am not one of them yet.*

Poor Cerridwen! She had been so glad to finally be with dragons again, after giving them up to stay with Elizabeth, and now this. Had she done something to upset them?

Although Elizabeth had not meant to send that, Cerridwen often picked up on her unspoken thoughts. *No, they say it has nothing to do with me. But I do not like secrets.* If Cerridwen had been human, she would have been pouting.

Elizabeth put her arm over the dragon's shoulders affectionately. *Neither do I, and I am glad you came here instead. I will always tell you anything you ask.*

Darcy studied the swans in shock. How could they possibly have turned out so well? It was a powerful tool that Lady Amelia had taught him, as shockingly improper as it might be. The question was how best to use it.

His thoughts were interrupted by the sound of hoofbeats and wheels on gravel. Real ones, not illusory this time. He shaded his eyes with his hand to see a carriage was coming up the drive, the top loaded with trunks and packages, as if the occupant planned on an extended stay. Could Elizabeth have invited someone without telling him? Then the answer struck him.

How could he have forgotten? It had not even been a fortnight since he had called on his sister in London and insisted she visit Pemberley. But then he had come home to the discovery that there were dragons in England, like the murderous ones who had killed his brother Jack in Spain. And one of them was in his own drawing room, bonded to his wife. Everything else, including Georgiana's arrival, had flown completely out of his head.

Now she was here, and he had not even warned Elizabeth, much less the staff.

The driver of her coach was staring at him in absolute horror. Or, more specifically, at the dragon just a few feet away.

With a quick excuse to Lady Amelia, he set off for the coach at a run. He had to get there before Georgiana spotted Cerridwen.

His sister was already stepping down from the carriage by the time he arrived, her face wreathed in smiles as he came into view. She threw her arms around him, burying her face in his chest, as if she still feared she might never see him again. Just as she did after every separation, no matter how short.

Darcy hugged her. "I hope your journey was easy." Especially as the situation was about to get complicated. She would not take it well that he had forgotten about her arrival.

"There were no problems," she said softly. "It is good to see you."

"I am glad you are here," he said, a slight prevarication, but well meant. "I have a great deal to tell you about."

She stepped back, straightening her bonnet. Her gaze drifted past him to the figures by the lake. "I am sorry. I did not mean to take you from your company." Then her eyes widened, and she gave a little shriek. She must have seen the dragon. Why had he not spoken faster? He caught her arm. "All is well," he said soothingly. "I know it is a shock, but I can explain."

She pulled away from him. "I want to go back to London. This instant!" And before he could stop her, she pushed past her companion and hurried back into her carriage.

Damnation. This was worse than he had thought. He clambered in after her. "Georgiana, listen to me. There is nothing to fear. Cerridwen – that dragon – is kind-hearted and gentle. She will not hurt you."

"But what if she can *tell*?" his sister whispered.

Not this again! "No one has ever been able to do so before. Why should this be any different?"

She curled herself into a ball on the bench, her knuckles white. "Because they are…" She took a deep breath. "In the old stories, dragons could always discover people's secrets."

This was difficult. "I am not an expert on dragons." To say the very least! But he could hardly reassure her that Cerridwen would not touch her mind, when he knew full well that Georgiana would be bound against revealing the presence of the dragons. Lady Amelia's dragon, who was to arrive the next day, might not prove as trustworthy as Cerridwen. "But I think it perfectly safe."

"I do not want that dragon to see me," she begged. "May I not simply return to Town?"

"But you just arrived. Would you not like a little time together first? And I would dearly love for you to meet my wife." How would he explain it to Elizabeth if Georgiana left without a word to her?

"I would not have come at all if I had known!" she cried. "Of course I want to see you, but not like this. And you have *guests*." She said it as if he had invited horrific monsters.

"Only Elizabeth's great-grandmother from Wales, and her friend Roderick, who is training me in illusion-casting." This was not the moment to bring up that Lady Amelia was a Fitzwilliam by birth. "And Cousin Frederica, who is staying at the Dower House, since her Talent does not allow her to be close to me. You need not spend time with any of them if you do not wish it." It might in fact be easier if Georgiana kept to herself, away from the constant discussions of dragons, Nests, and defenses against Napoleon.

"Can I remain in my room? And would you ask the dragon to keep away from me?" Tears began to run down her cheeks.

He could not bear it when Georgiana cried. Perhaps if he gave her a little time, she might realize the dragons would have no interest in her. "I will ask Cerridwen to keep her distance from you. She is hardly ever here these days, in any case."

"Thank you," she whispered. "I am sorry to be such trouble."

He took her hand and held it, wishing he could soothe her anxieties. But that seemed like a hopeless task.

Elizabeth watched with amusement as Lady Frederica Fitzwilliam, followed by Roderick, made a beeline for them as soon as Darcy had turned his back. Frederica could never resist an opportunity to deluge Granny with questions about dragons and magic. How long had she been hovering about, hoping Darcy would step away so that she could come closer without suffering the usual mage repulsion?

"What was it you told Darcy to do?" Frederica demanded of Granny.

The elderly lady snorted. "Nothing you could use, young lady! That technique will only work for Darcy."

"It would still be interesting to know," she coaxed.

Granny shook her head. "Not this one, child. Some things should remain private." Then her wrinkled face dissolved into a smile, taking any sting from her words. "Those swans look quite well on the lake, do they not? The last time I came to Pemberley, nearly eighty years ago, it was a muddy stream with dozens of workmen digging. Now you would never know it is not natural. I would think the lake an illusion, too, if I did not know better."

"Perhaps *you* could cast an illusion like that, but any image of water is far beyond me," Frederica said ruefully. "Roderick told me you can cast a waterfall, but I can hardly credit that."

Granny's face was wreathed with smiles. "I cannot resist a challenge." Across the lake, the field of daffodils was suddenly replaced by a rock face, with a narrow stream of water tumbling down into the water below.

Elizabeth studied the illusion. Every detail was there, from the sunlight glinting on the falling drops to the arc of ripples crossing the lake from where the water cascaded into it. It was completely believable, except where the ripples passed straight through Darcy's illusory swans.

"Astonishing," Frederica breathed.

With a sly look, Granny said, "You have magical Talent enough, yet you are unable to cast an illusion of water. Is it your lack of ability – or a lack of proper training?"

Elizabeth winced. Even though Granny was speaking about Frederica, Elizabeth's ability with illusions had proved to be disappointing. It was hard, after years of priding herself on her mastery of other magical skills. Of course, her training had been non-existent until recently.

Frederica flushed. "You will have to blame me, since the King's Mage taught me herself."

Granny sat back in her chair with a pleased expression. "The very same who gave Darcy his first lessons, and yet Roderick tells me he went about illusions completely backwards, using his head and not his heart."

Frederica leaned forward eagerly. "What does that mean, casting with your heart? Can you teach me how? Or will this only work for Darcy, too?"

Cerridwen bumped against Elizabeth's shoulder, no doubt bored with this conversation about human mage Talents. "Who is in that carriage? I have already put a binding on the two men outside it so they can tell no one of my existence."

"I was not expecting anyone, but I should go see who it is." Elizabeth shaded her eyes to study the new arrivals, but she could make out no details. "Roderick, I will hold you personally responsible if Frederica exhausts Granny with her questions."

The Welshman laughed. "As if I could stop her! Fortunately, Granny does not need me to defend her."

But Granny was looking at Frederica with approval. "Come, girl, sit down with me, and we will see what you can learn."

Frederica did not need to be asked twice.

Elizabeth left her to it, but halfway to Darcy, she stopped in her tracks at the sight of the woman taking his hand to descend from the carriage. What was Lady Anne Darcy doing at Pemberley? Darcy's mother, the distant, powerful King's Mage, who seemed to care for nothing except finding and breeding new mages. And to suddenly appear without any warning? Did she think everyday manners did not apply to her?

Then a chill crawled up her spine. Could Lady Anne have discovered what was happening at Pemberley? Had someone managed to get word to her about Cerridwen, or worse, about Granny? Frederica was bound against mentioning dragons, but she could have sent a letter telling her former teacher that she must pay an urgent visit here. Surely Frederica would not have betrayed her that way! The very thought made her stomach churn.

Then Darcy put his arm around Lady Anne, who leaned against his shoulder. No, it could not be! The woman might look just like Lady Anne, but the King's Mage would never appear in public in a simple dress and her bonnet askew, with wisps of golden hair escaping in every direction. Nor would Darcy have that protective look towards his mother, who needed no one's protection. And the King's Mage would never, ever have a tear-stained face.

Still, the resemblance was remarkable. Not merely the same hair color and height, but identical features, as if they had been cast from the same mold. This one was just a girl, though. She had to be Darcy's sister – and she was clearly distressed.

A crying girl appearing unexpectedly was a different story than the King's Mage coming to discover their secrets. Elizabeth's fear and anger evaporated as she continued forward with a welcoming smile, even though the timing for this visit was unfortunate. She had wanted to meet her new sister, but now they would have to spend their evenings speaking of trivialities instead of dragons and the war. There was nothing to be done for it, though.

As she approached, Darcy caught her eye with a slight grimace, and his voice spoke in her head. *I am sorry. I found out she was coming when I was away. I meant to tell you when I returned, but it slipped my mind when everything happened.*

Everything, no doubt, meaning his discovery that Cerridwen was a dragon, and their subsequent fight over her. At least that was behind them now, thank heavens! Making up had been sweet indeed.

Darcy said, "Georgiana, dearest, may I introduce you to my wife?"

The girl released Darcy with apparent reluctance. She turned to Elizabeth and curtsied, the tearstains even more apparent now.

"Welcome," Elizabeth said. "I am so pleased you could join us here. Your brother has spoken of you with great affection."

Miss Darcy glanced at her brother nervously. "I am happy to make your acquaintance." At least her voice was completely unlike her mother's, quiet and hesitant instead of self-assured.

Darcy cleared his throat apologetically. "We have encountered a slight difficulty. My sister, as it turns out, has a deep fear of dragons. Would it be too much to ask Cerridwen to keep her distance from Georgiana during her visit?"

"I will speak to Cerridwen," she said. Did the girl know her other brother had been killed by a dragon? It was a well-kept secret that dragons had caused the massacre of English troops at Salamanca, but both Darcy and Lady Anne knew the truth. Perhaps one of them had told her, or she might simply be afraid of all strange creatures.

"That would be helpful," Darcy said. He nodded to a dark-haired young woman who was now descending from the carriage. "May I present Miss Lowrie, Georgiana's companion?"

Elizabeth exchanged a curtsy with the newcomer. Miss Lowrie appeared only a few years older than Miss Darcy, certainly younger and more attractive than Elizabeth would have expected for a hired companion. She glanced at Darcy, surprised that he had not insisted on the traditional widowed lady in her later years. It was unlike him to defy convention that way, especially when it came to his younger sister.

"Oh, yes, brother," Miss Darcy said. "I told Belinda that she could pay a visit to her family while I was here, but she insisted she must speak to you first."

"Rightly so," Darcy said. "I have no objection to your plans, Miss Lowrie, but I am pleased you consulted me."

"I thank you. If it is no trouble, I will stay here tonight and set out tomorrow." A flush of color in her cheeks accompanied her words. Clearly the prospect excited her.

Miss Darcy tossed her head. "Which will give you time to tell my brother everything I have done since you reported to him last." Despite her words, the girl seemed more amused than disturbed by the prospect.

Miss Lowrie's dark eyes twinkled. "That is what companions do."

"You must be longing to refresh yourselves," Elizabeth said. "Would you care to come inside?"

After the two ladies were led upstairs, Elizabeth asked Darcy, "Will she be offended to discover I have limited time to provide her with companionship?"

"Georgiana? Not at all. She prefers to keep to herself. She spends most of her days practicing her music. Miss Lowrie's family is one of our neighbors, so I expect they will still call on each other."

Elizabeth took care with her words. "Miss Lowrie seems very young to be a companion."

He shrugged. "True, but she has known Georgiana all her life, and is one of the very few people my sister trusts. That is more important to me than her age."

She debated asking him more, but she had already learned that he did not like to talk about his sister. Instead she said, "What was it that Granny told you to do? It made such a difference in your casting."

Once again, he flushed, raising her curiosity to a feverish level. "Perhaps you should ask her." But he must have seen her outraged look, for he added, "Ask me tonight, when we are alone." And that smoky look was back in his eyes.

"Promises, promises," she teased.

He raised her hand and, turning it over, pressed a lingering kiss to the inside of her wrist that sent a spiral of desire down her arm. "I always keep my promises."

Chapter 2

S OMEHOW DARCY MANAGED TO persuade Georgiana to leave her room and come down to dinner, as long as she could sit between him and her companion. That part was easily arranged, and the girl seemed as comfortable as she ever was among company, which was to say that she hardly uttered a word to anyone else.

There were too many guests at the dinner table for Darcy's taste, too. Until tonight they had all clustered together at one end of the long table, with Elizabeth beside Darcy, but now there were enough guests that she had to sit at the opposite end, with an epergne blocking Darcy's view of her.

It was unbecoming to sulk simply because he could not be near his wife, but, dammit, they had little enough time left together.

And something seemed to be bothering her. Earlier she had been warm to him, even after Georgiana's surprising arrival, teasing him about Lady Amelia's advice. But tonight, when he brought her into dinner on his arm, she was stiff and her smile artificial. Was she offended that he had asked her to keep Cerridwen away from Georgiana? Or perhaps Lady Amelia or Georgiana had said something to upset her. Whatever it was, he wanted to fix it.

When Elizabeth rose at the end of the meal, signifying the departure of the ladies, she did not even meet his eyes. This was not good. Could she possibly have managed to guess the truth about Georgiana? He could not imagine how, but he did not understand that unusual Talent of hers. Or what her dragon was capable of. The idea made his chest ache.

He had to find out, so after a token glass of port with Roderick, Darcy suggested that they rejoin the ladies. He could not wait until he was alone with Elizabeth in her room. For all he knew, she might already have revealed the secret to the others.

In the drawing room, he went straight to her side and bent down to ask her quietly to join him outside. She gave him a cool glance, but nodded and followed him into the next room.

"Yes?" she prompted. No little touch to his hand or his cheek, as she so often did when they had a moment alone.

"Something is troubling you," he said.

"How observant of you." Her smile showed her teeth but held no warmth.

"May I ask what it is?"

"Last week, when you went to Nottingham for your meeting with the War Office..." She left the sentence unfinished.

"What about it?" he asked cautiously. Perhaps this had nothing to do with Georgiana after all.

Her eyes narrowed. "What did you think of Nottingham?"

He had no impressions of it, since he had never been there. "I thought only of returning to you as quickly as possible."

"How then, did you manage to call on your sister, who was in London?" she snapped.

Devil take it! He should have asked Georgiana not to mention that, but it was too late now. "The War Office asked me to disguise my destination, in case Napoleon's spies might be watching me."

"And since I might be a spy, too, you could not tell me the truth." Her words dripped with sarcasm.

He rubbed his forehead. "No, of course not. But my instructions were to tell no one."

"I suppose I am just like everyone else, then. Did it ever occur to you that I might have wished to go with you? What it would have meant to me to spend even a few hours with my family?"

He winced. "It would have drawn attention. I traveled by mail coach under a false name and spent the night in a part of town frequented by gamblers and thieves. No one knew I was there."

She tapped her foot. "Except Georgiana, because you did have time for her."

Her tone made his ire rise. "I am well aware I should not have called on her, that it was a risk. I was worried because she had not been answering my letters."

"So this journey, which was so secret could not tell me about it, was still known by your sister and Miss Lowrie. And, presumably, by your valet, and the coachman who left with you."

"They were only aware that I did not go to Nottingham."

"They still knew more than I did." She turned away from him. "If you will excuse me, I have left our guests for too long." She was out the door before he could stop her.

Damnation! The last thing he wanted to do was spoil even an hour of their last weeks together with a quarrel, but did she not understand that he had to follow the War Office's directives?

Darcy had prepared his words carefully for his arrival in Elizabeth's bedroom that night. He could not afford to blurt out the wrong thing this time, as he had so often in the past. And it was a good thing he had, for when he entered her room, she shot him a cold look which would have stolen his ability to think.

"I have considered what you said, and I understand why you are angry. I should have told you the truth." He watched closely but saw no signs of softening. "I tend to treat orders from the War Office as if they were a military command I could not refuse, but I need to rethink that."

Her shoulders relaxed, and a genuine smile peeked out. "Thank you. I want to feel that I can trust what you say." She patted the spot beside her on the sofa, an unspoken invitation.

Thank heavens! He sat, placing his arm around her shoulders and drawing her to him. How very right she felt beside him! "I would hate it if you lied to me, and I am sorry I did that to you. I know you have kept things from me, information about the dragons and about your family in Wales, but that is different from a deception."

She snuggled in close to him, and he thought his heart would burst with happiness and relief. "Well, I may have told you a few untruths in the beginning, before I came to love you."

He leaned down to kiss her lingeringly. "Things are different now." How wonderfully, unimaginably different from anything he had ever expected. "I will not hide the truth from you again."

She nibbled at his lip. "Does that mean you will tell me what Granny said to you this morning?"

He could not help laughing at how neatly she had trapped him. Good Lord, that had been one of the most embarrassing moments of his life! How was he even to explain it without shocking her? "Perhaps I should start with what Roderick taught me a few days ago. He said I should stop trying to picture the illusion I am casting, and instead think of how pleased you would look if I succeeded at it. It seemed a ridiculous idea, but it worked."

Her eyes opened wide. "That was your breakthrough? To think of me instead of the illusion?" She sounded disbelieving, as well she should. It sounded utterly ridiculous.

"Astonishing, is it not?" He lowered his voice. "Lady Amelia told me to take it one step further. Not merely to picture your face, but to think of an intimate moment between us, when I am focused on your pleasure."

Elizabeth's mouth fell open, her cheeks growing even rosier. "She said *that*?"

"Rather more colorfully, but yes," he said ruefully. "You saw the result, so I can hardly complain. Though whether I can manage it in front of the emperor of France is a different question entirely." And when his own life was on the line.

Her brow furrowed for a moment before her face smoothed into a teasing smile. She ran her hand slowly up his chest, pressing the fine linen against his skin and sending a trail of fire into him. Nipping his earlobe, she whispered, "Then I suppose the only way to prepare is to...practice."

Once again, she had amazed him. He lowered his head, trailing his tongue along her lips to tease them apart. If making love to his wife constituted training for his mission, he was ready to work very hard indeed.

Afterwards, as he held Elizabeth in his arms, she said, "Do you know, with all this disruption over the dragons and Granny's arrival, I have not had the chance to ask about your meeting with the War Office."

The sensuous lassitude that had filled him fled. How he wanted to avoid her question! But that had backfired before, and he did not want to make the same mistake. "There has been a change in my travel plans," he said reluctantly. "Apparently there is a spy at the War Office, but they have not discovered his identity yet."

She gasped. "Oh, no! Does Napoleon know about your mission?"

"They believe not. Several agents in France were betrayed, but not the men I will be working with."

She bit her lip. "This makes it even more dangerous, does it not?"

How could he answer this truthfully without frightening her even more? "They are taking great care. My new itinerary will be known only to two men."

"A spy in the War Office. I hate to think of it." She shivered.

"I expect they will catch him soon." At least he hoped so. It was one thing to risk everything to end the war, but not if he would be arrested as soon as he set foot in France.

"Thank you for telling me," she said resolutely. "Is there anything else you have been keeping back?"

His stomach clenched. Of course there was. Which should he honor, her request that he trust her, or his instinct to keep it to himself?

She frowned. "There is, I can tell."

"I would rather not say this, to be truthful. But I will." He drew in a deep breath. "There is a good chance Napoleon will be back in Paris in a few weeks. Which means my mission will start very soon."

And then her face crumpled, her bright eyes filling with tears. "No," she whispered as if in disbelief, her voice trembling.

He folded her tightly to him, helpless in face of the devastation he had caused by coming into her life – and of his many, many bitter regrets over leaving her behind.

Still heartsick over Darcy's news, Elizabeth stepped into Granny's room the following morning, seeking comfort in the same way she had as a child. Back then, her great-grandmother had always been able to cure whatever ailed her. This problem was beyond anyone's ability to repair, but at least Granny would listen and sympathize. And Elizabeth needed that understanding so very badly, so she could go on pretending to the rest of the world that everything was normal.

Granny sat in bed with a tray of hot chocolate. She lifted her cup with a hand that trembled slightly. "This is something I have missed in Wales – having someone bring me chocolate on a chilly morning! I suppose I could have learned to make it, but it would look very odd to the people there. I am enjoying this visit back to the lap of luxury."

Elizabeth kissed the dry, wrinkly skin of her cheek, wishing she were eight years old again and could crawl in beside Granny. "I am glad we can indulge you."

The elderly lady put a finger under Elizabeth's chin and studied her. "What is making your pretty eyes so red? Come tell Granny all about it."

Elizabeth pulled a chair close to her bedside and sank into it. "My husband will be leaving for France sooner than I thought. Only a few weeks, perhaps." She barely got the words past the knot in her throat. "And chances are that he will never return." Her voice broke on the last words.

Granny patted her hand. "I did wonder about that."

"I do not want him to die!" It was almost a wail. "I have done everything I can think of to improve his chances, but it is not enough. I cannot bear it." She buried her face in her hands, choking back sobs.

"What have you done so far?"

Elizabeth swallowed hard, struggling for the remnants of her composure. "I bonded to the land so I can feed him more power, and I taught him everything I learned from my books. And I conceived his child so he can draw on his land Talent while he is in France."

Granny nodded. "A good start. I may be able to teach him a trick or two that could help, but you are right, it is a dangerous situation."

It was not what she needed to hear. "I will appreciate anything you can do," she said, trying to sound grateful instead of hopeless.

"You are a dear child." Granny took a thoughtful sip of her chocolate. "Now, we must speak about your final bonding to Cerridwen."

What? Her final bonding was the last thing on her mind. Did Granny not even care that Elizabeth was losing her beloved husband?

It was a painful realization, but perhaps she simply did not. Granny had outlived three husbands and most of her children, and likely she thought Elizabeth was making a great deal of fuss over nothing. And Granny had other worries about the safety of the dragons.

If Elizabeth's heartbreak meant nothing to her, then there was nothing to do but to accept that bitter pill. She slowly straightened in her chair and raised her chin. "What about it?" She struggled to keep her voice even.

Granny gave her an indulgent smile that seemed out of keeping with her dismissal of Elizabeth's concerns. "The ceremony itself is a simple matter. The two of you appear before the Eldest, and you promise to protect Cerridwen and the Nest. They make a little celebration of it, and all the dragons come to watch. At the end, the Eldest offers you a boon of welcome."

"A boon," Elizabeth echoed. Did Granny think that Elizabeth was a child, to be cheered up by some trinket the dragons might give her when she was losing the man she loved?

"You can ask for anything. Oftentimes it is healing for a loved one, or something of monetary value – a farm or a flock of sheep to provide income for a companion who might worry about keeping a roof over their heads. Those of us who are wealthier are often given an Artifact."

"What did you get?" Elizabeth was intrigued despite herself.

With a rusty chuckle, she said, "I was difficult, naturally. I asked the Eldest to stop me from being forced into marriage. She did it, too, although not in the way I hoped."

"What do you mean?"

"She arranged my flight to Wales, gave me the tools I needed to escape my family, and sent me to the Gwynedd Nest."

"Truly? I always thought you wished to go there."

Granny sniffed. "I was young and foolish. I wanted them to keep my father from marrying me off while I stayed at my lovely fashionable home, but the dragons would not intervene in a human's mind for anything short of their safety. It turned out better this way. I could have returned to my family once I was wed to a man of my choice, but by then I liked my freedom in Wales too much."

Then realization struck her. If the dragons had made it possible for Granny flee from her family, could they not assist Darcy in escaping France alive? "How did they help you?" She held her breath.

A triumphant smile lit her wrinkled face. "Finally, the correct question! You always were a clever one. They gave me a minor spell of confusion to keep anyone from noticing when I left, and an Artifact that created what appeared to be my dead body. That was the only thing that would stop my family's pursuit."

Her mind raced. Something like that could help Darcy, too – but only if she could convince the Nest to accept Cerridwen and to complete her bond before he left for France. "How quickly can my final vows be arranged?"

Granny looked pleased. "It should not take long, once my Sycamore gives his blessing to Cerridwen leaving the Gwynedd Nest for the Dark Peak. He should be here later today, though his first priority will be speaking to your husband about the dragon attacks."

Once again, Granny had come to her rescue – and clearly she had known exactly what she was doing. Elizabeth threw her arms around her. "Thank you so much. This could make all the difference."

"Oh, tush, girl! You are the one who is doing everything." She held her finger up to her lips, her eyes twinkling. "I never said a word about boons."

"Not a single one!" Elizabeth agreed, beaming with impossible hope.

Chapter 3

ELIZABETH COULD HARDLY WAIT to see Granny's dragon again. Fortunately, Sycamore was already waiting in the oak grove at Pemberley when they arrived. Elizabeth alighted from the small open carriage and ran to him. His elegant form, with wings of metallic black and amethyst highlights, dominated the cleared area. How enormous he looked to her now, compared to Cerridwen! No wonder he preferred to sleep away from the house where he had more space.

She raised her hand to rub his shoulder in the way he had always liked. "Dearest Sycamore, it has been too long!" How she had loved spending time with him as a child in Wales! Playing together in the garden of Granny's house, whispering her secrets to him late at night, hearing Sycamore argue with Granny on Elizabeth's behalf when she had been caught in some mischief. He had even once let her ride him, with the thrill of the wind on her face and the patchwork of countryside rushing by far below her. Those memories had been hidden from her all those years, but now they were back, vivid with delight.

A joyous warmth flowed from his aura. "Little Lizzy, all grown up! And now Companion Elizabeth."

She beamed up at him. "And we are together again." A cause for celebration! She was looking forward to spending time with him while he was here.

But Darcy's expression was studiously neutral as he helped Granny down from the carriage. Was this difficult for him? He had struggled with accepting Cerridwen, and meeting a full-grown dragon was enough to trouble even the bravest of men.

Regardless of his feelings, he helped Granny to the waiting chair. He did not even flinch as Sycamore padded across the clearing to join his elderly companion, towering over Darcy.

Granny's expression softened as she reached out a gnarled hand to stroke Sycamore's side. He leaned his head against her arm with clear affection. Then suddenly the dragon stiffened and swung his head towards Darcy, sniffing the air.

Darcy stood his ground, though his fingers curled inwards as if readying for a fight.

Sycamore shifted his weight to face Darcy directly, lifting the tips of his wings in a manner that reminded Elizabeth of a dog raising its hackles. The dragon spoke in a husky growl. "That one. He reeks of the blood of the High Fae." This was a side of Sycamore she had never seen before.

Granny turned her head to stare at Darcy, but Elizabeth was already rushing to his side. "I assure you my husband is purely mortal," she said.

The dragon studied him. "Mortal, but blood-bonded to a woman of the High Fae. And one who bears the blood of the King of Faerie, may his bones rot while he yet lives."

"There must be some mistake," Elizabeth blurted. "My husband disapproves of blood bonds. I do not know what you are sensing, but—"

Darcy held up a hand. "The dragon is correct. I am blood-bonded to a fae," he said in a haughty, remote voice. "I know nothing of any connection to the High King, though."

Elizabeth stared at him as if he had suddenly turned into a stranger. "But everything you said about blood bonds—"

"I did not like doing it, but I deemed it necessary." His tone made clear this was not open to further discussion. "It has nothing to do with any of this."

He had a blood bond with a highborn fae lady – and he expected her to simply accept it without complaint? Anger and betrayal threatened to choke her. She turned to Sycamore. "Forgive my intervention, then. Clearly I do not know whereof I speak," she said icily, humiliation churning her stomach.

How could Darcy have done this to her? His distrust of dragons was bad enough, but this was worse, far worse. She dug her fingernails into her palms until it hurt.

"A bond to the blood of the Wicked King, may his flesh be cursed in eternity, is not a matter easily dismissed," grumbled the dragon.

Darcy looked taken aback. "I know nothing of her connections. She is not..." He straightened. "This is not something I can discuss except to say it is completely unrelated to the matters at hand."

The dragon set back on his haunches. "I require an explanation. A connection to the Wicked King, may his name live in infamy, cannot be set aside so easily."

Darcy lifted his chin. "These are secrets which are not mine to share."

Tension thickened the air, and it was not eased when Darcy's lynx padded out of the forest to stand by his side. Battle lines had been drawn.

And Elizabeth, heaven help her, no longer knew where she stood.

"Enough of this nonsense," Granny said irritably. "This is a major setback, it cannot be denied, but your posturing will not help. Darcy, the dragons harbor deep hatred for the High King of Faerie going back thousands of years, stronger than your enmity for Napoleon. Sycamore cannot ignore this anymore than you could if the dragons in Spain were his fellow nestlings. If you refuse to explain your bond, we cannot continue these discussions."

Darcy raised his chin, every inch the haughty aristocrat. "I regret that I cannot oblige you, but I will not break my word."

He might as well have drenched her in ice water. "But we need their help!" she cried. And if the dragons blamed her for Darcy's choices, they might not allow Cerridwen to stay with her, nor could she get a boon to save his life. Then she would have nothing but a faithless husband whom she had foolishly trusted. She shivered. How could a few words have destroyed everything she believed?

In sudden decision, she turned her back on Darcy, pressing her shaking hands together. "Sycamore, I will tell you everything I know about the attacks in Spain and Austria. Darcy's knowledge is more complete, but I daresay I am aware of most of it."

Darcy blanched. "Elizabeth, I told you those things in confidence!"

Sycamore's irritated snort sent out smoke and the acrid smell of newly forged metal into the center of the grove. "This is a waste of time. Lizzy, I am sure you mean well, but he has deceived you. Do you expect me to believe stories of violent dragons from a man who shares blood with the Wicked King? He is trying to trick us."

"Stop it, all of you!" Granny's voice echoed in the clearing. "Lizzy, not another word until I have spoken privately to Sycamore, and that goes for you, too, young man."

Now Granny was angry with her on top of everything else. Elizabeth could not bear it, standing exposed in front of all of them as her heart was ripped to shreds. She choked out the words, "Excuse me." Then she turned and walked into the woods, forcing herself to take one measured step at a time, rather than fleeing as she ached to do.

Away from Darcy and his pretense of affection. Only last night he had promised not to hide things from her, and now this. There was no possibility of recovering from what she had learned today.

This was the end of her life at Pemberley. Once again she would have to leave behind a land that was alive under her feet, whose power ran through her body. All because Darcy had chosen to bond with a fae lady and deliberately kept it hidden from her. Nausea gripped her.

She had never truly known him.

She stumbled down a narrow path along the stream, but even among the trees, there was no sanctuary for her. She could not return to the house like this, facing the servants when she could barely breathe or control the tears springing to her eyes. There was no point in hiding, either; Darcy's land bond would tell him where she was, no matter how she tried to disguise her presence. There could be no escape. Instead, she clambered down to the stream's bank.

All those tales of beautiful fae women who bonded human men to be their lovers – she would never, ever have imagined Darcy would be one of them. Her husband, who shared her bed and called her his love, while belonging to a woman whose extraordinary loveliness would never fade with age.

She would never have believed it, had she not heard the words come from his own mouth. What a fool she was!

How long had it been going on? She sank down on a rock that jutted out over the water, pulling her knees to her chest and wrapping her arms tightly around them as if it could ease the gnawing pain inside her or relieve the agony of betrayal. But nothing could do that. She could not even reach into the rich life of the land for comfort, because Pemberley was his. She had left her own land and her family behind to help him, all unknowing that he belonged to another woman.

Had all his warmth and affection been just a show to keep her supporting his mission? It must have been. She bowed her head to her knees.

How dare he keep such a thing from her, after his promises to tell her everything?

She closed her eyes, letting the burbling of the water fill her ears. It flowed from the Dark Peak, she knew that much, but where did it go from here? She would have to ask Darcy.

Darcy. Everything came back to him. Damn him!

"Elizabeth?" It was his voice.

She stiffened. The sound of the stream must have covered his footsteps. "Where does the river go from here?" she asked flatly.

Silence for a moment. "Into the Derwent, which flows into the Trent, and eventually the North Sea."

Of course he knew. She did not trouble herself to reply or even to pick up her head.

"We have come to an agreement. I shall explain my bond to Lady Amelia, who will then advise the dragons on whether I can be trusted." He sounded almost hurt. "I thought you might wish to hear my explanation, too."

Slowly she pushed herself to her feet, her joints aching. "I suppose I might as well listen." She did not try to sound anything but displeased.

"I am sorry I could not tell you sooner. I did not mean to take you by surprise."

She turned her head to look at him in disbelief. "Surprise? How would you feel if you discovered I was bonded to a fae lord? Never mind; you likely would not care, as long as it did not interfere with your precious mission." She spat the last word.

"Elizabeth, no! It is not that sort of bond!"

"*Not that sort of bond*?" she mocked, fury burning in her throat. "Then why keep it a secret? I gave up my entire life in Hertfordshire, my birth-blood bond to Longbourn, my sisters, my parents, my friends, all for you. I have been dedicating myself to saving your life. I showed you my Arabic books and taught you magic from them. I told you Cerridwen was a dragon. I nearly died bonding to Pemberley for your sake. And you could not even be honest with me! All that time you scorned my blood bonds, and you – you had your own secret one to a *fae*!"

He paled. "I am sorry. I swore an oath never to reveal this secret."

"You made a vow to me at our wedding, too! One which I clearly took more seriously than you did. Trusting you is not a mistake I shall make again."

He reached out a hand to her, but she ignored it. "Elizabeth, I can understand why you are angry–"

"Anger does not begin to describe it," she snapped. "Betrayal. Humiliation. I trusted you. I defended you to my great-grandmother, and you made me look like a fool. How could you do this to me?"

He looked away, appearing to study a nearby oak, taking a deep, harsh breath. "That was never my intention, as you will see when you understand more of my situation. If you wish to hear my explanation to Lady Amelia, you are welcome to join me. The rest will have to wait until later."

He turned to climb back up the riverbank. She followed, seething. Did he truly expect her to forgive him even for this? Did he care if she did?

She rested her hand on her abdomen, over the new life beginning in her. No, it would not matter to him. He already had what he wanted from her.

Even inside the small cottage, Elizabeth could not bear to look at Darcy. Instead, she watched Granny, who was ensconced on the chair by the hearth, the quilt from the bed over her knees.

Despite being the very image of a weak old lady, Granny's voice was strong. "This had better be good, young man. And I will remind you I am a truth-caster, so pray do not deviate from the facts."

"I would not have done so," he said coldly. "I may have kept a secret, but I hold my honor close."

His honor. Elizabeth curled her lip. What honor had he shown her by hiding this? She crossed to stand in front of the small window, where the light behind her might hide her expression in the dimness.

Granny snorted. "Then tell me about it."

Darcy folded his hands behind his back. "It begins with my sister, who is more than ten years my junior. When she was four, my mother visited her and then disappeared immediately afterwards. When she never returned, Georgiana believed herself to have been at fault. My father's main interest in her was the eventual royal dowry she was expected to bring. When she failed to develop a Talent, he considered her a complete loss. She had no playmates, just a series of nurses and tutors, and she became very attached to me. Since my father's death, I have been her guardian." His voice was clipped.

"I fail to see what this has to do with a fae lady," said Granny crossly.

"After ten years, my mother reappeared alive and well, with the shocking news that she had gone to Faerie on discovering that Georgiana was not her daughter, but a changeling."

Elizabeth sucked in her breath. It could not be. "Impossible! She is the very image of your mother!" The words burst out of her.

"A glamour set on her at birth, at a guess," he said. "My mother went to Faerie to rescue her true child, but failed. She disowned Georgiana completely, although at my insistence, she kept the matter private."

"How very like a Fitzwilliam," sniffed Granny.

Darcy ignored her words. "Georgiana went into a decline, withdrawing into herself, unable to sleep or eat. Our father was dead, she had been rejected by the only mother she had ever known, and she expected me to do the same. She could see no reason I would stand by her when we shared no blood, and she was not even human."

Granny narrowed her eyes. "She did not wish to return to Faerie?"

"To the people who had sent her away at birth, exchanging her for a different child? To a world she does not understand, where she knows no one? No. But she thought I would throw her out on the streets." A haunted look crept into his eyes. "To my mind, she was still my sister, the same girl she had always been, and nothing had changed. She did not believe me, saying I would eventually discard her as everyone else had."

It was a tragedy for Georgiana, without question. But it also meant heartbreak for Elizabeth if it had brought Darcy into the way of the hauntingly beautiful ladies of Faerie.

He cleared his throat. "I became sufficiently concerned for her well-being that one night, in a moment of incomplete rationality, I offered to swear blood brotherhood. I knew boys at school who had done such things on a dare, and, while I disapproved, I could think of nothing else to reassure her. She seized on the idea, and we exchanged blood. It helped, in that Georgiana recovered from her decline, but I also learned how very dangerous blood magic is. I was fortunate to survive. I swore never to touch blood magic again."

The bond was to *Georgiana*?

Or so he claimed. Could she even believe anything he said?

Granny snorted. "Good Lord, where is your sense of proportion? A blood bond to a high-ranking fae is dangerous. So is leaping off a cliff, but that does not mean it is dangerous to jump from a chair to the floor. Well, except at my age, perhaps. It does not mean all blood magic is a risk."

He looked down his nose at her. "Regardless, you wished to know how I came to have a blood bond with a fae, and you can see it has nothing to do with dragons or Napoleon." He turned to Elizabeth, his eyes narrowed. "Or with another woman."

Granny tapped her finger on her knee. "The question, then, is how your sister is connected to the High King of Faerie."

He turned up his hands. "This is the first I have heard of it. She does not appear to hold any loyalty towards Faerie. If anything, she seems afraid of it."

"Why?"

"I have not asked her, as she prefers to avoid the subject. I hope I may depend upon you to keep the matter of her birth between us."

Granny narrowed her eyes. "I will need to tell Sycamore, but dragons keep secrets better than any human."

Elizabeth could stay silent no longer. Her outrage would not permit it. "Did you intend ever to tell me?"

He gave her a pleading look. "I planned to do so before leaving on my mission, since you will be her guardian if I do not return. I wanted you to come to know her as a mortal first, as I did."

She was not ready to forgive him yet. Not even close. "You think you know everything, and you know so very little. Granny, what will Sycamore make of this?"

The old woman's eyes became unfocused. "Sycamore will speak to you, but he wishes to learn more about the changeling."

"Her name is Georgiana," snapped Darcy.

The discussion with Sycamore did not go well.

At least the dragon spoke directly to Darcy now that the matter of the fae bond had been explained, but it was clear Sycamore still did not trust him. His many questions about the dragon massacre dripped with incredulity. Darcy had no patience for it, not when Elizabeth was standing there with hurt and anger in her eyes. And he did not even want to think about how she would treat Georgiana now that she knew the truth. Most people feared and detested changelings.

Finally Lady Amelia interrupted. "Sycamore, I understand your reluctance to believe any dragon could behave in such an unnatural manner as to fight in battle, but there have been mad dragons in the past. Yes, humans can lie, but I assure you that the government would never admit to such a thing unless they were absolutely certain of their facts, and they are quite skilled in intelligence-gathering."

The dragon made a snorting sound. "The Wicked King, may his eyes be pecked by vultures, is fully able to perform a deception of this level. Why should I believe this man's word when he is no friend to dragons and unwilling to have his thoughts read?"

It was beyond enough. Darcy said, "Why should I believe yours? My brother was killed by dragonfire in the charge at Salamanca, and you think I should allow you to rummage around in my mind?"

Sycamore sat back on his haunches. In a gentler tone, he said, "I am sorry about your brother. I assure you no dragon in their right mind would ever commit such a horrendous crime, but that does not change your loss. If you are so certain of the truth of your story, why will you not allow me to read you so that I can see the evidence?"

He should not say it. He absolutely should not. But Elizabeth was angry at him and the dragon was calling him a liar, and he had no restraint left. "Because other dragons and sea serpents are working for Napoleon, and I have no reason to believe you would not report to him as well. The information in my mind could cost thousands of lives. I will not risk it."

A small puff of smoke escaped from the dragon's nostrils as he swung his head towards Lady Amelia. "This man does not understand dragons," he growled.

Had Jack seen similar smoke coming from the dragons in the moments before he was lashed by dragonfire?

"Of course he does not," she said irritably. "That is what happens when you hide your existence for hundreds of years. People are left ignorant of what you are."

The dragon turned back to Darcy. "I answer to no human except my companion, and certainly not to one who wages wars. Since you will not be read, I cannot assess the truth of your claims. If you require a more personal motivation, should you persist in this attitude of hostility to dragons, no Nest will allow your wife to take her final vows."

A gasp came from Elizabeth, and she turned her face away.

Lady Amelia made a clucking noise. "Enough, both of you. I am tired. We will try again another day, when feelings are not running so high."

Darcy drew in a breath to protest, but it was pointless. What difference did it make if the dragons did not believe him? There was no point in wasting time on this when he needed to talk to Elizabeth. Alone.

"Ah, I hoped I would see you tonight," said Granny with satisfaction as Elizabeth entered her bedroom. A small table was set up in front of the fireplace, and two footmen were carrying in trays of food.

"So Cerridwen told me," Elizabeth replied. "I had assumed you might be too tired for company, but I am happy to be proved wrong." As if the word happy could even apply to her now. Was it only that morning, in this very room, that she been delighted by the prospect of a dragon boon that could save his life?

"Dining in my chamber is one of the few benefits of extreme old age. Spending two hours over a formal dinner making social chit-chat is a waste of time and energy. I hope your husband will not object to your abandoning him to join me?" There was a touch of challenge in her words.

Elizabeth shrugged as she took a seat at the table. "I did not ask him." She had not the least desire to hear his opinion on the matter. Or on anything else. She helped herself to several dishes.

"Good for you! Do not let him dominate you."

Not a lesson she was in any danger of forgetting at the moment, nor one that she wished to discuss. "Are you certain this is not too tiring for you?"

"Not at all. I pleaded fatigue as the only way to stop those two ridiculous males from posturing at each other like a pair of peacocks. Truly, Sycamore should be outgrowing some of this impulsive behavior by now."

"Outgrowing?" Elizabeth asked. "But he is far from young, is he not?"

"He is well past his century mark, since the Dark Peak Nest does not allow dragons to bond as early as your Cerridwen did. That is still young for a dragon, though. Wisdom comes with age. He is troubled, too, by his worry about me. It is always a hard passage for a dragon when they lose their Companion."

Elizabeth dropped her fork, her heart sinking. "Is there something you are not telling me, Granny?"

The old lady waved her hand. "Nothing of note, but I am ninety-three years of age, and it would be foolish to think I will be on this earth much longer. Dragon companions are long-lived, thanks to our bondmates' healing abilities, but even that can only go so far. Sycamore would wrap me in cotton wool to keep me safe, but he knows I will not tolerate it, and it makes him cross."

Elizabeth took a bite of pheasant pie and chewed it thoughtfully. Would she, too, live to a very old age? "I never thought about what it would mean to Cerridwen if something happened to me. Or if we could not complete the bond."

"That is what I wished to speak to you about – this unfortunate situation with your husband. His attitude will stand in the way of your final companion vows. Leaving aside the question of the boon, Cerridwen is running out of time. She must either complete the bond to you or return to Wales. If we cannot find a way out of this mess, you may have to choose between giving up your bond to her or leaving your husband.

She closed her eyes, took a deep breath, and opened them. "Is it truly that serious?"

"I fear so. It is too risky for the Nests to allow so much knowledge to someone who is hostile towards them, especially with that odd connection to the High King."

Her chest tightened. Cerridwen had been her trusted friend all these years. She could not stand losing her, too. And how could anyone expect her to give up being a dragon companion? It was the stuff of her childhood dreams.

But Darcy, for all his faults, was the father of her child. "How long do I have before Cerridwen would have to leave me?" Her voice shook.

Granny appeared to consider this. "Given how stubborn Cerridwen can be, perhaps six months, or even a year, assuming the Nest allows her to stay here that long. The problem may resolve itself if your husband does not survive this mission of his. Then there would be nothing standing in your way."

Nothing except a broken heart and a memory of betrayal. If he came back alive, would she have the courage to leave him? Would she ever be able to forgive him if she lost Cerridwen on his account?

Tears filled her eyes. "I am not yet ready to give up. If the problem is his connection to Georgiana, would it help if I convinced her to let the dragons read her? She knows no state secrets."

"Would she do that? I thought she did not want dragons near her."

"I do not know, but it is worth a try," Elizabeth said determinedly. "I doubt my good opinion means much to her, but she loves Darcy dearly. If I can convince her it is in his best interest, she might agree."

"It cannot hurt to ask. What of your husband? He seems to care for you. I know how hard it is to get a Fitzwilliam man to listen to sense, but can you attempt it? He does love you, you know."

Elizabeth grimaced. "He says so, but at times like this I wonder if he means it."

"Oh, he does. His magic would not entwine with yours otherwise." She took a sip of wine.

"What does that have to do with anything?"

Granny patted her hand. "Entwinement only happens when a mage starts falling in love with a dragon companion. Your stronger Talent pulled his into alignment with yours, like a magnet with iron filings. That is why you can affect his magic."

"But I could alter his illusions before he ever thought about marrying me!" And then she remembered what he had said about being fascinated with her even before that, when he was so proud and aloof. Could it have been true?

Her anger softened, but just a little. "Well, I will speak to him, but not yet. I would only say all the wrong things and make matters worse. Tomorrow I may be calmer."

"Perhaps I will try in the meantime." Granny winked at her. "I imagine Darcy is too well trained to be rude to his elders, even if he wants to."

Darcy scowled as he strode through the corridor. First Elizabeth was nowhere to be found, and now Lady Amelia had summoned him to her private sitting room, likely for another lecture. And he was in no mood either to be summoned or lectured.

Still, he owed a certain respect to his great-grandfather's sister, so he did his best to greet her politely. At least her damned dragon was nowhere to be seen. "I hope you have recovered from our excursion earlier."

"Thank you, yes. Lizzy was kind enough to dine with me here so I could rest."

So that was where she had been, leaving him to eat with Roderick and a tearful Georgiana, still distressed over the revelation of her great secret. "How may I be of service to you?"

She waved to the chair across from her. "You can start by sitting down instead of looming over me. Then you can tell me why you oppose letting the dragons read you. Making them see the attacks are real would benefit us all."

"Or they might simply find another way to disbelieve me," he said coolly. "Cerridwen seems good-hearted, but she is very young. Of the four adult dragons who have touched my life, three of them massacred tens of thousands of Englishmen, including my brother, and then your dragon turned on me the instant we met, with threats and curses. You will forgive me if this does not incline me to believe dragons are trustworthy." For Elizabeth's sake, he had tried to overcome his hatred of dragons and to believe they could be honorable, but today's meeting had shattered that possibility.

She nodded. "Sycamore behaved badly; I cannot deny that. The shock of your fae connection was the reason, but it is no excuse. What you are presenting is any dragon's worst nightmare, that someone could force them to become killers, as the High King did to their ancestors. Regardless of your sentiments, we need their knowledge if we are to construct adequate defenses and stop what is happening in Europe."

"Obviously it would be better to have them as allies, but until I can absolutely guarantee that they will not give my information to dragons sympathetic to Napoleon, it is simply too dangerous."

"You do not understand. That is the last thing they would do."

"No, it is you who do not understand. If I knew fewer secrets, it would be simpler. As it is, I cannot permit the dragons free access to my mind; it would endanger far too many people. I cannot in honor do that." He was tired of explaining this.

"Men! How they always use honor as an excuse to avoid doing unpleasant things. Tell me, is it honorable for you to force Lizzy to break her bond to Cerridwen, after you have already taken her from her home and family?"

He gritted his teeth. "I am not the one insisting on breaking the bond. You must blame the dragons for that."

"They have offered you a compromise which you have refused." She shifted in her chair. "What do you think will happen when you force Lizzy to choose between you and Cerridwen?"

He lifted his chin. "She will be unhappy, but I am her husband." But he did not want her to be unhappy.

"Let us suppose Lizzy insisted you break all ties with your sister, which she would be justified in doing under the circumstances. What would you do?"

He would talk her out of it, but that was not an answer the old lady would accept. "I, too, would be unhappy, but my wife would come first."

"Would you ever forgive her for driving your sister away?" The words shot out like a knife. "Would you still trust her? Would your marriage still be as loving?"

No. It would never be the same. He opened his mouth to say they would learn to move past it, but the words would not come out.

Of course. The old lady was truth-casting, damn her. He could not speak a lie in front of her.

What could he say that was true? "Elizabeth would never request such a thing unless she had a good reason, and I would try to respect that reason."

Her upper lip curled. "A nice try. But listen carefully, because this is why Lizzy will choose Cerridwen. If some outside power forced her to choose between you, I suspect she might take you. But Lizzy is clever enough to realize that your marriage can never recover if you force her to make that choice. If you value her affection, you must start acting like a man who deserves her love."

His mouth went dry. "You think very little of me."

"I think you were raised by a Fitzwilliam mother who puts a ridiculous sense of abstract duty ahead of everything else, and you learned your lessons too well. She would tell you that your secrets are more important than your wife's love. I, however, have not yet given up on the possibility that you may have a heart under that overdeveloped sense of duty."

She was right about that. He did have a heart, and it was breaking.

After leaving her great-grandmother, Elizabeth followed the tinkling tones of the pianoforte to the music room. Now she wished she had spent more time with Georgiana, but as Darcy had warned her, the girl preferred to keep to herself. She rarely spoke much at dinner, although she seemed happy enough to chat with Darcy at other times or with Miss Lowrie. But she had always been reserved with Elizabeth.

It must be hard to keep a secret as monumental as hers.

She waited until Georgiana's fingers stilled on the keys before she said, "Good evening."

The girl straightened her shoulders, but she did not lift her eyes from her music. "My brother tells me you know the truth now," she said flatly.

"A bit, at least." No thanks to Darcy, who would have kept it a secret as long as he could.

Still avoiding her gaze, Georgiana asked, "Do you want me to leave Pemberley? I have no desire to impose myself upon you."

At that moment, she bore an undeniable resemblance to her brother, blood tie or no. "Nonsense," Elizabeth said briskly. "You are my husband's sister, and this is your home. Nothing has changed." Nothing she could admit to, anyway. It was disconcerting having a fae in the house, but that was not the girl's fault.

Georgiana's fingers danced up and down the keyboard in a rapid series of arpeggios, filling the room with a waterfall of notes. "Yet you clearly have something to say. What do you want of me, then?"

The girl's bluntness took her aback. "Yes, I came to ask something of you, but it is a complicated matter." So much to tell, and all of it so strange! Still, she did her best to summarize the events of the day.

To her credit, Georgiana took it calmly, her fingers continuing to move fluently over the keyboard as she listened. "I assume you have a reason for telling me this," she said.

Elizabeth took a deep breath. "I know you do not like the idea of seeing dragons, but it would mean a great deal to me if you would be willing to speak to them about your heritage. They have certain questions, and my ability to remain as Cerridwen's companion depends on the answers. That, and more."

Her playing paused. "I need not avoid them anymore, now that you already know the truth. I was only afraid your dragon would discover it. Does my brother wish me to do this?"

Elizabeth shifted from one foot to another. "He has not stated an opinion. He refused to let Lady Amelia's dragon read his thoughts about you because he is afraid of giving away secrets of his mission, which is why I am asking you to answer them directly instead."

Finally the girl raised her eyes to Elizabeth. "Why? If my brother does not wish it, why should I subject myself to questions from these dragons?"

"Because your brother is a stubborn fool," Elizabeth snapped. "His life is at stake, and I will leave no stone unturned trying to save him. The dragons may be able to help him, but unless we answer their questions, they will not do so."

"You mean his mission?" She gazed down at the keyboard. "He does not expect to survive it, does he?"

Elizabeth shook her head. "No, he does not."

"I thought as much, when he told me you would be my guardian if anything happened to him." Her voice trembled. "If that happens, I promise to be as little trouble to you as I can. To stay out of your way, if you wish it."

"No, I do not wish it! What I want is for you to do the one thing that might save your brother." Even if she was furious with him.

Georgiana's eyes were wide as saucers. "How can talking to the dragons possibly help *him*?"

She would have to spell it out, the thing she had been keeping secret. "When I take my final vows as Cerridwen's companion, the dragons will grant me a boon of my choice. I plan to ask them to bring your brother home safely. It is nearly my only remaining hope. But the dragons will not allow me to take the vows unless they can resolve the matter of his bond to you. No final vows, no boon. Darcy has refused to allow them to read his thoughts. Perhaps if you will speak to them... I ask this for his safety, not for my own sake."

Georgiana lifted her fingers from the keyboard and lowered the cover with exaggerated care. "Then I will answer their questions."

Chapter 4

Darcy trudged up the seemingly endless steep slope behind Elizabeth, mist blocking any view which might distract him from this miserable errand or from his wife's continuing cool distance. Yesterday had been bad enough after his revelation about Georgiana, but he had assumed they could talk about it and she would understand. Apparently he had underestimated her anger – or his sins.

Not that Elizabeth had given him any chance to apologize. After she had avoided him at dinner, he had not even seen her until late in the evening, when she had appeared in his study to inform him – not to ask him! – that she and Georgiana would be meeting with the Dark Peak dragons in the morning. When he had gently suggested that perhaps he should have been involved in such a decision, she had raised her chin and told him that since he had chosen to act in the manner which suited him best, without reference to her, she had resolved to do the same. And then she had swept out without another word.

He had not gone to her bedroom last night, telling himself she needed time to regain her spirits, but the truth was that he could not bear to see her anger or face the possibility that she would turn him away. His lonely bed was almost as unbearable, after all those nights of heavenly abandon, of making love to her and falling asleep in her arms, of waking there in the morning with a previously unknown joy.

He *missed* her, damn it!

Then, when he had come to breakfast at the same time they usually drifted downstairs together, she was already having a carriage readied and looked displeased when he announced his intention to accompany them. At least she had not refused, though perhaps that was only because Georgiana might not have stood for it.

So now they were here, together in body if not in spirit, speaking only when strictly necessary, and to maintain an appearance of cooperation in front of Georgiana. Not that she was likely to be convinced by it.

Finally the path leveled off, the mist falling away, revealing a long ridge with outcroppings to the side. Easy for a dragon to escape and hard for anyone else to see, especially in all the mist. Perhaps the fog was weather magic, designed to provide cover for the dragons. But there was no sign of the beasts.

"Where do we meet them?" he asked.

Elizabeth glanced up at a kestrel circling overhead. Cerridwen, no doubt. "They are on their way."

A trio of hawks materialized out of the mist, winging their way along the ridge. They glided in and landed some twenty feet away, where the kestrel joined them. One by one, the hawk shapes blurred and swelled into the now too-familiar forms of dragons.

Huge dragons.

At least two of them dwarfed Cerridwen, making her look like a doll beside them. He had thought Sycamore was enormous, but these were even larger. The third was only twice Cerridwen's size.

The small dragon – small! As if there were anything small about him, except by comparison! – approached them. "Companion Elizabeth, we meet again."

She inclined her head. "Honored Rowan, I am grateful to you for coming today on such short notice."

"We will always respond to the call of a dragon companion," said the dragon, his scales shimmering with dark red highlights. "I have brought two of the Nest who bear the wisdom of age. May I present Juniper, who speaks for the Eldest today, and whose poetry sings in the wind? And this is Hawthorn, whose Talents come to life in our greatest sculptures."

Darcy's lips tightened. How easy it was to present themselves as artists when their distant cousins had massacred an army. And naming themselves for trees? Ridiculous!

"It is a great honor to have dragons of such abilities travel so far for my small needs," said Elizabeth.

The red dragon said, with apparent amusement, "There is much interest in you at the Nest, Companion Elizabeth."

The largest dragon, whose form dominated the hilltop, spoke in a resonant voice that echoed off the rocks. "Companion Elizabeth, pray acquaint us with these other mortals."

"It would be my pleasure," Elizabeth said. "May I present my husband, Mr. Fitzwilliam Darcy, and his sister, Miss Georgiana Darcy? Miss Darcy has offered to answer any questions you may have about her, er, background."

Darcy strove to keep his face impassive. This was a waste of time. The dragons had made it clear that he was persona non grata, and he returned the sentiment heartily. What could Georgiana say that would change anything?

"What would you like to know?" Georgiana asked, her voice a little higher than usual. She was clearly uncomfortable, too. Devil take it, why had Elizabeth not left well enough alone?

The dragon studied her. "You are fae, despite your present form?"

Georgiana lifted her chin. "The body you see me in is mortal, but my blood is fae."

What? She was *mortal*?

"Are you of fae descent, then?" asked the dragon.

She shook her head. "I was created, not born."

Darcy caught his breath. Created? What did that mean, and why had she never told him any of this? Elizabeth's voice echoed in his memory – *You think you know everything, and you know so very little.*

The dragons, though, seemed unperturbed by this news. "You have the scent of the Wicked King, whom mortals call the High King," the dragon rumbled.

Georgiana's lips pursed, as if she had eaten something distasteful. "He is the one who created me, using his own blood and essence and a lock of human hair."

The dragon seemed unsurprised. "The first dragons were made in a similar manner. What is your present connection to the Wicked King?"

She glanced in Darcy's direction. "Elizabeth said you could read my memories. I would rather not speak them aloud."

The dragon lapsed into silence. Conferring mentally with the others, perhaps? Finally he said, "I regret we cannot honor your request. Without understanding your connection to the Wicked King, I cannot be certain he will not perceive me in your mind. It would be unwise for us to draw his attention."

Georgiana paled. "He can hear my thoughts?" Her voice shook.

The dragon's fluting voice softened. "That is unlikely, child, but my intrusion might catch his notice."

Darcy stared. Why was the dragon speaking so gently when he had made it clear Georgiana was his enemy?

"I hate him!" she cried. "I detest and abhor him! I wish I could...I could spit him through and roast him alive over a fire!"

A wave of calm seemed to emerge from the dragon. "Child, do not wish death even upon your worst enemy. It is your own soul that pays the price."

"I have no soul." Tears shone in her eyes. "I am nothing but a tool he created, no different from a hammer or a plow."

Darcy's stomach twisted in a knot. Did she truly believe that?

Cerridwen clawed at the ground. "She does have a soul. I have heard it."

The larger dragon turned to her. "Explain yourself, Nestling."

Cerridwen spread her wings wide, her chest expanding, as if she were about to declaim or perhaps to sing. What came out was not the dragon's voice, though, but the tinkling music of an invisible pianoforte, playing one of Georgiana's compositions. The notes flooded through the air, an exact replica. Apparently dragons truly did have perfect recall, but how could she produce that sound?

The dragons listened attentively. When the music ended, the large one asked Georgiana, "That is your music?"

Georgiana stiffened. "I wrote it and played it, yes."

"The nestling is correct. You do have a soul, child. Do not believe anyone who tells you otherwise."

Georgiana pressed her hand over her eyes. "He says... He says he is my father and I must obey him. But I will not. I will not!"

"We dragons are living proof that the Wicked King's creations can escape him," the dragon said soothingly. "He built us to be machines of war and enslaved us when we refused to fight. But we escaped to this world, where he cannot touch us. As long as you stay out of Faerie, his only control over you is the power of persuasion, and you can close your ears to that."

The dragon was slowly moving towards Georgiana, but there was no threat in its motion, only concern. When he reached her side, he held out his forelegs to her.

She threw her arms around the dragon, or at least the tiny amount she could reach, and burst into sobs.

Darcy froze. He had never seen Georgiana respond this way to anyone except him. How had this dragon whom she had just met earned her trust so quickly, when others could not do so even after years?

The other dragons drew close to Georgiana and began a low humming, lines of melody intertwining, the air around them seeming to vibrate.

They seemed to have lost any interest in Darcy. He sidled over to Elizabeth, who stood some feet away. "What are they doing?" he asked in a low voice.

"Nothing," she said. "Nothing magical, at least. I think they are trying to comfort her."

"But she is a threat to them."

"That does not mean they wish her to suffer," she snapped. "Can you not feel their auras, their desire to help her?"

The damnable thing was that he could.

This was not how dragons were supposed to behave. They were supposed to destroy anyone who was a threat, not encourage them to sit together and share a flask, even if he could see exactly that happening before his eyes. This made no sense.

Unless Elizabeth had been right all along, and he had been wrong. These dragons were like Cerridwen, not the monstrous ones in Spain.

In which case, they might be the answer to preventing future massacres like Salamanca.

His mind whirled as he took in the possibilities. Was it too late to make allies of them? He had rejected them, just as he had destroyed Elizabeth's trust in him. It had made sense to him when Sycamore turned on him, but now new evidence stood before him.

It was up to him to mend his own mistakes, to save his marriage, and perhaps his country as well.

"Elizabeth," he began, but she did not even look at him. He tried again. "I was wrong to judge all dragons by Sycamore's reaction. This shows me a different side of them."

Her chest rose in a deep breath, but she paused before looking at him, and even then it was only a glance. "I am glad you can see the truth when it stands before you." It was grudging, but at least it was an acknowledgment.

"I want to learn more about them. Will you teach me, you and Lady Amelia?" Would she be able to hear his apology in that?

She sighed, but there was no warmth in it, only resignation. "I will have to ask Cerridwen what I can tell you. They have secrets, too, and they know your loyalties lie elsewhere."

He winced. "My duty is to my country, but my loyalty is to you. I deeply regret causing you to believe otherwise. You deserve trust and honesty from me, and I must learn to reassess my former beliefs."

Now she turned to look at him, her dark eyes searching his. "Do you actually mean that?"

"I do. I wish I had told you about Georgiana. I should have trusted you not to reject her."

Her jaw dropped. "Reject her?" Her voice rose in disbelief. "Is that why you kept it a secret?"

He blinked. "Well, yes. Most people would want nothing to do with a changeling."

"If you judge most people by your mother, perhaps so. But I am not like that."

"I know," he said humbly. "I ought to have realized that."

Beyond them, Georgiana's voice rose in a song, one in a minor key. The words were carried away on the wind, but he could hear a clicking as the red dragon kept time with his talons. The greenish dragon named Hawthorn produced a little pan pipe from nowhere and played a harmony. Wait – a dragon playing an instrument? In harmony to a tune the dragon could never have heard before?

His understanding of dragons clearly lacked a great deal.

Elizabeth said quietly, "It is good to see her with them. I think she needed this."

God above, what a relief it was to hear her words, not so much for their meaning but for the sense that once more she saw him as being on the same side, that she might forgive him! Her distance since yesterday had felt like a nightmare, the kind where something precious was forever out of reach, no matter how much he chased after it.

Unable to stop himself, he reached out his hand and interlaced his fingers with hers. When she squeezed them in return, his heart swelled.

Tightening his grip, he said, "You are the best thing that has ever happened to me."

A small, tentative smile lit her face. "I do not understand, but I am grateful you feel that way."

If only he could take her into his arms! But this was not the place, and he did not want to risk ruining the moment by saying the wrong thing, so he simply said, "I do." And stood beside her in silence as Georgiana finished her song and resumed her conference with the dragons.

A few words drifted past, too soft to hear. Finally the large dragon rose, stretching its wings before folding them again, and then approached

Elizabeth. Georgiana remained with the other dragons, leaning against the flank of the green one, watching Darcy.

The dragon spoke only to Elizabeth, not even looking at him. "Companion Elizabeth, we have heard this child's answers to our questions. I will present them to the Nest so we may determine whether to permit you to take final vows."

Elizabeth bit her lip. "It is not enough, what she had told you?"

The dragon brought his forelegs together. "She has a kind and generous soul, and I trust she would not voluntarily help the Wicked King. But he could still influence her, and your husband is an unknown quantity."

She bowed her head. "I understand." Her voice quavered.

Darcy could not bear it. Suddenly decisive, he took a step forward. "I would make a request, if I may, Honored Juniper." Was that the right form of address, the one Elizabeth had used earlier?

The dragon blinked slowly, studying him. "What is your request?"

"I would like to prove my trustworthiness by being read."

Another blink of the enormous eyes. What was he thinking, this creature many times his size, far older and more powerful than he? "Has anyone coerced you to do this?"

For some reason, that amused him. "My wife attempted to persuade me, but without success. Your kindness to my sister has changed my mind."

Blink. "You understand this would be a deeper reading than merely the sharing of thoughts, and that I may see things you do not wish me to?"

Darcy swallowed hard, but he had come this far. "I do, and I ask only that you keep private those findings which do not relate to my wife's fitness to be a dragon companion."

"That which need not be revealed shall never be disclosed. Come, then. Place your hands on my talons and look into my eyes."

His heart pounding, Darcy followed his instructions, moving so close that the faint aroma of burning metal tickled his nostrils. Juniper's talons were large enough to fill his palms, smooth on top and ridged underneath, and thick with magic. The immense inhuman face loomed over him. Did flames ever come from between those sharp teeth? The dragon's eyes were large, gold-rimmed amber, and hypnotic.

Was the mist rising again? The world was losing focus around him.

You are doing well, said a gentle voice in his head. *It would be possible for me to move silently through your thoughts, but I will make myself known, so you will know what I have sensed and what is untouched.*

And he could feel it, a presence drifting through his thoughts. Bringing the events of the last few weeks to the forefront. Then back to his first meetings with Elizabeth and his decision to marry her. The choice to undertake his mission.

The presence flinched away from his memory of interviewing the wounded soldiers and sailors, leaving those unexamined. Instead it went to his mother, her reappearance and Georgiana's despair. Back to when his mother had been lost, and all the pain of the boy who believed his mother dead, an embarrassment to the Darcy of today.

The dragon comforted him. *It speaks well of you. A child should feel such a loss.*

Oddly enough, it helped. A small part of his bitterness toward his mother leached away.

Your mother has allowed herself to be enslaved to duty, putting it ahead of all else. There should be a balance in life. Laughter, hope, and love.

All he could think of was Elizabeth.

Yes, she can teach you to laugh more. There was a feeling of warm satisfaction.

Back to the idea of Cerridwen, then, and a sense of amusement as the dragon perceived his early hostility towards what he had believed to be a kestrel familiar. *We all dislike what we do not understand. Do you not find it so?*

Fortunately, while Darcy was still mentally blushing over how childish his behavior appeared in hindsight, the presence moved onto his knowledge of Faerie – sparse as it was. And his hearty dislike of it for the pain it had caused his mother and Georgiana. But the presence also understood a thought he always avoided like a poisonous snake – his deep fear of what might have happened to his true-born sister, the one he had never met, who had been traded as an infant for the Georgiana he knew.

There is nothing you can do, but the Faerie court does not mistreat their mortal children. They are like beloved pets to them. It is unlikely she is suffering.

But unlikely was not good enough.

No, it is not. Then the presence drew back, tugging at something in him, and suddenly he found himself in the dragon's mind, surrounded by a cathedral of well-organized thoughts, tinted by a strange light like the last moments of a sunset.

Forgive me for startling you. There are things I would say to you in private, but not where I might influence you unduly. Will you listen?

Shaken by the absolute foreignness of it, Darcy sent, *I will.*

Your sister, the one who is here, is not wrong to fear the Wicked King. We cannot protect her from him, but we can teach her how to protect herself, and we can set wards against him at your home. Would you be willing to permit us to do so?

Georgiana, threatened by the High King of Faerie. It was like a cold knife in his ribs. He would take help from his worst enemy for her sake. And this dragon was not his enemy. *Yes, I would be grateful.*

We will make arrangements, then.

Then he was alone in his own body again, with Elizabeth beside him, tears of pride shining in her eyes.

Chapter 5

G EORGIANA TURNED HER FACE away as she climbed into the carriage, obviously avoiding Elizabeth's gaze. Darcy, entering behind her, seemed lost in his own world, but that was hardly surprising after he had been communing with the dragon.

There was so much left unsaid, and Elizabeth suspected that if she left it to Darcy and Georgiana, none of it ever would be spoken. She had no intention of allowing that to happen. "Georgiana, thank you for agreeing to this. I know it was difficult for you."

The girl kept her head lowered. "It was good to meet them," she whispered.

Darcy blinked, as if suddenly aware of his whereabouts. "Georgiana, the dragon asked my permission to offer you training in how to protect yourself from the High King. I granted it, but it will be up to you if you wish to take advantage of it."

Her eyes flickered up at him for a moment before lowering again. "Yes," she said in a small voice. "I would like that."

"He also said they could set wards at Pemberley so that he cannot come there. Does that seem like a good idea to you?"

Now she did look up, a disbelieving smile warming her face. "Could they truly do that? It would be wonderful! Then I could stay at Pemberley all the time."

Darcy's brow furrowed. "But I thought you liked London."

She shook her head. "Oh, no. I only wanted to be there to stay safe from *him*. The High Fae cannot come to the city because of all the iron there."

"Then that is settled," Elizabeth said briskly, before Darcy could think to ask the next question of why the girl was afraid of being found by the High King. That was not a conversation to have in a carriage. "I would like to know, though, about the lock of hair he used in creating you. Do you know whose it was?" If the old stories were anything to go by, this could be a matter of great importance.

Georgiana's cheeks flushed a delicate rose. "Lady Anne gave it to him."

"She *gave* it to him?" Darcy rumbled disbelievingly. "Was it her own?"

"Yes. When she bargained with him."

Elizabeth's chin dropped. If there was any message that had been drilled into every child in England from the tales of Faerie, it was never, ever to bargain with the fae. What had Lady Anne been thinking? A sense of foreboding filled her. "What did she bargain for?"

"She wanted a living daughter. It had been years since Fitzwilliam and Jack were born, and she had despaired of having a daughter to carry on her magical work. He kept his word; she bore a daughter. He never promised to let her keep it," Georgiana said bitterly.

A typical fae trick. "Even so, she must have known it would be dangerous to give him her hair," Elizabeth argued.

Georgiana sighed. "She made him promise not to use it to harm her or any of her relations, and apparently she thought that was enough."

Elizabeth said slowly, "But if he used it to create you, was that not hurting her?"

"No, for he could have substituted any fae child for her baby." But she dropped her gaze.

"He must have had a reason," Elizabeth prompted. "It makes no difference to my opinion of you, but we need to understand his motives."

Georgiana's shoulders sagged. "It meant I can pass as mortal, that I can touch iron safely. He thought the knowledge I would gain of fashionable society and mortal magic might prove useful to him someday."

Elizabeth exchanged a worried glance with Darcy. "He wanted you to be a spy?" No wonder the girl hated the High King!

"I never agreed to it! I was only a helpless infant who knew nothing of his plans!" she cried. Then, with an obvious attempt to calm herself, she added, "Not a spy for information, more a resource he could use to understand the mortal world. The same reason the Welsh Nest wanted Cerridwen to live in England."

Cold ran down Elizabeth's spine. "I do not know what you mean."

"The Welsh dragons wanted someone who understood the behavior of the English. She just told me that."

That was more than Cerridwen had ever told Elizabeth! She was not about to admit to ignorance, but she would have some questions for Cerridwen later. "Lady Anne traded a lock of her hair for having a daughter and thought it would never rebound upon her?" How foolish could she be? The fae always demanded a high price.

The girl hesitated. "That was only part of the trade, but he never told me the rest. He was terribly pleased with himself about it."

Of course he had been; the fae delighted in taking advantage of mortals. Why had Lady Anne been desperate enough to take such a risk?

Darcy's brow furrowed. "Do you know when this bargain took place?"

Georgiana wrinkled her nose in distaste. "Nine months before my birth, if you can call it that."

Elizabeth calculated back. Darcy would have been, what, ten or eleven then? During that brief time when his mother had been training him to be her heir. A thought struck her. "Would they have chosen her as the King's Mage if she did not have a daughter?"

Darcy frowned. "It is not a requirement, but it would have been a strike against her. Especially since her sister had a daughter."

His cousin – and his first wife. Elizabeth hated thinking about her, even though she knew Darcy had never cared for her nor even spent time with her, because of their magical repulsion.

Had Lady Anne truly been so ambitious that she would bargain with the fae in order to become the King's Mage?

Darcy made a hissing sound between his teeth, and all the color leached from his face.

"What is it?" Elizabeth asked. Not that he lacked reasons to be upset, but this reaction seemed something stronger.

"Nothing," he said tightly.

Georgiana buried her face in her hands. "I am so sorry! I should never have said anything."

Elizabeth slid across the bench to put her arm around the girl. "I am very glad you told us. The truth can sometimes be upsetting to hear, but it is still better to have it out in the open." And she glared at Darcy, who was still sitting in stunned silence.

He tipped his head back and pressed his lips together for a long minute, and then said, "Pray do not blame yourself. This news has distressed me, but I am nothing but proud of how you have comported yourself."

"For someone who is not even a real person?" she asked in a small voice. "I let you think I was a natural-born fae."

"You are precisely the same person you have always been," said Elizabeth. "Just as it does not change my opinion of Cerridwen, either, to know that the first dragons were constructs." Not that she truly understood what that meant. She needed to learn more about the ways of the fae.

"It is irrelevant," Darcy said. "You are my sister, and that is all."

Slowly Georgiana straightened. "But if it is not me, then what is troubling you?"

Darcy sighed. "It may be merely a coincidence, but something else happened around that same time, and it raises an unhappy suspicion in my mind about the second bargain she made."

"What?" Georgiana's eyes were round.

"That was when Lady Catherine de Bourgh became ill."

Georgiana gasped.

Elizabeth asked, "Your aunt?" Why would that be relevant? People became ill every day.

"The very one. It was not a normal illness. She was out of her wits for months. And her Talent never recovered."

Georgiana's hand stilled over her lips. "She always said our mother had poisoned her."

Elizabeth looked from one to the other. "This simply does not make sense. Even if your mother wanted her sister out of her way, there are far simpler ways to do it than making a deal with the King of Faerie. Heavens, people do it all the time simply by spreading malicious gossip or setting up a compromising situation! Not to mention a mortal poison or arranging a carriage accident."

"You do not know Lady Catherine," said Darcy heavily. "You are fortunate in that. She was both immensely powerful and completely unscrupulous."

More secrets, just when she had thought they were done with that. Elizabeth opened her mouth to make a retort, then closed it again. This day had been difficult enough, and Georgiana was already deeply upset. If Lady Catherine was no longer a risk, questions about her could wait until later.

"Will we be able to finish the wards today?" Elizabeth asked the peregrine falcon on Roderick's shoulder.

Rowan glided to the ground and transformed, his currant-red scales gleaming against the dark green hedges, earning a gasp from the elderly gatekeeper who was hobbling out of the gatehouse. "Yes. Once the others are here, I will be able to close the circle."

"Good." Elizabeth had not been too concerned about the possibility of the High King coming to Pemberley until she had gone to Georgiana to ask about her fears. The girl had seemed less frightened once she was in her bedroom, and Elizabeth could recognize why: she had filled the space with iron. Candelabras and candlesticks everywhere, not a single one silver or brass, and none of them lit. Three different iron boot scrapers far from any exterior door where a boot might need to be scraped. A collection of bird ornaments painted in bright colors, but the shape of the cast iron came through.

It was a room designed to be poisonous to fae, who could not bear the proximity of iron. How sad that poor Georgiana had to live her life in such anxiety!

When Elizabeth asked her what the High King had done, Georgiana said, "The first time he came to me was to tell me who I was and that he expected me to serve him. After that, he started asking for things. Information about Lady Anne, mostly, but I could not tell him much, since she refused to see me. That made him angry, and he told me to question Fitzwilliam and Jack about her. The last time he wanted a lock of hair from both of my brothers." She sounded despairing. "He would not tell me why, but it would not be something good. He said he would punish me if I did not do it."

Elizabeth had caught her breath, her stomach churning. That hair could give him control of Darcy's body or mind. "And did you?"

Georgiana shook her head. "I cheated him. I had a mourning brooch from when my father died – my supposed father, that is – and I took the hair from that and told him it was Fitzwilliam's, since the color was right. I thought that would be safest, as he was already dead, and the High King could do nothing to him. That could not work for Jack, but he had just left for Spain, so I said I would write to him and ask him to send me a lock." She shivered. "Then I insisted on staying in London after that. He could not approach me there."

The High King's interest in Darcy's family – her own family now – was very disturbing. So

Cerridwen asked Elizabeth the next morning if she would be willing to assist with creating the wards right away, she agreed with alacrity.

Rowan had arrived shortly thereafter, and Roderick and Georgiana joined them. Then they had walked nearly ten miles around the borders of Pemberley to begin the process. Georgiana was flagging by the end, and so was Elizabeth. The child within her must be sapping her usual energy, for her legs ached more than she would have expected. But it was worth it. This way the wards would protect the entire estate.

The dragon had stopped them at uneven intervals. At each one Rowan would scrabble in the dirt and tell Elizabeth to call on her land Talent.

Then something would happen. Something powerful. A shining golden symbol, like a letter in an alphabet she could not read, would form over the ground before sinking in and vanishing. Elizabeth could feel each of them link with the last, forming a ring around Pemberley, a new power in the land.

"Are you certain that will keep the fae out?" Georgiana asked.

"The High Fae, yes. Stopping a lesser fae is nigh impossible, but they are no danger to you," said Rowan.

Roderick laughed. "Unless you mind having your boot laces tied together. We had a hob who loved to make us trip over our own feet."

Rowan's chest trembled with amusement. "Pranks, yes, against mortals. But they are blood-bonded not to harm any High Fae, so Georgiana is safe." The dragon swung his head towards the Welshman. "Friend Roderick, you have made this much easier by being an excellent anchor. Have you done this before?"

Roderick shook his head. "I have not been so honored."

Elizabeth interrupted, curious. "An anchor?"

"In this mortal world, dragons must stay near an anchor. For an older dragon, it must be a powerful one – the Nest, essentially. Younger ones can use smaller anchors. Permanent ones, like your Dragon Stones, or mobile ones, like companions. You are Cerridwen's anchor."

Elizabeth frowned. "But Roderick is not a companion."

"Friend Roderick took on being a temporary anchor for me by wearing an Artifact and giving it a drop of his blood. We call it the lesser bond. Ah, here are the others."

Elizabeth squinted, but it was still a moment before she could make out a pair of shapes winging towards them. Was a dragon's eyesight especially sharp? Then the falcons landed and transformed into Cerridwen and Sycamore, crowding the small space just beyond the gatehouse.

The gatekeeper blanched, clutching his withered hand in his good one, as if that would offer him some protection.

Elizabeth glanced up and down the thankfully empty road. Hopefully no one would come by before they were done, but... "Could we do this part elsewhere where there is less of a chance of being spotted by a passer-by?" Darcy would not be pleased if they had to put a binding on an innocent traveler.

"It is better here," Rowan said. "The traditional entrance to the estate has an important resonance. It will strengthen the wards to close a circle here."

The dragons, without any obvious instruction, shuffled to form the points of a triangle, slightly askew from the line of the road.

"Now, the rest of you, one each between us." Rowan turned to the gatekeeper. "You, sir, should stand at the center. You have resonance as well, as the keeper of the gate."

Elizabeth stepped between Cerridwen and Rowan. Who could blame the poor old gatekeeper for looking as if he were about to faint? This was an assembly such as she could never have imagined. Three dragons were enough of an impossibility, and here she stood with a fae changeling of royal blood, a disinherited Welsh mage-prince, and an old loyal retainer whose long service to Pemberley had been rewarded with the simple duty of opening and closing the gate. All performing powerful magic together.

"Companion Elizabeth, will you prepare the earth to receive the rune?" asked Rowan.

She let her Talent sink deep into the land once more. The soil under the gravel lane was tightly packed, but the roots of the lime trees lining it formed tendrils of life, while creatures too small to be seen and earthworms burrowed through it. She could sense the weight of the magic moving from the dragons around her, spiraling into the land. *Accept this Talent,* she told the land, *which will protect those who live here.*

Her Talent tingled as it raced through her feet. Keeping her attention in the earth, she nodded to Rowan.

The red dragon spread his wings, and the other two followed suit, creating a dome of gleaming scaled leather that surrounded their circle. Elizabeth's skin prickled as a vortex of power formed in the center, resolving into a glowing golden rune floating in midair. Slowly it sank down and touched the earth.

Elizabeth staggered. It was as if a giant bell had tolled, sending reverberations through the land. The links Rowan had created earlier were all joined now, full of power, a ring around Pemberley.

It was done, and surely such strong magic would keep them safe from the High King. Elizabeth reached out again with her Talent. The land was still the same, full of life, of dormice nesting beneath the grass, a rabbit racing through the shrubs, the deep roots of the lime trees undisturbed. The earth radiated its usual busy contentedness, not troubled by this massive work of dragon magic.

Georgiana's timid voice spoke up. "Is it true? He cannot come here now?"

"Not unless you or Companion Elizabeth grant him access. Not the Wicked King nor any of his minions." Rowan's tone held a reassuring rumble, his aura shining with pride.

"It is well done, youngling," said Sycamore judiciously. "It is not easy to set a ward on such a large area."

The red dragon ducked his head. "I never anticipated having to do such a working beyond the Nest, but I am glad of the opportunity."

"Indeed," said Sycamore. "It is a fine thing for the young to have a place where they need not be in hiding."

Elizabeth studied Granny's dragon, the one who had left the Dark Peak Nest for another where dragons were more accepted among the villagers. What was it like for dragons to be forced to hide their true natures except in the Nest? The Great Concealment had kept them safe, but at what price?

If Pemberley could be a refuge for them, that would be a fine thing. Just like it was now a safe haven for Georgiana – and for Elizabeth herself.

The dragons transformed and took flight. Georgiana chattered happily as they walked backed back to the house, as if the wards had set free a new side of her. Elizabeth shared an astonished glance with Roderick at the girl's changed behavior. She must have been truly terrified that the High King would come to her.

Inside, Georgiana went off to the music room to practice while Roderick accompanied Elizabeth to the drawing room, an unusual spring in his step.

"What was it like, serving as an anchor?" Elizabeth asked him.

"Energizing," he said. "Fulfilling. Despite a lifetime among dragons, I have never been so entwined with one before."

"Were you ever considered as a possible dragon companion?" It was something she had wondered about often, but been afraid to ask.

"To my everlasting regret, no. Dragons prefer female companions. Less warlike, you see. My sister almost became one, but the bonding did not work."

"It would be a difficult thing for a dragon, I suppose, if their companion went off to war," she said thoughtfully.

"They will not take the risk of bonding to a potential killer, even if it has been several generations since we have had to fight. Still, I would have loved to be a companion," he said wistfully.

"I am glad you had the opportunity to experience the lesser bond, then."

"It is a memory I will treasure. And to see another Nest, to meet with dragons who have not known me since infancy – it is a privilege I never hoped for. Much less expected, when I was sent here to fetch you back to Wales."

And Rowan thought it a treat to be able to come to Pemberley and be among humans. "Perhaps someday, when all our crises are past, you might come to visit again, both Pemberley and the dragons." It would be odd to bid farewell to him; he had become such a part of her life in the last few months.

"I would like that." He gave a rueful smile. "Though perhaps not when Lady Frederica is here. I thought she might burst with fury when she learned I would be included in the ward setting and she would not."

Elizabeth eyed him with sympathy. "I cannot believe she blamed you for that, though she does envy our connection with the dragons. Perhaps if you told her about what we did, it might ease matters."

His lips tightened. Clearly this was a painful subject. "Though I wish her well, it is unlikely I will ever see her again after I depart."

Chapter 6

"I HAVE BEEN THINKING it over," Granny told Elizabeth and Roderick the next morning after breakfast. "If Miss Darcy was created out of mortal hair, then most of her must be mortal as well. I wish I could consult the Eldest in Gwynedd about this. She has made a study of the stories of the High King."

"She would be the one to ask," Roderick agreed. "Though she has not been the most helpful about this situation with Cerridwen."

"That was of her own making," Granny sniffed. "She favored sending Cerridwen to England and would not send anyone to help Lizzy with the process after my daughter died."

Elizabeth looked up from her needlework at that, another of the Talent-imbued handkerchiefs she was racing to make for Darcy to use in France. It was such a relief to be on good terms with him again! "I have wondered why I was chosen. Surely it would have been simpler to select someone local as a companion." She hesitated. "Cerridwen says it was deliberate."

"Ah, yes. That was my idea." Granny's eyes went distant. "The dragons needed a better understanding of what was happening in England. Even fifty years ago, it was easy enough for a Welsh Nest to stay hidden, to frighten away or lay spells of confusion on any Englishmen who tried to enter their territory. But the English are more organized now, less superstitious, and much greedier. They believe there may be wealth in the mountains of Gwynedd, and they are determined to find it. The dragons do not understand that they will not stop coming this time."

Roderick added, "Their naïveté is understandable, given how many centuries they have been in hiding."

"True, but it does not serve them well now. I suggested that if one of their nestlings lived among Englishmen for a few years, she could provide useful insight in dealing with them. That required an English companion, preferably one among the gentry who would expose Cerridwen to English society. One of your sisters was the obvious choice."

That stung. "You wanted one of my sisters, but not me?"

"That was your father's insistence that it should not be you, so originally we tried for your sister Mary. But none of the nestlings we brought to meet her felt the connection needed for a bond. Then Cerridwen noticed you, since you were in the garden with Mary, and made it clear you were her choice. I tried to discourage her for your father's sake, but Cerridwen was determined. She said if she could not have you, she would take no companion. It is not unusual for a dragon to feel a strong affinity with a certain human, but she was particularly insistent. I suppose it should not have been a surprise when she refused to break the bond years later."

She caught her breath. "My father knew Cerridwen was a dragon?"

She snorted. "Of course he did. Ridiculous boy. He was under a binding against speaking of it, naturally, but he opposed the idea from the beginning. He knew dragon companions, adult ones, had to live near a Nest, and he wanted you to stay at Longbourn. He thought if he kept you away from the Nest long enough, Cerridwen would be forced to break the bond. Such a fool, planning to kill his own golden goose."

That sounded ominous. "What do you mean?"

"Why, he valued you for your land Talent, but the reason you are powerful is that you are a dragon companion. Without Cerridwen, your Talent would be little greater than his."

"But...my land Talent is not my own?" How mortifying! She had worked so hard at it, prided herself on it.

"It is both yours and Cerridwen's, your joined Talents strengthening each other." The old woman sighed. "Fortunately, Cerridwen was stubborn, and you escaped in time. That is good, since her growth is already stunted from her time away."

Her chest grew tight. Her dearest Cerridwen had suffered because of choosing to stay with her. And her own father had caused it. "Will she grow once she is part of a Nest again?

"It may take some time once you have taken your final vows, but yes." Granny's expression softened. "It should do her no long-term harm."

She was about to ask another question when Darcy strode into the room, his face grim.

He closed the double doors behind him. "Another dragon attack," he said harshly, tossing a newspaper onto the tea table.

"What?" cried Granny. "Impossible!"

Roderick jumped to his feet and grabbed the newspaper, his eyes rapidly scanning the headlines.

Elizabeth found her voice. "Is it certain?"

"Over half the Austrian army killed, and this time there were many witnesses. Now everyone will know that Napoleon can command dragons. There will be panic."

Half the Austrian army lost! Hundreds of thousands of men who would never go home again, gone in one fell swoop. Her chest grew tight.

"Roderick, what does it say?" demanded Granny.

"Five dragons. They flamed the Austrian army when it took the field, ignoring the massed French troops. Thousands of eyewitnesses." He glanced at Darcy. "Have you heard anything else?"

"A letter from the War Office confirming it, with one other detail. Napoleon has demanded an unconditional surrender, and the Austrians have agreed. What choice do they have, the poor devils?" Darcy rubbed his hand over his eyes.

Elizabeth blinked hard. She knew what he was not saying. England would be next. Now even more was riding on his mission.

All those dead soldiers, lost to their families. And the dragons, the poor peace-loving dragons in the Dark Peak, who had been so kind to her! They would be devastated, too. Cerridwen would be heartbroken.

Granny had that unfocused look in her eyes, and Roderick was fumbling to remove the pendant Rowan had given him. Cerridwen needed to hear this from her, not from other dragons.

Elizabeth swallowed hard and reached her mind out to Cerridwen, finding her much closer than expected, sitting in a tree outside the music room window.

We are listening, sent Cerridwen, with an image of two other birds perched near her. Young dragons in disguise, most likely. *They enjoy Georgiana's music.*

Could it only have been a day ago that they had heard Cerridwen reproduce that music?

Bad news, dearest, she sent, along with an image of all she had learned.

Shock, dismay, and then abrupt anger. And then silence, as Cerridwen took wing.

Poor Cerridwen.

But that was the least of Elizabeth's problems. "This means Napoleon will be returning to Paris soon," she said, her eyes fixed on Darcy. Was it already too late to take her vows and get a boon to help him escape?

"It seems likely," he said quietly.

Roderick wiped his forefinger with a handkerchief that came away stained with red. "Darcy, do you have an atlas where I can find the location of this attack? Rowan wishes to pinpoint which Nests are nearest to the battlefield, but I do not know where this place may be." He glanced at the newspaper, "Kleinreith, they call it."

"Yes, in the library. Are there so many dragon Nests in Austria that he is uncertain?"

"In the Alps, yes. More than here, at least." The Welshman paused, listening. "Rowan asks if he may come here to see the newspaper article with his own eyes, but he will not do so without your permission."

Darcy's eyebrows shot up. "Dragons can read?"

"Of course," said Granny irritably.

"Then he may come, I suppose, but it would be better if he took a different form, at least where others can see. The staff may already be hearing this news, and the sight of a strange dragon might frighten them."

"I will tell him so."

Darcy frowned. "How are you communicating with him? The Nest is too far for a sending."

Roderick touched the pendant which now hung outside his cravat. "This Artifact allows it, even at a distance. Rowan gave it to me so he could contact me about Mrs. Darcy, but it works in reverse, at least when I give it a drop of my blood."

Elizabeth studied the pendant. There it was, right before her, a complex Artifact made by the dragons. Something like that could make all the difference for Darcy when he was in France. She had meant to ask Roderick about the purpose of the gift sooner, but it had slipped her mind. It seemed impossible that it had been only a week since she first met Rowan.

Everything was happening too quickly, and there was still so much which she did not understand. And, thanks to Napoleon, she was running out of time.

The news from Austria hung over them like a heavy storm cloud. Even the servants were affected, tiptoeing as if a dragon attack on Pemberley might materialize at any moment. The war had always seemed very far away for them, but this had brought it close to home.

Elizabeth had requested a shortened dinner with only one remove instead of the usual two. With everyone in low spirits, there seemed to be an embargo on every subject of discussion that might provide distraction. How could they chat about the weather and other pleasantries when their world was falling apart?

Instead of the ladies withdrawing, the entire party moved to the drawing room. Elizabeth, unable to bear her helplessness, immediately sat down to her handwork. At least the bit of Talent-infused fabric in her hands might have a chance of helping to put an end to Napoleon's depredations.

"Are you certain you will not play, Lizzy?" Granny asked. "You were sewing all afternoon." The rustling of card shuffling came from the table where Roderick and Darcy had joined her in a game of loo, a courtesy to the old lady's love of the game.

"No, I thank you." She jabbed the needle into the fabric. It was already blood-spotted where she had pricked her tired fingers, but the appearance of her work no longer mattered. Only getting it done. Perhaps the blood would even help.

She hoped Mrs. Reynolds would find her a spinning wheel soon. At least spinning used different muscles. And she needed to purchase any other Talent-entwined fabric the mysterious midwife might have.

At the familiar tapping of a beak, Roderick tossed down his cards and went to the window to open it. The kestrel glided in and landed on the floor beside Elizabeth.

Close the doors, Cerridwen sent to her.

Elizabeth hurried to do so, and the falcon blurred into her true shape.

Cerridwen settled her glistening wings. "Is there any more news?"

"Nothing yet. We can only receive information from letters in the post and the newspapers, which are already two days old when they arrive." So many everyday things she had never explained to Cerridwen, back when she believed her to be only a magical falcon.

"You must tell me at once if you learn anything."

Elizabeth said, "I will. But what of the dragons at the Nest? Do they believe us this time, or do they still think we are mistaken?"

A puff of acrid smoke came from Cerridwen's nostrils. "They know the truth. We just received word that a dragon came through the Gate at a North African Nest carrying dozens of eggs. They recognized her as one of their own who had been gated to an Austrian nest as a hatchling."

Roderick's eyes were wide with horror. "But you can only go through a Gate once."

The dragon lowered her head. "She collapsed as soon as she dropped her burden. With her last heartbeats, she sent the message, 'Beware the emperor.' And then her body burst into flames, leaving nothing but ash."

A being who would have lived for centuries, gone. A shiver traveled down Elizabeth's spine.

Granny lowered her head. "May her memory and her sacrifice live forever." It sounded like something a dragon would say.

Darcy set down his cards without the slightest regret. The game was not an entertainment he undertook with any pleasure, especially after the disastrous news of the day, and Elizabeth had gone white as a sheet with the news. He hurried to sit beside her, taking her hand in his. "It is terrible, I know. Is there anything I can get you for your relief? A glass of wine?"

She shook her head. "I am well enough." Her voice was subdued, though.

If only he could help her in some way! The image of the dragon giving up her life to save the hatchlings would not leave his mind, either. He would do the same for the child Elizabeth was carrying.

Across the room Cerridwen stiffened, then rose to her full height, her wings extending, her eyes staring into the distance.

Roderick jumped to his feet just in time to catch a vase that her wingtip had toppled.

"Is something the matter?" Elizabeth asked.

"Hush," Lady Amelia said. "She will tell us when she is ready. Or not, if she prefers."

"But what is happening?"

"A sending, unless I miss my guess. One of a special sort."

Cerridwen's aura shifted then, from anxiety to satisfaction. A minute later, she drew in her wings and sat back on her haunches.

"News?" Granny asked.

"The Nest is going into Conclave," Cerridwen said. "And I... I am invited to join it." Her head swung to Elizabeth. "They are accepting you as my Companion."

Elizabeth's face lit up. "That is excellent news. What is this Conclave?"

"Later," Cerridwen chirped distractedly. "I must go now." As she shifted to her kestrel form, Roderick was already at the window, holding it open for her.

"At least that is one problem solved," Lady Amelia said as Cerridwen flew off. "And another begun. The dragons will be discussing what to do about this. I hope this Conclave will be a short one. We do not have weeks or months to spare."

Elizabeth's shoulders sagged. Why did that particular idea bother her, out of all the others? Darcy rubbed his hand over her arm in what little comfort he could give.

"I cannot imagine it will take that long." Roderick closed the window and latched it. "There is not enough information for them to make a decision."

Lady Amelia pulled her shawl around her shoulders, frowning. "For them, perhaps, but it is clear what I must do. Little as I like the idea, I must drag my ancient bones down to London and teach your ridiculous War Office chaps how to deal with dragon attacks – not to mention peaceful dragons."

"London?" Elizabeth cried, sounding horrified. "Will that journey not be too much for you?"

"It will be more painful than I like, but there is no choice. I had already been considering how to do it, since we can no longer afford to have the government acting in complete ignorance of dragons. This is the moment, since during a Conclave, the Nest cannot stop me." The old woman sighed. "And we must learn about the involvement of the sea serpents. Sycamore can speak to the ones in the estuary in London."

Darcy stiffened. "Dragons can speak to sea serpents?"

"Of course," Lady Amelia said irritably. "Sea serpents are their cousins."

"It would help enormously if we knew what had turned them against us," Darcy said.

Elizabeth shook her head fiercely. "But this will expose the existence of dragons here, and that cannot be undone. Even if you manage to keep my involvement secret, will it not endanger them?"

Lady Amelia made an unladylike noise. "Oh, the Nests would certainly oppose it, at least until they had given it consideration for at least a year or two, hidebound creatures that they are! It will not be the first time Sycamore and I have acted on our own, choosing to seek forgiveness rather than permission."

"I did not hear that," said Roderick pointedly. Then, more soberly, he added, "You are planning to violate the Great Covenant of Concealment. I do not disagree with your reasoning, but I must report your plans to the Gwynedd Nest. Unless you stop me from doing so."

Lady Amelia's eyes unfocused briefly. "Sycamore is already on his way here to bind you against revealing it. The Nest here will find out soon enough, but it will be too late."

Roderick nodded, as if this was exactly what he had expected. "They may still punish Sycamore, even if there is little they can do to you."

Suddenly she looked every year of her age. "Do you think I do not know that?"

Darcy said slowly, "I could not agree more with the necessity of informing the government, but could not someone else make the journey in your place? Roderick understands dragons and can travel more easily."

"Roderick could do a fine job if only they would listen to him, even if we could remove the binding that would keep him from speaking of it. But what chance would an unknown Welshman have of getting a hearing? No, it must be a dragon companion, because no one can ignore a dragon."

"Are there no other companions who could go, then?" Darcy probed. "Surely there must be others."

She frowned. "Fewer than there should be, and none of them are suitable to speak to the government. There are two decently born Scottish companions, but they have never been to England and would be perceived as barbarians. This is what happens when the Nests value staying hidden over everything else. They end up choosing commoners as companions, who cannot then advocate for them. Lizzy was supposed to be my heir in that regard, and if she had started her training on time, she could do it. But there is no point in crying over spilt milk."

Darcy sat down next to the old lady and said gently, "It has been a very long time since you visited London. Times have changed. You have a powerful family name, if people believe you are who you say, but no current connections beyond Elizabeth and me. They are, sad to say, unlikely to listen to you."

"Oh, they will listen. Perhaps not until I have Sycamore destroy Westminster as a lesson to them, but it will be no loss to dispose of that ramshackle mess." She sounded rather pleased by the prospect. "We will get all the people out first, of course."

And judging by what the dragons in Spain and Austria had done, it would be well within Sycamore's power. "Madam, I must protest. That will only lead to your arrest."

She cackled delightedly. "Dear boy, do use the mind God gave you! I may be physically feeble, but I am a dragon companion who has spent seventy-six years honing my skills. There is no one in London who can begin to match my power. Try to touch me – no, go on, try."

It was foolishness, but he obeyed her – or attempted to. His hand would not move. It was glued in place. So was his other arm. His legs would not budge, either. Panic swirled in him, but he pushed it down. "What is this?" At least his mouth worked.

Her smile was proud. "I may be aged and frail, but my Talent can still stop a regiment in its tracks." She lifted her hand, and his invisible bonds vanished.

Deeply unsettled, Darcy spread his fingers, merely to prove he could. "Impressive. Is this the sort of thing Elizabeth will be able to do after her final vows?" This could be important, should the war come to England.

She snorted. "It takes decades of work to control the power. At first, she will merely be a little stronger. If you are like my first husband, you may be in for some surprises, too. If you live that long, and you stay connected to Lizzy."

His throat tightened at that unpalatable truth. But he should be used to that by now.

Chapter 7

DARCY'S SLEEP HAD BEEN troubled by dreams of Austrian soldiers being cut down by dragons, but he forced those images away as he descended the steps of the portico towards the coach waiting to take Lady Amelia and her party to London. It helped to have his hand entwined with Elizabeth's, a necessary precaution with Frederica's presence. It was almost a pity that his cousin was leaving. It would take away his ready excuse to hold his wife's hand in public.

Not that he would have many more opportunities to do so, with Napoleon likely already heading to Paris.

Elizabeth embraced Lady Amelia, at least as well as she could while holding Darcy's hand. "I wish you did not have to leave so quickly."

"No choice," said Lady Amelia. "I must be gone before the Nest can interfere."

Elizabeth held up a finger. "I almost forgot. There is a woman in London, Rana Akshaya, an Indian mage. She recognized that Cerridwen was a dragon when I met her there, though I did not know it until later. My maid, Chandrika, used to be in service to her, so I asked her last night if she wanted to go to London with you. She declined, but said it was important that you should call on Rana Akshaya. Frederica can tell you more about her."

Lady Amelia cocked her head. "An Indian mage who can recognize a dragon in disguise? I wonder if she might be a dragon companion, too. I will indeed want to meet her."

"I hope your journey will be an easy one. I will miss you." Elizabeth's voice trembled. Was she thinking of how unlikely it was that her great-grandmother would live long enough to see her again?

"We will come to visit you, Lady Amelia, whether in Wales or London." The words came out of Darcy's mouth without forethought.

Elizabeth gave him an odd look, and he suddenly realized it would not be possible. He would be gone on his mission in a matter of days.

"See that you do. One day you might even break down and call me Granny," said Lady Amelia briskly. "Now give me your arm, young man, and help me up into this abominably high vehicle."

As Elizabeth gripped his shoulder, he used both hands to support Lady Amelia's elbows, bearing most of her slight weight as she stepped into the carriage. When she was seated, he said, "This is the best sprung carriage I own, and you will have four outriders to fetch you anything that will make you more comfortable." It was the least he could do. Every instinct still shrieked that he should escort the old lady to London himself, even though she had flatly refused his offer, saying she did not want to draw any attention to Elizabeth or Cerridwen.

Inside the carriage, Roderick spread a blanket over Lady Amelia's lap. After some protest, she had agreed to allow the Welshman to accompany her, although she planned to send him back immediately, claiming he would only harm her ability to portray herself as an English aristocrat.

Darcy stepped back from the carriage as Frederica came forward, a small satchel in her hand. Nodding to her, he said, "I thank you for undertaking this journey and making the introductions in Town. I know you were in no hurry to return to the King's Mage."

She winked at him. "Yes, but to have three days in a coach where I can pester Granny with all my questions? It is entirely my pleasure."

Lady Amelia's amused voice drifted from the carriage. "The King's Mage may not recognize the apprentice I will return to her."

The coachman shook his reins, and the carriage moved down the gravel drive, first slowly, and then picking up speed, in keeping with his instructions to make the ride as smooth as possible.

Elizabeth squeezed Darcy's hand, although she could have released it now that Frederica was gone, taking the risk of repulsion with her. "It will seem quiet here with all of them away!" She did not sound displeased, though.

"I, for one, am looking forward to having you to myself."

"And Georgiana, and Cerridwen, and your French tutors," she teased.

He matched her tone. "Perhaps we should hide in the cottage in the oak grove. Let them all think we have left." But she was right; there was still work to do, and Georgiana deserved some of his attention, too. While Elizabeth was by his side, he could tolerate anything. And he refused to think about how short a time they might still have together.

The reprieve was short-lived, though. Late that afternoon, as Elizabeth sat with Darcy in his study, Cerridwen returned in kestrel form, dropping a small pouch on her lap.

A gift of some sort? "What is this?" she asked the bird.

"You shall see," Cerridwen chirped with a sense of great satisfaction.

Elizabeth laughed as she picked up the pouch. "A mystery, then. How was the Conclave?"

Cerridwen perched on the desk and danced from leg to leg. "Open it, and it will answer your questions." How strange it was to hear her speak aloud in her kestrel form!

"Very well." Elizabeth opened the pouch and took out a heavy, intricately engraved globe of silver.

As it touched her skin, an illusion rose from it, a glowing miniature dragon, and a voice resonated throughout the room. "I am the Eldest, the voice of the Nest. Companion Elizabeth, we seek information on recent events. We request you to present yourself at the Nest that we may pool our knowledge. I particularly encourage you to bring your mate, whose insights would be much valued. He would be required to submit either to a blindfold or binding to avoid revealing the Nest's location. I await your reply via your companion. I am the Eldest, the voice of the Nest."

The illusory dragon vanished, leaving only a prickle of magic on Elizabeth's skin and a heavy, inert ball in her hand. Astonishing!

In a strangled voice, Darcy said, "Dragons seem to have a truly remarkable supply of Artifacts."

"We create them," chirped Cerridwen. "The Eldest of this Nest is very skilled at it."

"And is the voice of the Nest," Elizabeth added, amused.

"That phrasing means this is a formal request of the highest priority. It was the decision of the Conclave to speak to you." Cerridwen stretched her kestrel wings, flapped them a few times, and then looked around curiously. "Where is Sycamore? I cannot feel him."

Oh, dear. Elizabeth hated to disappoint Cerridwen, especially when she was so pleased with the invitation to the Nest. "Granny and Sycamore left for London while you were in the Conclave."

"London? Why would they go there?"

Elizabeth was still trying to come up with a way to explain it gently when Darcy spoke for her. "They went to speak to the government about dragons."

The kestrel stilled. "But that violates the Covenant of Concealment." Betrayal radiated off her.

"That was their intention," Elizabeth said softly. "They chose to do it during the Conclave so the Nest could not stop them." She would not lie to her dragon, not even for Granny.

"I must tell the Nest at once." Cerridwen took wing and flew out the window.

Elizabeth looked after her, but there was nothing she could do to help. Instead she wrapped her arms around Darcy's waist, drinking in the warmth and steadiness of his muscular form. What did he think of this invitation? He had seemed much calmer about dragons recently, but an invitation to walk straight into the lair of the Eldest, the most powerful dragon of the Nest, might give anyone pause. "I will go, but your attendance is up to you."

Darcy frowned. "I dislike the idea of being blindfolded, but any further mental binding is out of the question. I have quite enough of that already."

"I understand. I was blindfolded the first time I came near this Nest, and I cannot say I cared for the experience. The binding is actually much less trouble, and it is safer."

He stiffened. "You think I cannot be trusted with the knowledge?"

She released him, picked up the sphere, and handed it to him. "Tell me, if the government knew of the existence of these Artifacts, how forcefully would they question you as to the location of the Nest? Or suppose the French capture you, and want to find our Nest to create more killer dragons who will ravage England? I feel safer knowing I cannot tell anyone."

He turned the ball over in his hand. "Very well, I will consent to a blindfold, but only because I think it necessary that we share information. I would not want you going there alone, either, in these unsettled times."

She hugged him tightly. "There is no cause for worry, but I thank you." Then she kissed him.

The light from Darcy's lantern reflected from damp stone walls and stalactites hanging from the ceiling. After all his expectations, this dragon Nest was nothing more than a simple cave, not unlike half a dozen others in these hills. He played in a similar one as a child, imagining it to be a fortress, but even then, he would have thought a dragon's lair to be something grander. Apparently he had been wrong.

"Cerridwen says it is this way," said Elizabeth, pointing to an alcove. She had been looking around with every evidence of pleasure. Perhaps caves were a rarity in Hertfordshire.

Darcy held up his lantern. "That is a dead end."

"No, it is not," she said absently as she walked forward –

...Into the cave wall. And disappeared.

"Elizabeth!" he cried. "Where are you?"

Her voice sounded only a few feet away. "Right here. What is the matter?"

"Kee-kee-kee!" It was obviously laughter – and directed at him.

Illusion. It had to be. When Darcy reached out to touch the wall, his hand went straight through.

But the illusion was perfect. Even knowing it was not real, he had to brace himself to step through, half-expecting his nose to smash into the stone.

Instead, he found himself in a palace.

There was no other word for it. It was throbbing with magic and full of extraordinary art, elaborate carvings, giant swirling mosaics that formed dizzying images, and more silver than he had ever imagined seeing in his entire life. Sculpted faces, human, fae, and draconic, peered out from nooks and crannies, drawing him in, making him want to come closer, to examine them, to learn their expressions. The floor was a mosaic of tightly fitted tiles of differing hues, making a giant pattern he could not comprehend.

And he had wondered if the creators of this had the mental capacity to read a newspaper!

Cerridwen transformed into her true form and led them through an archway and down a long tunnel, a vast corridor sized for dragons, and every inch of it decorated. How long had it taken the dragons to create this massive work of art? Centuries, at the very least. It sang of ancient power.

Finally they reached another chamber, one of even more mammoth proportions. Darcy stifled a gasp at the sight of the creature inhabiting it. He had thought the dragon who read him was mythic in size, but this one was almost twice as big, as long as three horses standing in line. The beast was awe-inspiring by that alone, but the intensity of magic shrouding her raised the hair on his neck. If anything in the world was invincible, surely it was this dragon.

He glanced at Elizabeth. Did she feel it, too?

Cerridwen crossed her forelegs in a supplicant's position. "Honored Eldest, I present to you Companion Elizabeth and her mate, Darcy."

"I appreciate your prompt attendance." The Eldest's voice reverberated through the chamber, so resonant that Darcy felt it in his bones.

"I am at your service," Elizabeth said. "Both my husband and I are eager to do anything we can to stop these attacks."

The dragon's enormous golden eyes focused in on her. "Companion Elizabeth, will you share your knowledge with me?"

"Yes." And without hesitation, she stepped forward and laid her hands on the Eldest's talons, apparently without fear. Her fingers were tiny compared to the massive claw they rested on, but her face showed no distress.

The two stayed frozen, as if in a trance, apart from a small twitching of the tip of the Eldest's tail. But it would be wrong to say they were silent, since the dragon's aura shifted abruptly, almost violently, turning from initial curiosity and trepidation to deep pain.

Darcy swallowed hard, his chest tight. It was a struggle to watch Elizabeth engage with the dragon in a way that excluded him so completely.

After a few minutes, Elizabeth withdrew. "I am sorry," she whispered, her lips trembling. "I know it must pain you greatly, as it does me." She reached out her hand blindly towards Darcy, and he took it gladly, wishing he could pour his love for her through that connection.

The great dragon's head shifted quickly from side to side, as if she were shaking herself. "The truth is often painful." Turning those giant eyes towards him, she continued, "And you, Darcy. My nestmate Juniper has told me of what you shared with him about interviewing soldiers and sailors, but he would not allow me to see it for myself, since you had not given him permission to do so. He acknowledged not looking deeply, out of a belief that the attacks were illusions. Would you be prepared to let me see those memories, or do you prefer to answer verbal questions?"

Darcy straightened his shoulders. He was Fitzwilliam Darcy of Pemberley, mage and landed Talent. He could face another dragon peering into his thoughts. "I will share, but first I would like to hear what you have learned of these attacks."

The dragon seemed undisturbed by this challenge. "I am embarrassed by how little we know. You have already heard, I believe, of the dragon who sacrificed herself to save the hatchlings. Because of that tragedy, we have broken our long-standing rules and sent dragons from nearby Nests to the Silent ones, both in Austria and Spain." Her head sank down, and she lapsed into silence, the chamber filling with an aura of deep distress.

Darcy drew in a deep breath. "May I ask what they found?"

"It is a sign of our deep alarm that we have done this. It is one of our core beliefs that dragons may choose Silence. To visit a Silent Nest uninvited is a violation." The rest of her answer came as a sending so powerful it almost knocked him off his feet.

A giant cavern, as decorated as this one, but with signs of conflagration everywhere – scorch marks marring the artwork, ash, and melted glass. Empty. And an arch, which he somehow knew was the entrance to the breeding grounds in Faerie, demolished. Aloud, the Eldest said, "That is the one in Austria."

The visions were certainly not what anyone would expect from dragons voluntarily fighting for Napoleon. How had the Eldest received those images in the first place? More incomprehensible dragon magic, no doubt. "And in Spain?" His mouth was dry.

"One Nest abandoned and burned, and the other with only three young nestlings, their minds so knotted with bindings they could tell us nothing." Sadness, deepest sadness.

So bindings could be dangerous, as he had suspected. At least in some circumstances. "Where do you think the dragons went?"

The Eldest bowed her head. "How much humans have forgotten! Dragons cannot survive without their Nest. Only those young dragons with companions can leave it for more than a day or two. The dragons in Spain and Austria are gone. Three Nests, lost forever! All that knowledge, all the lore, all those lives. That we should live to see such a day!"

Her sorrow was overwhelming, making the very air seem thick and unwieldy. Somehow Darcy made himself say, "Your grief is mine as well. My apologies for my ignorance."

The dragon raised her enormous head. "A grief shared is halved. This is why we must learn everything we can. We must discover how a mortal has learned to make dragons turn to killing."

"I will do everything in my power to stop it." Including risking his own life to help kill said mortal, but the dragon would not want to hear that.

"The Wicked King has the ability to force dragons to do his will. He created a mechanism for it when he made the first dragons to be his most fearsome warriors, and it is our greatest weakness. That a mortal can do this is an untold disaster."

No wonder the dragons were suddenly ready to work with humans. Darcy said, "A tragedy indeed, one which must be stopped." Then he deliberately placed his hands on the dragon's rough talons.

The reading was less of a shock this time, apart from gazing into eyes that were the size of his head. As instructed, Darcy brought his knowledge to the forefront of his memory, as if he were preparing to speak about these things. She seemed most interested in the reports of the wounded from Salamanca, although it clearly pained her.

Finally she withdrew from his mind. "I am grieved that mortals have suffered so at the hands of dragons. We must put an end to this."

And he could tell that she meant it with every part of her being. "If I receive any further information, would you like me to send word?"

"I would be grateful for that. You have sources which we lack. If you tell Cerridwen, she will pass it along to me," said the Eldest.

Then Elizabeth stepped forward to stand at his side, just as it should be. With great determination, she said, "There is one more thing. I wish to take my final vows as soon as possible. It is overdue, and this is a time when the Nest may benefit from its companions."

"We can do it at this moment, if you wish it," said the dragon.

Her lips parted. "Yes, I do wish it. I want to be a full partner to Cerridwen."

"Then let it be done. It will be a cause for celebration during this bleak time. We cannot gather the entire Nest, as many of us are busy shoring up our defenses and planning new ones, but those who have met you will be glad to take a break for this auspicious event."

Darcy drew in a sharp breath. "Defenses? Against Napoleon and his dragons?"

"Eventually, perhaps, but also from uninvited mortals. Since Companion Amelia has decided to expose us all, we must prepare for the worst. We trust you as an individual, but not your leaders."

"I understand. Will your defenses harm the local people?"

"Not unless they decide to be foolish. We use no weapons, but if I create a wall of fire between the two of us, and you choose to run through it and are burned to death, that is on your conscience, not mine. We may create a rockslide to stop anyone from reaching the Nest, or employ illusion, glamour, or confusion spells. There are many ways to defend ourselves while hurting no one."

Lady Amelia had spoken of the dragon defenses in Wales. With the power of their magic and Artifacts, the dragons could make things very difficult for an invading army – if they so chose. If the government treated them as allies instead of enemies.

And now he, too, was unexpectedly in a position to be an ambassador of sorts, at least while he remained alive. "That shows great wisdom."

"We do what we must." The Eldest paused, then asked with seeming reluctance, "Have you any word from Companion Amelia?"

Elizabeth shook her head. "Only a brief note from a lady traveling with her to say that the journey was going well. I expect she is in London now."

"A terribly risky business. Companion Amelia has always been headstrong, but to decide on her own to break the Great Covenant of Concealment is beyond that. I cannot understand why her dragon agreed to such a step without consulting the Nest. This will impact all of us." Anger throbbed in her aura.

Darcy would not want that wrath directed at him. He could understand it, though, having seen this Nest. It now seemed outrageous that Lady Amelia had chosen to expose the dragons against their wishes.

At the time, though, he had only been grateful that she was putting England's needs first. Just as he had originally done, and only now he saw his error. There were so many aspects to this.

And more than anything, he needed Elizabeth by his side.

Chapter 8

ELIZABETH'S FINAL VOWS WERE arranged faster than Darcy had expected. The dragons he had met with Georgiana joined them along with several others, magic thrumming through the ground with each arrival. Darcy could not touch it, but its undeniable potency filled the room, like the charged air during a thunderstorm. The dragons began to hum, and the power grew even more intense.

It should have been more disturbing, being trapped underground with all these dragons, and stranger still to be more or less ignored by them. The entire room was silent except for that odd, reverberating humming. He should have expected it, since dragons only spoke aloud for the sake of humans. Instead, he felt lost, left out of the mental conversation. But there was such a sensation of celebration, of welcoming Elizabeth, that his natural discomfort eased.

He had expected something like a wedding ceremony, with vows exchanged, and he could not deny the idea had made him uncomfortable. But that did not appear to be the case. Instead, Elizabeth stood alone in front of the Eldest, with Cerridwen joining the other dragons. Now he could see why they called her a hatchling. She was half the size of the others.

Something must have happened, for after a few minutes, the Eldest spoke aloud as she gazed into Elizabeth's eyes. "You are now a full partner to your companion, and a part of our Nest. Let this be your second home and we your second family. And so it is done."

The vows were done? Had the whole ceremony happened in silence, and he had missed it?

Elizabeth's form seemed to glow for a moment, and then she staggered. Alarmed, Darcy stepped forward – but no, he tried to step forward, but his feet would not leave the intricately tiled floor. Instead, the room blurred around him, a surge of strange, potent magic singing in his veins.

It was like when he was lost in the land, when he let his Talent sink too deeply into Pemberley and struggled to find his way out, but this time he had not used his Talent at all. So why was magic scouring him from the inside out?

What had the dragons done to him? Had he been wrong to trust them? He needed answers, but he could not find the words.

The voice of the Eldest broke through his jumbled thoughts. "It is our custom to grant each new companion a boon to welcome them to our Nest. Do you have a request, Companion Elizabeth, or shall we choose for you?"

Elizabeth took a deep breath. "I have a request, perhaps an unusual one. You are aware that my husband will soon go on a dangerous mission to France."

The dragon rumbled, "We cannot help with his mission, since it involves killing."

Elizabeth raised her chin. "I know. I am asking for something different, that you assist him in coming home safely afterwards."

This. This was why she wanted him here, why she had wanted to hurry this process along. It stung his pride to see her begging the dragons for help, and yet, of all the things in the world she could have asked for, she had chosen his safety.

His head swam. Should he say something? Could he even make his mouth form intelligible syllables?

The Eldest's aura had shifted, and she did not seem pleased. "Does this request reflect your own desires, or was it suggested to you?"

Elizabeth's lips twitched. "Honored one, I strongly suspect my husband is furious with me for asking this, because proud men dislike needing help. It was my idea entirely."

The dragon's head swiveled in his direction. "Darcy, step forward. I would hear this from you."

Somehow Darcy managed to move, first one foot and then the other. It seemed to require an inordinate amount of effort to keep his balance while the magic sparked like lightning in his skull. "I knew nothing of a boon, much less of her plans." That had made sense, had it not?

The dragon's nictitating membrane closed slowly and re-opened. "And if you had known, would you have supported her request?"

The lightning sizzles in his brain made it hard to formulate a response. "With all respect, I cannot see any way in which you could help me, so I would see no point in asking."

"You have little faith," said the Eldest, with a sound that might have been a snort.

"I..." The rushing in his ears was growing intolerably loud, and his knees gave way.

The dragons' Nest. That was where he was. He had been telling the dragons...something, and then... nothing. And now he was lying on a pile of cushions in the enormous chamber of the Eldest, the scent of smoke and metal prickling in his nose. He raised his head, and Elizabeth's face appeared in his vision.

"Thank heavens! You frightened me," she said.

Darcy stared up at her. "What did they do to me?" he asked hoarsely.

She bit her lip. "The dragons? They did nothing. It was my fault, although unintentionally done. Taking the final vows gave me full access to my dragon companion magic. Somehow that unexpectedly affected you. I have had many years to adjust to the power, even though I could not use it, but you have not."

"They had control of your magic?" He did not like the sound of that.

"They say it is the usual process when a companion bonds as a young child. My body could not manage dragon magic then, so they...well, perhaps the best description would be that they put a bridle on my ability to use it. Usually it would have been removed when I was sixteen, but I never went back to the Welsh Nest for my final vows. It is gone now, which feels odd." She paused. "It is affecting you through our blood link, because I am increasing."

He struggled to his feet, his head swimming a little. "Not because our magic entwines?"

"Unlikely," the Eldest rumbled from behind her. "Many dragon companions can entwine their magic with their mates, but none has had this effect. It is unusual for a companion to come into their power after they are already married, though."

He blinked. Everyone knew entwined magic was highly unusual, but was it merely because dragon companions were rare?

"If I had been unbridled before I conceived, you would have grown accustomed to this gradually," Elizabeth said apologetically. "Instead it has hit you all at once."

She helped him to a chair that someone must have found for him, since why would dragons otherwise have a chair? If one could call it that when it was an elaborate silver sculpture with miniature faces of animals, fae, and legendary creatures. It looked more like a throne for the monarch of a magical kingdom than a place to keep him safe from having his legs go out from under him.

He sank down into it gratefully. Its comfort did not match its beauty, but it held his weight, and that was the important thing.

The enormous dragon rumbled, "I have been considering the boon you requested, Companion Elizabeth. We have nothing that can guarantee your mate's safety, but there are some tools which might prove useful to him."

Elizabeth nodded. "I will be grateful for any help."

"Indeed," Darcy said. He was willing to play along with this for Elizabeth's sake, but it was hard to see what a dragon in England could do to help him escape Napoleon's clutches.

"The first thing will permit brief communication between the two of you." The dragon produced what appeared to be two iridescent copper-colored dragon scales, matching the ones that covered her body. "They will become active each day at sunset. When both of you hold one of these, you will be able to send a message regardless of the distance. Only a very brief one – an image, a thought, a sentence. These will not work for anyone one else, just the two of you, and only when your mate is away from England."

Darcy straightened. Could this be true? Sending over a great distance had always been thought an impossibility.

Elizabeth picked up one scale and stroked it carefully, reverently. "You are generous."

The dragon said, "One thing. I must insist that you not use this in any way to further your desire to kill. It is not a tool to help with murder."

"I give you my word," Darcy said. It was too bad, though. How valuable it could be, if only the War Office could send him word this way! After all, the dragons would benefit from Napoleon's death, too. Perhaps it was worth a risk. "If I may ask a question, though – why are you so opposed to my mission? I respect your belief that killing is wrong, but it would be none of your doing, and I cannot believe you wish for Napoleon to remain free to force other dragons to fight."

Shocked surprise furled off the dragon. "Wrong? Is that what they have told you? We do not kill because it endangers our freedom."

"How could it endanger you?"

The dragon gazed at him in sorrow. "Because the moment a dragon kills, he becomes a slave of the Wicked King. That is the trigger that puts us into bondage."

"I... I do not understand."

"When the Wicked King created dragons, he wanted a perfect war machine. He made us intelligent so we could make decisions in battle, but that risked making us too clever to obey every order. Lest we turn our weapons on him, he set a trap in our very bodies. The first time we kill, it triggers in us a compulsion to obey him in all things. Our ancestors did not know that, so they accepted the rewards he offered for fighting in his wars. Thus they became his minions for life, and he used them to destroy entire kingdoms of innocent fae." Grief pervaded the air around her.

It was horrifying. "But you are free of him in the mortal world, are you not?"

"Unless we kill – or take action that results in killing. I cannot help your mission, even indirectly." Her voice was weighed with helpless grief. "I have more that can assist your safe return, but we must speak alone for that. You may leave us, Companion Elizabeth."

Her eyes widened. "Very well." She darted a quick glance at Darcy and left the chamber, looking back over her shoulder. The trust in her expression warmed his heart.

The Eldest settled herself, as if striving for greater comfort. "May I speak to you in your mind?" she asked.

"You may." He was surprised she bothered to make the request after sharing with him earlier.

Her voice moved inside his head. *I thank you. Speaking aloud tires me, as I am both out of practice and out of date.*

"Your spoken language is not at all lacking." But was the Eldest not speaking now, only inside his mind instead of aloud? Or was a dragon using some other language entirely, yet Darcy heard it as English?

It has been many years since I had a companion to practice with. A sense of sadness, an image of a woman in Elizabethan dress. *One does not forget, but it does not come as smoothly.*

It sent a shock through him. It was one thing to be told the dragons lived for centuries and that this was the Eldest, but knowing she had lived in the time of good Queen Bess made it real. "I am sorry for your loss." Was it appropriate to offer condolences for someone dead for over two centuries?

She lives on in my memory. But to the matter of your safety, there are ways I can help you, but only if you agree to be bound against ever revealing the information I give you to anyone, either human or dragon.

He blinked. "Is it enough if I give you my word?"

To my sorrow, no. We have learned that the most honorable humans can have their tongue loosened by threats to them or to those they love, and I must protect my Nest as you would protect your family.

Allow another spell to control what he could and could not say? Never. His mind was his own. It was bad enough having the one binding spell in place.

I can sense your discomfort with the idea, so I will say no more.

"You will not try to persuade me that it is only a small thing?" He had not meant to say that, but the words would not be held back.

Of course not. Only you can decide whether giving up your free will on whether or not to speak is an acceptable price.

At least the dragon understood his concerns. Even so, every instinct raged against the idea. "If I agree to this, will it truly bring me back safely?"

No. I would give you tools that could help you, nothing more.

No false promises, but no rescue, either. The disappointment made him realize how badly he longed to survive this mission, to return to Elizabeth, to meet his child.

If Lord Liverpool at the War Office knew how to use bindings, he would have bound Darcy long ago not to speak of his mission. It would be a tool they used on every spy and agent, and without asking permission. But this dragon, ancient, powerful, with the ability to tear him to shreds with its sharp talons or to roast him alive with its fiery breath, was offering him a choice.

A choice to live to see his child.

"Yes, I will accept the binding," he blurted out before he could think better of it.

You do not seem certain. Perhaps you might wish to consider it or to speak with your mate first. This dragon cared more for his opinion than all the fine gentlemen in the government who lectured others on their duty.

"I am as certain as I can be about a spell which affects my mind." And suddenly it was true.

The dragon inclined her head. *Then everything you learn from me in this conversation henceforth will be under binding.*

"I agree."

His skin tingled, not painfully, more like the mildest of repulsion, and then it faded away. He felt no different. Had something truly changed?

Here is the gift I have for you. The dragon held out her foreleg as if holding something in it, but there was nothing there. *You cannot see it, but you will be able to feel it. Take it.*

Feeling foolish, Darcy reached out for empty air, and his fingers touched metal. He grasped it, the invisible Artifact, and ran it through his fingers. It seemed to be a pendant, a chain with an attached oval of metal. He could see his fingers clearly through it, with none of the blurred edges characteristic of an illusion of invisibility. It made no sound as he poured it from one hand to the other, no clinking or clattering. "What is it?"

It is invisible, silent, without smell or taste. If you put a drop of your blood in the center of the pendant, you will take on those same properties for a day and a night. No one will see you, smell you, or hear you, not even your breathing. Nor can your magic be sensed. Only by touch can you be found.

Darcy's jaw dropped. "This can truly do all that?" It was the stuff of ancient stories.

We use them regularly. I have placed limitations on this one, though. It will work only for you, and only one time. I set it so it will have no effect on British soil, nor upon the sea. It is for your protection, and nothing else. Should you try to use it to harm another person or dragon, it will shatter in your hands and lose all effect.

Darcy stared at his seemingly empty hands. With this, he could walk out of Napoleon's palace without pursuit. This could easily make the difference between life and death, imprisonment or freedom. "I give you my word of honor I will not misuse it. This is truly a marvel. I have never heard of such a thing."

The dragon sighed. *We keep them secret, even from our companions. We created these amulets for our safety, but many humans would see the potential for misuse. They would use it to spy or steal or kill with no one the wiser. If your leaders knew they existed, they would want them for their soldiers and spies, and they would demand them from us, whether or not we were willing. We would be complicit in the crimes they committed with our magic.*

It was true. One of these amulets would allow anyone to walk up and kill Napoleon, or the prime minister, or King George. They would give ultimate power, and the government would not rest until they possessed them. "Yet you use them regularly. Why would a dragon need to hide when you can already change into any form?"

We hide from the Wicked King. Although we live in the mortal world, there are times we must return to Faerie: to breed and for the hatching of eggs. These amulets protect us from discovery.

From the High King, who could force them back into slavery. No wonder they had created these Artifacts, but the Eldest was right. These were too potent for humankind to be trusted with. For once, Darcy was grateful for the binding that would force him to keep this secret.

Chapter 9

To Elizabeth's relief, the Eldest had pronounced that Darcy should not travel until the following day and turned them over to Rowan's care. Elizabeth and Darcy followed the young dragon through a long corridor and out a different exit from the Nest, this one leading to a lonely moor, broken only by a few grazing sheep and a crumbling shepherd's hut.

The dragon gestured to the shepherd's hut. "We have prepared the Companions' House for you."

Oh, dear. It did not bode well if the dragons felt that this tiny shelter was suitable accommodation for their companions. Would the roof even be intact? Perhaps she should insist on something better. Even a rustic cottage would be an improvement.

Darcy's pace was still slower than usual, so Elizabeth arrived at the door first. She reached for the clearly visible latch string, but her hand grasped at empty air. She glanced back at Rowan, who was conversing animatedly with Darcy, so she gave the rough planks a testing push.

At her touch, the hut dissolved into an expansive gabled stone house, rising to a height of three stories. The tiny door was now a massive arch of wood and iron, one that would not have looked out of place in a castle, and large enough to drive a small carriage through.

Or a modest sized dragon.

Illusion, of course. The dragons would not want wanderers stumbling across a medieval manor house where one had no right to be.

The vast door opened at her gentle push. She stepped into a great hall with beamed ceilings far above and furnishings of heavy dark wood. Tapestries of dragons and humans covered the walls, surrounding an immense inglenook fireplace. It was like stepping five hundred years into the past, apart from the many sinuous carvings and sculptures like those in the Nest, clearly of draconic make. And a raised platform scattered with cushions, perfectly suited for dragon comfort.

She turned in a slow circle, ending facing Rowan. "Oh, my. Are we the only ones here?"

"Apart from the Kith who maintain it. Centuries ago, before the Great Concealment, companions were more common, and many of them made this their home. It has been a long time since a companion stayed here."

Kith. It took a moment for her traitorous memory to recall the name for the human servants employed by dragons. "Where are the other companions of this Nest?" She was eager to meet them and learn from them.

"You are the only one. Before today, we had none."

"None?" she cried.

"Taking companions is rare in these days of concealment, and our Nest has had such ill fortune with bindings in the last century that the Eldest determined we would make no more attempts."

She frowned. "What sort of ill fortune?" Granny had never mentioned this.

Rowan sat back on his haunches, radiating sadness. "First there was Companion Amelia, who no sooner made her vows than she left, taking Sycamore with her. Two unsuccessful attempts to bond followed that, and one human did not recover. Then there was a great disaster nearly four decades ago, when a bonding went wrong. It changed both the dragon and the mortal, allowing the human to misuse her Talents. Hornbeam still lives among us, though his mind and his strength have never been the same. The Eldest concluded our ability to bond must have weakened over time, making the risk no longer acceptable."

So she would be the last companion of the Nest? It was heartbreaking. "Yet the Eldest agreed to take me," she said slowly.

"You had already formed a bond, and that is the dangerous part." The dragon sounded wistful. "And there was no evidence you would turn our teachings against others, as in the last binding."

What had happened to that companion, and how had she misused her Talents? She wanted to ask more, but Darcy looked weary again and was surreptitiously holding the side of the table. The walk must have tired him. "Is there a room where my husband can rest?"

A young woman appeared at a side doorway. "I will show tha' the way, honored Companion." One of the Kith, presumably.

"I will check on you later, should you require anything further," the dragon said.

"I thank you for your assistance." Elizabeth tried not to sound hurried, but Darcy's hands were trembling where he clutched the table. He would never admit his own weakness, but she could do it for him.

"I pray you, lie back again," Elizabeth pleaded. "It has only been half an hour, and you are still pale." Given how much trouble he had coming up the uneven stairs, she doubted he would get far if he tried to get up.

Darcy's eyes darkened. "If I must be in bed, I would rather you were here, too."

She laughed. "You must be feeling better, but I still insist that you rest. Come, I will sit beside you, and we can pretend we are lord and lady of the manor, waiting for news from the Crusades. Although I should not say that; the Crusades are a sore spot for dragons."

"Truly? Why would they care?"

"It was the end of the Great Age of Dragons. The dragons counseled against seeking out holy wars in faraway lands, and the English kings listened – at first. But Richard the Lion Heart, whom the dragons call

Richard the Traitor, wanted a war, and he resented the dragons for opposing him. He did not like the dragons dispensing justice to the people, either; he thought that should be the prerogative of the King. He came back from his crusade carrying the banner of St. George the Dragon Slayer, claiming that all dragons were liars and should be killed. He spread false stories of dragon hoards to tempt people to hunt them. Eventually that led to the Great Concealment."

Darcy's brow furrowed. "I can see why he would not wish to share power with the dragons, but how could mortals kill them?"

"They cannot, unless the dragon permits it. But sometimes they prefer to die rather than to kill in self-defense, given the consequences." It was a dark thought, and not one she wished to consider at this time when dragons were being forced to become murderers. She rubbed her hand over the slight bulge in her abdomen. What a world to be bringing a child into!

Darcy did not miss the gesture. "Is anything wrong?"

"No, just thinking about the future." Perhaps this was the moment to bring up a sensitive subject. "Though I suppose I must think about some practical arrangements. Perhaps Mrs. Sanford will meet with me now. Having a nearby midwife who understands bonding to the land would be an enormous advantage."

His warm look faded into an expression of embarrassment. "A fine idea, although I have learned something unexpected about her. I would have told you, had we not been so preoccupied with the dragons." He paused. "Mrs. Sanford is my half-sister."

She wished she could let herself smile. Not because he knew, but because he was voluntarily telling her a secret. "I had heard rumors, but did not know what to make of it."

"I only learned of it after she helped with your healing. I am told my father had sent her away as a child, but after his death, Mrs. Sanford quietly came back to care for her ailing mother. She assumed I would insist that she leave if I ever discovered her presence, so she avoided coming to my attention – at least until my lynx gave her no choice."

"Did you speak to her, then?"

He hesitated. "My steward felt she would not be comfortable with that. Instead I instructed him to give her the deed to her mother's cottage and to tell her that it was not in payment for her help when you were ill, but because it should be hers by right."

Of course, he had fixed the problem, at least as much as he could. He always did. It was a shame, though, that he never had the chance to know his half-sister, but that could still change. "Well, I will meet her and try to persuade her to attend me. Perhaps now that she knows she can stay, she will not be so shy of me." And she wanted to find out how the midwife had learned to spin her land Talent into fabric.

"I would not wish Georgiana to be aware of the connection," he said in a low voice. "She worries so much about not being my true sister that I fear what she would think if she discovered it."

Poor Georgiana! It would be hard for her to learn that Darcy had a blood sister living right on the estate. "I shall not tell her."

Darcy pushed aside the heavy bed curtains and swung his feet over the edge, wincing at the sore muscles in his legs. The sun through the mullioned window looked to be near its zenith. He must have slept nearly round-the-clock, despite the creaky bed and the coarsely woven, too-short nightshirt someone had found for him. And his stomach was grumbling.

He was alone, but somehow he knew Elizabeth was nearby, her sparkling presence imbuing the air. Was this one of the changes in his Talent the dragon had predicted?

He rubbed his chin, the stubble scraping against his hand. It would be too much to hope for a shave, much less fresh attire. If there was any to be found in this place, it would doubtless be from a previous century. Nothing to be done for it, though, besides shrugging himself into yesterday's clothes and doing his best to tie a simple knot in his cravat. His fingers seem to lack something of their usual dexterity, as if he were recovering from a severe illness.

At least there was a comb, so he made himself as presentable as he could. Then he set off to follow that ineffable sense of Elizabeth in this ancient house.

He found her in the great hall sitting at a trestle table with a sturdy young woman. "Ah, there you are!" she exclaimed. "I hope you are well rested."

He grimaced, knowing better than to mislead her. "Rested indeed, although I feel as if I had been through a particularly bad drubbing. Better than yesterday, though."

The woman stood. "Tha' must be hungry. Shall I bring tha' summat to eat, then?"

His stomach growled. "That would be most welcome."

As she bustled out of the hall, Darcy asked, "Human servants among the dragons?"

Elizabeth nodded. "They are called Kith, local people with a bond to the Nest. They provide service to the dragons in exchange for protection. Food during poor harvests, healing, that sort of thing. I was just asking her about it."

So there were common folk who served the hidden dragons. Curious, but it made sense. The few people who scratched out a living in the poor soil of the Dark Peak likely needed all the help they could get.

Elizabeth reached out her hand to him, and he could not resist leaning over and tasting the sweetness of her lips. How fortunate he was to have her!

When she finally broke off this kiss, she said archly, "I see you are much improved."

He laughed. "Indeed. Can we travel today? I am anxious to return home." Especially as there might be a letter from the War Office. And grave dangers to come, but he would not think about that now.

"I suppose we must. Though I must admit, if it were not for that, I would not mind spending a little more time exploring this house and everything in it."

Darcy nodded. "It is an odd place, but pleasant. Very quiet, as if the walls absorb sound."

She tipped back her head to gaze at him. "Like your cottage in the oak grove. The heart of Pemberley."

The cottage where they had first joined together in love, sharing their passion on the simple, narrow bed. "*Our* cottage. I will never think of it without remembering our time there."

A becoming blush rose in her cheeks, but the sound of approaching footsteps silenced whatever she might have said. Instead, she looked at the table before her. "I wonder when an outsider last saw this place. Probably not since the binding that failed. How strange that it would be empty for so long."

It was the serving woman, now carrying a wooden platter loaded with dark bread, cheese, and a bowl of some sort of stew. She placed the dishes in front of him. "Sorry 'tis so simple. We had no warning of your arrival."

Peasant fare had never looked so appealing. "This is perfect." He bit into a slice of bread, finding it gritty, but with a pleasant, tangy flavor. The cheese crumbled at his touch and carried the sweet aroma of sheep's milk. He followed it with a swallow of small beer from an ornate flagon that would have been hopelessly old-fashioned in his grandfather's day. Shaking his head, he chuckled.

"Is something the matter?" asked Elizabeth.

"The strangeness of it. Yesterday I was an educated gentleman of our modern scientific age, and now I am a squire in the Middle Ages." He gestured around the hall, the blackened beams overhead, and the food before him. "Eating as my many times great-grandfather might have done, and drinking from a goblet at least that old – and all of it after a consultation with dragons. As a boy, I would pretend to be Guillaume D'Arcy, who would have known dragons, and now I am living his life. This is not the world I was born to."

She cocked her head and studied him. "Perhaps it is the world which you were born for, though. The Age of Concealment is over, for better or for worse. You could be a bridge between the ancient world of dragons and the fine society of London, bringing modern science to the dragons and dragon magic to our mages. Perhaps a human natural philosopher could help the dragons solve their problem with bonding companions."

It was a revolutionary notion. His father had told him his only purpose in life was to care for Pemberley and the Darcy family name. His mother's one concern was that he should beget more mages. Apart from the War Office, no one had ever asked him if he wanted to do something else.

Nor had anyone told him what it would be like to become a father, to suddenly have a responsibility for the world his child would be born into.

"And intriguing thought, but first I must face Napoleon. I have some questions for the dragons first, about how my Talent has been changed."

"That may have to wait. The Nest has gone back into Conclave, to discuss what they have learned from us and decide on their next steps. Cerridwen says it will last for days, perhaps weeks."

He wanted to protest that he did not have time to figure this out on his own, but it would do no good. "I suppose we should return home, then. They will be wondering at Pemberley what has happened to us."

Chapter 10

Mrs. Reynolds came to the drawing room that afternoon with a question. "Mrs. Darcy, I know you prefer not to be troubled with household matters, but a situation has arisen which you may wish to be aware of."

Oh, dear. A pregnant housemaid, most likely, or some other difficult situation, but at least it would take her mind off her worries. Pemberley was so quiet with Granny, Roderick, and Frederica gone, and Darcy was already off in the clearing learning to control the changes the dragon binding had made in his ability to cast illusions. And her thoughts were not good company, not when a letter from the War Office could arrive at any moment. "What is it?"

The housekeeper looked back over her shoulder. "Cassie, you may come in now."

A lean young woman crept into the room, her eyes darting about. If she was with child, there was no sign of it in her thin form. She bobbed a curtsy.

"Mrs. Darcy, Cassie is one of our kitchen maids, a good girl and hard worker. Today she came to me – quite appropriately – with an unusual story. Go ahead, tell Mrs. Darcy. You are not in trouble."

The girl wrung her bony hands. "I've a touch of the Sight, madam, not much, but I can see the wee ones, the fae. My mum is the same way."

"It is a gift," Elizabeth said gravely, to avoid frightening her more. It was true, too; she had always wished she could see them.

"There have always been wee ones who stop by here, a hobgoblin or two for the most part, but in the last few days, there have been more, over a dozen of them, and they seem to be planning to stay." She cast a glance at the housekeeper. "I thought Mrs. Reynolds should know."

"Quite right," Elizabeth said. The girl had no reason to lie, but it did not make sense. They had just warded Pemberley against the fae, after all. Or at least she had thought the spell was successful. She must be missing something. "Are they doing any harm?"

"No madam, leastways not that I've seen. One old hob is always grumbling and complaining, but he's not hurting anything."

"Have you any idea why they are here?" It was baffling.

The girl shook her head. "No, madam. They do not talk to me."

Well, this was clear as mud. Silently Elizabeth sent to Cerridwen. *Dearest, apparently Pemberley is suddenly overrun with fae. Could the wards have failed?* She shared the memory of Cassie's words.

A ripple of laughter echoed in her head, remarkably like Cerridwen's old kestrel kee-kee-kee. *Lesser fae, all of them. They are there* because *the wards are keeping out the High Fae.*

I do not understand.

Cerridwen sent the mental equivalent of an impatient sigh. *There are those among the lesser fae with reason to fear the High Fae. You have provided them with a safe haven.*

Trading one problem for another, apparently. *Are they a danger to Georgiana? Or to the rest of us?*

No danger, especially if you treat them well. A series of images flowed through Elizabeth's head before Cerridwen withdrew from the sending. Apparently she had said all she wished to.

Elizabeth drummed her fingers on her thigh. "Cassie, some people feel that if they see a fae, it is wise to offer them food."

The girl ducked her head. "I never gave them anything but my own food, I swear it! But I had to. Otherwise, they can be tricksy. I never took anything that wasn't mine!"

Even if it meant going hungry, apparently. "Mrs. Reynolds, pray arrange to provide whatever food Cassie recommends for our new guests. It is not to come from her own portion. Cassie, you have done us a service by bringing this to our attention. I hope you will keep us informed if you notice any other changes."

Her face brightened with an astonished smile. "I will, madam, I promise."

"If we are to have fae among us, your Sight will be most valuable to us."

The housekeeper nodded, clearly pleased with this decision, or perhaps simply that she did not have to make a choice about how to deal with invisible creatures. "I will make certain of it, Mrs. Darcy."

Elizabeth watched after them as they left, chewing her lip. Had she done the right thing? Not that there were many choices. The lesser fae went wherever they pleased, and nothing she could do would stop that.

Then a thought halted her, a reminder that this could affect Georgiana. Would these lesser fae recognize her as a changeling? What if they reported on her to the Wicked King? Good heavens, she was sounding like a dragon now, calling the High King of Faerie by their title for him. Next she would start finding inventive ways to curse his name each time she mentioned him. The thought made her smile.

But Georgiana needed to be warned, and it should not wait until Darcy returned to the house. Elizabeth sought her out first in the music room where the girl spent much of her time, and then, when that proved empty, in her bedroom.

Georgiana's room looked different, but it took a moment for Elizabeth to realize why. Then it struck her. All the iron was gone, the candlesticks and figurines and boot scrapers. She must trust the wards were keeping the High King away.

The girl still looked nervous to see Elizabeth, though, rubbing her hands in her skirts. "Is something the matter?" she asked.

Elizabeth chose her words carefully. "Nothing is wrong; I just wished to obtain your opinion on something. I have been informed that a number of lesser fae have come to Pemberley."

The girl's eyes flickered from side to side. Or was she looking at invisible fae? "Yes, I know," she said nervously.

"Are you able to see them?" Elizabeth prompted.

The girl nodded.

Was it always this hard to get answers from her? "I wonder if you might know why they are here, or what their intentions may be."

"All I know is what they tell me," Georgiana said apologetically. "They can only speak the truth, but they may be omitting matters of importance."

Just like the old tales, then; the fae were truthful but skilled in manipulating their words to give a misleading impression. "And what do they tell you?" Elizabeth asked.

Georgiana flushed. "That they wish to serve me, to prove their loyalty to me. That they fear the High King."

They wished to serve *Georgiana*? This was too deep for Elizabeth. Perhaps Darcy might be more successful in getting an explanation from his sister. For now, she would do better to focus on the practical side. "Will there be consequences for the rest of us?"

A creaky voice answered from the empty air. "We have promised the great lady that we shall harm no one here and will offer assistance as we may, in keeping with our natures."

The great lady? What did that mean? It was beyond disconcerting, conversing with a being she could not see. "How long do you intend to stay?"

"Why, this is our home now."

Forever, then, or at least as long as the wards remained active. Well, Pemberley could afford to feed them, and perhaps some good might come of it for Georgiana. It was always wise to stay on the good side of the fae, even the relatively weak lesser ones, so a gracious response was called for. Carefully, since all the stories agreed that the fae, like dragons, hated being thanked. "Your answers have eased my mind. My staff has been instructed to offer food for you. If there are any difficulties, I hope you will inform me."

"Indeed, Lady Companion," the voice said.

How had he found out that she was a dragon companion? Georgiana was bound against telling anyone. It was a good reminder that the fae often knew far more than people thought they did.

Georgiana said in a low voice, "I am sorry to have brought this upon you. If you wish them to leave, I will ask them to do so."

Good heavens, how easily Georgiana could blame herself for anything! "I do not mind their presence at all, and if our wards keep them safe from those who would harm them, I am glad of that. My concern is solely to understand what is happening and to make certain everyone at Pemberley, both mortal and fae, is treated fairly and with respect."

The girl's shoulders relaxed. "I hope it will not make trouble for you."

"No trouble at all," Elizabeth assured her. "We have already successfully added a dragon to the household, so including lesser fae should not be a problem." At least she hoped so.

Two days later, Darcy led Elizabeth to the edge of a field where hay bale targets had been set up. He raised her hand to his lips and caressed it lightly before releasing it. Walking hand in hand with her was something he treasured even more, when he knew how little time he had left to do so. But he refused to let any worry into his mind right now. He was with his beloved Elizabeth on a beautiful day, and he intended to make the most of it – or at least as much as he could from a brief outing designed to study the sound of gunfire. Which was not much.

Her eyes danced under the edge of her bonnet as she gazed up at him. "I do not know how much help I will be, since I am far from expert at recognizing the sound of artillery."

"You should stop interfering with my excuses to spend time with you," he said in mock disapproval. "Besides, that is why Wilkins is here." He gestured to where his valet stood at the end of the pasture next to a stack of firearms.

Wilkins raised a hand in salute, and then lifted a long rifle to his shoulder, his head turned towards Darcy in expectation.

Darcy touched Elizabeth's arm, simply for the pleasure of it. "This will be real gunfire. Listen to it and pay special attention to the timing between the sound and the appearance of the smoke. And how the smoke changes. That is what I will be trying to imitate."

"Not something I noticed on those rare occasions when my father had a hunting party," she said with a laugh. "I will do my best, though."

Darcy nodded to Wilkins. The valet fired, a fine shot that thunked right into the bale of hay.

"That was a real bullet. Now he will simply hold the gun while I make the illusion happen. It will look different, of course, since I cannot make the gun kick back, but I only need it to seem convincing at a distance." Darcy gathered energy from the air, plaited it together in his mind, and cast it out.

And almost stumbled at the explosion beside him. No, not an explosion, just the sound of one.

Elizabeth clapped her hands over her ears. "That was far too loud!" she said. "Did you intend that?"

"No. It should have sounded no different." At least he was discovering this now, not when he was standing in front of the French Emperor. "The dragon magic seems to be having a bigger effect on my Talent than I expected. Let me try again."

He gestured to Wilkins to lift the rifle again. This time he reduced the energy he put into the cast. A little too quiet now, but better. At least the smoke had come out beautifully. Odd that the dragon magic had more influence on his sound illusions than on the visual ones, but he was glad of it. People did not tend to question whether gunfire was real.

Or perhaps he noticed it less with his visual illusions because he had been practicing them daily as the dragon magic built up in him. This change was more sudden.

He cupped his hands around his mouth and called to his valet. "Reload and fire again, if you please."

Elizabeth seemed to have recovered from her surprise. "This is fascinating. I had no idea you could do this."

"I practiced it often at Netherfield, but not since then. The sound of gunfire comes easily to me – it is familiar and not complicated. I cannot cast a believable human voice, or even a cat's meow."

"Is that what you were doing when you and Bingley went out hunting? Everyone wondered if he was a terrible shot, since it seemed like there was far more shooting than was required to kill a few birds."

"Gossiping, my love? Well, guilty as charged. And poor Bingley – he is actually a crack shot, better than I am. At least when he is allowed to use a gun that is loaded, unlike at Netherfield. Here, watch again."

Wilkins pulled the trigger, and the crack of the rifle split the air.

Darcy cast again, a better effort this time, despite using less of his Talent than usual. A single shot, and then a barrage of illusory gunfire, with smoke rising from each one. Like an attack that might distract guards. The air currents made it harder, getting the smoke to linger just long enough, but it was a creditable effort.

"What do you think?" he asked Elizabeth.

"I would be convinced," she said. "Does it feel different than it used to?"

"Without question. Before I could manage no more than three separate shots." And this had been at least a dozen. "I wonder what other surprises your dragon magic has in store for me."

But no surprise could be as miraculous as the joy he felt when Elizabeth beamed at him.

Chapter 11

THEY RETURNED TO THE house in time for Darcy's meeting with his steward. Elizabeth settled herself in the library with her Arabic book on magery. There was still one segment she did not understand.

She had not even finished a page of it when a maid came in with a message. "Mr. Darcy requests your presence in his study, madam."

Foreboding washed over her, echoing through her with a sense of horror. Her shoulders tightened. Darcy's meeting should have taken at least an hour, and he never sent for her, instead preferring to join her wherever she might be. He would only do this if he wanted to ensure they had privacy, even for that first moment when she saw his face.

Which meant his face would be showing something. The time for his mission must have come.

She tried to swallow, but there was a lump in her throat that wanted to choke her. She needed to do her duty, to act as if nothing was wrong. Forcing back the ready tears that fought to spring into her eyes, she pasted a smile on her face as she set her book aside. "Very well."

It was not as if this was a surprise. They had known it was coming very soon. But it was hard not to feel as if everything had changed, as if each step she took was bringing her closer to her doom.

Elizabeth knew the second that she reached the study that she was not wrong. Darcy's face sported new lines tugging at the corners of his eyes, even though he stood as proudly as ever.

She would not make him say it. Closing the door behind her, she asked, "When must you leave?"

"Tomorrow."

"So soon?" The words escaped her.

The corner of his mouth quirked. "It is not my choice. Time is of the essence, they say."

He had not moved to embrace her, instead staying behind his desk. Perhaps he could not let himself soften right now, either. "What reason will you give for your journey?"

He lifted a letter from his desk. "They have arranged it all. I have a small estate in Ireland, and the steward there has been found to be stealing. I must go to oversee the investigation and hiring of a new one. I will sail from Liverpool, in theory."

In theory, but not in reality. "I suppose it is better if I do not know all the details."

"Most likely." Now, finally, he came out from behind the heavy desk that stood between them. He took her hands in his and leaned down to whisper in her ear. "I will be traveling under the name of Edward Harcourt."

She bit her lip until it hurt. He was telling her this so that if the news-papers reported that Edward Harcourt had been killed, she would know what it meant. Through her suddenly dry mouth, she said, "Thank you."

He continued to whisper. "You will receive letters from me, purportedly from Ireland, to keep up appearances. They will all be written in advance, though."

And she would have to pretend she was not worried about him. "Is there anything I can do to help you prepare?" Having a task might make it easier. No, what was she thinking? Nothing could make this less painful.

"My valet will handle most of it, but you could inform Mrs. Reynolds of my plans." He hesitated. "Perhaps, if I do not ask too much, could we dine privately tonight?"

A chance to be alone with him, with no servants looking on? "Yes, of course." And then her façade crumbled as she moved into his arms.

This would be their last day together. She wanted to steal every moment of it.

Elizabeth was wearing her brave face when Darcy found her in their private sitting room, her eyes still red-ringed, but she welcomed him with a smile that only looked slightly forced.

"Thank you for arranging this," he said huskily. He had hurried through his last preparations, final instructions for his steward, breaking the news to Georgiana, and scribbling quick responses to letters that would otherwise never be answered, just so that he could have this time.

How had he ever thought he could do this? It had seemed simple back at Netherfield, when he was still reeling from the knowledge of Jack's death and the dragon attacks. He would marry Elizabeth, get her with child, and then head off to France without a second thought for either his wife or baby.

He had not known then that she would teach him to care about living again. Nor what it would mean to learn to love her, and then abandon her to a future alone. Not to mention breaking his own heart by giving her up.

"When do you leave tomorrow?" she asked.

"First thing," he said. "It will be a full day of travel." He tried to chase the image out of his head, of walking out the door of Pemberley for the last time, and their final farewell.

She raised her chin. "I think it would be best if we said our goodbyes here in the morning, then. Perhaps it is weak of me, but I am not certain I will be strong enough to keep my composure in front of the staff when you leave. It will be hard enough to pretend that I am not worried about you while you are gone." Her voice trembled.

He went around the table, already set with food, and took her hands. Gently he raised her to her feet. "It is not weakness. It shows that you care, which means everything to me. It will be easier for me, too. I never imagined parting from you would be so hard." He took her precious form into his arms, all too aware this would be among the last times he could do so.

She pressed her face against his shoulder, and then raised her head to seek out his lips. He met them with a desperation and hunger that surprised even him. How much he needed her!

Then his hands, as if of their own accord, began to tangle with her buttons, and he forgot everything but her.

The waiting dinner was long forgotten.

The next morning, Elizabeth dragged herself out of bed. Sobbing would not bring Darcy back. She poured water into the basin and splashed it on her hot face, letting the cool wetness soothe her swollen eyes. But nothing could reduce her fear and pain.

Perhaps if she went back to bed, she could escape through sleep. But then she would only dream of Darcy in danger, and she could not spend the next few months hiding from reality.

She needed to face facts. Because of her efforts, Darcy was better equipped to succeed in his mission. With the help of the dragons, he even had a chance to survive it. But it was no more than that: a chance. He would be in enemy territory with the entire might of the French state turned against him, and his English accent would betray him from the moment he opened his mouth.

Her breath caught in her throat. No, she was not going to start crying again. She had responsibilities, to practice the exercises Granny had given her, to work with the dragons on setting up defenses, to strengthen her bond to the land so she could send more power to Darcy. To care for the child growing within her. To take her place as the mistress of Pemberley.

She rang for Chandrika to help her dress. The maid carefully said nothing about her reddened eyes, just rubbed a little powder under them to disguise the shadows. "Will you be wanting a breakfast tray, Mrs. Darcy?"

The cowardly side of her wished to accept. But she had a role to play, that of a wife whose husband was merely attending to business in Ireland, not risking his life. For his protection, she had to put on a brave face and not draw attention to his absence. She raised her chin. "No, I will go downstairs."

Convincing herself to eat something was a different matter. Even if her appetite had not fled with Darcy, she had been distinctly queasy in the mornings of late. The very smell of coffee was enough to make her want to run away. She should ask Mrs. Reynolds to stop serving it, since Georgiana never drank it. But she soldiered on, ignoring the generous spread of food on the sideboard in the breakfast room, settling on tea and toast with honey.

It seemed so empty there. Only last week, Granny, Roderick, and Darcy had all broken their fast with her, and Frederica had been just a short walk away. Now all of them were gone, all but Georgiana, who spent most of her time in her rooms. She was alone.

She had managed only a few bites of toast when Mrs. Reynolds came in. "Mrs. Darcy, would you have time today to consult with me about a situation?"

Anything that could distract her would be a blessed relief. "Of course. Is something the matter?"

The older woman hesitated. "Nothing is wrong, as such, but some of the staff are growing distressed by the presence of the fae."

"Cassie told them?"

"It has become hard to miss. If you would be willing to accompany me to the servants' quarters, it would be easier to show you than to explain."

Mystified, Elizabeth followed her up the narrow steps to the top floor, where the maids' sleeping quarters lined a long corridor. Mrs. Reynolds gestured her in the first door.

Elizabeth stepped inside the bedroom. While not large, it was more spacious and brighter than the tiny spaces tucked under the eaves at Longbourn. The furnishings were simple but sturdy.

What could be the problem with the room? Everything seemed in order. Even the hairbrushes were lined up perfectly, and the room was spotless.

Too spotless. The small windowpanes gleamed as if polished. The curtains looked freshly pressed. The walls showed not a trace of dirt, not even a shadow of the soot in the corners of the ceilings. The room had been scrubbed within an inch of its life.

She narrowed her eyes and turned to the housekeeper. "Either you are working the maids to the bone or we have a brownie."

"More than one, most likely. All the maids' wing is like this, and Miss Georgiana's rooms as well. The stables, too, I am told."

Elizabeth frowned. Brownies never came to wealthy households, preferring to stay where they were needed most. Had the safety offered by the wards outweighed that preference? "Why does this distress the staff? It would seem to reduce their workload."

"They fear losing their positions," Mrs. Reynolds said sharply. "Why would you pay good money for work that is being done for free? The staff here receive reasonable wages and are treated well; they are unlikely to find another job like this. Nor one that allows them to be near their families."

Elizabeth rubbed her hand over her forehead. If only she knew more about the fae! "No one will be dismissed," she said tiredly. "I intend to learn more about this, and I will speak to our staff later."

Elizabeth found Georgiana practicing the harp. If anything, the music room sparkled even more than the staff quarters. The very air seemed scrubbed clean, like the first breeze of a summer day. It was the only public room of the house she had seen so far that had the touch of brownie cleaning. Was it because Georgiana spent most of her time there?

Georgiana smiled as she rose to make her curtsy. Perhaps the girl was finally becoming a little more comfortable with her. That would be a pleasant change.

"I apologize for interrupting your practice. It sounded lovely," Elizabeth said.

The girl absently caressed the pillar of the harp. "It is a fine instrument. My brother gave it to me last year."

Elizabeth smiled at her warmly. "I expect it was more the musician than the instrument. I do not wish to keep you from it, though. I wondered if any of the lesser fae are about, and if you might be willing to help me communicate with them."

"There are always some near me, unless I send them away." Georgiana sounded quietly confident. "I always ask them not to attend our family dinners, so that we have privacy there."

All the things she had not thought of, like whether there was a crowd of fae watching them eat! Having invisible guests was an uncomfortable thing. "Mrs. Reynolds tells me that some rooms here have been cleaned by brownies. Do you know anything of that?"

"A little." Georgiana beckoned with her fingers to an empty corner of the room. With her gaze fixed in that direction, she said gently, "It would please me if you answered my sister's questions."

How far did the little fae's obedience to Georgiana go? Elizabeth said carefully, "It would make me more comfortable if I could see who I was speaking to."

A small creature in a tattered black skirt and patched leather vest rippled into view. She was barely taller than Elizabeth's waist, with long, pointed ears and spindly fingers that clutched a rough twig broom. "What d'ye wish tae know, mortal?" she asked in a hoarse voice.

The sight of this being from the old tales made the hair rise on Elizabeth's arms. "Is it true that brownies have been offering cleaning assistance here?"

The brownie glanced at Georgiana before responding. "Aye, when t'spirit moves us."

Elizabeth had the sense that she was biting back a harsher response. "You have been doing a fine job of it. It creates a small problem for me, though. While your assistance is clearly well meant, I cannot accept your aid without recompense."

The brownie hissed at her, revealing sharp uneven teeth. "We help those who help us. T' great lady who gives us her protection; t' folk in the kitchens and stable who put out food for us. We dinna serve *you*."

Reasonable at one level, yet a little too close to unpaid servitude for Elizabeth's liking. Still, the fae had clearly been offended by her question. "As long as it is by your choice."

"Nae one compels us." The brownie seemed a little less hostile now. "And we can defend ourselves."

"I am glad of it. I am not familiar with the ways of the fae, but I am willing to learn. I wish us to live together here in harmony."

The brownie snorted. "We serve t' great lady, but there can be nae harmony while t' High King tortures our people."

"My dragon would agree with you," Elizabeth said slowly. "You have answered my questions well."

Now all she had to do was to convince the staff to accept the situation.

The staff were all gathered in the servants' hall, murmuring to each other. At Elizabeth's entrance, they stood and shuffled into rows. Oh, dear. She had hoped for more informality. But this was Pemberley, not Longbourn, and they still hardly knew her.

"Good evening." She moved to stand at the head of the room. "I thank you for coming. As you are no doubt aware, we have had an influx of lesser fae among us. I have spoken to one of them, and they have promised to do us no harm. But I am aware you may have other concerns about how this will affect you."

She watched for a reaction, but it was just worried looks, so she continued. "There will be no changes in the staffing here, no reductions in position or salaries. For those of you whose workload has lessened, I have instructed Mrs. Reynolds to find new tasks for you. She will consult the rector to see if there is charity work which could use extra hands."

She could see the visible signs of relief on the faces nearest her. "It will be an adjustment, but I am determined that none of you will suffer for the presence of the fae among us. Mrs. Reynolds will, as always, assign your particular duties, but if you have any general questions, I will do my best to answer."

An older footman stepped forward, and she nodded to him.

He ducked his head. "These fae. The elderflower brought them, didn't she?"

Baffled, Elizabeth studied him. His accent was not particularly thick, certainly not enough for her to misunderstand his words, but what on earth did he mean? None of the other servants seemed confused by his question. "Pardon me, did you ask about elderflowers?"

Mrs. Reynolds moved closer to her. "He means the dragon. It is a way to avoid using the word, because of the binding."

Yet another local custom she needed to learn. But of course they must think it was Cerridwen's fault. A dragon had appeared at Pemberley, and less than a fortnight later, the house was overrun with lesser fae. How could she explain this so they could understand – and not blame her for it? "Not directly. You have no doubt heard that Lady Anne Darcy was trapped in Faerie for many years. We recently discovered that one of the High Fae has been threatening her children. When Cerridwen learned of it, she placed a protection on Pemberley to keep him away. But many of the lesser fae also fear him, too, so they have come here for their safety. We did not expect that, but it is the price of keeping Mr. Darcy and Miss Darcy safe from the High Fae."

Mrs. Reynolds frowned. "Mrs. Darcy, is there any risk to the staff from this High Fae?"

"Not now, since he can no longer enter Pemberley, and his interest is only in the Darcys. Beyond that, I cannot say, though I would not wish to be the one standing in his way. He is very powerful." The staff might panic if they knew it was the High King himself.

The housekeeper nodded decisively. "So we are safer now, too."

"Thanks to Cerridwen, yes. Are there any other questions?" Of course they must have questions, but apparently none they would voice to her. "Mrs. Reynolds will keep me apprised, of course, should any new problems arise."

After she bade them good night, the servants turned to each other, putting their heads together to whisper as Elizabeth turned to climb the stairs, with Mrs. Reynolds following behind her.

Once they reached the great hall, she turned to the elderly housekeeper. "Will that satisfy them?"

"I hope so. I thank you, Mrs. Darcy, for keeping everyone on. It is generous of you."

"Will any of them wish to leave anyway? A dragon is enough of a shock, and then to add in the fae – I could not blame them if they did," she said wearily.

Mrs. Reynolds seemed to consider. "One or two, perhaps. More because of the fae than your dragon. They are quite proud of her, and that they are in service to a dragon companion. The only complaint I have heard on that front is annoyance that they cannot boast to their families about it."

It was almost enough to make her smile. Almost, but not quite. "What was that about elderflowers?"

The housekeeper's expression cleared. "It is a tradition here, that anyone who sees a dragon will then plant an elderflower by their doorway as a sign to their neighbors who are also under bindings, and to honor the dragons. Because elderflowers are sacred to dragons, of course."

That was news to Elizabeth, but there were certainly many elderberry bushes in the village and the hedgerows – and around the Dragon Stones. No doubt this explained why elderberry preserves and elderberry wine had been appearing on her trays so frequently since Cerridwen had taken on her true form.

But for now she was simply exhausted. She had hardly slept last night, and the pain of Darcy's absence seemed to sap the strength from her bones. "Pray keep me informed if there are any further problems, Mrs. Reynolds. I think I will retire early tonight, with a tray in my room, if that is not too much trouble." She could not face making conversation with Georgiana over dinner.

"Not at all, madam," the housekeeper said.

She should not complain, though, not when Darcy must be far more uncomfortable, somewhere in a coach partway to London or wherever it was they planned to take him to catch his ship. Somehow not knowing made it even worse. At least he was safe while he was still on English soil, but that would not last.

Finally she was in her bedroom, where she could throw herself on her bed and bury her face in the pillows. These next weeks and months, waiting to hear the worst, were going to be a nightmare.

Chapter 12

B Y THE NEXT MORNING, loneliness hung on Elizabeth's shoulders like an iron weight. She had not realized how rich she had been in friends at Pemberley. A week ago she could have spoken to Darcy, Granny, Frederica, or Roderick about the matters on her mind. Now there was no mortal with whom she could discuss any of it – her land Talent, magery, or dragons.

There was one person at Pemberley who did know about land Talent, though, and shared her interest in pouring magic into yarn and fabric. A woman who had once saved her life, and whose help she would need later in her pregnancy. Darcy's base-born half-sister, the midwife – who had made it clear that she wanted nothing to do with the Darcy family.

Elizabeth was determined to change her mind. She needed Mrs. Sanford as a midwife, and she desperately wanted her as a friend.

The midwife lived in a cottage near the top of the hill. Elizabeth was glad of the effort it took to climb the steep path, since it distracted her from wondering how she would be received. She wanted this to work.

The door opened to her knock, and Mrs. Sanford stood behind it, frowning at her. "Mrs. Darcy," she said flatly. Her slight resemblance to Darcy, mostly around the eyes, gave Elizabeth a pang.

This was not promising. Elizabeth gave her an engaging smile. "I hope you will forgive me for calling without an invitation. Or, for that matter, a proper introduction. I owe you a great deal for saving my life."

Mrs. Sanford studied her, and then opened the door to let her in, with seeming reluctance. "Your husband's lynx left me little choice in the matter."

Elizabeth stepped inside the tidy room. "He brought you to the house, that is true, but you chose to help heal me."

There was no softening in that stern face, nor did she respond.

Then it struck Elizabeth what it must have been like, to have Darcy's lynx force her to go. The midwife would have made the natural assumption that Darcy had sent him. "I must apologize for that, though. The lynx was acting on a suggestion from my familiar. My husband knew nothing about it."

One corner of her mouth turned up. "I am certain you mean well, Mrs. Darcy, but the lynx is Mr. Darcy's familiar and acts on his behalf. Even when it comes to showing his teeth and forcing someone out of their home – and into a place where they are forbidden to go."

Oh, dear! That did sound bad. "My husband did not even know of your existence. If he had, he would have sent a servant, not his lynx."

Now her lips bowed downwards. "I could have refused a servant's request. But that is neither here nor there; it has always been the case that the Darcys make the rules at Pemberley, and the rest of us have little choice but to follow them."

This was a poor beginning indeed! "I would not be pleased either, to be hauled off by a wild creature under someone else's command. Would you be willing to take my familiar's word for it that it was solely her idea?"

Her eyes narrowed. "Your dragon, you mean?"

She nodded. "I did not know whether you were aware of her identity."

"It was rather obvious, after she shared her power during your healing."

Elizabeth wavered, wanting to know how the midwife guessed Cerridwen's true nature, but that could wait. "I believe she meant you no harm, but we could ask her directly."

Mrs. Sanford sniffed. "It does not matter. You must be here for a reason. I assume you want me to leave." Her tone was bitter.

Elizabeth stared. "Leave? But this is your house!"

Her face crinkled as if she had smelled something noxious. "Leave Pemberley, of course."

Recoiling, Elizabeth exclaimed, "Good Lord, no! Why would I want that!"

"To strengthen your husband's precious Talent, of course. Because there can only be one Talent bonded to the land. Because only a true-born Darcy can be permitted to touch the power of the earth." Scorn dripped from her voice.

"That is just silly. I am bonded to the land, as is my dragon, and neither of us were born a Darcy."

"You do not think my Talent lessens your husband's bond?" Her tone was skeptical.

Elizabeth laughed. "Have you seen his Talent in action? Does it look diminished? Where I grew up, I taught all the tenants to give blood to the earth, and it never harmed my own bond. Besides, why would I object when you use your Talent to help the other tenants? Not to mention saving my life with it."

"But they say only one person can hold the Talent within the estate."

"You and I are living proof that is not the case. Personally, I think they claim that to protect the inheritance laws, to keep younger sons from trying to take part of an estate."

Mrs. Sanford studied her in silence, her dark eyes so like Darcy's that it made Elizabeth's heart ache. "You are not what I expected. I will grant you that," she allowed. "If you are not going to evict me, then why are you here?" It was grudging, but no longer hostile.

Should she even say it? "I came for the same reason any other woman calls on a midwife. I believe I am increasing."

Her eyes widened, her jaw falling slightly. "And you want me to attend you?"

"You are, by all reports, an excellent midwife; you have healed me before; and most importantly, you understand the issues of bonding to the land. Why in the world would I go to anyone else?"

Mrs. Sanford sank down onto a chair as if her legs had suddenly decided not to support her. "Surely your husband will wish to handle the birth rites."

Elizabeth took a deep breath. "He is away for some months. I hope he will return in time for the birth, but babies do not always keep to a schedule. That is why your help would be invaluable."

She looked stunned. "He would miss the birth of his heir, the bonding to Pemberley?"

Elizabeth steeled herself. "It may not be possible for him to do otherwise." And she had to prepare for that.

"When is he due to return?"

"That is uncertain." Elizabeth raised her chin, trying to keep the wobble from her voice.

Something flickered in those familiar dark eyes. Pity, perhaps? "Is this one of *those* marriages?" she asked darkly. "I hoped he might care about more than your dowry."

Bother those tears that came so readily these days! Elizabeth blinked them back. "He does care, but business calls him away."

"Do not make excuses for him. I know his sort all too well."

It was a bitter disappointment, but there was no point in arguing with this woman. She would have to find friendship – and a midwife – somewhere else. "I fear I have made an error in coming here. Pray forgive me for taking up so much of your time." Elizabeth marched over to the door.

"Wait! I will help you, if you wish it."

Elizabeth turned back slowly, her hand still on the latch, her chest aching. "Why? You are clearly angry, and no doubt have good reason for it."

"My anger is at your husband, not you. And he is not the one who needs my care."

"It is not his fault he must be away." Why did she care so much that this woman understand that?

Mrs. Sanford tsked. "If you wish to believe that, you may."

"It is true!"

Her eyes flashed. "It is also true that a rich man can show a purse of gold and be brought to your side whenever he wishes."

"Not from behind French lines in Europe!" The words slipped out. Elizabeth clapped her hand over her mouth.

Mrs. Sanford stood stock-still. "Is that where he is?"

"I should not have said that. It is a secret," Elizabeth said in a low voice. "I pray you, tell no one." If only she could do a binding, like Cerridwen! It would be a disaster if this angry woman revealed it.

"A healer never reveals the secrets they hear," the midwife said slowly. Then she straightened. "I think you had better sit down and tell me more about your condition."

Half an hour later, Elizabeth was still there, sipping an herbal tisane the midwife had prepared for her. "This is tasty," she said. "Fennel?"

"With raspberry leaf, nettle, and chamomile. Good to strengthen your womb. I will give you some to take with you." She hesitated. "I must ask this. Are you aware of who my father was?"

Elizabeth set down the cup carefully. "I was given to understand that old Mr. Darcy had two families, although my husband appears to have been unaware of it until meeting you."

"Hardly surprising. We were forbidden to go anywhere near the great house, and he sent us away before we were old enough to disobey." Her lips tightened. "Off to school and then into the Army for my brothers, and a position in London for me. He provided for us, as long as we never returned."

"But you came back."

"As soon as he died, to care for my ill mother. When no one said anything, I decided to stay. Quietly."

Then she had only been here for five years. "How did you manage to bond to the land?"

"My mother's work. She teased a little information from the old man and buried my afterbirth in the garden. She knew my brothers would be taken away, but she thought he might let her keep a daughter. When I returned, the power was here."

"Where are your brothers now? Are you in contact with them?"

A shadow crossed her face. "I have not seen them since we were children, but we write occasionally. Robert's last letter mentioned he had met the other Darcy boy, Jack, in Spain. Said he was a surprisingly decent sort, given his upbringing." Her face paled. "That was his last letter. He was at Salamanca, in the massacre."

"I am so very sorry," Elizabeth said softly. "Jack Darcy died there, too." Jack, whose father had refused to buy him a commission because it was too dangerous, but he had sent his two base-born sons into the Army. Now the two half-brothers had died together.

"They met the same fate." She looked up. "There will be talk, you know, if I am attending you."

"As if there has not been talk about me since I arrived! That strange Mrs. Darcy with her books and old clothes and now her dragon," Elizabeth said ruefully. "Unless it troubles you, I do not care about a little gossip."

"It does not bother me. No one here minds my oddities, since they are useful, and everyone loved my mother." She shrugged. "I understand you can feel the power in the cloth I make. I wonder if you would be willing to test something for me, purely for my own curiosity."

"Of course. At home I used to grow my own flax and spin it into yarn with my Talent."

The midwife got up and opened a chest, pulling out a small pile of fabric. "Would you mind closing your eyes? I would like you to hold two pieces to see if you can tell the difference between them."

It seemed harmless, and now she was curious, too. "Happily." She closed her eyes and held out her hands, palms up.

Bits of fabric settled in them. Wool, by the feel, with magic in each. She raised her left hand. "This one is stronger. What is it?"

"Open your eyes."

Elizabeth looked down at her hands. Two identical scraps, except one was blue and one white. "The color?"

"They are from the same looming, but I dyed that one with woad I grew in the garden."

She nodded slowly. Another step for adding in the power from the land. It made sense. "Would you teach me how someday? I know nothing about dyeing."

The midwife smiled for the first time. "If you wish."

Chapter 13

A WEEK. ONLY A week. Just seven days alone at Pemberley since Darcy had left, but it felt like forever to Elizabeth. Fear for him was her constant companion, since she had few others.

She had hardly seen Cerridwen, who was always at the Nest these days, getting to know her new nestmates. Elizabeth missed their closeness, but she could not beg Cerridwen to come back simply because she was lonely and sad. Not after all the years Cerridwen had spent alone, without any other dragons for company, for her sake. It was Elizabeth's turn to bear that burden.

Mrs. Sanford had called on her once, with more herbal teas and a tonic to help the baby's growth, and Elizabeth saw Georgiana every day at the breakfast table and dinner. Her sister-in-law was still shy of her, and had plenty to occupy herself between her music, the lesser fae, and her companion, Belinda Lowrie, who had returned from her visit to her family now that Georgiana planned to remain at Pemberley instead of returning to London. The two always had their heads together, chattering and laughing in a way Georgiana never did with Elizabeth.

There were always her books, but every morning had an empty space which had been taken up by her lessons in magery with Frederica. Even though she had rarely succeeded in learning much, she had enjoyed that stimulating time. Now Frederica was in London, and likely to remain there.

She spent the time instead taking long walks through the recently planted fields of Pemberley, sending her Talent down into the earth to encourage the crops to grow. She was still learning the land's needs here, but she could sense how it welcomed her attention. Her spirits were lifted when the tenants were happy to see her, knowing she would improve their harvest. But she gave the oak grove and cottage at the heart of Pemberley a wide berth, with all their memories of Darcy.

When she finally trudged back to the house, there was a carriage in front of the portico, a plain one of the sort that could be rented at any coaching inn. It had come to the main entrance, though, so it had to be a visitor for her or Georgiana.

Could it be news from London? She hurried her pace and practically ran up the steps and into the hall, where a familiar golden-haired figure was handing her bonnet to the butler.

Frederica had returned!

Tears rose to Elizabeth's eyes as she embraced her friend. "I am so glad to see you!" What a relief it would be to have her friend there again!

Frederica untied her bonnet and handed it to a servant. "I apologize for failing to warn you I was coming. I left in rather of a hurry," she said with a laugh.

"Not at all! I am delighted you are back. I hope you will stay here in the main house, since Darcy is away." The reminder of his absence left her hollow inside.

"Gone already? I had not realized that. I am so sorry."

"Just a few days ago. You may have passed each other on the road," she said, trying to make light of it. "Come in and have some tea. I am eager to hear all about Granny in London."

Frederica flounced into the drawing room and flung herself onto the sofa. "I can tell you less than I would like. Granny thought it could damage my reputation to be seen as her ally, so she told everyone it was all Darcy's doing that she was there and pretended to barely know me. I had to call her Lady Amelia!" This last seemed to have added insult to injury.

"But you made the introductions?"

"Yes, to Lady Anne, at least. At first she was tremendously pleased with me for discovering Granny – until Granny announced that she was a dragon companion. I expected doubt or perhaps shock, but she was outright terrified. White as a sheet, she backed as far away from Granny as she could. I have never seen anything ruffle a hair on her head before!" She shook her head in disbelief.

It surprised Elizabeth, too. "I suppose some people find dragons frightening," she said slowly.

"They certainly do! Granny had Sycamore materialize in Grosvenor Square – oh, the screaming as people fled! And Sycamore just sat there on his haunches and looked amused. After that, Lady Anne dragged me off for an interrogation – and I do not use that term lightly – about everything I had seen here and learned of Granny. But then she did not want me around, either, not when she had your sisters to play with."

An unexpected wave of longing for her family swamped her. "Did you see Mary and Kitty?" Any news of them would be a relief.

"Only for a moment, when I first arrived. The repulsion, you know. Lady Anne is pleased with Mary, but said Kitty lacked cleverness. Of course, she seems to think the same of you, which is odd."

Elizabeth laughed. "Not really. I went to some effort to convince her I was a stupid country girl. I did not care to be interrogated, either."

Frederica's eyes brightened. "Well done! Anyway, then I had to go home to my father's house, where I have not lived for years. He is in the government, so he told me a little of what happened next. There was supposed to be a polite demonstration of Sycamore's ability in Hyde Park. At least it was polite until a frightened soldier took a potshot at Sycamore and the bullet bounced right off his scales. Granny froze the entire regiment in their tracks and their guns grew so hot that they dropped them. She called the officer in charge a fool who deserved to lose the war, and he could either take her seriously or she would burn Westminster to the ground."

Elizabeth gasped. "Oh, my! At least she showed a little restraint."

Frederica chuckled. "Not for long. Something else must have gone wrong, for there was a fire at Westminster the next day – not a big one, no one killed, but it must have been Sycamore. It was a fortunate thing for me, since my father went storming out of the house without giving orders that I must be kept inside. So I announced I was going shopping, bought a ticket on a stagecoach, and came here."

Elizabeth held up her hand, unable to keep up with the torrent of words. "Wait! Why would your father make you stay in the house?"

Frederica made a tutting sound. "Oh, that. He announced it was time I married, and he had sent for that nuisance Mortimer Percy, who has been waiting for me for years despite my frequent refusals. No need for any courting, of course, since we would never be in the same room except to conceive a child. What I would not do for one of those dragon silver rings to stop repulsion! Not that I would marry Mortimer Percy, anyway, ugh. I was just writing a note to Granny to ask her to rescue me when the news about Westminster came, and I seized my opportunity." She looked tremendously pleased with herself.

Elizabeth could not help laughing at her effervescent friend, despite her concern over the turmoil in London. "You have had quite an adventure! Well, I am glad you are here, though I imagine you are sorry to miss all the excitement Granny is creating in Town."

Frederica leaned forward. "Not really. I wish I knew what she was doing, but I would rather be here with the dragons. The ones I can talk to, that is. Where is Roderick? He must have reached here days ago."

Oh, dear. "I received a note from him in London, saying he was returning directly to Wales, and thanking me for my hospitality." It had been a disappointment to her, since she enjoyed his company, but she suspected it would be more of a blow to Frederica.

Frederica's face froze, and for a moment she did not say a word. Finally, stiffly, she said, "How very like him. He did not even bother to say goodbye."

In fact it was not at all like Roderick, who was unfailingly calm and polite. What had happened on that long carriage ride with just the three of them, Frederica, Roderick and Granny? "I am sorry for that."

"It is unlikely I will ever see him again," she said icily. "How is Cerridwen?" The abrupt change of subject only revealed the depth of her distress.

Poor Frederica! Not that she and Roderick ever had a real chance, the fashionable aristocratic lady and the disinherited Welshman, not to mention the inevitability of repulsion between them once Roderick returned the dragon silver ring he had worn at Pemberley. But still, it was clear her heart had been touched. Not to mention her pride.

"Cerridwen seems well, though I hardly ever see her. She seems to want to make up for all those years when she was deprived of the company of other dragons."

"Pity. I have been hoping to speak to her about something." Frederica frowned.

Perhaps this was an opportunity for distraction for both of them. "We could call on her. I do not know if they would let you into the Nest, but I think you would find the Companions' House very interesting." And the dragons would be eager to hear Frederica's report on the events in London.

Her eyebrow arched gracefully. "The Companions' House?"

"Oh, yes! A great deal has happened since you left, and I must tell you all about it, once you have recovered from your travels."

"I doubt my curiosity can wait that long, but I would like nothing better than to see this Companions' House," she said stoutly. "Oh, but there is one thing I must tell you. Rana Akshaya is coming here. She called on me to announce her intentions. I am not certain she understands that she is supposed to wait for an invitation, or even to warn you of her arrival."

So the Indian mage was going to visit Pemberley. No doubt Cerridwen was the main attraction, but it would give Elizabeth a chance to learn more about her than Chandrika was willing to reveal. "I had best send her an invitation, then, just to make things proper."

"A good idea." Frederica took a sip of tea. "Now, tell me everything that has happened here."

Frederica hurried to the Great Hall of the Companions' House. How exciting this was, staying at the very place which had once been home to the companions of the old stories! Even if they would not let her into the Nest, it was still thrilling. And she had let a full-grown dragon read her memories and be present in her mind. What an experience!

And now she was going to put her cards on the table. Most likely it would fail, but that would be no worse than never trying.

Juniper, the one who had read her earlier, was waiting for her on one of the raised platforms, towering over her. And she had thought Sycamore was a giant compared to Cerridwen!

"You wish to speak to me again, Lady Frederica?" asked the dragon.

She took a deep breath. There was nothing to lose, after all. "Yes. I have a proposition for you."

"I am happy to hear it."

"I am told your Nest has several young unbonded dragons, yet only one companion. I would like to propose myself as a possible companion. I know this is not how it is usually done, but I can offer certain advantages that could be very useful to the Nest in this troubled time."

His chest rippled with amusement. "No, this is not how it is done, but it is generous of you to offer." He was refusing, even if gently.

She would not give up so easily, not when she had longed for this her entire life. "It is not generosity, as my reasons are quite selfish, but will you at least listen to why I think it is a good idea? You can still refuse afterwards."

More chest rippling. "I do like your spirit. Very well, I will hear you out, although this is not as simple a matter as you may think." He settled back on his haunches and crossed his forelegs.

She took a deep breath before launching into her prepared speech "I was the apprentice to the King's Mage for three years. I worked with the royal family, since I was responsible for protecting them. They know me and trust me. I can request an audience with the Prince Regent, who is my brother's dear friend, and it will be granted. The Prime Minister is an ally of my father's, and has known me since I was a child."

"That shows impressive connections, Lady Frederica, but not why you should be a dragon companion."

"Because these are the people who need to understand what dragons are! Who will be making the decisions on whether you are viewed as an ally or an enemy, and you have no other way to reach them. They are frightened by the very idea of your power, but I am in a position to persuade them to meet my dragon companion and to talk to them. I can help them see you as individuals and as potential friends. My connections can help you forge an alliance."

His aura flickered with concern. "Am I to understand that you would not use those connections on our behalf unless you are made a dragon companion?"

"Of course I will still use them! If I am ever released from the bindings, I will write letters to those who will read them, telling them about my experiences here. But a letter or even a visit from someone who likes dragons is not the same as knowing someone you trust has bonded themselves for life to a dragon – and who can introduce you to that same dragon."

"Companion Amelia is already speaking to some of those people."

"Not to the royal family, and not as their friend. And, frankly, she is not doing well as an ambassador. Her concern is with the War Office, who talk to her because they have no choice. They are afraid of her – and of Sycamore. This does not bode well for your future relationship with the government. I could approach them in peace, not as a threat. That is the road to an alliance."

Juniper studied her. "You make a persuasive argument. But a dragon cannot simply bond to any human. There must be a certain compatibility of mind and personality, or the bond will not take. And your plans would require a dragon with maturity and temperament to conduct sensitive negotiations."

She raised an eyebrow. "Unlike Sycamore?"

The scales on his chest glinted in his amusement. "Sycamore would not have been our first choice."

She hurried on. "In fact, it might be best if my companion were a very young dragon, even a nestling. A full-size dragon is intimidating, whereas humans are drawn to small childlike creatures. A nestling could not speak for the Nest, so any serious discussions would have to occur over a distance. Sometimes delays of that sort reduce the likelihood of impetuous decisions."

He cocked his head. "You have given this a great deal of thought."

She smiled. "I have thought of little else since I learned Cerridwen was a dragon."

He rose, uncurling his tail. "I will consider what you have said, though even if the Eldest were to approve, it is unlikely we could find a suitable match. Do not get your hopes up."

"I knew you were likely to refuse before I asked, and I shall not resent it if you do. But if I never posed the question, I would always have wondered what might have happened if I had."

"Why have you not taken the first step to becoming a companion, then?"

Now she was getting somewhere! "Out of ignorance, I imagine, since I have no idea what that step would be."

"Ah, has so much been forgotten? Those who wish to become companions signal their intent by giving their blood at one of our anchors. The ones you call the Dragon Stones at Pemberley would do. Any dragon who feels an affinity to your blood will respond."

"That is all? I shall do so immediately."

The amused ripples returned. "Not too much blood, in your enthusiasm. Just a taste."

She laughed. "Yes, I am rather too enthusiastic about this!"

He inclined his head, as if preparing to leave, and then he said, "You told me your reasons were selfish. May I ask what they are?"

She relaxed. This was simple. "Because I want to be a dragon companion. As a child I fell in love with the stories of dragons, and I can think of nothing more exciting or fulfilling than to spend my life with a dragon."

His eyes glinted. "There are certainly worse reasons, Friend Frederica."

Chapter 14

DARCY SQUINTED AT THE triangular shape on the horizon. Could it be a sail? The rising moon cast little light over the dark sea. But yes, it was a boat. He was certain of it.

Stiffly he rose to his feet. His legs ached after crouching on the pebble beach for hours, keeping his profile hidden below the small hillock behind him. He picked up the smuggler's signaling lamp and opened the shutter, revealing a narrow opening that cast light only out to sea. As he had been directed, he swung it back and forth five times, replaced the shutter for a few minutes, and then repeated the actions.

His heart pounded. Would they see it? Was it even the correct ship? If no one came, he would have a very long walk through the desolate marsh back to the nearest village come daylight, and yet another delay to his mission. It was galling to have to rely on smugglers, but they were the only ones who could reach France.

Yes, it was a boat, growing closer. And then a dinghy was lowered over the side and two men climbed into it. They were coming for him. He waited impatiently as it crawled nearer.

As it reached the shore, one of the smugglers jumped over the side and dragged the dinghy up onto the pebbles. He gestured to Darcy with a sharp swing of his head.

Darcy hefted his small trunk and began to carry it to the boat. Apparently not fast enough, for the ragged sailor clad all in black grabbed it from him and tossed it in the boat as if it weighed nothing. Darcy held tight to his satchel as he clambered over the edge. Without a word, the smuggler pointed to the bench where he should sit. Clearly silence was the order of the day.

When they reached the ship, Darcy climbed an unstable rope ladder up the side and over the rail. No sooner had he reached the deck when another smuggler hurried him to a small hatch in the deck.

"Down there. And stay out of sight until we're at sea," he hissed.

At the bottom of another steep ladder, this one thankfully made of wood, Darcy had to stoop to pass through the dark cramped passageway below the deck. The only trace of illumination was the dim moonlight angling through the open hatch above. He could barely make out the outlines of crates and barrels, and the stuffy air reeked of old liquor and mold.

The floor suddenly rocked beneath him, and he caught his balance on the edge of a crate. A good thing he was wearing gloves, or he would have a handful of splinters. Carefully he felt his way through the cargo hold until he found a barrel he could rest his weight against.

And he had thought traveling by mail coach was barely tolerable. It was nothing to a smuggling ship. But at least he was on his way. The sooner he reached France, the sooner he could return to Elizabeth.

Assuming he lived that long.

The ship rose and fell more now, so they must have reached open water. It felt as if he had been in the hold for hours.

Darcy made his way back up the rickety ladder and gulped down his first breath of fresh salt air. After the darkness below, the moonlight on deck seemed bright, revealing one man at the wheel and four others coiling ropes and hauling on the sails in the brisk wind. It was a larger boat than he had expected, although nothing to the great ships on the Thames, and it rode low enough in the water that spray occasionally misted the deck.

No one seemed to notice him, or perhaps they were paid not to. He made his way to the wheel and spoke to the man behind it, reminding himself of his alias. "Good evening. My name is Edward Har—"

The smuggler threw up his hand to silence him. "Don't want to know your name, nor your business neither. You're just a package I'm delivering, nothing more, nothing less."

"I thought you worked for the War Office."

He spat on the deck. "I work for gold. Someone paid me well to haul you over, and I asked no questions. If that Corsican bastard pays me more, I'd deliver you straight to him."

Darcy sucked in a breath. "You sail under the Union Jack."

The captain, if he could be called such, guffawed. "Only until we pass the blockade. Then we fly the French colors. Not that we've seen hide nor hair of a blockade ship of late, nor the Revenue neither. Better hope our luck holds." He spat again. "Now stay out of my way."

Luck? So the smugglers did not know that British ships were hiding in port, those which had not already been sunk by sea serpents. The creatures never seemed to attack fishing boats or small vessels, so they could well be ignorant.

He retreated to a storage bench near the rail, pulling his coat around him to keep off the spray, his arm looped through his satchel. No need to tempt the smugglers with a little extra profit by taking his belongings.

Not that his own gold was in it; that was sewn in the hems of his coat and tucked in his boot heels. The War Office had been thorough.

There was nothing to do but wait. To keep himself alert, he revied in his mind the plans for reaching Paris once the smugglers set him ashore near Calais.

Eventually he began to doze lightly, his chin dropping to his chest.

A thump startled him awake. The boat lurched, and he grabbed the railing to keep his balance. Not the smooth up-and-down of the waves, but as if they had struck something.

Or something had struck them.

The sailors were on their feet, clinging to the mast and conferring in urgent tones. A string of curses flowed from the captain.

Then a giant scaly head rose above the boat. For moment, Darcy could only think that a dragon had somehow come after him, but the long sinuous neck of it told him otherwise. This was a sea serpent.

Horror rose in his throat as a giant tail coiled around the other side of the boat. This was the end. He was going to drown in the Channel, his mission over before it had begun. He would never hold Elizabeth in his arms again, never meet their child.

She would never even know what happened to him. Nor would the War Office.

This was one place where magery could not help him. Neither an illusion nor invisibility could keep him from drowning – but was there a chance he could get word out? He slipped his hand into his inner pocket and rubbed the dragon scale between his fingers. It was the wrong time. Elizabeth was no doubt asleep, but he had nothing left to lose.

Simple. Keep it simple. And so he sent the very image before his eyes, the sea serpent looming over the boat. But there was no connection, no sense of Elizabeth at the other end. He redoubled his efforts. If this was the last thing he would ever do, he might as well use all his power.

The giant head swung in his direction. Huge, gold-ringed eyes shone in the moonlight, seeming to stare straight into him with a piercing curiosity. Had it sensed what he was doing? Or could it smell the dragon scale?

Lady Amelia had said the serpents were cousins to the dragons. Darcy scrambled to his feet, pulling energy through his link to Pemberley and sending it towards the serpent. *I am a friend to dragons.* Images of Elizabeth and Cerridwen. Of himself in the Nest, of his meeting with the Eldest. He held up the dragon scale with one hand.

A familiar hypnotic sensation entered into his urgent fear, like the time when the dragon had read his thoughts. This time Darcy opened his mind wide, showing anything that could possibly convince the giant creature to spare him.

I come to stop Napoleon, who forces the dragons to fight, who has made serpents attack ships.

Bafflement. Perhaps the serpent did not speak English? He tried again in French, with no better results.

The timbers of the ship creaked loudly around him, the crew shouting in despair.

Darcy gave up on words and scrambled to put his plan into images. Napoleon. Wanting to protect the dragons. His determination to stop the carnage.

Approval flowed toward him. The serpent understood. Darcy took the first deep breath he had managed since the creature had appeared, but water was already rushing into the ship. Once more he held up the scale, even more desperately.

Then the captain shouted, "Stop him! He is in league with the beast!"

Pain exploded in his head and all that was left was darkness.

Darcy awoke to a pounding headache, as if artillery were firing inside his brain. His eyes refused to focus. He was somewhere dim, his back resting on something hard and uneven. As his vision gradually improved, he made out the walls of what seemed to be a cave, one whose walls reflected a rainbow of colors and an odd green glow.

At least he was not underwater. Or drowned.

He remembered the sea serpent. His dragon scale – what had happened to it? He had been holding it in his hand. Was it now at the bottom of the Channel? Had he lost the one tie he had to Elizabeth and England before he even had a chance to use it?

Desperately he reached for it, but it was not in his pocket, nor in the leather bag hung around his neck. Every movement hurt, but he forced himself to sit up and feel the rock around him. And then he saw it, gleaming, beside his boot.

He grabbed it and held it tightly, its warmth reassuring. But now his head was swimming as well as stabbing with pain. Then a rush of magic scoured through Darcy, making him break out in a sweat.

Suddenly his head no longer hurt, and he could see clearly. He reached back to touch the back of his head. There was not even a bruise there.

What had happened? Where had that power come from? Darcy struggled to his feet and turned in a slow circle. The chamber he was in appeared to have only one exit, but if this was like the dragon Nest, there was no telling what might be an illusion.

He had to find an exit so he could complete his mission. And then a way to escape from France afterwards, now that the smugglers were no longer an option for returning to England. But he was alive, which was more than he had expected when the serpent had crushed his ship. He even still had his satchel, for what little good that would do him.

He set off into the next chamber. It was no different, but the following one was filled with deep pools of water separated by a wide pathway. The air was fresh, with a slight breeze, not cold and dank as he would have expected. His footsteps echoed in the empty space.

The third chamber was different. Not in appearance, though it was darker, and he struggled to see the far end, but in its presence, heavy, weighted with magic, and deeply familiar. He had sensed something similar in the Nest, in the presence of the Eldest.

It was like dragon magic, but with a different flavor, like the tang of sea air. And it was full of grief.

A giant figure waited in the back. Its head rose above a coiled body, part of which rested in a pool of water. *Who are you, friend of dragons?*

So this sea serpent could use words, unlike the one on the boat.

Yes. I chose to bond to human sailors so I could explore all the seven seas.

Had the serpent heard his unspoken question? And how could he answer without either lying or revealing his name? "I am an Englishman, traveling to France. My wife is a dragon companion, and I am descended from other dragon companions."

I can taste that, and it is why you were brought here, rather than being left to drown.

He had come within an inch of death, and now he was at the mercy of this huge creature. It was terrifying, but perhaps also an opportunity. "I am grateful for it. May I ask you a question, or is that forbidden?"

You may ask, and I may choose to answer.

He worded it carefully, in case there were bindings in place. "Which is your enemy, the British ships you have been sinking, or the one who has ordered you to do so?"

The serpent sank back on its coils. *The question is a clever one.*

The back of the cave, formerly shrouded in darkness, grew bright, revealing half a dozen deep alcoves. Most were empty, but one contained a few large eggs, carefully clustered together in a shallow pool. Lazy swirls of steam rose from the water.

Another held a deeper pool that glowed in aqua hues as a long thin shadow moved through it, perhaps a yard long. An infant serpent?

Then a different image formed as in his head, of this same cavern, but the alcoves were piled high with eggs, the deep pools full of wriggling shapes playing together, while young serpents wandered the floor in small groups, clearly interacting silently, a vibrant community.

This was what you would have seen, only a few seasons ago. Now they are gone, all our hatchlings and eggs. For every three ships we sink, he returns one to us. When we refuse to sink one, he gives a hatchling to the Wicked King, to be raised in enforced servitude and all its hatchlings after it. I am not proud of it, but we value our young more than your ships. Regret filled the air.

Darcy inclined his head. All those drowned sailors, who also had families who loved them. "As any parent would. I will have a child soon, and I would do anything to protect him." But this was it, the answer the War Office had been seeking so desperately, of why the formerly peaceful serpents had gone to war.

He had to risk another question, to confirm what he already knew. "The one who ordered you to sink the ships, who stole your eggs, is it the Emperor of France?"

The serpent shifted on its coils. *I am unable to answer that.*

A binding, then. "Let me ask this, then. Could you deny it, if you chose to?" Were sea serpents bound by the fae obligations to speak only the truth?

I choose not to deny it, friend to dragons.

Napoleon, in league with the High King of Faerie, so despised by the dragons. How would they respond when they learned the French Emperor was giving him sea serpent eggs? Was this how he was forcing dragons to fight for him?

"Stopping the French Emperor is my goal. It is why I was crossing the Channel, to put a plan in place to end his power."

The serpent studied him. *On behalf of the dragons?*

"I am sent by my government, but the dragons know of it. They wish to see Napoleon gone, but they cannot support my mission, since it requires killing. But I, like you, will do anything to protect my unborn child."

The serpent tossed its head. *Dragons are trapped by their very nature, by the price they must pay for bloodshed. I am not. I wish you success on your mission, friend of dragons.*

"First I must reach France. Am I there now? Could you tell me how to get there?"

We can take you close to it, but I dare not ask any of my fellows to come near the shore. Can you swim?

"A little," Darcy said, though he was considered a strong swimmer when it came racing across a lake. Swimming the open water of the Channel, fully clothed, was an entirely different question.

The serpent slithered towards him. *Stand still.*

Darcy forced his body to obey, grateful now for his experience in the Nest with the dragons and their mysterious ways. A few months ago, he would have been hard put not to flee for his life.

Especially when the serpent opened its massive jaws, only a few feet from his head. Good God, it was enormous, large enough to swallow him whole if it chose! But he stood his ground. The dragons had proved trustworthy, and he needed any ally he could get.

Even when the cloud of sea serpent exhalations enveloped him, cold, clammy, and smelling of fish and seaweed. And so heavy with magic he could scarcely breathe, much less move. The inside of his nose stung as if attacked by hornets. It scoured his skin, not just his exposed face and hands, but all over his body. The power seemed to infuse his very bones.

What had the serpent done to him?

That will keep you safe in the water.

Darcy blinked. Safe from other serpents or from sharks, or would it make him buoyant? Either way would be a gift. "I will do everything in my power to remove the danger to your eggs."

The sea serpent inclined his head. *Your service will not be forgotten. Now my brother will take you as near to France as he dares, and the people on the shore will help you, if you tell them you were brought by one of les* serpents de mer. *May good fortune smile on your efforts.*

"It already has. I am grateful for this opportunity." Beyond grateful, in fact.

He was alive for only one reason – because of the dragons. If he had not married a dragon companion, if the Eldest had not given him that scale, he would be dead and his mission over before it had even begun. He wished he could tell Elizabeth that she had already saved his life.

Chapter 15

Frederica had to suppress the desire to skip as she climbed the path to the clearing with Elizabeth. She would have liked to run, but that would be unfair to Elizabeth, who tired easily these days and seemed in particularly low spirits today. But how could she restrain her excitement? Against all her expectations, she was going to meet with a potential companion! Cerridwen had brought the news this morning that there was a nestling willing to consider her, only a few days after she had spilt her blood on the Dragon Stones.

But she should be more considerate of Elizabeth. "Do you wish to stop to rest for a little?"

"No, I am perfectly well. And we are practically there." But she was frowning.

"Do you disapprove of this? My desire for a companion?"

For the first time since they left the house, Elizabeth truly looked at her. "No, I am delighted for you. And for me – I would be so glad not to be the only companion of the Nest." She hesitated. "I am sorry to be out of sorts today. I had a bad dream last night, and somehow I cannot shake it from my mind."

Relieved, Frederica said, "Oh, it is so annoying when that happens! What did you dream?"

"I was on a ship being attacked by a sea serpent. I keep seeing it, all those teeth as the head came towards me, and hearing the creak of the wood as the ship broke up." She shivered. "It was remarkably vivid. I could even smell the salt air."

"That sounds terrifying! I am glad we have dragons here instead of serpents. I do not think I would like them."

Elizabeth seemed to relax a little. "I prefer our dragons, too."

But as they entered the clearing, Elizabeth's frown returned at the sight of the large sea-green dragon standing beside the Dragon Stones. "That is not my favorite dragon, though," she said in a low voice. "Quickthorn tends to be irritable."

But Frederica's gaze was already fastened on the small dragon beside Quickthorn. Why, it was barely the size of a fawn, and utterly beautiful, with scales of russet and auburn.

Elizabeth stepped forward. "Honored Quickthorn, it is..." She seemed to stumble for words. "Good of you to join us here today. May I present Lady Frederica Fitzwilliam?"

Frederica tore her eyes away from the little dragon in time to see Quickthorn toss her head. She made a quick curtsy. "It is an honor to meet you."

"But not as much of an honor as it is to meet the nestling," said the dragon. Irritable, indeed!

Frederica pulled out the manners she had misplaced in her joy over the nestling. "That is, perhaps, more exciting, since there is a chance he might become my companion, but I am honored and pleased to meet any dragon."

"Why?" It was a demand.

That was easy, even though the question made her nervous. What would happen if Quickthorn disapproved of her? "Because you fascinate me. I feel inexplicably drawn to dragons and want to know more about you, to learn how you see the world and why you hold your beliefs."

"Not because of the power it would give you?"

"That would be nice, but it would take years and much study. From what Elizabeth – Companion Elizabeth – tells me, I would have to learn to use my Talent anew, so I would be weaker, at least for a long time. And to learn to use it well, like Companion Amelia, takes decades of hard work. I am not a particularly attentive student."

"What do you use your Talent for now?"

"The odd illusion and some sendings, and more recently for truth-casting. The only thing I am particularly good at is weather magic, and that is not useful except for keeping the rain off. An umbrella works just as well."

"You could stop a drought by making it rain," the dragon challenged.

"Only if I am willing to cause a drought somewhere else by stealing their rain," she retorted. "Some people may not care about that, but I do."

She had not meant to say that about the weather. Then it struck her. "You are a truth-caster, too, are you not? Or can all dragons do it?"

"Only a few of us," said the dragon grudgingly.

"No wonder you are so grumpy, then," she said with more candor than tact. "It can be unpleasant to know what everyone really thinks all the time. I suspect I would like people better if I knew less of their inner thoughts."

Quickthorn drew her head back in surprise, but the displeasure in her aura lessened. "I would not argue that point. This nestling is Agate, and he has agreed to meet with you. Nothing more than that; this is merely to see if you are compatible."

"It is a great pleasure to meet you, Agate," she said. Then, when he said nothing, she glanced back at Quickthorn. "I thought dragons from this Nest were named for trees."

"We have used all the tree names, so the new generation has gemstones as their mortal use-names. Agate has just been granted his name for this meeting."

Mortal use-names. "Does that mean you use different names among yourselves?"

Quickthorn huffed. "Of course. Our true names have meanings the human tongue cannot comprehend."

"That makes sense." Frederica turned back to Agate. "What would you wish to know of me?"

The larger dragon spoke for him. "We will begin with a brief sharing, you and I, with Agate listening in, so he can sense your mind."

Her second sharing! "Very well."

Quickthorn held out her forelegs. Agate scampered close to the larger dragon and leaned against her side.

Frederica grasped her talons, glad that she needed no instructions this time. Quickthorn's eyes gazed into hers. How beautiful they were, all amber with sea-green flecks! And then the dizzying sensation of another presence in her head began – with a sense of nervous watching at the edge. Was that Agate?

Think of the first time you saw a dragon, Quickthorn commanded.

Eager to please, Frederica drew on her memories of seeing Cerridwen in dragon form for the first time. It was a happy memory, but somehow the timid watcher seemed more anxious. Had she misunderstood? She switched to her first meeting with Cerridwen-the-kestrel, when she had tried to feed her too much plum cake because she wanted to be friends. But the disquiet continued to increase until suddenly it vanished, leaving only Quickthorn in her mind.

She could feel the dragon withdraw, too, and her spirits sank. It was obvious it had not gone well, but what had she done wrong? Was there anything she could do to fix it?

But now that her mind was her own again, she could feel fear in Agate's aura. Fear of her. She turned to Quickthorn. "What am I doing that is frightening him? That is the last thing I wish to do!"

An annoyed puff of smoke issued from Quickthorn's nostrils. "It is not you. He has known all his life the price of a companion bond gone wrong. He sees poor Hornbeam every day, with his mind twisted and his magic depleted, stolen by his former companion. It is only natural for him to fear the bond."

"But..." Frederica said helplessly. Agate was such an amazing creature – and so frightened! She dropped to her knees, to meet his eyes on his own level.. "I would never wish to do anything to harm you. If bonding is so dangerous to you, then it should not happen." She could not, would not risk that beautiful young dragon! Nor could she bear for him to be afraid of her.

"Well spoken," said Quickthorn. "But his fear is natural. The companion who injured Hornbeam was of your family, and like you, she desired very much to bond." She snorted. "It was not an ideal match. Hornbeam should have refused."

Of her family? She could not mean Granny, and there was no other. But she had not known Granny was a dragon companion until recently. Had another Fitzwilliam secretly taken on a dragon bond – and harmed their companion? Or perhaps it had been centuries ago, given how long-lived dragons were. "Who was it? When did this happen?"

"More than three decades ago. Her name was Catherine. Lady Catherine Fitzwilliam, you would have called her."

Frederica's mouth went dry. "She who is now called Lady Catherine de Bourgh?" Oh, now it all made sense, terrible, terrifying sense.

"I do not know what you mortals call her now," Quickthorn snapped. "I curse her name."

"I will join you in that," said Frederica fervently. "I never knew she was a dragon companion. She has done terrible things to humans, too. But I am deeply grieved to learn that she also harmed her dragon." And horrified. Was that how Lady Catherine had gained her unnatural powers? She shivered.

Elizabeth's voice sounded from behind her. "What was it that she did? Darcy told me only it was very bad."

"She influenced people's minds, forcing them to do what she wished," Frederica said. Even after all these years, nausea still rose in her at the thought. "The king's madness? That was a result of her meddling."

Elizabeth's jaw dropped. "But no one can do that!"

"No human mage has that skill," Quickthorn retorted, "but it is intrinsic to dragons. Except for Hornbeam, who had that ability ripped from him by his companion."

Frederica pressed her fingertips against her mouth in horror. Injuring her own dragon companion for her benefit! At least it explained Lady

Catherine's horrible Talent – and why the nestling was terrified of bonding.

Decisively she turned back to the nestling. "No wonder you are afraid! And it does not matter how many times I might tell you I would never do such a thing. The very idea horrifies me. I am grateful to have met you, and would wish to know you better, but you should never, ever bond to someone you fear. That is just wrong." Tears filled her eyes at giving up the dream of being a dragon companion, but this was the right thing to do. The right thing for Agate, and that was most important.

The nestling came forward and laid his head on Frederica's arm. "I was willing to risk it because of the benefits it could bring our Nest, but our minds do not mesh. I honor your decision." And then he waddled back to Quickthorn, leaving Frederica biting her lip to keep back sobs.

"A wise choice," Quickthorn told her. "You are too strong-willed for a nestling; you would dominate him without meaning to."

Frederica nodded jerkily. "I am still grateful for this opportunity – and for your honesty."

Two days later, Frederica pushed away a tinge of disappointment as she found Quickthorn alone by the Dragon Stones. When she had received the sending from Cerridwen telling her to go there again, she had hoped against hope for another potential companion, one who was not afraid of bonding. But apparently that was not to be.

At least she did not have a witness to her disappointment this time. Elizabeth had been out walking the fields when the sending came, so she would never know Frederica's hopes had been raised. It was just as well, since Elizabeth had been in such high spirits today after finally connecting to Darcy last night using her dragon scale.

Frederica was determined not to wallow in her disappointment. Quickthorn was interesting, and any chance to talk to a dragon was more than she had once dreamed of. But why had the dragon called her here? "Honored Quickthorn, I am glad to see you once again."

"I suppose that must be true, since you cannot lie to me," the dragon grumbled.

"I am always pleased by the opportunity to meet with a dragon, especially another truth-caster," she said. "You are the only one I know apart from Companion Amelia, and she seems to carry the challenge of truth-casting more gracefully than I do."

"Or than I," said the dragon. "But most mortals do not like my company."

Frederica considered this challenging but no doubt perfectly true statement. "Well, I do. You speak your mind, and I like that. I do not demand that everyone be cheerful all the time."

The dragon peered at her. "Why are you so different from the others?"

She shrugged. "My mother always said I was born different. But it is not just that." She paused to think. Why did she like this particular cranky dragon? "I am always blurting out things I should not say, but I mean no ill by it. Well, at least not most of the time; only if someone truly deserves it. And when you read me, when you came with Agate, I felt no malice in you. I was bitterly disappointed when you said I should not try to make a bond, but I could tell you were saying it for Agate's good. As you should."

"Why did you want to bond to a nestling?"

It did not matter now. "I did not particularly want a nestling, really. I just wanted to be a dragon companion, and I thought the Nest would be more likely to permit it if I showed them a way it was to their benefit. A nestling might help me convince human skeptics more easily. But for myself? I had no great desire to wait for a young nestling to mature enough to be a true companion."

"Then you would not refuse a dragon who was older?"

"I would be happy if any dragon were willing to take me as a companion." Could it be that the door was not completely closed, that Quickthorn had another potential match to propose? She could not hold back her excitement. "Is there a possibility of that?"

Quickthorn scratched at the ground with her back leg, an odd embarrassment emanating from her. "I am not what you wanted, neither very young nor at all agreeable."

It took a moment to sink in, that the beautiful sea-green dragon was offering herself. Frederica just barely repressed the urge to jump up and down and clap her hands. "You would be perfect for me."

"You mean that." The dragon sounded surprised.

"I do! I have thought a great deal about what you said, that I would dominate a nestling. You would never let me dominate you, and you understand me."

"Our minds work along similar lines. I saw that when I read you. That is important, for a successful bond."

Frederica thought her smile just might split her face open if it got any wider. "What would I need to do? Should you read me again, to be certain you can trust me?"

"If you wish to proceed with this, yes. We must both be sure. The Eldest has already given her blessing to the attempt." She paused, then added grudgingly, "She wants more of us to take companions, now that the Great Concealment has been broken, but she thinks you will not consent. She has never considered me as a possible companion, because no mortal would want me."

"Then she is wrong, because I want you!" Frederica said stoutly. "And I still want to help humans to accept dragons. They will find you appealing, too, only in a different way."

A snort of smoke. "As long as I do not speak to them."

Frederica cocked her head. "There is the truth-caster problem, yes. I always thought people simply disliked me. Once I learned about truth-casting, I realized that was why I made them uncomfortable, because they found themselves saying more than they wanted to me." It did hurt still, all those years of rejections, but there was no need to explain that to another truth-caster.

"We are indeed uncomfortable company. But perhaps we can find a way, you and I."

Frowning, Elizabeth walked back into the drawing room. She had gone to the cottage in the oak grove before sunset, specifically so she could have access to all her land Talent when Darcy connected with her. But how was she to make any sense from Darcy's new sending? It had been a long walk back to the house by lantern light.

Frederica was already dressed for dinner, her bright expression fading at the sight of Elizabeth. "Oh, no! What is the matter? Was he not there?"

"No, I felt him," she said slowly. "But I do not understand what he tried to say."

"The words were not clear?"

"It was a perfectly clear image – of Napoleon carrying huge eggs from a cavern, and a sea serpent looking on." She shivered, remembering the frightening serpent in her dream. "It felt ominous."

"That is odd. Were they sea serpent eggs?"

"I can only assume so, since the serpent was nearby, but I do not know."

Frederica wrinkled her brow. "Why would he send you that? We already know the serpents are working with Napoleon."

"It is mysterious. But I will tell Cerridwen, in case it is something he wants the dragons to know."

"A good idea," Frederica agreed. Then, more cheerfully, she said, "And I have some news of my own. Quickthorn has offered to bond with me. I will be a dragon companion after all!"

"What?" Elizabeth cried, embracing Frederica. "That is fabulous news. I know how much you have wished for it." Quickthorn might not be a favorite of hers, but she was glad for her friend.

Frederica beamed. "I am beyond delighted. Quickthorn may have some challenges as an ambassador to humans, but I am determined to find a way. And it would be some time after the bonding before we could travel away from the Nest."

"If you tell people she is a descendent of Blackthorn the Sea-Green, companion of Ethelrida the Wise, they will be so impressed that they will take her bluntness in stride."

"Is she indeed? She never mentioned that to me." Frederica laughed. "No one will ever call me Frederica the Wise, that is for certain! Perhaps Frederica the Impulsive. And you will have to teach me everything you know about being a dragon companion."

"That will be quite a turnaround, to have me instructing you! Perhaps you will prove a more apt pupil than I am." Elizabeth was still frustrated with her lack of progress on her mage skills despite all of Frederica's lessons.

"Perhaps it was my poor teaching rather than my student," Frederica said with her usual frankness. "Or we simply have not found where your mage Talent lies."

Elizabeth doubted that. And she still needed to solve the mystery of Darcy's sending. Waiting until tomorrow's sunset and his next message was going to be hard.

"Georgiana, Mrs. Reynolds came to me with an odd concern," Elizabeth said. "Apparently some of your brother's old clothes are missing. I was wondering if it might be the doing of the lesser fae. If so, I would be happy to arrange for other clothing for them." Not that she was actually concerned, but one of the maids who had discovered the discrepancy had almost resigned her position already over the presence of the fae at Pemberley, and she would like to exonerate them if she could. Darcy would not be happy if they lost staff over this.

The girl licked her lips, as if the question made her nervous. "I was the one who took them, not my fae, but there is no need to worry. I will bring them back."

Georgiana had taken them? That made no sense at all, unless something she did with the fae required a boy's clothing. "If you find yourself in need of clothes you can move more easily in, we can arrange for that."

"No, I..." Her eyes darted from side to side. "I suppose I might as well tell you." She opened the door to her bedroom and gestured Elizabeth in.

Her bed was covered with scattered items of Darcy's clothing. And half of them were moving, as if in invisible hands. Elizabeth sighed. "I do not understand."

"Pray let yourselves be seen," Georgiana said, with a hint of command in her voice.

Elizabeth's vision seemed to waver, and then there were half a dozen fae, ranging from a tiny redcap to a trio of hobgoblins, all with the odd proportions and pointed ears that marked them as denizens of Faerie. Even after her encounter with the brownie, it still gave her goosebumps to see these creatures from old tales with her own eyes – and because they were rubbing Darcy's clothing over their hands, their faces, and anywhere else they could. One female hob had three of his cravats tied around her arm, making her look like a strange maypole.

"What are they doing?" she asked, half-choked by the strangeness of it all.

"They are taking his scent," Georgiana said, as if there were nothing unusual about it. "They will share it with the lesser fae in France, so that they know to look for him and help him."

Elizabeth turned to stare at her sister-in-law. "They can do that?"

Suddenly Georgiana's new confidence seemed to fade. "They say they can. They know how much I want it."

"But I thought they came here for the safety of the wards. How can they go to France?"

The hob with the dangling cravats said in a scratchy voice, "We have our ways, which are not for mortals to know."

"I see." It was still disturbing, though she often felt that way about the fae. "I am glad to know of it." She turned and left them to it.

Outside the door, Georgiana asked, "Are you angry with me?"

"Of course not. Anything that might help him is a good thing." Then she smiled. "I may have to come up with a different story for Mrs. Reynolds, though."

Chapter 16

D ARCY'S ICY HANDS TREMBLED as he piled up the last of the brush and driftwood he had collected. The great serpent in the cave had been correct that he would not drown, but he had said nothing about nearly freezing. Each time Darcy had sunk beneath the waves, he had been able to breath as easily as in open air, a truly miraculous experience. But swimming through the cold, rough Channel was still a battle, leaving him exhausted, sore, and chilled to the bone.

The land under him was dead to his Talent, so he reached deep inside for the power of Pemberley, drawing it over hundreds of miles through his tie to Elizabeth. It was weaker than what he was used to, but it was there, more than enough to let him create flames in the heap of sticks. Fire, his earliest mage skill, the one that still came to him more easily than any other. He groaned with relief as the heat reached his aching fingers.

What next? The serpent had told him to speak to the people on the shore, but he was on a deserted stone beach with a white chalk cliff rising far above him, one that stretched as far as he could see in either direction. He was going to have to do some serious walking if he wanted to find anyone, and that would be impossible with his sodden clothing hanging heavily from his shoulders.

There was no help for it. He stripped down to his shirt and underclothes, dumping the seawater from his boots and wringing out the rest before putting them back on. They were lighter now, at least. And his satchel looked intact, though if the water had soaked through the oilcloth enclosing his safe-conduct, there would be trouble. An Englishman with no papers would not get far in France.

If he even was in France – and could find his way past these cliffs.

Then he spotted a distant figure atop the cliff. Friend or foe? It hardly mattered if he could not find a way off this cursed beach. Darcy waved to catch his attention. The man swung his arm, pointing to Darcy's left.

At least it gave him a direction, though with no guarantee he would not be arrested at the end of it. He stomped out the fire and set off, the effort of walking on the uneven gravel warming him. Finally he came to stream that cut through the cliffs, creating a narrow ravine down to the sea.

He climbed along a steep path worn beside the stream, his thighs aching as he scrambled over rough boulders. Was he actually off English soil? That meant he could try to reach Elizabeth tonight using the dragon scale the Eldest had given him. It had only been six days since he had seen her, but it felt like forever.

And he needed to tell her about the sea serpents. The dragons would want to know – and the War Office, too, though how Elizabeth could explain it to them without involving the dragons was unclear. If, in fact, he could communicate it to Elizabeth at all.

The ravine gradually widened, the path becoming smoother. Then the man he had glimpsed on the cliffs came stomping towards him. A man who would either help him or turn him into the authorities.

Life or death. Success or failure. He was growing tired of this choice.

The man was short, his skin wrinkled with age and leathery, as if he spent all his time out of doors. His clothes were heavily worn and hung loosely, and he seemed displeased by the sight of Darcy. Not a good sign.

Darcy's heart pounded. "Je suis envoyé par les serpents de mer." *The serpents sent me.*

The man gave a sharp nod, jerking his thumb to indicate that Darcy should follow him.

He exhaled in relief. Two problems solved, since the man both knew about the serpents and spoke French. But he needed to be certain. "Suis-je bien en France?" he asked. *Am I in France?*

The man averted his head and spat on the ground. "Normandie."

Normandy? Well south of where he had intended to land. All the hours of planning from the War Office, the routes he had memorized, the names of the towns and potential contacts – all useless now.

Now he had to find a way to Paris, and his map of France was in his trunk at the bottom of the Channel, along with his other clothes – including the power-infused shirt he had intended to wear when he confronted Napoleon, the one Elizabeth had sewn for him from the fabric made by his half-sister. At least he still had the two handkerchiefs Elizabeth had embroidered, even if they were soaking wet. He had kept those in the pocket closest to his heart.

Somehow he would have to find attire suitable for a gentleman in this desolate land. If he ever managed to get dry, something which seemed impossibly distant.

The man led him to a hut built into the hillside, a spiral of smoke rising from the narrow stone chimney.

Darcy ducked his head as he went through the door, an unpainted slab of wood hanging on leather hinges. The acrid smell of burning peat assailed him in the dim interior, a smoky single room with rough furnishings. But beggars could not be choosers, and he was indeed a beggar now.

A stooped old woman stood by the rustic hearth, looking for all the world like a witch in an old tale. She stared at him in shock. No doubt he clearly came from a different world, even when disheveled and soaking wet.

The man growled in a thick accent, "Envoyé par les serpents." Then he stomped out, the door falling shut behind him.

The woman burst into a flurry of words, as voluble as her husband was silent, but Darcy could barely understand it. "Je ne comprends pas ce que vous dites," he said tiredly. Would this dreadful day never end?

She cocked her head, then spoke more slowly, but he still made out no more than one word in three. Some local dialect, no doubt. But she brought out a rough nightshirt and gestured to him to remove his wet clothes.

He would wear anything that was blissfully dry. Once he had changed into it, she ladled up a bowl of fish stew and pointed to the table. Chatting incomprehensibly throughout, she collected his soaking attire and took it outside.

Only then did he realize how hungry he was, having eaten nothing since leaving England. The stew was delicious to his starving tongue. He would happily have refilled it several times, but he doubted these poor fisherfolk could spare even this much.

Regretfully he pushed the empty bowl aside, taking stock of what little remained to him. His watch was ruined, of course. Fortunately it was not his own, a gift from his father upon developing his land Talent, but one the War Office had given him with 'E. Harcourt' engraved upon it. His satchel held a surprise, though, a happy one – everything within it was completely dry. It was as if the seawater had never touched it. He said a silent word of thanks to the sea serpents for their magic.

His boots, turned upside down to dry, would never be the same, and his hair was sticky with salt. How did people without servants deal with these things? He would have to wash it in the stream. No one would believe him to be Mr. Darcy of Pemberley if they saw him now.

His stiff muscles groaned as he rose and padded barefoot outside to the brook. The old woman was hanging his clothes on a line. She pointed him to where the water collected in a pool, no more than a few inches deep, but enough that he could collect it in his cupped hands and rinse out the worst of the salt. It was a far cry from the ewer of hot water his valet would pour over his head.

If he ever made it back to England, he would never take his valet for granted again.

When the woman offered him a rough cloth to dry his hair, he asked, "How do I get to Paris from here?" He enunciated each word slowly and carefully.

"Paris?" She sounded as shocked as if he had suggested traveling to the moon.

Perhaps he should lower his standards. Only a path led to this hut, not a road, nor even a cart track. "Somewhere, an inn, perhaps, where a *diligence* stops," he said using the French word for stagecoach.

She shook her head, baffled.

"The nearest town, then."

She smiled. "Ah oui! Demain." Then she went off into a spate of words, from which he took the meaning that she would direct him to the town tomorrow, when his clothes were dry.

She was right, of course. Even if he managed to find the strength, he could not set off in soaking clothes. And it was almost sunset, when he could try to reach Elizabeth through the dragon scale.

It took Darcy three days to reach civilization. First a long, wearying trudge in boots that pinched abominably after their soaking to reach the so-called town. It consisted of five small cottages. He hired another old man – France seemed completely depleted of men of fighting age – to take him to the next town in a slow ox-drawn wagon. He had not realized how much he would stand out simply because of his age and good health. His newly ill-fitting boots proved a boon in the end; the farmer seemed to think his limp was a war wound.

They did not reach their destination until dark, where the promised inn proved to be a widow who let out her spare room to visitors. But it did have a *diligence* which came by once a week.

By sheer luck, he only had to wait two nights.

He remembered the *diligences* from his trip to France when he was ten, not that his mother had allowed him to ride one, but he had been intrigued by the odd shape, like two stagecoaches mashed together over four wheels, often with a small cabriolet attached for those who preferred to ride in the open air. Now, when he finally had the chance to ride in one, he spent the journey pretending to doze to avoid conversation until they arrived in Rouen.

Thank heavens! It was recognizably a city, even if the pointed spirelets above the famed astronomical clock and the colorful half-timbering made it look obviously foreign to his English eyes. And everyone here seemed to speak recognizable French.

The *diligence* was greeted by a crowd of boys shoving advertisements for hotels on the unwary travelers. Darcy chose one for its address on the Grande Rue St. Jean, which seemed likely to be in a better part of town. The Grande Rue, though, proved to be barely a yard wide, but the hotel seemed acceptable enough, if not the sort of establishment a high-ranking gentleman would patronize. Fortunately, his rooms looked out the back, with a view so that he could see the setting sun. He would not know the exact moment it touched the horizon, which was when the dragon scale would become active, but he would be ready.

If only he could go straight to Paris! He had lost too much time on this journey already, thanks to the sea serpents and landing in a singularly unpopulated part of France, but there was no way around it. He could not arrive in Paris with no luggage, only one set of suitable clothing to his name, and that having been more worn for the better part of a week. He would have to stay in Rouen long enough to obtain a few more clothes if he was to make the appearance of a gentleman.

He had paid an extra fee for a private manservant. When the man arrived, Darcy explained his situation in clipped French, with the tale of a shipwreck and lost luggage. He would need new clothes, but also a map of France and one of Paris.

It was almost sunset, so he sent a servant off to begin making the arrangements, telling him he was not to be disturbed under any circumstances for the next half-hour.

Because this was his chance to communicate with Elizabeth, and that took all his concentration. The first night, at the hut, the shock of feeling her vibrant presence within him was so astonishing and welcome that he forgot what he needed to say. Her words sounded in his head –*Are you safe?* – as if she was speaking aloud, and it was all he could do to say yes and that he loved her before the connection faded, leaving him bereft.

After that, he had prepared his messages more carefully. The Eldest had not misled him – a simple sentence or an image was all he could hope to convey. Which was quite a challenge, when he needed to communicate a complex concept like Napoleon using sea serpent eggs to force them to do his bidding.

He had decided to divide the message over three nights. The first time he had sent an image of Napoleon stealing eggs from the sea serpents. The second was a French Emperor giving the eggs to the High King. Tonight's would be the trickiest.

He can only pray that Elizabeth would make sense of it.

He slid the scale from the leather pouch around his neck and rubbed it between his thumb and forefinger. For some reason it always felt warm to the touch, warmer than a human. And then Elizabeth was there.

He did not let himself get distracted by her beloved presence, much though he longed to. He sent his image, Napoleon handing an egg to a serpent with a sinking ship in the background.

Her shock was palpable. He could practically hear her indrawn breath and could imagine her stunned look. She had understood!

I will tell the dragons, she sent.

The scale went still in his hand. Would he grow accustomed to this, that sense that she was there and then vanished?

Tomorrow he would use his message to tell her how much he loved her.

The bored ticket-seller at the inn where the *diligences* stopped leaned on a crutch as he studied Darcy's papers. "Good enough. Coach or cabriolet?"

The sudden memory assailed him of his first journey to France, as a boy of ten who wanted only to be back in his silent cottage at Pemberley, away from the noise and conversation and too many changes. He hated the entire trip, but Jack had loved it.

Jack had chattered endlessly, full of questions. Why did they have to travel in that stupid private carriage when anyone could see it would be more fun to ride in the cabriolet perched on the top of a *diligence*? Why could he not play with the French boys out in the street?

His mother's answer was the same every time. "Because you are an English gentleman and a Darcy of Pemberley."

Jack had been curious about everything – no, not everything. He had been bored by the grand cathedrals, the vast quiet spaces where Darcy had finally felt a little peace. In the bloodthirsty way of little boys, Jack had been disappointed by the lack of guillotines and tumbrels carrying aristocrats to their deaths. At least he could gawk at the square where the Bastille had stood and imagine the fighting in the streets.

Even then Jack had wanted to be a soldier. Their mother had indulged him by taking them to a review of French troops, going so far as be-friending a French general. She invited him to dine in their suite, where Jack had pestered the poor man into telling him about the battles he had commanded.

Jack had never had the chance to ride in the cabriolet of a *diligence*. He begged to go back to France when the Peace of Amiens was declared, but by then Lady Anne was lost, presumed dead, and their father had refused to allow fifteen-year-old Jack to travel with only servants. Darcy, who by then also had to fear repulsion, had no interest in the trip.

Had he known how little time he had left with Jack, Darcy would have dropped everything to go with him.

All he could do for Jack now was to purchase a seat in the cabriolet in his honor.

He was joined in the open-air seat by an old dowager and her female companion. The young woman gave him a shy smile that reminded him of Georgiana, but once the *diligence* was moving at speed, the wind rushing past made conversation impossible. Another advantage of riding in the open cabriolet.

It gave him a wider view of the countryside, too, as the *diligence* sped from town to town. So many fields left fallow, and the ones under cultivation worked only by women and old men. He had seen few younger men on the streets of Rouen, apart from the ones missing arms or legs. France was paying a high price for Napoleon's wars.

From Écouis to Gisors and finally on to crowded Paris, its imposing stone edifices towering on each side of the streets like the imperial capital Napoleon had made it. He steeled himself to have his *passeport* questioned, but when he disembarked, no one seemed to care about the incoming passengers except a ragtag group of young boys offering to carry trunks.

He let one of them lead him to the Hôtel de Suède, the Sweden Hotel, which the War Office had recommended because its staff and most of its guests were Swedish. Darcy's accent would not stand out as much there. The innkeeper, who was indeed Swedish, examined his papers carefully before agreeing to provide Edward Harcourt with a suite of rooms and a manservant.

After his all-too-brief sunset moment of loving connection with Elizabeth, Darcy spent the evening penning his letters of inquiry, the ones that would alert his co-conspirators to his presence in Paris. In the morning, he would give them to the innkeeper to post.

Only then, when there had been nothing left but to wait, did it occur to Darcy that something had been distinctly odd about his early trip to France with Jack. Why had Lady Anne decided to take her two young sons on a tour of revolutionary France, when only a year earlier there had been blood running in the streets of Paris as the Terror raged? She told them it was for their education, to broaden their horizons, but that made no sense, either. She had never taken them anywhere before, not even to London.

Had Lady Anne disguised a secret diplomatic mission for the government by taking her children with her? Possibly, but she had not been the King's Mage then. Perhaps she had only wished to escape her sister, the traitorous Lady Catherine, for a time. Certainly his mother had seemed more at ease on their journey, as if a great worry had been taken off her shoulders. Rather unusual, given the dangers that lurked in France at the time.

What was his mother thinking now? She had already lost Jack at Salamanca and her true daughter had been stolen by Faerie. Did she have any regrets over sending off her only remaining child to what the government saw as an almost certain death in France? Unlike Elizabeth, she had given him no advice on how to try to survive.

If he lived through this, he intended to be a very different parent to his own children.

Chapter 17

ELIZABETH SCOWLED AT THE letter she had just received from Lady Anne Darcy. It was full of advice, but not the sort of motherly guidance that she might have welcomed, or even sympathy over the absence of her husband or delight in the news of her pregnancy. Did she have no interest in the prospect of her first, and perhaps only, grandchild?

No, this missive was all about the great importance of Rana Akshaya's visit to Pemberley, how much depended upon the Indian mage being pleased with her reception, and how disastrous it might be if Elizabeth somehow offended her – along with a list of questions Lady Anne wanted her to ask Rana Akshaya should the opportunity arise. If only she could just throw the letter in the fire!

"Can you believe this?" she exclaimed to Frederica. "She has no faith in my ability to be a hostess, and a moment later she wants me to interrogate my guest!"

Frederica looked up from her own letter from the King's Mage. "Hah! Apparently Lady Anne told Rana Akshaya that she would accompany her here, and Rana Akshaya refused to allow it. Her own home, even if she had not been here for years! Oh, she must have been furious! She desperately wants to know Rana Akshaya's secrets."

"As if she does not have enough power of her own as the King's Mage?" Elizabeth gave an unladylike snort.

"To be fair, I think it is more that she is afraid of what Rana Akshaya might do. That she will turn out to be someone who misuses her power, like Lady Catherine. She is always terrified of that." She grimaced. "Knowing now what Lady Catherine did to her dragon, I understand better. Do you suppose Lady Anne will fear me once she finds out about Quickthorn?"

"We will be in the same boat if she finds out I am a dragon companion." Elizabeth paused, then added, "I do not suppose she mentioned Granny to you."

Frederica frowned. "Not so much as a word. I imagine Granny is avoiding her, but still, I wish we had some sort of news! Who knows what mischief she might be up to with the War Office?"

The thought had been troubling Elizabeth, too. Granny could be unpredictable, but without Darcy, Elizabeth was in the dark about what the War Office was doing. How could she be an effective advocate for humans with the dragons when she knew so little? If only Granny would write to her!

She looked down at Lady Anne's letter again. As if she had not already been dreading Rana Akshaya's arrival! Her hands were full enough already, between learning to run an estate far larger than she had ever known, dealing with the fae running everywhere, trying to convince the dragons to help protect England, and the fatigue natural to her condition.

She had lost the better part of a week to Frederica's bonding to Quickthorn, which had taken place much sooner than she had expected, just a day after Frederica agreed to it. Happily, Frederica had recovered quickly, but it still had taken time and energy Elizabeth could ill afford.

No, that was not true, either. She was simply nervous about Rana Akshaya's visit. She had never hosted even an ordinary dinner party at Pemberley, and now she would have foreign royalty visiting for heavens only knew how long, a woman whose traditions she did not know and with whom she had never had a complete conversation. It would have been hard enough if Darcy were still here. Doing it on her own seemed an impossible challenge.

Just the preparations had been burdensome enough. Chandrika had warned her that the great Rana would require a room larger than any of the usual bedrooms, so Mrs. Reynolds had undertaken to convert the huge state parlor into a grand bedroom. If Rana Akshaya was, as Elizabeth guessed, a dragon companion, the parlor would be large enough for a full-size dragon. Then there were the special foods Chandrika insisted the great Rana would expect. It was nerve-wracking.

Even before this aggravating letter from Lady Anne.

As if on cue, a footman appeared. "Forgive me for interrupting, Mrs. Darcy, but there are carriages approaching. Grand ones."

Elizabeth groaned. "I am coming." She hurried out to the portico, with Frederica trailing after her.

The footman had not overstated the case. Trust Rana Akshaya to simply appear with no notice! But who else could possibly be in this cavalcade? She hoped the stables would manage to find room for them all.

If only she had some idea of why Rana Akshaya had come to Pemberley! How was she to avoid missteps when she could not even see the path ahead of her?

The first carriage came to a stop in front of the house, and a uniformed footman opened the door and lowered the steps. The first to emerge was a young man dressed in the Indian manner whom Elizabeth recognized as Rana Akshaya's translator.

Without any greeting, he turned to offer his hand to a shadowy figure inside the coach.

Rana Akshaya emerged slowly, taking each step with care. As before, her face was hidden behind a veil, and her figure was wrapped in flowing embroidered fabric. She paused when her feet touched the ground, raising her head as if studying the sky. Her servants formed a line beside her.

Elizabeth moved forward and made a deep curtsy. "Welcome to Pemberley, Rana Akshaya. We are honored by your visit."

The Indian woman spared her a glance. *At a time like this, we must all stand together.* It was a sending, not speech.

Did she mean they must stand together as dragon companions? "Indeed we must. I believe you are already acquainted with Lady Frederica Fitzwilliam, who is also a guest here."

As Frederica came forward, Rana Akshaya murmured something in her own language. Her translator said, "The great Rana is pleased to –"

Rana Akshaya silenced him with a wave, and spoke in her own resonant, lightly accented voice. "Is the King's Mage aware that you have bonded?" Apparently she could tell simply by looking at Frederica.

"I have not told her, and I do not believe anyone else has," said Frederica. "It only just happened."

"You are to be congratulated."

Frederica curtsied. "It is the greatest honor of my life."

Elizabeth girded herself to do her duties as the hostess. "You must be fatigued after your long journey. Pray permit me to invite you inside. We have prepared rooms for you according to Chandrika's suggestions."

"Your companion is already on her way. I will await her here." Rana Akshaya gestured in the direction of the Nest, which no one had shown her. It was a reminder of how much her powers outstripped Elizabeth's own.

What was the proper protocol for standing outside with foreign royalty who declined to follow the usual rules? Should she order chairs and refreshments to be brought out? It could take a quarter of an hour for a falcon-shaped dragon to fly from the Nest to Pemberley, but if Cerridwen was already in flight, it might be less. "As you wish."

As one, the Indian servants stepped forward and arranged themselves into a neat half circle around the mage. A moment later, the welcome sight of Cerridwen in kestrel form appeared overhead. She shifted shapes in midair and glided to the ground as a dragon.

Thank heavens! Cerridwen's presence was bound to distract Rana Akshaya. Not that Elizabeth disliked the Indian woman, but she was barely an acquaintance, and the Indian mage said the most unpredictable and mysterious things.

Rana Akshaya made her slight bow to Cerridwen. A shiver ran down Elizabeth's arms – there was magic in use. The Indian mage must be sending to her dragon. What was she saying?

A small leather bag appeared in Cerridwen's talons, and she held it out to Elizabeth. "The message is for Rana Akshaya, but it is keyed to you. The Eldest wishes you to hear it, too."

Elizabeth raised her eyebrows. It contained a familiar heavy silver sphere, like the one that had called her to the Nest along with Darcy. A sharp pang of missing her husband stabbed through her. But she had a task now, and she would do it. She poured the Artifact into her gloved hand.

Nothing happened. Cerridwen spoke in her head. *It must touch your skin.*

Of course. She had not been wearing gloves that first time, in Darcy's study. Quickly she stripped off one glove and set the intricately engraved globe in her palm.

The last time the illusion that rose from the sphere had been tiny. This time it was much larger, an image of the eldest nearly as large as Elizabeth herself. She almost expected her hand to sink under the weight of it, but of course it was completely insubstantial.

And then the illusion spoke in the familiar echoing tones of the Eldest. "Greetings, Rana Akshaya. I am the Eldest, the voice of the Dark Peak Nest. We look forward to learning more about you. Under ordinary circumstances we would joyfully invite you into our Nest, but given recent events, we must be cautious. Therefore, we ask you to remain within the boundaries of Pemberley, the estate of Companion Elizabeth, and present your business to our young dragons, who will then communicate it to us. We intend no rudeness by this; but until we know what has led to the destruction of the Nests in Europe, we must take precautions. Cerridwen will direct you to our anchors at Pemberley. May our meeting be the beginning of an auspicious new era."

The illusion faded, leaving her hand tingling.

Rana Akshaya straightened, seeming to grow an extra inch or two. "What is this about Nests being destroyed?" Her voice reverberated with outrage.

Cerridwen spoke. "Three Nests burnt and empty. They were home to the dragons who attacked the armies. None are left alive."

This time Rana Akshaya definitely swelled with size, impossible as it might be. "Then I must meet with your dragons immediately."

Elizabeth's mouth went dry. What might this powerful, angry mage do to her if she said the wrong thing? Lacking any other answers, she fell back on her best manners. "Do you not wish to refresh yourself first? It is a long journey you have had."

"Immediately," snapped Rana Akshaya.

That was clear, at least. "Very well," Elizabeth said. "I will take you to the Dragon Stones. It is a long walk up a steep hill, nearly half an hour." Perhaps that would give the older woman pause.

"*You* will remain here. This is a matter for dragons, not mortals."

Suddenly a whirlwind of dust formed around Rana Akshaya, seemingly out of nowhere, starting at her feet and moving up to encompass her entire body. It thickened until it hid her completely, and then just as quickly as it had appeared, the dust settled to the ground.

Rana Akshaya was gone. In her place was a large falcon.

Elizabeth stared, open-mouthed. It could not be.

"Lead the way, Nestling." Rana Akshaya's voice came from the falcon, only slightly distorted. She spread her wings and leapt into the air.

Cerridwen's edges blurred and then she took flight as a kestrel, heading towards the Dragon Stones.

It was utterly impossible – and apparently true. Rana Akshaya was not a dragon companion, but an actual dragon.

Dizziness swept over Elizabeth, making her stagger. Everything was spinning. Was it the shock or some strange foreign magic?

Frederica found her voice first. "I thought dragons could not take human forms convincingly."

Chandrika spoke from behind Elizabeth. "The great Rana is an ancient and very wise dragon. She spent many years mastering this skill."

Of course. Rana Akshaya always wore a veil, covering her body with flowing fabrics that would disguise any mistakes.

It still made no sense. Elizabeth said slowly, "But only young dragons can travel far from their nests."

"True. The great Rana has paid the price."

"But how?"

Chandrika shook her head. "Only the great Rana can tell you that. She has loosened the bindings on me so I may answer your questions, but that magic is beyond my knowledge."

And it was Elizabeth's terrifying task to play host to this powerful Indian dragon.

The ground was still showing a distressing tendency to move under her. If only she could sit down! Then Chandrika's hand came under her elbow. "Mrs. Darcy, pray permit me to take you inside."

Everyone was watching her, the semi-circle of Rana Akshaya's servants and the grooms by the line of four carriages.

"Yes, let us go in," she said weakly. Somehow she managed to raise her voice to reach the others. "Mr. Hobbes, the butler, will direct you as to unloading your baggage, and the housekeeper will take you to your rooms."

Then she let Chandrika lead her inside.

Chapter 18

ELIZABETH WAS STILL RECLINING on the fainting couch when Rana Akshaya entered, back in the form of a veiled woman. She was alone, without any of her entourage. Elizabeth considered rising to curtsy, but her last attempt to stand had led to a fall, and one bruised hip was enough. It was enough of a challenge to keep her eyes open.

"Chandrika tells me you took ill when I placed a binding upon you," Rana Akshaya said.

A binding? Of course, Rana Akshaya would have bound her against revealing her dragon nature. Elizabeth said, "I do not know if that caused it. I have other reasons to be unwell. And Lady Frederica does not seem troubled by it."

Rana Akshaya stepped close and placed a palm on Elizabeth's cheek. Magic trickled through it, a cleansing energy that scoured her before withdrawing. "I removed it. Does that change anything?"

Indeed, the dizziness had faded completely away, and Elizabeth's body felt like her own again. She sat up and gingerly shifted her legs over the edge of the fainting couch. "Much better." She had to bite down on the urge to thank her.

Rana Akshaya frowned. "My apologies. It was an overly broad binding, applied in haste, when I was in a disturbance of spirits. I have replaced it with a smaller specific binding, tuned to your particular condition."

"My...condition?" Could the dragon tell she was with child?

"Your Talent is complicated. A dragon companion, but also bonded with two lands and two Nests. And carrying an egg with the blood of fae royalty. Yes, most complex."

Darcy's bond to Georgiana's fae blood was present even in their child? "What does that mean?"

"I cannot tell you, for in my country we would not permit our companions to have even a single land bond, and certainly no connection to the fae." There was clear disapproval in her voice. "Your Talent, with its many roots, is likely to be unpredictable. But perhaps it makes you suited for the unprecedented role you must play."

Carefully, Elizabeth said, "I do not have the honor of understanding your meaning."

"You stand at the crossroads in a time of great change, Elizabeth Darcy. The meeting between two colonies of dragons, lost to each other for many ages, would by itself be a great event, but coming at a time of threat to your Nests and an end to their Great Concealment, it is even more. And you are at the center of all these changes, with the power to influence the course of dragon history."

Was Rana Akshaya trying to flatter her, to win her over? "Then I am singularly unprepared for it. Until a few months ago I believed dragons were long extinct, and even now I know little of them."

Rana Akshaya studied her. "Sometimes the outsider is the one who sees most clearly." And with those mysterious words, she turned and walked out.

Rana Akshaya was a dragon – and staying at Pemberley. Elizabeth had thought dealing with the influx of lesser fae at Pemberley was the strangest problem she would ever run across, but this outdid them. What was she supposed to do with the Indian dragon?

Why had Cerridwen not warned her? She must have recognized Rana Akshaya's true nature when they met at Netherfield, but Cerridwen had told her nothing, not even when she knew Rana Akshaya was coming to Pemberley.

Her dragon, and indeed the Nest, had been playing their cards close to their chest. And Elizabeth had thought they trusted her.

Now she was expected to play hostess to her, with no idea of what was expected. Irritated, she tried sending to Cerridwen, but apparently her dragon was too busy to respond. Elizabeth grimaced.

But her dragon had not been the only one keeping secrets. Chandrika must know, too. Sudden burning anger rose in Elizabeth's throat, fury and betrayal. The maid had helped her dress, arranged her hair, and prepared her baths – all while hiding her true purpose, and no doubt telling her mistress all Elizabeth's secrets. True, Elizabeth had known all along Chandrika was likely spying on her, but somehow this felt worse.

It was time to put an end to that. She had liked Chandrika, but it was time to have a maid who served no one but her.

First she had to find her. Would Chandrika be in Elizabeth's rooms, as was proper for her maid, or would she already be with Rana Akshaya's retinue? Perhaps she had already decided to leave Elizabeth's service. Elizabeth headed upstairs to check.

Chandrika was right where she should be, laying out Elizabeth's evening gown, one of the new ones from Frederica's milliner, a lovely confection in rose and gold. She looked up. "I am glad to see you looking better, Mrs. Darcy," she said in a muted voice.

Elizabeth had no patience for polite chit-chat. "Chandrika, now that Rana Akshaya is here, do you not wish to return to her service?"

The Indian woman raised her eyes, her expression oddly blank. "Has my work been less than satisfactory, Mrs. Darcy?"

"No, or I would have sent you back to London long ago. I will be hard put to find a maid whom Cerridwen likes better. But I thought you would wish to be with your countrymen and old friends." Somehow she managed to bite her tongue on the accusations that wanted to spill out.

"I have been happy to serve you, and would prefer to remain as I am."

Her simmering anger would not be repressed. "At Rana Akshaya's behest, no doubt, so that you can continue to report to her on my doings."

Chandrika lowered her head. "I have told her very little about you. A companion is of little interest to the great Rana. She wished to know about the Wise One."

Elizabeth let out a sharp breath. Oh, the irony! Chandrika had not been spying on her, but on Cerridwen. "Nevertheless, I cannot have that. I need a maid who does not serve another mistress."

The Indian woman looked crestfallen. "I understand," she said softly. "I cannot blame you, when you have reason not to trust me. But if you would ever be willing to give me another chance, I would do everything in my power to prove my loyalty to you."

"Why?" Elizabeth studied her, puzzled. "Are you afraid of Rana Akshaya's displeasure if you leave my service?"

"I do not intend to return to her. If you do not want me, I will seek another position, or see if your Nest will take me on to serve their dragons."

What was she missing here? "Is there a reason you do not wish to return to Rana Akshaya? Has she been unkind to you?"

"No, not at all. But she is a very great dragon, so far above me. I did not realize before I came here, working for you and your Wise One, that there was another way. I could never talk to her like this. Cerridwen has spoken to me more than Rana Akshaya has in my entire life. I want to choose that for myself." She took a breath. "Until now, my entire life was preparation to serve Rana Akshaya on this journey. I did it because it was my duty and it had to be done. Now that she no longer needs me, I want to have a life of my own."

Her words struck Elizabeth hard. Her own childhood had been carefree, but once her land Talent had emerged, her father had told her that her task was to make Longbourn profitable again. She had dedicated herself to it, until her duty had changed to helping Darcy survive his mission. Now the Nest expected her to host Rana Akshaya indefinitely, with no instructions on how to do so. Someday she would like to make some choices, too. "But surely you must wish to return to your own country, to your family."

"I have no country." Chandrika's voice was low. "I was sent as a child to be raised in a household of your countrymen, so that English would be as natural to me as my own language and English customs familiar to me. Even before I came to England, I did not fit in with my family, and there was never an expectation that I would return."

Elizabeth started at that. Had it truly been a one-way trip for Chandrika? "You will not go back with Rana Akshaya?"

"She cannot go home again. I do not know where she will decide to settle, but it will not be anywhere near India. That was part of the price."

"The price you cannot explain?"

"I cannot..." Chandrika hesitated. "Forgive me; I keep thinking there must be bindings to stop me from saying these things. I do not know how it was done, but she had to cut all her ties with her Nest and abandon her claim to the throne."

"Her claim to the throne? What throne?" There was so much she did not understand.

"She was the Rana of our land for five centuries, through generations of human rulers. Now her only subjects are those of us who came with her. It was a great sacrifice."

And apparently one that had taken decades of planning. "Why? Why would she give up so much to come here?"

"To learn about her enemy, that someday her knowledge can be used to gain our freedom. She blames herself for failing to see the dangers of allowing the English into our lands, for all the suffering that has come of that."

Her enemy? Elizabeth swallowed hard. She had believed Lady Anne, who told her Rana Akshaya had come to learn about English mages. But if the Indian mage...no, the Indian dragon saw the English as her foes, it changed everything. Did the Nest know? Were the English dragons her enemies, too, or only the people?

"Does Rana Akshaya intend to harm anyone here?"

Chandrika stepped back. "Of course not. She cannot, no more than any other dragon. She wishes to discover how the British can be defeated by the humans in my country."

It struck her, then, how unaware she was of what had happened in India. "I know almost nothing of the situation in your country. Have the British treated your people so badly?"

"Yes." The single word was strong, fervent, and clearly heartfelt. "Why else would I have agreed to leave my home, to give up everything for the great Rana's goal?"

"I see." It was disturbing to know, and she would have to ask more about it, but it did not solve her immediate problem. "I have been pleased with your work. I do not know, though, how I can trust you not to report on me in the future. I wish I could."

Chandrika wrung her hands. "Perhaps your Wise One would be willing to put a binding on me, so that I can tell the great Rana nothing about either of you."

It was tempting. She had grown used to Chandrika, and she had seen a new side to her today, but she did not like the idea of using a binding for her personal convenience. "Instead, would you be willing to answer some truth-caster questions from Lady Frederica?"

Chandrika's face brightened. "I would be happy to do that, if it means I can stay."

"I will have to consult with Cerridwen, too. This decision is as much hers as mine," Elizabeth cautioned.

"As it should be," Chandrika agreed. She gestured to the dress she had laid out. "Will this suit for dinner tonight?"

Elizabeth tickled her cheek with the plume of her quill pen. How could she warn Granny about Rana Akshaya's secret without giving it away to the government spies in London who were no doubt reading any mail addressed to Lady Amelia? Placing the tip of her tongue in the corner of her lips, she wrote, *Rana Akshaya has proved even more interesting than I had anticipated. She was interested in my falcon, but now that I know her better, I would say she has the very spirit of a falcon, somehow contained in a human body. I have never known anyone like that, but perhaps it is common among people in India.*

How desperately she missed Granny! Now, more than ever, she wished her great-grandmother were here to advise her, but there had still been no news from her in London. Were it not for the occasional mentions of her in the newspapers, Elizabeth might have feared for her life, but Sycamore would have returned if there had been some terrible problem. But the question remained – why had Granny been so silent?

She finished the letter and pushed it aside, saving it to show to Cerridwen before sending in case the dragon would find it too revealing of their secrets.

As if she had somehow heard the thought, the kestrel appeared at the window. Chandrika opened it for her, and Cerridwen took her true form by the hearth, visibly larger than she had been even a fortnight ago. Clearly she was catching up on her growth now that she was part of a Nest again. Perhaps that was why she was spending so many of her nights there rather than at Pemberley.

Elizabeth longed to ask her what had happened with Rana Akshaya, but she knew better than to pester her dragon with questions immediately. Instead she said, "Cerridwen dearest! I have missed you."

Cerridwen tossed her head. "You will see a great deal of me now, and Quickthorn, too. The Eldest has decreed that one of us must always be here while Rana Akshaya is in residence. Though what she thinks I could do if any problems arose is quite beyond me!" She sent an image of herself next to the Indian dragon, who was at least four times her size.

"You could tell the Eldest about it, I suppose," Elizabeth said. "Chandrika, will you excuse us?"

Expressionless, the maid nodded and left the room.

"Is something the matter?" Cerridwen asked.

Elizabeth said carefully, "Did you recognize that Rana Akshaya was a dragon when we met her in Hertfordshire?"

"Of course."

"Why did you never tell me?"

Cerridwen turned to gaze into the fire. "You did not even know I was a dragon at the time."

"But later, especially when you knew she was coming here, you still said nothing."

The scales on the dragon's neck rose. "I was under Silence when we met. Rana Akshaya was the first dragon to speak to me in two years, and she asked me politely not to mention her presence unless I thought it needful."

Elizabeth caught her breath. Poor lonely Cerridwen! "No wonder you kept it to yourself."

"I did tell the Eldest, when Rana Akshaya asked for an invitation to the Nest." Cerridwen ducked her head. "She was not pleased with me. She said my first loyalty must be to the Nest."

"I am sorry. That must have been unpleasant." Elizabeth crossed to sit on the floor beside her dragon and stroked Cerridwen's flank.

"I am still learning how to be part of a Nest. It has been so long, and I was only a small nestling then." The dragon laid her head on Elizabeth's lap.

It was likely safe to ask a question now. "How did the meeting with Rana Akshaya go?"

Cerridwen's chest rippled with amusement. "Not at all as planned. The Eldest had given us gifts and a speech of welcome to give, but Rana Akshaya insisted on hearing about the Silent Nests and the attacks instead. The news about the Wicked King's involvement with Napoleon distressed her greatly. We never got to our inquiries about the Nests in India, though I did learn one thing. They do not have Gates; we had to explain how we communicated with the other Nests. Though I suppose it makes sense, since the Gates were only created when the Nests went into hiding."

That was news to Elizabeth. "I thought Gates had always existed."

"No. It was one of my forebears who built them, along with his companion." She preened a little.

Elizabeth could not help smiling. "You must be proud of that. Will there be more meetings with Rana Akshaya, then?"

Cerridwen sighed. "Many more, apparently. She is clearly displeased to be met only by our youngest dragons, but the Eldest will not budge on that, not until she is certain Rana Akshaya has nothing to do with the attacks on the Nests. Only Quickthorn, Rowan, and I, and we must report only to Juniper, who will tell the Eldest, in case Rana Akshaya uses some magical influence on us. It feels very strange, since Rana Akshaya is such an ancient dragon, older even than our Eldest, and we are mere hatchlings in comparison."

It was unusual for Cerridwen to speak so openly about dragon politics. Elizabeth decided to take advantage of it. "If she is so old, how could she travel away from her own Nest? I thought older dragons could not take companions."

Cerridwen raised her gold-ringed eyes to her. "The Eldest is very eager to learn that, too. If there is a way to travel without a companion, it would change everything."

Elizabeth wrinkled her brow. "Chandrika said something about it, about how she cut her ties to her Nest. But there is more I must tell you." She briefly summarized her earlier discussion with the maid. "What do you think?"

"She has always seemed to feel kindly disposed towards me," Cerridwen said slowly. "And if I want to find out more about how Rana Akshaya left her Nest, it is better to have her here."

She stroked the dragon's side thoughtfully. Her nestling was growing up.

Chapter 19

THE NEXT DAY DARCY set out on errands in Paris. His manservant had procured a guidebook for him and given him a recommendation for a tailor, since nothing Darcy had bought in Rouen would do for even the most casual presentation to a member of the aristocracy, much less the emperor.

After being measured and looking at far too many fabrics – never a favorite activity of his – he headed for the fashionable shops. Also not one of his hobbies, but the War Office said it would look more suspicious if he did no shopping, so he browsed through several stores, looking for a perfect gift for Edward Harcourt's non-existent stepmother who had supposedly sent him on this errand to France.

But he could not resist a fine silk handkerchief embroidered with wildflowers. Elizabeth loved them, often pointing out the violets and cowslips near the cottage at the heart of Pemberley. A large present was out of the question, as it was all but certain that he would have to abandon his luggage to make his escape. But a handkerchief could fit in his pocket, and it represented his hope that someday he would be able to give it to her.

There was one other thing he wanted to do for Elizabeth, and it involved being in just the right place when the dragon scale awoke. That afternoon, he followed his guidebook's instructions toward the Seine, where he could see the towers of Notre-Dame rising over the rooftops of Île de la Cité.

A pair of soldiers stopped him at the bridge and demanded his papers, something that seemed to happen more frequently in Paris.

How did the French stand it, having to prove their identity again and again? Not that most of them got a quarter of the attention he did, but still, he could not imagine the English tolerating it. But he was accustomed to the procedure now, and so far his safe-conduct had not been challenged. He chatted with them amicably, agreed that the *Code Napoléon* was much fairer to the common man than anything in England, and gave them a coin to drink to the emperor's health. Then he crossed the Pont au Change and made his way toward the towers.

The buildings to his west were casting long shadows, but he still had time, so he paused in front of the great cathedral. He had seen engravings of it, of course, but it could not compare to the majesty of the ancient building, its square towers jutting towards the sky. Elizabeth would enjoy seeing these memories.

Then he strolled inside and found a pew which gave him a view of one of the rose windows. He gazed at it as the last of the light disappeared, studying every inch of it so that it was set in his mind. Then he took out the dragon scale and held it between his fingertips, waiting. When it finally came to life, he poured the image he had created through the link, the rose window and the glory of Notre Dame in the fading afternoon sun.

He could feel her gasp of pleasure. Her wordless gratitude and her love, the precious gift she had given him. And then she was gone.

Now the nave was dark except for the flickering candles lit by the faithful. He made his way between the tall pillars out into the square, warmed by his memories of Elizabeth.

He had to find a way to survive this and get back to her, so that someday, when there was peace, he could bring her here.

Finally, it came, after nearly a week of waiting, wondering if the conspirators had lost their nerve or, even worse, been discovered and arrested. A servant brought the response, demanding that he present himself to the Duc de Velaudin to explain the letter he had sent.

Darcy's manservant helped him into his most formal attire and accompanied him to Velaudin's stately townhouse. He was shown into the august presence of the duc, who haughtily informed him that he did not believe a word of Edward Harcourt's story and believed him to be an English spy. Exactly in keeping with the script the War Office had set up.

Darcy played his part, protesting his innocence and suggesting that the question be taken to the Minister of Police, who had approved his *passeport* and safe conduct.

"The Minister of Police!" cried Velaudin scornfully. "I will take it to the emperor himself. He is the only one I trust in these matters. I will set up the audience."

The secretary beside him referred to a piece of paper. "He is reviewing the troops in front of the Tuileries tomorrow."

"Inform the emperor's chamberlain that I wish to approach him then, with this Englishman." Then Velaudin looked scornfully down his beaked nose at Darcy. "You will meet me there, and His Imperial Majesty will judge you."

Darcy bowed. "It will be my very great honor."

And so they concluded their piece of theatre, performed for the benefit of hangers-on and servants, to convince them that the Duc de Velaudin could not possibly be conspiring with an Englishman.

Even if he was.

Darcy tried to hide his jubilation as he left Velaudin's townhouse. A troop review was perfect. Outdoors, in the great open square where he could bring his horses charging through. Where illusory gunshots would produce chaos. His chances of both success and escape would be much better outside than at an indoor public audience. And he had avoided the worst possible outcome – a private audience with Napoleon, which would be almost impossible to escape.

Since time was short, he stopped to make his final arrangements and to pay a second visit to the area around the Tuileries, refreshing himself on the locations of streets and potential hiding places. He could not choose the angle for the horses to come from until he knew where the troops would be, but he could consider possible options.

If he was very fortunate, by this time tomorrow, Edward Harcourt would be no more, and Darcy would be on his way back to England.

He would do his duty to the best of his ability. Drawing on the power of Pemberley and the dragon magic inside him would make his illusions strong. He had the dragon Artifact to assist his escape, and his plans for leaving Paris were as solid as he could make them.

And yes, there was still a good chance he would die tomorrow, but he would not dwell on that. Particularly when his final contact with Elizabeth before facing Napoleon was coming soon.

The message took no effort. *Tomorrow afternoon, my love.* Flavored with all the affection he could pour into it.

A gasp, a moment of fear, and then something that felt like an embrace. *I love you.* And then she was gone.

If only the connection lasted a little longer! But he should be grateful it existed at all, that his final memories of Elizabeth could be something beyond her tear-stained face that morning in her bedroom.

A knock at the door made his pulse quicken. Could their plan have been discovered, even at this late date? Had the conspirators lost their nerve? He opened it, fully expecting to see soldiers on the other side.

But it was only a liveried messenger with another letter. No, not just a letter, but a formal, sealed document, tied with a ribbon. He gave the boy a coin and sent him on his way.

The seal showed Napoleon on his imperial throne. Dread filled Darcy as he opened it. The formal language commanded him to appear with the Duc de Velaudin at the Tuileries palace the following morning for a private audience with His Imperial Majesty Napoleon, Emperor of the French, King of Italy, and Protector of the Confederation of the Rhine.

He stared at it in horror, his blood turning ice cold. There it was, in black and white. His chances of survival had just dropped to the same abysmal level that they had been when he first accepted the mission, before he had met Elizabeth and learned to hope.

It was a death sentence.

He would never see any of them again. Not Elizabeth, nor their child, nor Pemberley, nor England.

Dropping the paper, he dug his fingernails into his palms until it hurt. He still had a task before him. His brother had died to stop Napoleon. Could he do no less? Tomorrow he would save countless lives across Europe and avenge Jack's death. He would protect England from invasion and make the world safe for his child.

It was worth the price. It had to be.

Chapter 20

THE TUILERIES WAS ENORMOUS, a palace on a vast scale, with an interior designed to impress, every inch decorated with marble, sculptures, and larger-than-life paintings in gilded frames. If Darcy could have felt awe, he would have. But inside he was numb, his mind racing to the confrontation ahead of him, all the possible plans for distracting the guards. How could he prepare when he did not know where their audience with the emperor would take place? Would there be windows that the soldiers could be drawn to? If not, there was little he could do beyond sounds and mist. Did such an effort even have a chance of success, or would his sacrifice prove useless? The only person he might be able to ask was Velaudin, but the plan called for him to remain disdainful of Darcy until the end. Both of them needed to play their parts.

After showing his invitation and his papers, Darcy mounted the grand staircase between two lines of soldiers, and then followed a page through a series of elaborately adorned rooms before reaching a large hall filled with men in uniform. Dozens of them stood, and more sat in chairs along the walls. The ceiling bore a giant painting of Mars driving his chariot, looming over Darcy with the knowledge that there was no escape from this place.

His papers were checked yet again, and they patted him down, searching for weapons. Then he was directed into the next room, where exquisitely dressed men and women awaited their audiences. Darcy's new clothes did not come close to meeting their sartorial standards. Velaudin was across the room, chatting with a several others and ignoring Darcy. If he was nervous, it did not show, but the young man beside him – presumably the cousin who was to help him – was pale and drawn.

Chatter rose around him, and there was hardly room to move. He received supercilious looks from those who deigned to notice his existence. His skin itched. It was a far cry from his beloved silent cottage in the woods. And there was no escape. The room had only two doors, one into the guardroom and one on the opposite side, leading to wherever the audiences were held.

The inner door opened, and three men walked out, looking pleased. A chamberlain called a name, and an attractive young woman and a much older gentleman went through. They were out again in less than five minutes. The parade continued, new petitioners entering the august presence as the previous ones emerged.

Darcy gave a tiny tug on his land Talent. The power of Pemberley rose to meet him. Good. He needed to be ready. And the dragon Artifact hung on his chest, safely invisible, ready for his touch. It would do him little good here in this crowd, where there was no clear path. But if a chance arose, he would be prepared to seize it.

The next time the chamberlain entered, he called out Velaudin's name. Darcy made his way across to him and entered behind the would-be assassins. Into the imperial presence.

Every eye was on Napoleon, including Darcy's. He felt like the needle in a compass, twirling to face true north. It was almost as if the other people in the room faded into the background, the courtiers and secretaries and soldiers.

Only the emperor stood out as an individual, despite standing off to one side of the salon in front of the fireplace instead of sitting in the great chair under a canopy – not a throne, but close to it. He was dark-haired and no more than average height, shorter than most of the guards around him, with features more suited to a merchant than an emperor. He should not have looked majestic, but he exuded an intense magnetism.

The sight of Velaudin making his bow shocked Darcy out of his strange fascination. He hurriedly followed suit, and as Darcy's gaze moved away from Napoleon to the elaborate carpet underfoot, he realized his mistake. He should have been examining the room, not the man.

As he straightened, he tried to remedy his error. Two large windows to his left – thank heavens! A door in the middle of the opposite wall, presumably leading to Napoleon's private apartments, given the two guards standing in front of it. And many people – they were outnumbered by far.

Velaudin was speaking, and Darcy dragged his attention to him. "This *Englishman* claims he has permission to try to contact my cousin's daughter regarding an inheritance. He has a safe-conduct, but it may be forged. We cannot be too careful of our enemies."

One of the secretaries handed Napoleon a paper which he glanced at. The emperor said, "It all seems in order." His words were quick and businesslike, as if he found the matter uninteresting.

Then he turned to Darcy, his eyes fastening on him, studying him closely. "Have you anything to say for yourself, M. Harcourt?"

A frisson went down Darcy's spine. Something was odd about this, but what? Perhaps it was just that the emperor's face was so familiar from engravings and caricatures. "Your Imperial Majesty, my only interest in France is to fulfill my stepmother's commission to find her long-lost daughter. I sent all the paperwork through the embassy several months ago." Why had Velaudin not given him the signal to produce his illusions?

Napoleon was still studying him, with eyes that seemed almost like molten metal. "You interest me, M. Harcourt," said the emperor. "I wish to know more of you. Step forward."

Darcy's heart pounded, but he obeyed. Two of the guards stood on either side of him, prepared to seize him if he should make an untoward move. "Your Imperial Majesty honors me."

"You are a landed Talent, I am told."

"Your Imperial Majesty is well informed."

Napoleon's nostrils flared. "Have you ever been tested for magery?"

"No, Your Imperial Majesty." It was even true. His mother had always known he had that ability. But how had Napoleon thought to ask that question? He was not a mage or even a Talent, or Darcy's skin would be burning.

"What do you know of the fae?"

This was unexpected. Cold sweat broke out on the back of his neck. Why did the duc not give the damned signal? "I am told by those with the Sight that there are lesser fae on my estate. And I have heard stories, of course."

"And dragons?" Muffled gasps came from around the room.

"Dragons? I have read about the attacks in Austria, of course." His heart thudded. Someone had betrayed him. How could Napoleon possibly know otherwise? Suddenly it was harder to breathe, as if the air itself had grown heavier, warm and full of a rich scent redolent of spices.

"You know more of dragons than that, Englishman. You wear their work around your neck."

How could Napoleon see his pendant?

Then, inexplicably, he relaxed. It did not matter, did it? The emperor did not seem displeased, only curious, and who would not be? There was no reason to distrust him. He was so interested in what Darcy had to say. Perhaps he should simply tell him everything. How could he be emperor if he was not also wise? Relief filled him; yes, this was the answer.

Darcy was so tired, though. What had happened to all his energy? At least he had his bond to Pemberley to draw on. He pulled at it, sucking in all the energy he could, through his child in Elizabeth's womb.

Elizabeth. Her presence was there in the power of Pemberley, yanking him back to himself. To the reality that Napoleon was his enemy – and had somehow taken control of his mind.

Which still wanted desperately to believe anything the French Emperor said.

He was the rope in a tug o'war, with Napoleon pulling one way and Elizabeth anchoring him at the other, swaying back and forth. His breath rasped in his throat as the room seemed to close in on him. The only thing he could see was the emperor's eyes.

"You will answer my question." It was the voice of trust, of honor, of every hope Darcy had ever held.

No. He was here for a reason. But those mysterious eyes drained his resolve. He had to get away from them, this very instant. Panic made his skin clammy.

Then old instinct took over, the instinct that had kept him out of trouble so often as a child. He retreated into invisibility.

"Seize him!" cried Napoleon.

Darcy ducked down as the guards reached for where he had been, scuttling backwards. He was free of the grip on his mind!

But there was no way out of the room. They would discover him in minutes simply by touch. He could not afford to wait for Velaudin's signal to start the attack.

He had rehearsed it so often in his head that he could launch the illusions without effort, pulling on Pemberley's strength and picturing Elizabeth's face before him. And there they were, the sound of guns outside, created by his Talent. Smoke from gunfire that did not exist. Shouting, as if the palace was under attack. Almost effortless, after all his practice.

The guards ran to the windows.

"No, you fools! Block the doors! Find him with your hands." Napoleon sounded furious, but Darcy dared not look in his direction. His eyes were dangerous.

Instead, he began the second part of the plan. Mist everywhere, especially around the guards, to confuse them.

Then the sound of gunfire disappeared. Desperate, Darcy cast it again, but nothing happened. What had gone wrong with his illusions? He tugged hard on the power of Pemberley – and found nothing.

It was gone. His link to Pemberley via Elizabeth had vanished, as if someone had cut it with a knife. Terror rose in him.

"There he is!" cried the emperor, pointing straight at Darcy. "Seize him!"

His invisibility had faded, too. Darcy broke into a cold sweat as he tried to grab the power in the air to plait it, but it slipped from his fingers.

Then he remembered the handkerchiefs Elizabeth had made him, the ones into which she had sewn her land Talent. He had tucked them inside his sleeves as she had told him to, though more because he had promised to do so than because he expected to need them, not when he had all of Pemberley to draw on. They were pressed against his arms. And yes, he could feel the magic in them!

He let Elizabeth's power flow into his skin from the fabric she had labored over and tried again. Now his body faded from sight once again, and the gunfire sounds were back. But he had to be careful; the magic in the handkerchiefs was limited, and pulling energy from the air required a calmness of mind he had no hope of summoning.

A body pushed past him to the left. It was Velaudin, going to tackle Napoleon. At last! His cousin was there, too, winding the garrote around the emperor's neck and squeezing.

Darcy thickened the mist until he could barely see them, hiding their attack from the guards. But something shifted, and the garrote was suddenly empty, the two assassins staring at each other in confusion. How could the emperor have vanished from their grasp? And he was not just invisible, as Darcy was, but completely gone.

And then another impossibility, as a falcon took wing, flying up towards the high ceiling, landing on the canopy above Napoleon's throne.

A falcon?

There was no time to think. Darcy had to stop him, and quickly, with only the bit of magic he had left. He cast fire upwards, and the canopy exploded into flames.

Now the shouts became screams, as real smoke poured into the mist illusion. The fire spread to the painted walls, crackling fiercely. Thick smoke blanketed the room, blocking everything from view and making him cough.

There was nothing more he could do, and he would die if he stayed. He pushed his way into the crowd trying to escape from the room, people pressing against him on both sides as they tried to cram through the doorway. The sharp crack of glass shattering sounded behind him as he reached the doorway, coughing as the smoke filled his lungs.

Just as he went through, something bumped him in the back. Then a hand grabbed his coat, yanking him back. "Got him!" a soldier cried. He pushed down the woman in front of Darcy to make space to get a firmer grip. "Guards, over here!"

Desperately Darcy tried to pull away, but the soldier was determined, grappling to hold him. With the advantage of being able to see his opponent, Darcy lashed out with a punch to his chin that rocked him back and loosened his grip. But another man struck him from behind, making him stagger.

This was no time for fighting by the rules. Darcy kicked back at him, hitting with his elbows, his knees, whatever he could reach, throwing himself to first one side, then the another. But there was no place to go, and so much pressure from the escaping crowd. People screamed in terror.

A haughty aristocratic voice directly behind him snarled, "Out of my way this instant, damn you!"

The guards' grip on Darcy slackened, as if by habit of obedience. He seized his moment and pulled away, ducking sideways into the mass of moving bodies. But they had caught him once already without being able to see him.

Then he realized that being invisible was no protection in this throng. That was how they had caught him, because it made him stand out as an apparently empty place in the otherwise solid swarm. He blew out through his lips to dismiss the spell, and his body popped back into view. In its place, he cast mist over the crowd, but it would not thicken.

He had exhausted the handkerchiefs. Now there was nothing but the crowd's eagerness to escape to protect him from recognition.

He ducked his head as he forced his way through the chaotic rooms full of people yelling, down the grand stairway, pressed close with other bodies fleeing the flames. Out into the courtyard, where Napoleon's triumphal arch gazed down at the shouting crowds as if in mockery.

People poured into the courtyard from every direction, drawn by the noise and the fire. Darcy had to elbow his way through them. This was a disaster. Once word got out that an English mage had been speaking to the emperor when the fire broke out, the mobs would be howling for English blood.

Finally he reached the Rue de Rivoli. As he crossed it, he glanced back at the palace. Fire was still pouring out the windows. A young man grabbed his arm, asking what had happened.

Of course. He must have looked like he was fleeing from the palace, and that was dangerous. "Fire in the palace! No one knows if the emperor is safe." And he forced himself to chat for a minute with the Frenchman before setting off at a pace that he hoped looked relaxed.

But he might never relax again, not after this catastrophe.

Once he was a few streets away from the Tuileries, he increased his pace, following his carefully made escape plans in a daze. He went to the modest boarding house where he had taken a room the previous day for the sole purpose of leaving a change of clothes and an easily carried satchel of useful items. He struggled out of the tight formal coat he had worn for the emperor and into an outfit that would suit a common tradesman.

He hurried to the square from which the diligences departed, expecting to be stopped and seized at any moment. Using the new identity papers he had hidden away until now, he purchased a seat on the next coach to leave, one headed east. Not a helpful choice for him, since the Channel was to the northwest, but it might throw off any pursuit. At the first opportunity, he intended to switch to a less-trafficked line, where he would be less likely to encounter another Talent. His new *passeport* did not list him as a Talent, so running into anyone who experienced repulsion to him would risk immediate exposure.

He climbed into the open-air cabriolet section. The smell of smoke that still clung to his hair and skin would be too evident inside the closed carriage. At least the damp, chilly air meant he had it to himself. Over the tops of the nearby buildings, a wide plume of smoke rose from the Tuileries.

How much of the historic palace had he destroyed? How many people had died in the flames? And all of it for no reason. Had he only stopped to think of the significance of Napoleon changing into a falcon, he would have known better. But he had been desperate and disbelieving, so he had used the first tool that came to mind.

Fire was harmless to dragons. And unless there was some other un-known creature that could shift shapes to a falcon, Napoleon was a dragon.

His stomach lurched as the diligence swung into motion. And then there was nothing else he could do, no action he could take to make himself safe. All he could do was to sit there until the coach came to a halt.

No. There was one thing he could do. He could test his connection to Pemberley, the one that Napoleon had somehow broken. Could he have destroyed it permanently? The horror of the very idea roiled his stomach. How had Napoleon managed to cut off Darcy's blood tie? Dear God, had he somehow harmed Elizabeth when he did it?

He was almost afraid to try. Closing his eyes, he reached out to the land he loved.

And it answered. The oak grove, the clearing with the Dragon Stones, the moors and streams, all the power was there. And that meant Elizabeth and their child were safe, too.

But his relief was tempered by the full horror of the day. His mission had failed. Napoleon had escaped – and it was a worse disaster than any the War Office had ever imagined.

Chapter 21

ELIZABETH THOUGHT THE SUN would never set on this interminable day. Her heart had been in her throat since Darcy had pulled the power of Pemberley through her late that morning. She had felt it flowing, a constant stream of pulsating magic that went through her without touching her, flying invisibly to France to create illusions.

And then it had stopped, leaving her completely ignorant of the outcome. Had Darcy been captured – or worse? Had she somehow signed his death warrant by failing to give him enough power? She would not know if Napoleon had been killed until the news reached England, which could take days.

All she wanted to know was if Darcy was alive. And sunset, when the dragon scale became active, would provide the only answer she might get. Would she feel his presence, or would there be nothing there?

She could not bear to sit and wait, so she excused herself and headed outside. Frederica would have been happy to accompany her, of course, but it was easier to be alone. Anxiety ached in her throat as the sun approached the horizon. Would this be the night that she heard nothing?

The chill of the evening had set in, so she headed for the walled rose garden. She could sit on the marble bench under the pergola, but the soil called to her, asking for her Talent. She sent back the sensation of regret and the promise of more later; she could not deplete any of her energy that might be needed for the contact. But the land's disappointment was palpable, so she tried to make up for it by kneeling in the dirt and working it with her fingertips – not at all magical, but at least it showed her attention.

And it distracted her a little from the frantic worry.

Then it came, the special tug with Darcy's unique flavor, that sense of an oak grove in summer, and relief flooded her. He was still alive!

But then the tug intensified, dragging power through her, through their unborn child, just as it had earlier. Rivers of energy, all washing through her from the land, through Pemberley's bond to its master. She dug her fingertips deep into the soil.

What was happening? This was even more than he had pulled through her before.

He had to survive. Desperate, she poured all her powers through their bond, begging the land to give her more.

The draw of magic abruptly stopped. A cry left her lips.

Then another slight tug, and his voice, faint with distance, just at the edge of her hearing. No, not words, but images, coming from him.

Napoleon, held fast by two men, a garrote around his neck. Then the garrote falling loose, empty, as the familiar form of a kestrel took the air; and Napoleon nowhere to be seen, the men who had been holding him staring at each other in disbelief.

He controlled my mind. It was Darcy's voice.

Then the images faded, and she was alone, collapsed on the ground between two rosebushes, her mind spinning. Napoleon. Who had turned into a falcon.

Utterly impossible, and yet it explained everything.

His ability to find and control dragons, his uncanny knowledge of his enemy's battle strategies, his strange magnetism that caused even those who disagreed with him to follow him. All possible for a powerful dragon who could shift forms to fly over a battlefield before the fighting started.

Darcy had faced him and was still alive. Still alive! He must have drawn all that magic to overcome the distance between them, to give her that crucial message.

And she was too giddy to consider the consequences.

Giddy. Oh, dear, she had overdrawn her life force! And she was too far from the house to hope that they might hear her call out. She dared not try to move.

Thankfully, shuffling footsteps on the gravel path alerted her she was no longer alone. It was Edwards, the gardener.

"Mrs. Darcy, be ye in need of help?" he asked in his heavy local accent.

"Yes, very much so. Pray ask Lady Frederica to join me at her earliest convenience, and have tea with honey sent to me. Quickly."

"Here, madam?" He sounded dubious.

"Yes, here." Looking foolish by taking tea sitting on the garden path was the least of her worries. First she had to stay alive long enough to pass on Darcy's shocking message.

So she simply lay there in the dirt, letting the land's power trickle into her. Perhaps she could manage to walk to the bench, but for her child's sake, she would not take the risk. Had the baby felt all the magic pouring through him?

A bonnetless Frederica arrived at a run. "What happened?" she demanded.

Elizabeth looked up at her, feeling foolish lying on the ground. "I had a sending from Darcy. A true sending, not just the link."

"At this distance? No wonder you are drained! But he is alive?"

"Yes." She rubbed her hand over her forehead. "But apparently Napoleon is..." It was too ridiculous. She could not say it.

"Dead?" Frederica exclaimed excitedly.

"No. He escaped, by turning himself into a falcon."

It was beyond belief.

Frederica paled. "Napoleon... changed into a falcon?" Her voice rose on the last word. "Are you trying to tell me the Emperor of France is a dragon?"

Torn between disbelieving laughter and tears, Elizabeth raised her palms helplessly. "That is what Darcy sent me."

Frederica sat down on the bench with a thump. "I suppose that explains how he can command dragons."

"I suppose so." No, it was too ridiculous a notion. But what else could Darcy have meant? A sudden unexpected longing for him pierced her, and she ached with the need to have him beside her. Instead he was somewhere in hostile territory, under the rule of a mad dragon. Her stomach did a flip-flop.

Then it happened again.

Once again she pressed her hand to her waist, this time in a different kind of disbelief.

Frederica stared at her in consternation "What is it? Are you ill? Where is that dratted tea? I told them to hurry!"

"No, it is just the babe quickening. All that Talent flowing through him must have woken him up." What an odd feeling!

If only she could share it with Darcy.

The world came crashing back in at that thought, tearing her away from the miracle happening inside her. "We must tell the dragons. Can you call Quickthorn? I dare not try to send to Cerridwen while I am so weak." And then she would have to decide what to do next. Send word to Granny, most likely, since she knew no one at the War Office, and they would not believe her anyway.

Frederica said, "Quickthorn is on her way. And look, here comes your tea."

"Impossible!" announced Quickthorn, for at least the third time.

Elizabeth ignored her, inasmuch as one could ignore a dragon four times her size. She had finally made it to the bench, with her heavy shawl wrapped around her and lanterns lit on either side. And Cerridwen next to her, rocking back and forth and radiating distress.

She was not the only one. After Quickthorn's initial urgent sending to the Nest, other dragons had arrived, two in falcon form and Rowan, who was still young enough to be able to take his true form briefly away from the Nest. Elizabeth had just told her story yet again and allowed Rowan to read her, too, so he could take her memories back to the Eldest.

All of them, in falcon form or dragon, were exuding deep shock and horror. And terror.

"Are you certain?" asked Rowan.

"I am certain that is what Darcy sent me, and since Frederica and Quickthorn are both here, I cannot be lying," Elizabeth snapped. "And I can think of no reason why he would not tell me the truth."

Rowan sank back on his haunches. "My apologies, Companion Elizabeth. This is such frightful news that we all seek to find a way to disbelieve it, because the truth is so unpalatable."

"Why?" Frederica asked. "It is shocking, yes, but why does it frighten you so?"

The dragon lowered his head. "Because Napoleon, or the dragon masquerading as him, is a killer, which means he is in thrall to the Wicked King, cursed be his name. It means our greatest enemy has a powerful foothold in this world which has been our refuge. None of us are safe any longer. A killer dragon can destroy us all."

"But you already knew that Napoleon was in league with the Wicked King, from what the sea serpent told Darcy," Frederica argued.

"We thought him human then. A human with the backing of the Wicked King could do terrible things, yes. A dragon in his service, with all of Europe at his command, could bring the end to this world."

Elizabeth shivered. An end to the dragons, or an end to everything? Napoleon, either as a human or a dragon, had shown great callousness to slaughter.

Cerridwen leaned her leg against Elizabeth's. "This was the missing piece," the dragon said heavily. "Now we know the meaning of my vision. Some dragons disbelieved it before, because they could not imagine any power great enough to cause such devastation. Not any longer."

To no one's surprise, Elizabeth was summoned by the Eldest the following day. The Nest was a hive of activity, with more dragons in the main rooms than Elizabeth had ever seen before. She followed Cerridwen through to the chamber of the Eldest.

The room was unchanged, but the great dragon's aura weighed on it with deep concern tinged with despair. If only she could offer some comfort! But that was not possible. Cerridwen had not been herself since the news had come, either.

After exchanging greetings, she allowed the Eldest to read her memories of the previous evening. When it was done, the Eldest said heavily, "I wish to ask a favor of you. Would you permit me to intrude upon your connection with your mate this evening? I would use it to take the memory directly from his mind."

"I expected you would wish to do something like that," she said.

"You do have the right to refuse. The scale by which you connect was a gift to you."

"I do not object." Even if she would prefer not to give up her brief moment with Darcy, this was obviously more important. "How do we go about this?"

"You are generous, Companion Elizabeth. I will need to hold you against my body, with both of us touching the scale. It will mean remaining here through sunset."

She nodded. "Cerridwen warned me I might need to stay at the Companions' House overnight, so I came prepared."

The Eldest dropped her forelegs, releasing Elizabeth from the odd embrace she had held her in while the scale connection activated. "Well, that was curious," the ancient dragon said.

Elizabeth craned her neck to look up at her. "Were you able to see anything? I could not tell." To her, it had merely been an incomprehensible rush of Talent, with a slight flavor of Darcy's oak grove in summer.

"Enough to be certain the French Emperor is no mortal, and almost certainly a dragon. A killer dragon, with all that implies. What is puzzling is why he did not put a binding on Darcy to keep him from revealing this."

That was indeed odd. "A good question. Napoleon must have a companion, since he is far from any Nest. Is there a way to tell who it might be?"

The Eldest lowered his head. "To a mortal? No. If one of us were in his presence, we would know."

She knew better than to suggest that killing Napoleon's companion could force him back to his Nest. It did not matter, anyway, if they did not know who it was. And perhaps Napoleon was like Rana Akshaya, mysteriously able to leave his Nest with no companion.

"What will happen now?" she asked. The question had been pounding at her all day.

The great dragon sank back on her haunches. "That is a difficult question, and one that is too large for me. I must consult with other Nests."

Elizabeth had already heard this from Cerridwen, that dragons with companions from around Britain would be invited to the Dark Peak to discuss this news, along with how to manage the end of the Great Concealment. "Will Rana Akshaya be invited to speak to them, too?" If the Indian dragon was to be excluded, Elizabeth wanted to prepare for the explosion likely to follow.

"I think we shall have to, as some of the other Nests would like their own reports on her. But I fear I must also ask you for more assistance than is our custom with companions."

She had not expected that. "I am glad to offer any help I can."

"We need messengers to bear our invitations to Nests across Britain, men who can travel long distances quickly and are willing to be under binding. Our Kith are not accustomed to such journeys and lack good horses. Would there be any in your service who would be able to help?"

"Without a doubt." Pemberley had plenty of grooms and manservants who would be glad to take a trip for extra pay, and the brownies were keeping the stables clean. "But would it not be simpler to send the messages through the Gate?"

"Many Nests do not have Gates, and it takes time and enormous energy each time we must change the direction of the Gate. We have already exhausted our Gate dragons with sending out word of Rana Akshaya's arrival."

She nodded, though she had almost no understanding of the Gates, or even how many Nests there might be. "How many riders will you need?"

"Perhaps three, if you can spare them. Cerridwen will give them their instructions." The Eldest settled back on her haunches. "I will be frank with you, Companion Elizabeth. Our Nest has never hosted even a minor Conclave. We are one of the smallest Nests, since we are so close to the lowlands, but these events have forced us into the forefront of dragon affairs. We may need your help again if many companions arrive. We do not have enough Kith to manage more than a few guests at our Companions' House, nor have they any experience in doing so."

At last, a problem she could actually solve! "My housekeeper at Pemberley was rescued by dragons as a child. She is accustomed to running a large household and would be greatly honored to provide advice on the needs of managing the Companions House. She could help with providing supplies and servants if needed."

"If you think she would agree, that would be a burden off my shoulders."

"I will speak to her, then." Not that she had any doubts of Mrs. Reynolds' answer.

But what would Darcy think? He had left a calm, well-managed estate. Now they were overwhelmed with lesser fae, not to mention Rana Akshaya and her entourage taking over the state rooms, Quickthorn in residence in the ballroom, and now Elizabeth was loaning staff to the Nest right and left.

She swallowed hard, fighting back the tears that came so easily these days. Darcy could be as angry as he liked about the changes, as long as he came home to her.

Chapter 22

D ARCY LEFT THE *DILIGENCE* in a small town, choosing that over a city where there might be soldiers stationed. A nearby baker pointed him to a house that let out rooms to travelers, and Darcy bought several sugary pastries for use if he overextended his Talent.

After a cursory examination of his papers, a room was deemed to be available, and Darcy took his purchases there. He closed the door and settled himself to wait for the moment the dragon scale would come to life. Then he drew even more power than he had earlier, far beyond what he had ever used, to try to send word to Elizabeth. Sending so much over a great distance was unheard of – and beyond risky – but he had no choice. Chances were good he would be caught long before he reached the Channel, and getting word to England that Napoleon was a dragon was critical.

Without that, his entire mission was worse than a failure. It had made matters worse. Beyond the people no doubt killed in the fire, attacks on British troops would be redoubled.

The room was spinning around him by the time he was done. He choked down the pastries, hoping it would be enough to recover his life forces. Afterwards, he spent half the night lying awake and praying that Elizabeth had received his message. For all he knew, he might have exhausted his strength on an impossible sending that went nowhere.

In the morning, he had just finished dressing when the old man who had rented him the room burst in without even knocking. "What is it, my good fellow?" Darcy asked.

"Get out of my house!" the man spat, shaking with fury. "I will not have an Englishman under my roof, not after you tried to kill our emperor."

Shock rushed through him. How had he been discovered? Then he realized it was not a personal accusation, but one that would be leveled at anyone from Britain. He tried to sound confused. "What is this nonsense about killing Napoleon?"

"One of your countrymen tried, but our emperor was too clever for him, and all of you can rot in hell for all I care! Out of here, you son of a whore, or I will bloody your nose for you!"

As if this decrepit old man could lay a hand on him! But Darcy could not blame him; he would be equally incensed if a Frenchman had tried to kill the King. He slung his satchel over his shoulder and strode out of the house.

He would have to be even more careful now, when his very nationality made him a target. If only he could pretend to be Flemish or Austrian – but his papers would put the lie to that. Fortunately, the sleepy ostler at the stable where the *diligence* stopped either had not heard the news or did not care, for he sold Darcy a ticket.

Now he was on a different coaching route, an indirect, minor one where there would be fewer soldiers watching the road. In the afternoon, Darcy swung out of the small diligence, his legs aching. The seats were not designed for someone of his height, and on top of that he had tried to hunch down to avoid drawing attention and kept his nose buried in a book – a French book he had no interest in – to avoid conversation. Now his neck was stiff, too.

His muscles protested as his boots struck the pavement. Rolling his shoulders to loosen them, he followed the other passengers into the inn with more eagerness than the unprepossessing building deserved. He was parched enough to enjoy even the cheapest wine. But he also kept a hold on his tie to Pemberley's power, in case trouble arose.

But first, the necessary. He made his requests to the host and then followed his directions from the crowded taproom to the back of the inn, winding through a narrow brick passageway that could use a good cleaning.

A few minutes later, he turned back, his stomach grumbling. At least that would be easy to fix; the food had been good even in the poorest auberges in France. No wonder everyone hired French chefs in England.

An excited voice in the taproom caught his attention. "An Englishman? On the *diligence*? Mon ami, we can avenge the attack on the emperor – and our fortune is made!"

Were they talking about him? Darcy pressed himself back against the rough wall.

"What do you mean?" Was that the coach driver?

"Look at this! Five thousand gold napoleons for the capture of an Englishman, last seen in Paris. Another five hundred francs to anyone who assists his capture! Tall and dark-haired, just like this one, might be traveling under the name of Harcourt or Darcy. It must be the blackguard who tried to kill the emperor!"

"Hah! We'll teach him a lesson he won't forget!" another man cried.

Good God! He had expected a price on his head, but five thousand gold napoleons was a fortune beyond belief. Anyone would turn him in at the mere hope of it. What smuggler would carry him to England when they could sell them for a thousand times more than his fare?

There was no time to think of that now. He had to escape. If he set foot in that taproom, he would never see England again.

Or Elizabeth.

There had to be another way out of the inn. He carefully retraced his footsteps down the dark winding corridor, past closed doors. Then light poured in, along with smells of cooking food and the sound of clanking dishes.

The kitchen. It was bound to have a back door. With any luck no one there would have heard the news yet. If he stayed silent, they would not discover he was English.

Pulling up the collar of his coat, he strode into the kitchen. There it was, just beyond the hearth. Ignoring the two women who turned to stare at him, he hurried through the door, finding himself in the back of the stable yard. A groom was harnessing fresh horses to the stagecoach.

Dare he try to get his satchel? It was in the overhead netting inside the *diligence*, so he would have to open the door to reach it. Too much of a risk, even if he could stay invisible for that long. And there were more grooms in the stable, so taking a horse was out of the question.

There was no choice. He would have to leave here on foot, with nothing more than the clothes on his back. At least he still had plenty of French coin, traded in Paris for his English gold. God only knew how he would get back to England, but first he had to avoid capture.

He cloaked himself in invisibility and walked out to the road. They had passed through a forest just before the inn; that would have to do as an escape route.

After walking for hours, following one path and then another, sometimes cutting across a field or meadow, Darcy found an abandoned hut. The latch was broken, and the door hung open, but it was shelter of a sort, and it was almost time for his connection to Elizabeth.

When the scale came alive, though, it was not Elizabeth. Or not only Elizabeth; he could sense her there, but also another presence, one he had felt in his mind before. The Eldest of the Dark Peak Nest.

The dragon's voice resonated in his head. *Think of what you saw of Napoleon.*

Nothing could be easier; he had revisited the scene hundreds of times already, trying to comprehend it. He spewed it out to the Eldest in all its details.

The dragon's touch in his mind was rougher than he remembered it, either because of the distance or the need for haste. Then, quickly, it was gone, and Elizabeth, too.

He sank back into a corner of the hut, regretting the lack of his precious moment with Elizabeth, but relieved that this heavy knowledge was in the hands of the Nest. Would Elizabeth somehow find a way to inform the War Office, too? Not that it would make much difference; all the might of the British Army and Navy could not hold against Napoleon the dragon.

He touched the silk handkerchief in his pocket, the one he had purchased for Elizabeth, as if it already carried an essence of her.

Once it was full dark, he built a small fire with sticks collected near the hut. He used his identity papers as kindling, since they were now a danger to him. Anything that identified him as British would put his life in danger. He would be better off claiming to be Swedish and saying that he had been robbed of his *passeport*.

The flames cast little warmth but relieved the chill a bit. It did nothing to take his mind off his empty stomach, but he curled up in front of it, his coat wrapped as tightly around him as he could manage. Finally, he drifted off into a fitful sleep.

He awoke abruptly to the sound of barking in the distance. Wild dogs hunting in the forest?

He scrambled to his feet in sudden realization. Hunting, yes. Hunting for him. Of course the villagers would not let five thousand gold napoleons slip through their fingers. They would turn over every stone to find him. Including sending out the dogs. They would have his scent, too, from the satchel he had left behind on the *diligence*.

He had to get away from here. But how? He could not outrun a dog in the forest. No matter how far he went, they would smell him. If he climbed a tree, they would bark at it until someone came.

Unless he used the dragon Artifact, the one that would block him from any sense except touch. The dogs would not smell, hear, or see him. It would let him escape this – but at a price. Once used, it would never work again. But if the dogs found him and he was captured, it would be too late.

His fingers itched to open the pendant, to save himself right now, but he waited. Perhaps they would lose his trail, or he might be able to fight his way out. He would wait until the last minute to use the Artifact.

The barking grew louder, definitely closer. Two different barks, and perhaps other dogs who might be silent.

Then an unearthly yowl filled the air, high-pitched and vibrant, a sound he recognized. Darcy froze. Even if there were lynxes in France, they would be in the wilderness, not this small patch of forest near a village.

A flurry of yipping from the dogs, another scream of outrage from the lynx, and the sound of scrabbling. And then silence.

Had the lynx frightened off the dogs? Could he be so fortunate?

Then an image formed in his head. *Come.* A presence he knew as well as his own voice.

How could his lynx have found his way to France? True, he had followed Darcy all over England, but surely he could not swim twenty miles of the English Channel. If lynxes could swim at all.

But his familiar had never led him astray, so he cautiously emerged from the hut. His lynx sat outside in the dim moonlight, looking completely at ease apart from the blood dripping from the side of his mouth. Apparently the dogs had not escaped unscathed.

You saved me, he sent. Would his lynx understand those words?

Yes. Come. The lynx padded off, along a trail only he could see.

Darcy followed.

Darcy would not have survived the next few days without the lynx, who led him to wild apple trees and abandoned fields where a few turnips still grew, who brought him fish in the evening which he roasted in a fire, and once even a loaf of bread he must have stolen. In his old life, Darcy would have scorned bread that had been carried in a lynx's mouth. Now it was a precious gift.

Each night his familiar went back and marked the trail they had followed, presumably to deter any scent trackers. No sensible dog would go near to what smelled like a lynx's den.

He was weary, footsore, and tired of sleeping on the cold ground, but he was making slow uneven progress towards the west, or at least his best guess at that direction from the position of the sun. His map and compass had been in the satchel he had left in the diligence. If he was correct, eventually he would reach the coast. Then the hard part would begin, finding his way to the friends of the sea serpents, in the hope they would find a way to take him across the Channel without turning him in for the reward.

Then one night a squadron of soldiers trotted past the hedgerow where he was sheltering, set up an encampment not two hundred feet away, and began to search the area around him by lanternlight, swearing all the while about the damned Englishman and what they would do to him when they found him.

Darcy tried not to breathe. How could they possibly know he was here? They had no dogs. Could they have smelled the smoke from the fire he had cooked his fish in? Quickly he created an illusion to cover the remaining coals and made another of impenetrable brambles to hide himself. It must have worked well enough, for they did not find him. He sent a message to his familiar, telling him to stay away. Even a wild lynx had no chance against a dozen soldiers.

He would have to take greater care. No more fires. He waited until they were all asleep before he cloaked himself in invisibility and sneaked away. That day he took no rests, trying to make the greatest possible distance. His stomach growled, but he was not quite hungry enough to eat raw fish. By tomorrow, he suspected he might be.

But despite his hunger and fatigue, Darcy was exhilarated by his narrow escape, confident that he had left the soldiers behind. As always, the best moment was at sunset, when the dragon scale came to life and Elizabeth entered his mind, all warmth and pleasure, even when he reported no news. As usual, her message was to stay safe.

He gathered some leaves behind a stone wall to make himself a place to sleep. The lynx curled up next to him, sharing his welcome body warmth. If Darcy ever went on the run again, he was going to make certain to have a blanket with him. And a jug to carry water; the tiny flask in his pocket was not enough to keep him going between the occasional streams he passed.

Then the soldiers came again.

By the fourth night, Darcy was almost expecting them. He had tried everything to throw them off, changing his direction, walking inland instead of making his way to the Channel, retracing his own steps on the path and having the lynx cover his new tracks, and never a trace of fire. Today he had even told the lynx not to follow him, in case somehow the soldiers could sense his magical connection to his familiar. Yet still the squadron came trotting across the field.

He drew back into his makeshift hiding place between an ancient tree and a stone wall.

How did they do it? It was incomprehensible, and incomprehensibility usually meant magic. Could one of them be a mage, tracking him by repulsion? No, for then Darcy would feel it, too. It had to be some kind of unknown Talent, one without repulsion.

Still, whatever they were doing, it worked only to a degree. They kept discovering his general location, yes, but whatever magic they used could not bring them exactly to him. And why did they only come at night?

If only he could understand it, perhaps he could find a way to defeat their uncanny ability. Escaping from them would be harder now, with his belly too hollow to risk creating an illusion. He would keel over from exhausting his reserves. Without his lynx, he had eaten only a few berries all day.

He remembered his mother saying that some magical powers could not cross running water. What if he found a stream and walked through that?

He had passed one earlier, not far away. It would mean being in plain sight, though. He would have to travel at night, with all the attendant risks.

It was as good, or as bad, a plan as any. He leaned back against the tree and waited, giving the soldiers several hours to set up the tents and retire for the night. Once the moon was high in the sky, he crept over the stone fence and tiptoed into the woods, wincing at each tiny sound of dry leaves or twigs underfoot.

When he was certain he was safely away, he cut back to the road, retracing his steps from earlier in the day until he reached the stream. He clambered down the bank and stepped into the water. His boots would not keep it out for long, but there was nothing to be done for it. Better wet feet than captured.

He headed downstream, picking his footing carefully to avoid twisting an ankle in the uneven streambed. At least he would be getting away from roads and paths that would be easy to follow.

He trudged on for hours, as the stream met a larger one and eventually widened into what might be called a river. He had to stay in the shallow water near the bank now, his stomach churning with emptiness and his muscles aching. His life as Mr. Darcy of Pemberley seemed like a faintly absurd dream.

Dawn broke, and by good fortune the fields around him were fallow, with no sign of human habitation. Still, it meant taking even greater care to avoid being spotted, and he needed to rest. Desperately. He had walked all day and most of the night.

Finally he found a hollow in the bank where he could hide himself. He collected some branches and brush to cover himself. Then he curled up in the hollow and fell asleep, cold and achingly hungry.

He stayed there until sunset, when the dragon scale grew heavy in his hand. Elizabeth's presence filled him, replete with love and support.

It was a brief heaven-sent moment of connection, and Darcy longed to luxuriate in it, but he sent his prepared message. *Working to get home to you.*

Her reply came immediately. *Stay safe, no matter what.*

Then it ended, no matter how he tried to hug the sensation close to him. Now he was back to being hungry, achy, and filthy. He left his hiding place long enough to forage a handful of berries from nearby brambles. If only he knew more of what he could eat in the wild! If he ever made it back to England, he would learn that first. Starving was highly unpleasant. If he found nothing on his own tomorrow, he would have to call his lynx, even if it meant the soldiers would find him again.

Once it was full dark, he could continue down the river. Sooner or later it would lead to a town where he might be able to steal some food.

Then he heard hoofbeats. Again. Curse them! Quickly he huddled to the ground as they passed him, splashing through the shallows along the river's edge.

Damnation, how had they found him? He held his breath. Would they keep going?

"No, too far, blast him!" cried a voice in French. "Come back and go slowly this time. He will not escape us again."

Darcy's head sank back. This was very bad. His hiding place would not hold up to even a cursory inspection, and he could not summon the reserves to use his Talent.

The sounds of the men thrashing through the underbrush surrounded him. "He must be here somewhere!" The voice was triumphant.

This was it. He had used up all his narrow escapes, and there was only one option left, the one he had hoped to save in case he needed to sneak aboard a ship. The dragon Artifact, the one that could hide him for a day and a night. Without it, he would be captured. Once in prison, escape would be impossible. This was his only chance.

Careful not to disturb the branches around him, he reached up and tugged out the invisible pendant that hung around his neck. Snapping it open, he pressed his forefinger against the sharp point inside until he felt the skin part.

And his body faded from view, just like when he made himself invisible. It worked!

He had to leave his little hollow, though. Sooner or later one of the soldiers would stumble over it, and they could still find him by touch. No, the safest place would be in the river.

Now the dangerous part. Even if they could not see him, the branches he had to move were visible.

"Look, there!"

Darcy froze, halfway out of the hollow. A shot rang out, and something slapped his right shoulder. But God, they had hit him, shooting blind! Warm wetness trickled down his chest.

His luck had run out. He bit his lip to smother a cry of pain.

"Do not shoot less you have to! The emperor wants him alive."

"I thought I saw something move."

It was like a hot poker deep in his shoulder. He stumbled to the water, stepping in to stand knee-deep, and pressed his hand against the wound.

The soldiers were everywhere around him, half a dozen of them carrying lanterns and pacing up and down the river. A tall, thin lieutenant stood on the bank, studying something in his hand. "Something is wrong. It says he is right here."

"Could he be hidden from sight?" an older soldier asked.

"Possibly. There are mages with that ability." The lieutenant broke off a long branch and began sweeping it over the water.

That could be his downfall. The Artifact would hide him from any sense except touch. But if he moved, that mysterious device the lieutenant held would know it.

There was only one choice. He crouched down and submerged himself, moving as slowly as he dared to reduce ripples that might give his position away.

The branch whistled past, just over the surface of the water.

That had been too close.

Damn, it was cold! He held his breath as long as he could, then rolled onto his back and moved his lips to the surface. Air, blessed air! But he could still hear them stomping around the riverbanks, swearing.

On and on. His arms and legs began to cramp with cold, but at least it eased the pain in his wound. The Artifact might hide him for a day, but he would freeze long before that. Would they never give up?

"It must be broken. He was here, but clearly is gone." The tall lieutenant's words sounded distorted and distant through the water covering Darcy's ears.

"No matter," said the older one. "Tomorrow at sunset he will use his powers again, and it has always led us true then. This time we will surround him rather than try to follow him."

Sunset. Somehow they were sensing his evening contact with Elizabeth.

They tromped away, grumbling and cursing, but he did not move. It could be a trap. What if they only went a short distance and then returned? Darcy waited until he could barely move his fingers before creeping out of the water half-frozen. How would he make it through the night? He could not risk a fire.

His legs were not working properly, and dizziness almost claimed him more than once, but somehow he dragged himself as far as a hedgerow. It was likely the best shelter he could find, so he forced his way inside it, the brambles tearing into his skin.

He curled up there, shivering, the cold sunk deep in his bones. Could he possibly survive the night in his soaking clothes?

At least dying of cold would be less painful than whatever death Napoleon had planned for him.

Chapter 23

ELIZABETH FROWNED AT THE two-day-old newspaper. It carried a brief report of a failed assassination attempt on Napoleon and a fire that had destroyed his apartments in the Tuileries, but its headline was about the dragon companion Lady Amelia Fitzwilliam who was offering her assistance to the War Office in setting up defenses against invasion. The ensuing article failed to mention Granny's advanced age or Welsh connections. According to Frederica, it was solely meant to reassure the worried populace that they had matters well in hand. There had still been no direct word from Granny in London, which was a worry in itself.

But it was nearly sunset, and she had no more time to read. It had started to drizzle, so Elizabeth wrapped herself in a cloak and hurried out to the covered arbor. Would it be more of the same tonight, with Darcy reporting he was trying to get home? It had been a week since he had sent the message about Napoleon. If his escape had been going according to plan, it should have taken him no more than a day or two to reach the Channel.

At the last two sunset contacts, she had sensed a hint of desperation in him, but perhaps she was only imagining it because she was worried about the delay. Tonight she intended to ask what was going on. Not knowing was driving her mad.

She took out the dragon scale and rubbed it, letting its smooth warmth and the reflection of the fading light in its iridescent colors soothe the edges of her anxiety. Soon. Any moment, and he would be there.

The scale flared to life, the dragon magic thick between her fingers. She reached out. *What is happening?*

Nothing.

No response, no beloved presence, no sensation of oak trees in a summer grove.

She rubbed her hand over her suddenly tight chest. This was it, what she had dreaded every day as sunset approached. The night when he did not answer.

It was not the end, she told herself fiercely. She had prepared herself for this, too, with all the reasons Darcy might not respond on one particular day. He could be in company where he could not take out the scale. He might be seizing an opportunity to escape that happened to fall at sunset. Or someone could have stolen the scale from him. It did not mean he was dead, that she was a widow.

Except that she knew it was the most likely explanation. Darcy would have done his utmost not to miss their connection. Somehow he would at least have touched the scale, even if he could not compose a message. If he had not, something was terribly wrong.

She sank back on the bench, rubbing her arms and rocking back and forth, as if anything could comfort her in this agonizing moment. It could not be. It could not.

How could she live in a world without him?

Frederica gave it half an hour. It was not unusual for Elizabeth to dally a little after her contact with Darcy, but the rain was coming down in buckets now. And she had read the newspaper, too, about the massive manhunt for Napoleon's attempted assassin.

A word to the butler was enough to send the footmen out searching for Elizabeth. Just to look for her, of course, and report back without speaking to her. It did not take long for Hobbes return with the news that Mrs. Darcy was in the arbor in the rose garden.

She put on her pelisse and headed out into the storm, using just enough weather magic to keep the worst of the rain off her. At least the rose garden was nearby.

There she was, curled into a ball on the bench in the arbor. Frederica's heart sank, both for Elizabeth and for her poor cousin in France. This had always been the most likely outcome, but still, it was heartbreaking.

She put her arm around Elizabeth. "Come, let us go inside," she said gently. "For your child's sake. We cannot have you falling ill." She knew better than to suggest doing anything for Elizabeth's own health.

"There was nothing," Elizabeth choked. "And do not tell me there may be other explanations."

"I would not dream of it. Come now. The conservatory door is open, and there is no one there to see you." She knew that for certain, since she had told Hobbes to keep everyone away.

Elizabeth did not move.

Best to call in the reinforcements. *Quickthorn? Could you tell Cerridwen that Elizabeth is terribly distressed? Darcy was not there for their sunset sending, and she thinks he must be dead. And I cannot get her to come in out of the rain.*

I will tell her to come. And for once there was no sarcasm or irritability in her dragon's sending, just sympathy.

"Now you have to go in, for Cerridwen will be here soon, and she will be terribly cross if you are still out here in the rain," Frederica told Elizabeth.

"Nothing matters," Elizabeth sobbed.

"Well, then, nothing can matter inside, too. Come." And this time she pulled on her hand.

Apparently Elizabeth did not have the stamina to fight, for she followed, right out into the downpour, not making even an effort to shield her head. They were both dripping by the time they reached the conservatory. She led Elizabeth like a child through the rows of fruit trees, into the main house, and to her rooms.

There Chandrika took over, taking off Elizabeth's wet clothes and leading her towards an already drawn hot bath.

Elizabeth balked. "No. Just let me go to bed."

"I cannot, Mrs. Darcy. We must get you warm, for the baby's sake," said Chandrika firmly. "I will hold your hand as you step in."

Frederica suspected they would be using that argument a good deal.

She had envied the love Darcy and Elizabeth had shared, and she grieved the lost potential when Roderick had refused her. Watching Elizabeth now, she wondered if she had been the lucky one.

Then she went downstairs and informed the butler that Mrs. Darcy had just received news from home of the death of a dear friend, and that she would likely not be herself for a few days. He would spread the news, and no one would remark on her behavior.

It was a good thing being a truth-caster did not preclude telling lies.

Chapter 24

THE THROBBING IN HIS shoulder yanked Darcy out of sleep. He opened his eyes, blinked, and closed them again. This had to be a dream. Why else would there be the tree roots over his head? And surrounding him, too, forming the rounded walls of small chamber. A room filled with child-sized wooden furniture.

He dug his fingernails into his palms, willing the dream to fade. But when he looked again, nothing had changed. A fire burned merrily in an undersized hearth, with a tiny pot over it giving off an appetizing aroma. His stomach rumbled. When had he last eaten warm food?

A squeaky voice said, "Ah. You are awake; good." The voice came from the middle of this empty underground chamber, where no one stood.

An invisible speaker in a strange burrow where everything was too small for a human. There was only one answer, and it terrified him. "Am I in Faerie?" he choked out.

Faerie had cost him his mother for over a decade. Faerie could steal a dozen years from his life. His baby would be nearly grown by the time he returned. Elizabeth might have remarried, thinking him dead...

A rusty chuckle. "Nay, we are still in your mortal world."

Relief washed over him. Anything was better than Faerie. He tried to sit up, but a vicious stab of pain in his shoulder made him collapse back down.

"Allow me to help you." Invisible hands slid behind his back. "Let me do the work." The hands pressed upwards.

Darcy still grunted with pain, but this time he managed to reach a sitting position. "Who are you?"

"Names can be dangerous. I am a friend of a friend."

He was not about to trust a fae with vague answers. "Are you a friend of Napoleon?"

A tsking sound. "I care nothing for mortal rulers." A bowl wafted through the air and was set in front of him.

"A neat evasion, as Napoleon is not a mortal." Devil take it, would this pain never ease?

"Then no, I am no friend to Napoleon."

The smell of the food, the aroma of meat and roasted vegetables, almost made him dizzy. "Will this food have any magical effect on me? Or otherwise harm me?" He was so hungry he might eat it anyway.

"How sensibly distrustful you are! It is plain mortal food, without any spells, potions, poisons, or traps. It will not hurt you."

He could not help himself. He shoveled it into his mouth as quickly as he could with the tiny spoon. It tasted better than anything he had ever eaten. A second bowl appeared, and he demolished that, too.

It almost made him feel like himself again, despite the pain in his shoulder. Still, something nagged at him. "Napoleon's men are hunting me, and they have a tool that will lead them to me. Even here."

"Not to you, but to this." The leather pouch holding his dragon scale suddenly pressed against his chest as if a finger was pushing into it. Then the pressure eased, and the voice became annoyed. "Horrid iron bullet. It stings, even from this distance." A spitting sound.

"They are tracking what I have in the pouch?" The one thing he could not bear to give up.

"That bit of dragon, yes. They have a dragon lodestone."

He had never heard of such a thing, but it might explain how Napoleon had found the dragon Nests. "You are certain?"

"I overheard them speaking of it. They are close, even now."

Damnation. That would explain why they found him at night. When the scale became active at sunset, it would lead them to him again.

Perhaps he could hide it somewhere. But then the soldiers would find it and take it for themselves. They would do that eventually, no matter how well he hid it.

That scale was his only connection to Elizabeth and to England. She would assume the worst if he suddenly stopped answering. She would worry terribly. But he could not flee from the soldiers again, not with this wound.

Could he steal one last chance to contact her? Elizabeth had begged him to do whatever would keep him safe, even if it meant hiding for months.

She would want him to get rid of the scale that was endangering him. Even if his chest ached at the thought of losing that moment of connection to her, leaving him completely alone among his enemies.

Using his left hand, he slowly lifted the chain over his head and balanced the pouch in his hand. "I must hide this somewhere, then. Or better yet, put it on a *diligence* that will carry it far away and lead the soldiers to hunt somewhere else." But if he had this much trouble sitting up, how could he sneak into town, much less disguise himself to get close to the *diligence*?

"Clever, for a mortal. If you wish it, it shall be done."

"By whom?"

"I, or one of my kin," the fae said obligingly. Too obligingly.

Darcy weighed his words. "I do not understand why you would wish to aid me with no expectation of return."

A cackle of laughter. "Oh, how it pains me to explain myself to a mortal! The payment has already been made. You placed us under an obligation to you, and by this service, I lessen that debt."

He struggled to understand. "Because I tried to stop Napoleon?"

The spitting sound again. "Nothing so trifling."

It had not felt trifling to him.

A softer, gentler voice spoke. "You created an obligation by your kindness to her whom you call your sister."

Cold washed over him. How did these French fae know about Georgiana? "She is my sister in every way that matters," he said stiffly.

"Ah, they said you were proud, and so you are, even with a bullet in your shoulder! We cannot fix that, since it is iron, but a mortal healer will be here soon to remove it."

His mind seized on the least important part of his words. "Bullets are made of lead, not iron."

"Not this one." The kind fae sounded amused. "They use iron bullets when they are hunting fae. Likely they were unsure of your mortality and took no chances."

It made sense, but... "A human healer will betray me to Napoleon."

"This one shall not. But first we must take that bit of dragon far from here. The *diligence* is a good thought, but better to have someone take it even farther and throw into the sea. Then they will believe you gone."

His hand closed over the pouch. It had saved his life on the smugglers' boat. He had hoped it would help him find a sailor willing to take him back across the Channel. And it tied him to Elizabeth.

Now it was a target on his back.

He still hesitated. Elizabeth would be frantic. "Would it be possible for you to get a message to my sister, telling her that I gave this up? And perhaps even about the dragon lodestone?" Georgiana would know to tell Elizabeth.

A deep sigh. "I suppose so."

Slowly he opened his fingers and held it out. "Take it."

The slight weight lifted from his palm. Now he was completely on his own.

The healer proved to be a lady perhaps a few years younger than Darcy. She arrived the following day, just as his invisibility from the dragon Artifact was wearing off, and just in time. His shoulder might be no worse, but he could not say the same thing for his mind. According to the kind fae, Elizabeth had in fact not been by his bedside throughout the night. Nor had Star, the faithful spaniel whom he had been given as a pup when he was six. Since the fae did not lie, he had to believe her. Then again, he was talking to an invisible fae, which was at least as unlikely as Elizabeth mysteriously appearing and disappearing here when she was far away in England.

He would ask her when she came back, if she did. Or perhaps Star would know.

The woman kneeled beside him. "What is the matter?" she asked, her French accented with some other harsher sounding tongue. Flemish, perhaps, or German? Elizabeth's French always sounded accented to him, too, although in a different manner.

Her dark hair, pulled back in an intricate style which suggested a degree of wealth, or at least the services of a lady's maid, reminded him of Elizabeth, too, though this woman's curls were... His mind failed him in finding the words.

"I need you to pay attention," she said. "Tell me what happened."

"They shot me." He pointed to his shoulder, but he was forgetting something important. Oh, yes. "Are you going to sell me to the emperor?" Not that it really mattered. His chances of getting home now were almost nonexistent.

"No, of course not," she said. "This may hurt." She peeled away the blood-soaked linen over his torn flesh and bent forward to examine it, probing it gently with her finger. "The wound is clean, with no bleeding. The surgeon always says it is better to leave a bullet in place if it is not causing bleeding, since cutting it out can do more damage."

Whatever would heal fastest. Had he said that, or only thought it?

"It must come out," said the creaky voice, the kind one. "The iron is poisoning him. He has only a trace of fae blood, but enough that it is destroying his mind."

"He will need a surgeon, then. I can deal with minor wounds, but cutting out a bullet? I do not even know where to begin."

"You must do your best, Infant," said the voice sympathetically. "He has a price on his head, so getting a surgeon would mean a death sentence, and we cannot come near that iron. He will die if the bullet remains and die if we get a surgeon."

She drew in a sharp breath. "Then I suppose I will do my best. If you wish me to try, that is."

He had nothing to lose. And perhaps Elizabeth and Star would come back to talk to him again. "I would be in your debt."

She glanced towards the corner where the voice had come from. "This would be easier for me if he were asleep," she said in a subdued voice. "Otherwise someone will have to hold him down."

"I will make him sleep, Infant," the voice said.

Unseen fingers brushed over his forehead, and darkness fell.

His shoulder burned when he awoke. Pain shot down his arm, which was bound tightly in a sling. The woman had been right, that removing the bullet had made his injury worse. Now he would be more helpless than before.

The woman's hand was pressing on a bandage over the wound. "How does it feel?"

"It hurts. But I can think clearly again." And that was an enormous blessing

"Do not try to move that arm. Give it time to recover. There will be more bleeding, I suspect. I did my best, though I made it up as I went along."

"I thank you for your efforts, Madame...."

"Mme. Hartung," she said.

"Thank you, Mme. Hartung." His lips were too cracked to smile. "I could hardly call you 'infant.'"

She laughed. "The fae at home named me that when I was barely walking. They saw no reason to change it when I grew up."

So she was allied with the fae. "What happens to me now?" he asked in a low voice. Somehow it was easier to ask another human, one he could see. "Will they allow me to stay here while I recover?"

"They will, because of their debt to you, but the soldiers know you were nearby. We will need to find a way to take you farther away, where they will not be hunting for you."

Suspicion pricked at him. "Why would you help me? If I am caught, it could go very badly for you."

She looked down at her left hand, where a gold ring circled her finger. "My husband was forced to serve in Napoleon's army for years. When he was ordered to fire upon our own people in Prussia, he fled rather than murder our countrymen. But when he sought help from them, they turned him in rather than risk angering Napoleon, even though my husband was the kaiser's own cousin." Her voice shook. "I help you because no one helped my husband."

He hardly knew what to say. "You do me great honor. I had not expected to find an opponent of Napoleon among the French."

"There are many who wish he would give up his dreams of conquest, but I am Prussian, not French. My husband and I were sent here as hostages. I am no servant of the emperor of France."

"I am sorry for your situation," he said awkwardly. Even if it was fortunate for him.

"Do you have a wife waiting for you at home?"

Despite the burning pain and the hopelessness of his situation, the corners of his lips turned up at the thought of Elizabeth. He touched the pocket that held the silk handkerchief, as if it were a talisman. "I do. She is expecting our first child."

The woman nodded. "Somehow we will find a way to get you back to her."

Chapter 25

THREE DAYS. THREE ENDLESS days that had lasted an eternity, since Elizabeth had last felt Darcy at the other end of the dragon scale. The last two evenings she had gone to the oak grove at sunset, as if being in the center of his power when the dragon scale activated could make a difference.

It did not. There was only silence.

Each morning she arose after hardly sleeping, exhausted from crying, wondering if this was the day she should don a black dress. It felt wrong to be wearing colors when she was grieving so bitterly. Why had she not tried harder to stop him from going? Now she would never see him again. All she would have was her too-brief memories of their time together. It seemed an impossibly thin thread to sustain her for the rest of her life.

But she had to dress in her normal colors, for she could not explain to the world why she believed Darcy to be dead. The cruel tyranny of keeping up appearances forced her to pretend everything was normal. If, by some tiny chance, Darcy was still alive, she would not endanger him by admitting to his mission.

Only Frederica and the dragons knew what had happened, though Chandrika had likely guessed the truth. No one else knew her world had ended. Not even Georgiana, who had not been told about the dragon scales in the first place.

Which was why, when Georgiana paid an unusual midmorning visit to her sitting room, Elizabeth tried to force a smile to her frozen lips. Then she noticed a peculiar expression on her sister-in-law's face, pained and frightened. "Good morning, Georgiana. Is something troubling you?"

"A fae brought me a message today," she said slowly. "It came from a hobgoblin in France. He sent this, with instructions that I should give it to you." And she held out a dragon scale, the match to Elizabeth's.

Elizabeth's head swam. There it was, the proof she had dreaded.

Nothing mattered anymore. Not appearances, not anything. She bent forward, putting her head to her knees, gasping for breath. Darcy was gone.

Georgiana's words seemed to come from a great distance. "What is it, Elizabeth? Because there is more. My brother is hurt." There was a hitch in her voice.

Hurt?

Elizabeth lifted her tear-soaked face. "He is...alive?"

Georgiana gave her an odd look. "Yes, but he is injured. A bullet wound in his shoulder, he said. Poor Fitzwilliam!"

Somehow she stumbled to her feet. "Will he survive?"

"The fae who told me seemed to think so, but the message had passed through multiple hands. And there was another part, too, that I did not understand."

Alive. He was alive! A mere bullet wound seemed like the slightest trifle, if it meant she might see Darcy again someday. "What is that?"

"He said the French emperor has a dragon lodestone." She held up the dragon scale. "That is how they tracked my brother, by following him whenever he used this for magic, so Fitzwilliam told them to take it far away from him. I hope that makes more sense to you than it does to me."

That was why Darcy had not responded, because he had sent the scale away for his own safety. The rest of Georgiana's words seemed to float right past her, for all the sense she could make of them.

Nothing else mattered as long as Darcy was alive.

Frederica came to stand beside her. "What is this dragon lodestone? How does it work?"

Georgiana turned up her hands. "I do not know. The fae did not explain anything."

"Perhaps that is how Napoleon is locating the Nests," Frederica said.

Elizabeth found her voice. "Did they say where he is? And if he is safe?"

The girl shook her head. "Just that he was recovering. I tried to ask questions, but he would not stay. I wish I knew more."

A light frisson of magic tingled Elizabeth's arm, the one near Frederica. She must be sending to Quickthorn.

"Can you send a message back? Perhaps find out where he is?" Elizabeth asked haltingly.

Georgiana bit her lip, as if expecting to be scolded. "I do not know how, and when I asked my own fae, they said that is not how these things work." Her voice shook.

Somehow Elizabeth managed to salvage a bit of her shredded composure. "Georgiana, I cannot tell you how grateful I am to know this much. Your connections have proved most valuable today, and I thank you for it."

He was alive! And that meant everything to her.

Elizabeth looked up as the butler's voice came from outside the closed doors of the drawing room. "Sir, are you certain you would not like to take a few minutes to refresh yourself?"

"No time," growled an unfamiliar male voice.

With a sigh, Elizabeth pursed her lips and blew to dismiss the illusion of a mouse sniffing at Cerridwen's back leg. Pity, as it was one of her best yet of a moving creature.

A knock sounded on the door, and Hobbes intoned in his most disapproving manner, "Madam, Colonel Fitzwilliam has come to call. Are you at home?"

Frederica jumped to her feet, her eyes wide. "My brother," she hissed to Elizabeth.

Elizabeth raised an eyebrow. "Yes, Hobbes, pray admit him." At least it would be a distraction. More than a week of worrying about whether Darcy's wound had festered, and if she would ever have news of him again. Every day, when Georgiana said there was no news, was another disappointment.

The doors opened to reveal a man who was dressed for travel. Even with his greatcoat removed, he was covered with spatters of mud and dust. A blood-stained bandage circled his left sleeve.

"Richard!" Frederica hurried towards him as if to embrace him but stopped short. "Good heavens, what a mess you are!"

"Comes of riding straight through from London, with no sleep and a nasty skirmish with the highwayman."

"Some people take the stagecoach," she said pointedly. "Elizabeth, may I present my brother Richard? Although you might not believe it at the moment, he is usually quite tidy and presentable. Richard, this is Mrs. Darcy."

"Welcome to Pemberley, Colonel. My husband has mentioned you often."

He made a perfunctory bow. "Charmed, madam, but there is no time for niceties. We received information that it is unsafe for you to remain here, so I must beg you to permit me to escort you from this place to safety."

"Richard, you cannot simply announce something like that! What is the matter?" Frederica demanded.

Oh, dear. Ever since sending word to Granny – by private courier, no less –about Napoleon's true nature, Elizabeth had been expecting...something. "Does this have something to do with the letter I sent to Lady Amelia?" Elizabeth hazarded.

"Letter? I know nothing of a letter. No, this is news fresh from Napoleon's court, or at least only a few weeks old. The emperor has put an enormous bounty on Darcy's head, and also any member of his family. Assassins have been sent here."

"French assassins in England? Richard, have you been drinking?" Frederica scoffed.

"Not according to one of Boney's aides, who has nothing to gain from telling us that you need protection. Apparently Napoleon is furious over something Darcy learned and will do anything to stop it from getting out."

Elizabeth's chest tightened as she exchanged a wordless glance with Frederica. "I already know the secret Darcy discovered."

He swung to face her, seeming to truly see her for the first time. "You know? How? Not even the War Office has heard a word from him!"

How could she explain it without mentioning the dragon scale? "It was a brief sending. My Talent entwines with his, and he used the link through our unborn child for it."

He seemed to accept her explanation. "What did he learn?"

She wet her lips with the tip of her tongue. "Napoleon is a dragon in human form. He can take on other shapes. My husband saw him change into a falcon."

He stared at her in disbelief. "Ridiculous! As if a dragon could—"

Moving almost as quickly as a kestrel, Frederica clapped her hand over her brother's mouth. "Before you say anything further about dragons, I strongly urge you to look over at the hearth. Very strongly," she said sweetly.

The colonel, with a thunderous expression, turned his gaze on the fireplace where Cerridwen rested. His eyes bulged. "I am not seeing that," he moaned.

This was more than enough for Elizabeth. "Yes, she is a dragon, but my immediate concern is that you have news of my husband that you have not yet related to me."

His color rose, though he kept glancing at Cerridwen. "Madam, I will be glad to do so, but dragons are a grave danger."

"Not this one," said Elizabeth sharply, struggling not to strangle the news out of him. "I have been bonded to her since I was eight years old. Now, about my husband."

The colonel straightened his shoulders, but his eyes kept flickering towards Cerridwen. "We know very little. The attack on Napoleon failed. Darcy escaped, but the two Frenchmen did not. They revealed his true name under questioning, and no, I have no idea why anyone was foolish enough to tell it to them in the first place. There is a huge manhunt going on for him, but he has not been found. Or at least not as of the last word from France."

Elizabeth's heart turned over. The colonel's news was no more recent than what she had heard from the fae, but it was a reminder of the grave danger Darcy faced.

Frederica said, "We received a message through a fae – oh, yes, Richard; there are a great many lesser fae lurking here unseen – that Darcy was shot in the shoulder, but he lived through it."

The colonel cursed under his breath. "Shoulder wounds are bad. Never trust the fae, though; they are always up to something. When did you hear this?"

She counted on her fingers. "Ten days ago, perhaps. Less than a fortnight, for certain."

It had been over two long months since Darcy had kissed her farewell in her bedroom. A month since he had been on the run, in pain from his wound. She could not bear to think of his suffering.

"He must be having trouble returning. He was given names for escape routes, but none of them can be trusted not to turn him in for a reward of this size. Much as I dislike the idea, it would be safest for him to go into hiding there."

"You can do nothing to recover him?" Frederica asked.

The colonel gritted his teeth. "What could I do? How can we perform a daring rescue in a hostile country when we have no idea where he is? He might even have left France, for all we know. It would be hopeless."

A clear, floating voice said, "I can narrow it down, if that helps. I cannot tell how far away he is, but I know in which direction he can be found."

Elizabeth gaped at Cerridwen. Why had she never told her this before? What else did she know?

Cerridwen spoke in her head. *If I thought it could help, I would have told you. This Richard has an army and might be able to use the information.*

The colonel swung to face Cerridwen. "Are you certain? How closely can you locate him?" He demanded.

Frederica said firmly, "Pray forgive him, Cerridwen, for his ignorance of dragon protocol. Richard, they dislike direct questions from strangers. She will offer you what she wishes you to know."

Colonel Fitzwilliam's mouth opened and shut with an audible clash of teeth. But manners must have been drilled into him at a young age, for he made a precise bow in Cerridwen's direction. "My apologies for my lack of knowledge. I shall strive to do better."

Cerridwen tilted her head in acknowledgment.

The colonel rubbed his forehead, succeeding only in smearing mud across it. "But to the problem at hand, Mrs. Darcy, I must urgently request that you depart this place immediately, and I offer you my escort."

Elizabeth shook her head. "I cannot leave. The whole purpose of my marriage was for Darcy to draw on his land Talent through me, and that requires me to be at Pemberley. I have no objection to taking precautions, though."

"Precautions are not enough when French soldiers know they can earn a fortune and the emperor's personal favor simply by killing you. And since Napoleon knows Darcy's name, we must assume he is aware you are the source of his power, too. What better way to weaken Darcy than to dispose of you?"

"But what if his life depends on accessing my power?"

The child inside her chose that moment to kick, as if reminding her that there was another life depending on her, too.

Would she have to leave for her child's sake? It would be an unbearable choice. "Are you so certain it is a risk?"

"Certain enough to ride day and night to get here. Quite certain."

The butler cleared his throat. "Pardon me for speaking out of turn, madam, but a Frenchman came here two days ago seeking employment. We sent him away, of course, but he did seem very interested in looking around."

Elizabeth's stomach churned, and this time she could not blame it on the child. Someone truly wanted to kill her. A memory assailed her, one she had thought little of at the time. "Yesterday, as I was walking alongside the stream, I heard a gunshot that sounded quite nearby. I assumed it was a poacher."

The colonel's face paled, making the mud stand out starkly. "Were it not for bad aim, I might have been too late. There is no time to lose. We will leave for Matlock at first light. Until then you should not be alone, and I must ask you to stay away from windows."

"Matlock?" asked Lady Frederica. "Would they not know to look there?"

"Perhaps, but the good thing about living in a drafty old castle on top of a hill is that it is remarkably easy to defend."

Elizabeth's mind raced. Matlock, where she would be a stranger with no bond to the land. But perhaps there was another alternative. "Cerridwen," she said slowly. "The wards on Pemberley keep out High Fae. I wonder if they could be set to keep out unknown mortals, too."

Cerridwen's eyes unfocused for a long moment. "Rowan says they can be."

"Then I will ask for that to be done. It will make for some challenges, but it will keep French soldiers out." There would have to be changes in the estate, with deliveries left at the gatehouse to be brought in by trusted servants. The staff had already adjusted to worse. "And we have other defenses we can use, too." A castle might be easy to defend, but Pemberley had three dragons in residence who could set illusions and a host of lesser fae who were willing to fight for Georgiana.

The colonel frowned. "I would prefer to have you under my protection."

"I appreciate your concern, Colonel, but I will be safe here, and I would rather see you put your efforts toward rescuing my husband."

Colonel Fitzwilliam flushed. "If your dragon can tell me where to find him, I will go after him myself."

Cerridwen studied him. "I cannot tell you where he is. I can point you in his exact direction, but I have only a vague sense of how far away he is. If I were closer, I could lead you to him, but that is impossible."

His eyes narrowed. "So dragons can track people, but not from a distance."

"Not any dragon, and not any person. Only me, for I have tasted his blood."

Elizabeth winced at the appalled expression on the Colonel's face. "Just a drop or two, spilled by accident."

"Not by accident," Cerridwen insisted. "I knew something terrible would happen if I could not track him, so I clawed his face and tasted his blood."

This was clearly not helping the colonel see dragons as anything but bloodthirsty murderers.

But Darcy's cousin was clearly both determined and courageous. "Then will you travel with me, to show me where to find Darcy so that I can save him?"

Irritation rolled off the dragon. "I cannot go anywhere without my companion, and she must remain here."

Frederica jumped in again. "Richard, dragons cannot survive away from their Nests unless they are accompanied by their companion. The only exception is if they are flying from the Nest to their companion. You will have to find another solution."

Cerridwen walked to the window and unlatched it with her foreleg. Then she transformed and flew out.

The colonel goggled at the sight, working his jaw. Finally he said, "A dragon. Does Darcy know about this?"

"He does," Elizabeth confirmed. At least it was true that he knew about Cerridwen, but how would he feel if he knew just how many dragons were staying at Pemberley? "I am grateful to you for coming all this way to deliver your warning. Dare I hope you will stay with us for a time?" He looked ready to collapse.

"I thank you, Mrs. Darcy. If you will permit it, I would like to remain here for a few days to see if I can provide any suggestions on your defenses here. Darcy would expect it of me."

"You would be very welcome."

Frederica turned to the butler, still hovering by the door. "Hobbes, would you be so kind as to inform Mrs. Reynolds that Richard is here, injured, hungry, and tired?"

Hobbes bowed. "Of course, your ladyship."

As the butler disappeared, the colonel rounded on his sister. "Not fair, Freddie, setting old Reynolds on me! If she insists on a surgeon, I will wring your pretty little neck."

Frederica smiled at him. "It was my pleasure completely. By the by, you may see other dragons here as well. They are all perfectly civilized, though perhaps less polite in company than you might wish."

The colonel paled under the mud stains. "More dragons?"

"Three of them are often here, with another who visits with some regularity," she said coolly, as if there were nothing at all unusual about the situation.

He swallowed hard. "This will be interesting. You have a great deal of explaining to do, little sister."

Once the colonel was taken off to the room that had been prepared for him, Elizabeth turned to Frederica. "You did not tell him about your bond to Quickthorn."

Frederica grimaced. "I would rather not, if I can avoid it. Richard is a darling, for all his occasional bluster, but he will be angry enough when he discovers he is bound against speaking about Cerridwen. If he knew I was a dragon companion and could not tell the rest of the family, it would trouble him deeply. That is, if he did not strangle me first for taking on the bond to start out with."

"He does not seem to need any more reasons to dislike dragons. Bindings do tend to make things more complicated," Elizabeth agreed. It was frustrating enough that she could write so little about the truth of her life to her sister Jane. She longed to see her face to face, but it would be even harder then. As it was, Jane's letters to her sounded increasingly worried, asking her if anything was wrong. "Do you think he might have heard anything about what Granny and Sycamore are doing in London?"

"Indubitably. Richard is a terrible gossip, and he knows everyone." Her eyes twinkled, but then her expression sobered. "Are you worried by what he said about the French assassins?"

Elizabeth shrugged unhappily. "A little, but I want to see what the dragons and the fae can do to help us before I give up." She hesitated, but the thoughts would not stay inside. "But if I must leave anyway, I could go to France with Cerridwen. We could pinpoint Darcy's location and bring that information to Colonel Fitzwilliam."

"Absolutely not!" cried Frederica. "Have you forgotten your condition? You could lose the child, or be unable to return until after the birth, so it will never bond to the land. What if Darcy needs to draw on his land power through you, and you are not here? That is not even counting the risk of arrest and other dangers!"

"Let us also not forget the danger of my child growing up fatherless," Elizabeth retorted. Even though she knew Frederica was right.

"Darcy would not want you to do this. Not to risk your child's bond to Pemberley, the continuance of the Darcy line," Frederica argued.

It was true, every word of it. Darcy would be furious that she was even considering it. But how could she live with herself if he never returned, knowing she might have prevented his death?

And how she ached to see him, even if only for a moment, even if she could not touch him, just to know they were breathing the same air.

"I know," she said heavily. "It is just so hard."

Frederica's expression softened. "If I could go for you, I would."

Elizabeth nodded jerkily.

When Elizabeth retired to her rooms for the night, Cerridwen was drowsing by the fireside, having clearly returned from the Nest.

Elizabeth had ordered the room rearranged as Cerridwen grew, replacing the inlaid cabinet and the vanity with delicately curving legs with heavier furniture less likely to be overturned by a stray dragon wing or tail. She liked the look of it, the feeling of history it gave, and thought she would keep it this way even after Cerridwen outgrew the space. She had never had the opportunity to make a room her own before, and the process was exciting.

One thing she would not change, though, was the hand-painted chinoiserie wallpaper with its exquisite depictions of trees and dragons. She loved that.

She would keep the canopied bed with the elaborately carved headboard, too, the one where Darcy made love to her so often, where she had slept in his arms. She wanted those memories.

They might be all she would have.

She tiptoed past her sleeping dragon. It was good to see her back there; Cerridwen had spent the last two nights elsewhere, ever since Colonel Fitzwilliam arrived, and had seemed distracted and unhappy even when Elizabeth had seen her talking to the colonel about what illusions could be useful for trapping French assassins. Most oddly, she had seemed to be avoiding mental contact with Elizabeth.

She did not appear angry, though. If Elizabeth had done something wrong, it would have been obvious in her aura. But she was still worried.

The dragon opened one gold-ringed eye. "There you are."

Elizabeth dropped down to sit beside her. "Yes, I am here, dearest. I have missed you."

Cerridwen's chest rose and then fell. "I have been struggling, all in vain."

This was worrisome. "What is the matter? Can I do anything to help?"

"I fear you must." She lifted her head and laid it across Elizabeth's leg. "I am so very sorry. I have tried everything. I asked the Eldest whether I could form the lesser bond to that soldier, even though he does not like me, or to someone else, but she said it was impossible. Then I tried to see if I could give the taste of Darcy's blood to another dragon. It did not work with Rowan or Quickthorn, and then Juniper said it was too dangerous even to try with an older dragon. There is nothing for it."

It took a moment for this deluge of words to penetrate, and then Elizabeth's heart went out to her hard-working dragon. "Have you been trying to find a way to rescue my husband? How good you are, sweet Cerridwen!" No wonder she had been in low spirits. Did she think Elizabeth would blame her for her failure?

"But I could not do it." There was a painful intensity to her aura. "I did not want this, not for you."

"What did you not want?"

"To have to take you with me. To France." The words echoed through the room, off the chinoiserie wallpaper, taking on a weight of their own.

If only she could! "Dearest, you cannot know how much I want to go help him, but I must remain here. It would not be safe, for me or the child I carry. Or for you, when they have those dragon lodestones."

"I can keep you safe. Whatever might happen, I would only be a thought away."

"What if Darcy needs the power of Pemberley, and I am not here to give it to him? Or if I cannot return in time for the birth? The baby must be bonded to the land."

Cerridwen raised her head to study her with grim determination. "There are no guarantees, but we must still do it."

It made no sense. Cerridwen liked Darcy well enough, but that did not account for this insistence. "Why?"

Her head slumped down again. "My visions say so."

"Your foresight?" Elizabeth stared at her. "But you never mentioned going to France before."

"I cannot control when the vision comes to me," the dragon snapped. "When that soldier spoke of taking me to France, that was when I knew the price if I did not go."

"What is the price?" Elizabeth asked. Cerridwen had always refused to reveal the contents of her mysterious visions of the future to Elizabeth.

The dragon shivered. "Death. Destruction of the Nests. A return to enslavement. England in flames."

Well. She had guessed as much, but it was still brutal to hear. Elizabeth stroked the dragon's iridescent scales comfortingly. "And if we go?"

"It becomes less likely."

In other words, either she risked her child's bond to Pemberley, or she let it be born to a country under attack, a land in flames, where dragons were forced to serve Napoleon.

It was a terrifying choice, though every inch of her longed to find Darcy. But what of the risk of losing Cerridwen? "The dragon lodestone," she said slowly. "Will the French not be able to hunt you down with that?"

"The Eldest says the lodestone can only find me when I am in my true form. As long as I stay a falcon, I will be safe."

Elizabeth held up her hands. "But what of me? I do not even know where to begin such a journey. How to reach France, between the blockade and the sea serpents, or how to obtain the travel papers I would need." The War Office had handled all of that for Darcy. How was she to find a ship to take her across the Channel? Suddenly it seemed quite impossible.

"The Eldest plans to help us."

"How can the Eldest know?" she asked. "She has not left the Nest in centuries."

"There are Kith who transport items between Nests, things that cannot go through the Gates, including a shipmaster in Hull who serves us. The Eldest has already sent word that he will be needed." Already Cerridwen seemed brighter, as if she sensed Elizabeth's agreement.

The Nest had already begun planning this, before she had even agreed to it, because Cerridwen had said it was necessary. That was the power of a foreseer, even a young and inexperienced one. Goosebumps rose on her arms.

She was going to France in the middle of a war.

Chapter 26

AND THEN THE ARGUMENTS began.

Colonel Fitzwilliam led the way, absolutely determined that Elizabeth would not go to France, or, if he could not stop her, that he would come along to defend her. Never mind that he could barely speak French, at a time when Englishmen in France were being attacked on the streets merely because their fellow countryman had been part of the assassination attempt. But he would not stop insisting until Elizabeth said she would simply slip away without him – and that Cerridwen would cover her tracks if he tried to follow her.

She placated him with promises that she would do no more than locate Darcy and would then return home, give the colonel the information, and let him handle any rescue that needed to be done.

Then Frederica took a turn, insisting that she and Quickthorn should accompany her. There would be safety in greater numbers, and her truth-casting and illusion abilities could be useful, especially if Darcy was imprisoned. Quickthorn herself joined in the fray, pointing out how young and inexperienced Cerridwen was, and the importance of including a dragon with greater knowledge of the world.

It was harder for Elizabeth to deny this, because deep down she would have liked to have her friend with her. She almost said yes, but then reconsidered. She herself was fairly confident of her ability to pass as a commoner, especially with the Marseille accent that colored her French, the one that had made Darcy's French tutors wince. She had grown up traipsing the fields of Meryton, making friends with tenants and spending long periods of time living with the Arabic-speaking apothecary and his family. Lady Frederica Fitzwilliam was every inch the aristocrat, and that would show, from her perfect posture to her upper-class conversational French.

Frederica did not accept this easily. Quickthorn was even more argumentative and would not give in until Elizabeth agreed to let the sea-green dragon taste her blood, giving her the ability to track Elizabeth much as Cerridwen planned to do with Darcy. Not that Elizabeth wanted anyone to come after her if she got into difficulties, but if it would soothe Frederica and Quickthorn to think that they could, she would permit it.

Then Frederica and the colonel joined forces, with the argument that Mrs. Sanford should go with her. "She said you might reach your time in as little as two months. You may need her help, and she could support you as it gets harder for you to move about," Frederica pleaded.

This time Elizabeth just laughed. "Two months at the very earliest, she said, and much more likely three months or more! I intend to be back long before the baby is born, and even if I fail at that, there must be plenty of midwives in France. Women there have been giving birth for centuries, you know. It would only make me look suspicious."

It was not that she wished to go alone. In fact, the idea terrified her. But taking someone with her would only add to her danger. And she would have Cerridwen, if any problems arose. She steadfastly refused to think of the potential difficulties from which not even a dragon could extract her.

At least Mrs. Reynolds did not argue with her when Elizabeth told her she was going to France to find Darcy. "For everyone else, though, they are only to know that I am going to visit my family."

"Of course, madam." The old housekeeper bit her lip. "If I may ask, has there been any word of Mr. Darcy? I have been praying for him every night."

Elizabeth hesitated, but she knew how much Mrs. Reynolds loved him. "We believe he is still alive, although likely a prisoner. Cerridwen, who can sense his location, says he seems to stay in the same place, as if he is locked up." There was no point in distressing her with the news of his gunshot wound.

The housekeeper wrung her hands in her apron. "You are very good to go after him, madam. How may I be of service to you?"

"I will be traveling as a commoner. Could you find me a few dresses that would suit a farmer's wife or a servant? Nothing fine or new; something that will keep people from noticing me."

The housekeeper studied her from head to foot, no doubt calculating whose clothes might fit her, especially in her current condition. "I will arrange that immediately. If you want the staff to believe you are going to see your family, we will have to pack a different set of trunks for that, too."

She had not even thought of that, but Mrs. Reynolds was right. "I will be taking Chandrika into my confidence, so she can work on that, too." Which only raised another problem – how was she to explain her departure to Rana Akshaya? The Indian dragon kept to herself, but Elizabeth could hardly leave her without a host. Perhaps Frederica would be willing to stay at Pemberley in her absence.

"Very good, madam. And I will instruct Cook to pack up some local food for you – dried fruits and nuts. For the sake of the babe."

Tears sprang to the corners of her eyes. "Thank you, Mrs. Reynolds."

Another week! According to Cerridwen, the Nest's shipmaster had reported it would take that long to make some minor repairs before they could depart. Another seven days of waiting while Darcy was likely suffering, his life at risk every single hour. Another week apart, when she could hardly bear how long it had been already. Another week closer to her confinement, a high price to pay.

She stroked her hand over her belly, now prominent despite her loose skirts. Her pregnancy had not been visible when Darcy left, just a barely palpable bulge. Would it shock him to see the difference in her? She had been so careful to hide from everyone that she was more easily fatigued now, often behind on sleep from the lively creature within her who seemed to delight in kicking her ribs. If it was a boy, he was sure to be a sportsman, with his unending energy.

How she wished Darcy had been here to see the changes in her! And how she longed for his embrace. She should have appreciated every single one of them when he was still here.

And here came those blasted tears again! She had never been such a watering pot before she was increasing, and she detested how everything made her cry now. She hurried from the drawing room before anyone could see her and into the library, always empty at this time of day.

The room was dark, with no candles lit, but she did not care. She could see well enough to find her way to Darcy's favorite chair and to stand behind it, gripping the back as if somehow it held a residual essence of him.

If only he were there, where he would be safe, and with her!

She could picture him, his tall form filling the leather chair, his dark curls resting on the top, soft and springy, and his scent of soap and spice rising from it.

"William," she whispered despairingly.

As if her mental image had heard her, his head turned, his cheeks hollow. "Elizabeth?" He sounded astonished.

Her heart pounded with disbelief. She blinked, and the image began to fade around the edges, and then evaporated into the mist. Despairing, she cried, "No! Come back!"

Her knees buckled, her cheek rubbing painfully against the leather back of the chair as she slid to the ground, tears flowing down her face.

"Pardon me, madam, did you call?" It was Daniel, the footman. "Madam?"

"Over here," she managed to say.

He appeared around the chair, his expression of dismay almost comical. Finding the mistress collapsed on the floor was not part of his usual duties. "Do you require assistance, madam?"

Even through her tears, she wanted to giggle. Of course she needed assistance. "If you could make the room stop spinning, that would be very helpful."

Spinning. Dizzy. Giddy. She knew what needed to be done.

"Shall I fetch Mrs. Reynolds?" He sounded worried.

"No. Tea with honey, right away, and something to eat. And Lady Frederica." Had they not just played this scene? But this time she had not even realized she was using her Talent. Yet here she was, her life force depleted to the point where she could not even pick her head up.

But for that momentary sight of Darcy, she would have suffered more – whether it was real or not.

The sound of running footsteps announced Frederica's entrance. "Elizabeth? What happened? What did you do?"

With extraordinary effort, Elizabeth turned her head a fraction of an inch. "I am not quite certain, but I did too much of it. I was imagining my husband sitting in that chair, and suddenly he was there."

Lady Frederica gulped. "You created an illusion of Darcy? When you can barely manage a mouse? No wonder you are depleted."

If only her head would stop spinning! "Not an illusion. I saw him, and he saw me. I cannot explain it."

"That is impossible! There is no kind of sending where you can see each other."

Elizabeth's forehead throbbed. "Not a sending. Something different."

Rapid footsteps tapped into the room in a moment later, Mrs. Reynolds thrust a cream-filled goblet and a spoon into Elizabeth's hand. "Eat," she ordered. "Tea is coming, and more food."

Elizabeth tried to take the glass, but her hand shook so badly that Frederica grabbed it away. "You are in terrible shape," her friend informed her, scooping out a spoonful of trifle and holding it to Elizabeth's lips as if she were an infant.

Which, at the moment, it seemed she was. She opened her mouth and let the cool softness run into her mouth. "Currant trifle?"

"It was the first thing to hand," the housekeeper said briskly. "Old Mr. Darcy always told us time is of the essence in these matters. Now eat."

Elizabeth accepted another dollop of trifle from Frederica. Of course Mrs. Reynolds would be familiar with the situation; she had served two generations of mages.

The next person who barreled through the library door was not a mortal at all, but Rana Akshaya in her human form. "You must never, ever do that again," she commanded, her words a threat.

Elizabeth choked down the trifle in her mouth. "If I ever discover what I did, I will make every effort to avoid it, I promise you."

"This is not a joke, Companion Elizabeth. You shook the foundations. You could have killed all of us."

"Oh," Elizabeth said weakly. "But I was not even using my Talent."

Rana Akshaya glared at her. "Are all English companions so ignorant? Do they not teach you what can drain both companion and dragon alike?" With an annoyed sound, she stripped off her glove and laid her hand on Elizabeth's cheek. "Look at me."

She was too weak to disobey. Heat spiraled into her, scouring her clean, filling her with light, just as it had that long-ago day at Netherfield when Rana Akshaya had healed her.

The Indian dragon lifted her hand, and the spinning in Elizabeth's head was gone. Not just that, but she felt as if she could get up and run a race. Something was odd with her eyesight, but a vigorous shake of her head took care of that.

"Now listen to me, little companion," Rana Akshaya ordered. "You could easily have completely drained your dragon with a trick like that. We cannot afford to lose the Seer because of your carelessness."

Horrified, Elizabeth jumped to her feet. "Is Cerridwen hurt?"

"You were fortunate this time, and she is only weakened. I will tend to her next. Do not play with fire again." And she swept from the room.

"But…" Elizabeth said to her retreating back. Instead she turned to Frederica and Mrs. Reynolds, both of whom had gone pale. "What did I do?"

Frederica said, "I have never heard of any foundations, much less shaking them."

"It hurt Cerridwen, too." A horrifying thought. "I must go to her immediately."

Elizabeth found Cerridwen in the ballroom. Rana Akshaya was there, along with Quickthorn, so Elizabeth hovered just outside until the Indian dragon was finished with whatever magic she was doing.

As soon as Rana Akshaya left, paying no attention at all as she hurried past, Elizabeth ran in and threw her arms around Cerridwen's neck. "I am so sorry, dearest! I never, ever intended to hurt you!"

Cerridwen leaned into her. "I am perfectly well now. What happened?"

She tried to remember. "I do not know! I was missing Darcy, picturing him sitting in his chair in the library. Wishing he were there. Remembering how it felt. And then…he was there. For just a moment. He looked at me and said my name. Then he faded away."

"What of your Talent?" It was Quickthorn, speaking from behind her. "What were you trying to do with it?"

"I was not even using it! At least not that I was aware of. Just wanting… him."

Cerridwen's presence grew stronger in her head, probing her memories. "You tried to bring him here," she said slowly.

"Not intentionally! How could I? I know that is impossible."

"But you wanted it."

A huff of smoke passed over Elizabeth's head as Quickthorn lumbered forward to stare into her face. "You must never do that again. Not ever. Do not even let yourself have that wish, not if you want to live."

"I have already heard this lecture from Rana Akshaya," Elizabeth said crossly. "What does it mean, that I shook the foundations?" She had never heard of such a thing, not even in her Arabic books.

Quickthorn snorted. "The world sits on certain foundations which keep us in our place. In a very few places, the foundations have been altered, as in Faerie rings, permitting us to leave our world. It is a dangerous thing, not undertaken lightly, as it can cause a collapse of reality around the ring if done without great precautions being taken."

"But how could I do such a thing? I am a poor excuse for a mage; Frederica will tell you so! And I was not even using my Talent!"

In an unusual display of tact, Frederica murmured, "You are good at sending, even if we have not yet found any other part of magery that comes easily to you."

The air buzzed with energy. Elizabeth could practically see the sendings shooting back and forth between Quickthorn and Cerridwen. What were they saying?

Cerridwen tossed her head, then spoke in Elizabeth's mind. *Can you come to the Nest tomorrow? Apparently this requires the Eldest's attention.*

She could hardly refuse. Perhaps she could ask some questions of her own, too.

Chapter 27

T HE COMPANIONS' HOUSE WAS completely unchanged from her previous visits, of course, just as it had been for hundreds of years, a medieval manor house from an olden tale. Except for one thing. This time someone else was there. A young girl pored over a book at the large trestle table in the great hall, as a familiar figure beside her rose to his feet.

"Roderick!" Elizabeth cried as she hurried forward to greet the Welshman.

He grinned. "Mrs. Darcy, it is a very great pleasure."

"What are you doing here? Do not tell me you have been made a companion!"

His smile slipped slightly. "Not I, but Bronwen here. When the Dark Peak sent out a call for dragons from other Nests to attend their conclave, the Gwynedd Nest felt she was too young to travel on her own and sent me as her escort. May I present Bronwen ferch Rhys to you?"

The girl, who looked no more than twelve, rose and curtsied.

Elizabeth returned the gesture. "I am delighted to meet another companion, and my congratulations on your bond."

Bronwen ducked her head. "I was only chosen last year, so I am not very good at it yet."

"You are no doubt already better than I!" Elizabeth said with a laugh. "I never had any training."

Roderick cast her an amused look. "You learned on your own. Bronwen, pray continue your studies while I walk with Mrs. Darcy."

Elizabeth studied him. "If you know which room I should use, you could take me there. Apparently I will be here for at least another day." The Eldest had said five days, but she intended to argue for less. Time was already far too short, and she would not permit another delay in her journey to rescue Darcy.

"The Kith were preparing the corner room, so that is likely it." He gestured towards a narrow stairway leading out of the great hall.

She headed that way, looking back over her shoulder at him. "How long have you been here? Why did you not let me know?"

"About a week. We were the first companions to arrive, but several others are here now, too. It is good to see you."

She stopped in the middle of the steep steps and turned to face him. "An impressive distraction. I wonder that you did not simply lie, since I am no truth-caster."

He gave a reluctant smile. "Habit, I suppose. I will tell you when we are in private, if you must know."

"That is fair," she said, and began to climb again.

The room he took her to was smaller than the one she had stayed in on her previous visits. No doubt that had gone either to Roderick or one of the other companions. Excitement stirred in Elizabeth at the thought of meeting them. There was so much she could learn from them!

But first there was the matter of Roderick, who was lounging in the doorway. She narrowed her eyes at him. "I suppose you are avoiding Frederica."

He shrugged. "Rowan told me she was back at Pemberley." It was an admission.

"Did you ever think of simply talking to her?" She had no idea what had happened between them, but she hated seeing Frederica's pain, and Roderick was neither cruel nor unreasonable.

He focused his eyes on the mullioned window that let in wavering daylight through uneven panes. "Sometimes there is no good solution, and trying to find one only makes matters worse." Then his eyes swung to her. "What brings you to the Nest?"

She decided to accept the change of subject, at least for now. "Training, of a backwards sort. Apparently I have a Talent which is unsafe, and the Eldest has decreed that I must be taught how to avoid using it."

He nodded, looking unsurprised. "One of the Forbidden Talents?"

Now he had her complete attention. "Is that what it is? No one will tell me anything except that I must never do it, and it is infuriating."

His eyebrows rose. "Can you tell me what happened that made them worry?"

She related the story of seeing Darcy in the library, and the accusation of shaking the foundations. "Does that mean anything to you?"

"I know that Forbidden Talents exist, but they do not talk about them. Iorweth the Bold had one of them. He was companion to your Cerridwen's grandsire, Taliesin the Seer. Whatever Iorweth's Talent was, it killed them both, turning the Nest and the land around it into wasteland. Many died, both dragons and people."

"That would explain why they are worried, but I wish they would tell me what this Talent was supposed to do." It was frustrating to be treated like a child – and that the one ability she possessed was one that was too dangerous to use. But there was something else she wanted to ask him about. "Have you heard anything from Granny in London? We have received no news from her at all, apart from a brief letter early on, saying only that she was well and enjoying London. It was literally three sentences long."

He winced. "Writing is very hard for her these days, and she would not have felt safe putting anything more important in a letter, which would almost certainly be opened and read. We have not heard even that much. No doubt she is trying to avoid revealing the location of the village."

"I do wish we knew more! Colonel Fitzwilliam, Lady Frederica's brother, told us his friends at the War Office are complaining about Granny's autocratic ways, but that they are all too desperate for any help she could give them to argue with her. They do not understand truth-casting, but they are disturbed by what they see as an uncanny ability to discover things they would rather she did not know. He was not involved with her case, though; this was just gossip that he had heard."

"It could be much worse," Roderick said. "She would do best to stay in London for now. The Eldest of Gwynedd is furious with her, as are all the dragons. He would have put Sycamore under Silence, had not others convinced him that we could not afford to remain ignorant of what he has learned. I fear neither of them will be welcomed back after breaking the Great Covenant of Concealment."

"I was afraid of that."

"And you – you have been through a great deal since we last met. If you are willing, I would be eager to hear about what you have discovered in your contacts with Darcy. I have heard it all third hand, of course, but things are sometimes strangely misunderstood at a distance."

Her back was beginning to ache, so she sat down in the old-fashioned carved chair before she related the story yet again. Then she added on her plans to leave for France.

His eyes widened. "Surely you cannot go alone! If need be, I will come with you myself."

"Not you, too," she teased. "Is there something about a woman who is increasing that makes everyone think she is incapable of setting one foot in front of the other?"

"But—"

"I have already had this argument with several people and won in every case, so do not waste your breath!" But perhaps it would be worth putting one thought in his head. "Have you met Rana Akshaya yet? She will be remaining at Pemberley even though I am leaving, and I think you would find her very interesting." And Frederica would also be there, keeping an eye on Rana Akshaya and serving as a chaperone for Miss Darcy, but she need not mention that.

"Not yet. She does not come to the Nest, and I am told she does not care to be approached by mortals."

"There is some truth to that. I barely see her, even though she is my guest." She frowned. "Does Quickthorn know you are here?"

"I imagine every dragon in the Nest is aware of it," he said wryly. "That would include Lady Frederica's companion, though she has declined to take any notice of me."

Had Quickthorn told Frederica that Roderick was here? She would certainly know he was a sore point for her companion and might have kept it to herself.

But keeping a secret like this was not something Elizabeth could do.

Frederica was waiting in the drawing room when Elizabeth returned. "How did it go?" she asked without preliminaries. "Did you solve any of your mysteries?"

"I am still mystified." Not least by the decision by the Eldest to bind her against speaking of her new Talent that she could not use in any case. "But I have had many lessons in how to feel the foundations beneath me."

"It sounds like a lot of work."

"It was, but I also had the opportunity to meet some companions from different Nests, and that was very interesting. I had not realized that the Nests differed so much in size, from those with only a handful of dragons to one in the Highlands with nearly fifty. Most have no Gates."

Frederica sat up straight. "The other companions have arrived? Perhaps I should make a trip up, too."

This was why she could not keep Roderick's secret. "I was very glad to speak to them," she said slowly. "I was surprised to find Roderick is there, too, as an escort to a young companion from the Gwynedd Nest."

Frederica's face froze for a long moment. "I... see. Like the proverbial bad penny. I assumed he would hide away in Wales forever."

Elizabeth took pity on her and pretended not to notice her distress. "I hoped he might have word from Granny, but he had heard nothing, either.

And the dragons of the Gwynedd Nest are even angrier at her than the ones here."

Frederica accepted the distraction with apparent relief. "Let us hope she is doing some good, then, at least enough to earn forgiveness. And you – now that you are back, how long will you be able to stay?"

"Hardly at all," Elizabeth said. "The ship is almost ready, so I will leave here the day after tomorrow. Assuming your brother does not decide to keep me under lock and key, that is," she teased.

She laughed. "He would not dare, and besides, he wants to know where Darcy is almost as much as you do."

It only reminded Elizabeth of how she missed him at every moment. She had to find him. There was no other option.

Captain Thirtleby held out an envelope. "Welcome aboard, Mrs. Darcy. Here are your papers, in the name of Mme. Marie Dubois. You'll need them in France. *Passeport*, they call them, and everyone must have them."

Elizabeth took it gingerly. "How did you manage to get these?" It had taken the War Office months to set up Darcy's papers.

He grinned. "I know a good forger."

Perhaps she should not have asked. She changed the subject. "This ship is bigger than I expected." The towering sailing vessels she had glimpsed on her occasional trips to London were larger, of course, but she had only seen them at a distance. Somehow she had assumed this one would be more like the fishing boats pictured in engravings of seaside villages. But it was just as well it was not small, given her unexpected entourage.

"And as solid as she can be," said Captain Thirtleby proudly. "Plenty of room for both of you, and the elderflowers, too." He nodded to the pair of falcons perched on the mast, using the same code word for dragons as the common folk at Pemberley. Hardly surprising, since he was counted among the Kith of the Dark Peak Nest. "Always glad to have them on board. They keep the serpents away."

The dream of a sea serpent head hovering over a ship floated through Elizabeth's thoughts. "Have you had many problems with them?"

He chuckled. "Saw one on our last run, but I managed to keep away from it by hugging the coast. Hence the repairs – we took a good scrape on a shoal. Gave me a few extra grey hairs, it did! So I'm very glad to have the elderflowers this time. Wouldn't like to cross the Channel without one these days."

Colonel Fitzwilliam snorted. "Not worried about the blockade, then?"

"Not a bit! I've friends among them, and they know I'm an honest trader. Not that I'll turn down a particularly profitable cargo if someone offers me one, but that's not my business."

Frederica said, "I have just been informed that there may be a way to mark a ship as friendly to, er, elderflowers, even when they are not here. It might offer you some protection from serpents."

The captain's eyes lit up in his weatherbeaten face. "Is that so? I certainly want to know more about that, your ladyship! It could make all the difference."

Elizabeth turned to Colonel Fitzwilliam. "Thank you for your help in getting me here. If you wish to go ashore, I should be safe while we wait for the tide." The colonel had grudgingly agreed that the newly augmented magical wards defending Pemberley were adequate against French assassins, but letting Elizabeth leave those wards to travel was a different matter. He had organized their overnight journey with military precision, in conjunction with Cerridwen and Quickthorn providing illusions, going so far as to switch carriages at an inn. But at last he was satisfied that no one had followed them to Hull. He might frown every time the subject of dragons came up, but he was perfectly happy to use their abilities to protect Elizabeth.

He was not looking at her, staring instead at Frederica. "I have changed my mind. I will sail with you and Freddie."

"I thought you were prone to seasickness! And what is the point of merely going there and straight back? I will be perfectly safe between Captain Thirtleby and Cerridwen. I only agreed to allow Frederica to come because Quickthorn was so excited about flying over the sea."

His lips tightened. "It has nothing to do with you. I will be sorry to be on board when the boat begins to rock, but I need to know about these preparations to keep ships safe from sea serpents."

She laid her hand on his sleeve. "Colonel, you do realize you will not be able to share any of this information, no matter how useful it is?"

He lifted his chin. "Sooner or later, Mrs. Darcy, that will change. The more I know about the defensive capabilities of dragons when that day comes, the more lives we will save."

Clearly he had too much faith in the willingness of the dragons to work with the military, but she doubted anything she could say would change his mind. "Then I will hope we have calm seas for your sake."

What would it be like to be in the middle of the Channel, with nothing but water in every direction? Would she be seasick, too, or would she thrill in sailing before the wind? As dark as the situation might be, she could not help but be cheered by the prospect of new sights and adventures.

She was going to find her dearest love.

Chapter 28

Puzzled, Elizabeth looked down at the compass in her hand and then up again at the French stone manor house before her. In the last week, she had crossed the Channel and over a hundred miles of France, following Cerridwen's directions. This was the location her dragon had pointed her to that morning. There was nothing else nearby, only fields and a few outbuildings.

It looked nothing like a prison. No one was guarding it, and the sole person in sight was an aged gardener bending over a flower bed. Elizabeth had prepared herself for so many possibilities of what she might find, most of them involving imprisonment, but it could be that Darcy was still free and lying low. He might be hiding in a cave or a shepherd's hut, or even living in a hedgerow. Without identity papers, he could not stay at an inn or in a town. But what could he possibly be doing in someone's country retreat, complete with turrets and topiary?

She sank back against a stone fence, exhausted and footsore. Her journey had been simple enough until the last two days. The *diligence* had not been comfortable, but it had taken her to the town closest to where Cerridwen had sensed Darcy's presence. No one had questioned her story of going to stay with her uncle or even asked to see her forged papers. Apparently common pregnant women were above suspicion. But after that she had only the direction Cerridwen gave her, with no knowledge of local roads or lanes. She could hardly ask someone how best to reach a destination she could neither name nor describe.

She rubbed her aching back. Two days of following dead-end lanes and tromping across fields, circling around copses and impassable hedgerows had left her feet swollen and blistered. Only her eagerness to reach Darcy had kept her going. Now finally the end was in sight.

If impossible to believe.

A jab under her ribs told her the baby was awake. It was always quieter when she was walking and liveliest when she tried to sleep, but this time it felt like a reminder that her child needed its father. She had a job to do.

If Darcy was even here. What if Cerridwen was wrong? Elizabeth had come all this way based on her belief in the dragon's ability to find her husband. What if it was only Darcy's body buried in the garden here?

No. She would know if he was no longer alive. She had to believe that.

They must be holding him prisoner, here in this unassuming country house. Why else would he have remained here for weeks on end?

Her chest ached with the desire to reach out to him with her mind, to feel his presence. If only she dared to try a magical sending to him! But the dragons had warned her against using her Talent in any way, since they did not know what forms of magic Napoleon's men could sense.

No, she would have to do this the hard way, the way she would have before she discovered her mage powers. She pushed herself off the wall, wincing at the stabbing pain in her feet, and smoothed the skirt of her humble dress.

She made her way to the kitchen door and knocked, a timid rap suitable for a servant or a beggar. She had left her lady's manners behind in England.

The top half of the door opened to reveal a red-cheeked woman of middle years, her white apron tidy and clean.

"Forgive me for disturbing you," Elizabeth said humbly. "I am a poor traveler on my way to my family, and I wondered if you might be generous enough to allow me to sleep in your barn tonight. I will be happy to work for it; I can mend or clean."

"Oh, you poor creature! You must be exhausted, walking in your state. Come in and sit by the fire to warm yourself, and later you shall have a pallet to sleep on." She opened the lower door and shooed Elizabeth in.

"The saints bless you, sweet lady! But will not the master of the house object? I would not wish to cause you any trouble."

The woman chuckled. "No need to fret! My mistress is a kind lady, and she would not hear of leaving someone in your condition to sleep out of doors. Now sit down and put your feet up on the stool. They must be so swollen, no? When I was with child, I could barely put my shoes on!"

Elizabeth sank down gratefully. "I would not even recognize these feet as mine, if they were not attached to my legs."

"Oh, *ma pauvre petite*! Is this your first?"

Since coming to France, Elizabeth had learned that speaking about her condition was an easy way to forge a connection, so she settled into her prepared litany of difficulties. Her aching back, her husband who was taken to be a soldier and never heard from again. Not being able to pay her rent, and traveling to an uncle who needed her to keep house for him.

The cook, who introduced herself as Mme. Laurent, kneaded bread dough as she listened sympathetically and told her own tales of challenging pregnancies. She was pleasant and interesting, but Elizabeth struggled to hold her impatience in check. Darcy was nearby and likely suffering.

Finally she dared to ask a question. "You seem busy. Is it a large family you serve?"

"No, only my lady and her two children, imps that they are! And her poor cousin who was injured in the wars and now tutors the imps."

But somewhere there must be a prisoner, too, but of course the cook would not mention that to a stranger. "You must be feeding many servants, then." She gestured towards the bubbling pot on the hearth.

She sniffed. "Hardly any. My lady had to let most of the indoor staff go after her husband was killed, apart from the nurse and the lazy girl who works upstairs. But some of the nearby folk do not have enough to eat, and they know the pot here is full every evening. That is what I expected when you knocked."

This made no sense. If they were keeping prisoners here, they would try to keep visitors away, not encourage them.

Unless the cook was a very skilled liar, Darcy was not here. Elizabeth would have to keep looking. Perhaps he might be hiding in a disused outbuilding or one of those vast hedgerows. Yes, that must be it.

But it was growing dark, and she could not hunt for him without a light. She would accept the hospitality of the cook for the night, gain all the information she could about the environs, and set out fresh tomorrow morning. With any luck, Cerridwen would come to her and give her more precise directions.

Having a plan helped to ease the well of disappointment in her. She refused to think of what it might mean if she could not find Darcy. Cerridwen had never let her down before.

Still, after two days of walking, she would be grateful for a night of rest. Or at least as much rest as the child within her would allow her.

The cook stood in front of the rain-streaked window. "Surely you will not leave in this downpour! You will be soaked to the skin in no time and lucky if you do not find yourself ill. You can stay here until it stops."

Disheartened, Elizabeth picked up another dirty plate and began to scrub it. "You are very kind." She tried to sound grateful, but how could she forget how quickly the days were passing, every hour bringing her that much closer to childbirth and having to return home empty-handed.

But making herself sick by hunting in the rain would cost her even more time. The memory came to her of her sister Jane, sick at Netherfield for days after a soaking. How long ago and far away that seemed, when she still disliked Darcy, knew little of mages or dragons, and thought to spend her entire life at Longbourn! And now she was in France in disguise as a common woman, her hands stinging from the caustic kitchen soap. She would never again take scullery maids for granted. How long did it

ABIGAIL REYNOLDS

take them to scrub all the dozens of dishes from an everyday dinner at Pemberley?

She had met the lady of the house this morning, an attractive young woman only a few years older than her, who inquired kindly about her pregnancy and offered her a pair of old slippers for her swollen feet. It seemed impossible that this was a prison. Still, it would not hurt to turn every stone.

So when she finally dried the last dish, she asked, "Is there anything else I can do to help? Perhaps an empty room that needs airing?" Something that would get her out of the kitchen and into the main part of the house where she could search for any hints. At least it would feel like she was accomplishing something, even if she doubted she would find anything. "I can clean fireplaces." At least she had seen maids do so.

The cook snorted. "With that big belly of yours? I think not. Here, you may take the tray up to the children, since that lazy girl is late again. The imps are even more terrible when they have not eaten, and poor Kapitan Kupillas will not be pleased."

Elizabeth pictured a stern older Prussian gentleman. She would have to take care not to draw his attention; he was unlikely to be as trusting as the cook. "Where are they?"

"Upstairs to the second floor and then along the corridor to the end. You will hear the imps before you see them."

Perfect. The vague instructions would give her an excuse to wander about and see what she could discover.

She collected the tray and headed up the narrow dark servant stairs and then out through the door. The suddenly brighter light made her blink.

This was clearly not the finest part of the house, with stone walls and minimal decoration. Most likely rooms for guests and perhaps even servants. All the doors were closed.

Balancing the tray on her hip, she quietly lifted the latch on the first door and eased it open. Empty and clearly disused. The next was the same, and the third had furnishings under Holland covers. No sign that prisoners had been kept here.

She was reaching for the fourth door when a deep voice with a harsh German accent snapped, "What are you doing?"

She ducked her head, her heart racing. "Forgive me, sir. Which is the room with the children?" She held out the tray in evidence of her errand and raised her eyes pleadingly.

To a tall man with an icy expression, in a dark blue military uniform, not a French one, with gaunt cheeks and a mustache.

And Darcy's deep, dark eyes.

The tray slipped from her suddenly nerveless fingers and smashed to the floor.

Little Alexandrine was reading aloud haltingly when Darcy heard doors opening and closing over her piping voice. He tensed. No one came to this floor except on errands to the schoolroom and nursery.

His heart began to pound. Someone was searching the house. How had they tracked him here? He had not used even the smallest bit of Talent in the months since he was shot, but somehow they had found him.

There was no escape, not with only one working arm. He would have to brazen it out. He stood, reminding himself to use the Prussian accent Mme. Hartung had so painstakingly taught him, and stalked out into the corridor.

A woman, a poor one by her dress and heavy with child, was sticking her head in one of the unused rooms. Looking for something to steal? It was a relief. He should be annoyed, but for him, a mere thief rather than Napoleon's soldiers was the best news in the world. But with his fear suddenly gone, anger entered into its place, so he barked, "What are you doing here?"

She froze, the picture of guilt. Then she held out her tray of food. "Forgive me, which is the room with the children?"

Her voice resonated in him. It must be her accent, one from the south of France like Elizabeth's, and she was much of Elizabeth's height. Devil take it, why did he see Elizabeth in every woman? It only made him ache for her more.

Then she raised her eyes to his. Fine, dark eyes, so utterly familiar, but dulled by fatigue instead of sparkling with laughter.

And suddenly, filled with shocked recognition. The tray of food crashed to the floor.

Her hand flew to her mouth.

He wanted to believe it, wanted it more than anything in the world, but it was insanity. His mind had finally gone, from all his hopeless dread and loneliness. The impossible effort of pretending to be a Prussian nobleman, of not speaking a word of his native language in months. But every instinct shouted out to him that this was Elizabeth.

Her voice cracked as she said in English, "William? Dear God, is that you?"

His body realized the truth before his mind, striding forward to grasp her with his good arm and hold her to him, as if he could pull her essence into himself. Elizabeth was here!

It was so very, very right – and even more wrong. The coarseness of her dress, the smell of mud and harsh soap instead of lavender, but underneath that the ineffably feminine scent of Elizabeth. Above all, the strange shape of her, the bulge that was down between them.

His child.

It was beyond belief; it was heaven on earth.

His lips sought hers out, desperate for even more intimacy, and then he knew it was no mistake. He knew the taste of Elizabeth's kiss, how their mouths fitted together, how her body shifted in his embrace. It truly was her.

The sharp pain in his shoulder brought him back to reality. That they were in Napoleon's France, that Elizabeth was in danger, and he was making it worse by exposing her.

He stiffened, ending the kiss abruptly. But he could not bring himself to let her go, not so soon. "What are you doing here?" The English words felt strange in his mouth.

"Looking for you, of course." She laughed softly, tears spilling from her eyes. Her fingers brushed his upper lip. "A mustache, my love? It tickles."

That hit him with a true jolt. He had to protect them both. He forced his hand back to his side. "All Prussian officers wear them," he said in his Germanic accented French. Then, in a low voice, he added, "There is a spy in the house. A maid who reports to the government."

Elizabeth's eyes widened. "The lazy girl, the cook calls her." But she must have realized the danger, for she stepped back.

Just in time, as footsteps pounded up the stairs. The maid burst into sight. "What happened? I heard a crash."

He had to protect Elizabeth, no matter what. In his most haughty manner, he said, "Nothing of import. This clumsy woman dropped the tray." From the corner of his eye he saw Elizabeth kneeling down to pick up the spilled food, her head lowered.

"Stupid girl!" cried the maid, kicking at a roll that had bounced across the floor. "Clean that up immediately."

Darcy had to fight to keep silent as the maid chastised his Elizabeth. But he could only keep her safe from the spy by playing his role, so he turned his back and marched into the schoolroom.

"Look, Kapitan!" cried Alexandrine. "I have finished the entire page!"

His life had been turned upside down, Elizabeth was in danger, and yet the children had noticed nothing.

Why in God's name had she risked everything to come here? He ought to be furious with her, but all he wanted was to hold her in his arms again and never let her go.

Elizabeth returned to the kitchen in a daze, mumbling a confession about dropping the tray. The upstairs maid, the lazy girl, came to take a new one upstairs, once again scolding Elizabeth for her clumsiness. Elizabeth barely registered it.

Her mind was spinning. Darcy was here, he was free – or so it seemed? – and he had held her and kissed her. Oh, how she wanted to go racing up there simply to be with him. She had so many questions for him, so much to tell him, and no way to do it without risking their safety.

She spent the afternoon devising schemes to contact him, but it was pointless. She had to wait for Darcy to take the first step. He knew the house and its inhabitants, what was possible and what was not. He would find a way somehow.

Several hours later, Mme. Hartung came down to the kitchen to discuss the menu with the cook. Elizabeth listened with half an ear as she worked on the mending the cook had given her. At least that was a servant's task she was competent at, after all her years sewing her land Talent into handkerchiefs for Jane.

Mme. Hartung approached her, and under the guise of inspecting her work, whispered, "Go to the carriage shed when all the house is abed. He will be there."

Elizabeth caught her breath. The lady of the house knew Darcy's secret? Of course she must; she had claimed he was her cousin. But she must not show her surprise. "Merci, madame," she murmured.

Tonight. She would be alone with him tonight.

Chapter 29

DARCY OPENED THE SHUTTER on the lantern a fraction of an inch, just enough to lighten the worst of the darkness inside the carriage shed while leaving plenty of dark shadows to hide in. It was a good location for a surreptitious meeting. The large double doors were bolted from the inside, leaving only the small entryway on the side. Most of the space was taken up by the small carriage that had first brought him here from the fae burrow, half delirious with pain. He winced at the memory.

Soon Elizabeth would be here. It was a miracle – and a disaster. Elation and anger had been battling for supremacy since he had seen her this afternoon, the joy of touching her and speaking to her fighting with his anger that she would take such a terrible risk, both for herself and their child. Why had she not waited at Pemberley as she was supposed to? What madness had brought her to France?

What was happening in England to cause her to come after him, and how had she found him when Napoleon's troops could not? And there was the dread of telling her about his arm – and the disaster he had created with his failure. The husband she remembered had never known what it was to go hungry for days, to be hunted like a dog by men who wanted him dead, or to be in constant pain from a wound. And all for nothing. His love for her was deeper than ever, but he was not the same man she had married.

The side door opened a few inches. Elizabeth's face peered around it, and then she stepped inside and pushed back the hood of her cloak.

She was here, and that was all that mattered. None of his plans, the worries about someone following her, nothing except his Elizabeth. She was a magnet that drew him, the flame to his moth. He strode forward even as she ran towards him.

Then his good arm was around her, holding her tightly. She was real, and she was here, and he was complete again.

He could not hold her close enough. How had he ever managed to leave her, to give up this connection that filled him with such joy and warmth? His need for her roared through him, for the delight of her laughter, the sheer dancing pleasure of her presence, and the desire that raced through him at her touch. He buried his face in the softness of her hair, breathing in the essence of Elizabeth as if he could never get enough.

All his cares disappeared in the intoxication of her. He sought out her soft lips – and tasted salt. She was crying. Now he could feel the trembling in her shoulders. "Oh, my dearest love," he whispered. "What is the matter? Did someone hurt you?" He could not tell her all was well, for it most certainly was not.

She took an uneven, gasping breath. "Nothing. It has just been so long, and I did not know if I would ever see you again." She straightened and moved back a little, as if remembering where they were. "And you...are you well?"

"As well as I can be." His eyes roved down her body in the flickering shadowy light, and he brought his hand to rest on her swollen abdomen. "I can hardly believe this. He has grown so much." His child, right there beneath his fingers.

"He is a little rapscallion, always kicking and moving around," Elizabeth said fondly, covering his hand with her own. "But he is quiet now. Or she."

How intimate it felt, their fingers together, covering the child they had made. In the midst of this disaster, it was a moment of pure life-giving connection. "I wish I had been there for all of it."

She wiped her eyes. "You are here now." And then her hand went to his right elbow, and ran down to the fingertips hanging limply by his side. She had noticed, before he even had time to tell her.

He braced himself. "I was shot in the shoulder."

She nodded slowly. "The fae told me, the one who came with news of the dragon lodestone."

So the creature who rescued him had followed his request. Darcy forced himself to go on. "The wound healed, but my arm lacks any real strength." It was nothing compared to all the men who had lost arms or legs in the war, but it was still not his favorite subject.

She caught her breath. "Will it get better in time?"

"Mme. Hartung thinks it may, but I can hardly consult a doctor." He could hear the harshness in his own voice. But how he had hated this, giving her the bad news.

"I am so sorry, my love." Her eyes gleamed brighter in the dim light.

Damn. The last thing he wanted was to cause her pain! Gently he rubbed a tear from the corner of her eye with his thumb. "I hoped it might improve before you learned of it."

"It does not matter," she said fiercely. "You are alive. And free?"

"I am not a prisoner, but were I to leave this place on my own, that would quickly change." And it was not freedom to be stuck in a house, dependent on the charity of a stranger, unable even to defend himself with his useless arm.

"You were right to stay here," she said softly.

"I have no choice," he said, sudden anger rising inside him. "Do you know what they are doing to Englishmen here? Bloodthirsty mobs attacking them on the streets, their revenge for the attempt on Napoleon's life and the burning of the Tuileries. Innocent people have been killed because of my mission." He struggled to modulate his voice, to sound like the civilized gentleman he once had been. How could he, though, when she had placed herself in such peril?

She shuddered. "There were rumors of that at home, but I did not know whether to believe them."

"Believe it. You are in danger here." There was so much he wanted to ask her, so many unimportant details, or simply to hold her to him, but they could be interrupted at any moment. Business had to come first. He lowered his voice to a whisper, just in case anyone might be listening. "I must know. Has the War Office been informed about Napoleon?"

"Of his shape-shifting? I sent word to Granny, who is still in London. And I told your cousin, Colonel Fitzwilliam, when he came to Pemberley."

"That is something, at least," he said bitterly. "Otherwise it would all have been for nothing. Leaving you, being trapped in France, getting shot."

She shook her head. "That is not true! Yes, Napoleon still lives, but what you learned about him is vital. The sea serpents, too, and the device to find dragons. It is so important."

He barely suppressed a sound of derision, one directed at himself, not at her. "A slight help at best. Did you know that Napoleon has now set his sights on conquering England next instead of Russia? The newspapers here are full of it, whipping people into a frenzy. They say he plans to cross the Channel in the spring. All because of the attack on him." It would have been better for Britain if he had never left Pemberley. Why had he never considered the consequences that might follow a failed mission?

She gasped. "No. I had not heard that."

Of course they would have kept it out of the British newspapers. Otherwise people would panic. "And now you have walked into the trap with me. Why are you here? You were supposed to stay safe at Pemberley, you and the child. You should not have risked this."

She gripped his hands, her eyes wide. "It had to be done. Cerridwen had a vision of a disaster if we did not hunt for you."

The disaster had already happened, as far as he was concerned. "You are more important to me than any vision," he said urgently. "We must get you back home." As if even Pemberley was safe now.

But that was the problem. There was no safety to be had anywhere, not while Napoleon was at large. And Darcy had a wife and soon-to-be baby to protect. A child who needed to be born at Pemberley.

She laid her hands against his chest. "We will both go back together," she said fiercely.

No doubt she meant well, but it was a ridiculous hope. He had been working day and night to come up with an escape plan, and the best he had would take many months. And that was assuming Napoleon's troops did not discover him first, when Elizabeth seemed to have no trouble doing so. "How did you find me? Who else knows I am here?"

"Only Cerridwen, who can track you. I followed her directions."

Another life risked pointlessly. "Cerridwen is here, too? The dragon lodestones will find her, and then you." And him, too, but that mattered less.

"Those can only work at a short distance, according to the Nest. And Cerridwen has been careful. She does not even speak to me via sending, simply flies to me as a falcon. The Eldest says it is safer if we do not use our Talent."

"But the risk – you should not have come." He was repeating himself, but how could he bear it if she was taken by the French, all because of his errors?

She drew in a sharp breath, as if he had hurt her. "Should I have stayed safely home, knowing it meant England going up in flames?" Her voice shook. "There was never a choice, not when it came to you. Not for me. And I *missed* you."

Something inside him cracked open, past all the misery and hopelessness of the last months, something raw and agonized. "I cannot tell you how much I have longed for you, or what it means to have you here beside me. I have gone days without eating, been so cold I thought I would never be warm again, been shot and lost half my blood. But none of that hurt as much as missing you." He pulled her in again with his good arm, pressing his cheek against her head. How could he ever let her go again?

She gulped. "Oh, my love!" And then she wound her arms around his neck and brought her mouth to his.

The feathery touch of her lips was a gift, an acceptance, a welcoming he had not known he needed. And then she deepened the kiss, sending a surge of desire coursing through him. All the pain he had been holding back, all the nights alone dreaming of her, all the aching pain of his failed mission – it all became fuel for his desperate hunger for her.

And he could tell she felt it, too, from her quick gasps of breath to the way she arched against him, as if she could never be close enough to him. This was how it should be, the two of them together, lost in their love.

He needed more, so much more. "I wish there were somewhere we could be together." How he ached to be part of her again, to feel her skin against his! But it was impossible.

"The carriage," she gasped. "We can manage it in there."

Oh, the temptation! "It would hardly be comfortable for you, especially now." But he wanted her to contradict him. "It is too risky. We might be caught."

"If someone finds us, they will not be the least surprised that a rich gentleman has convinced a poor woman to share a little sport." Then her wicked, teasing smile broke out, the one he had not seen in so long. "And I will be most uncomfortable if we stop now. "

He could not have agreed more, as he prayed it would not be a disappointment to her, between the circumstances and his having only one hand. All he had was his love for her, and that would have to be enough to overcome their disadvantages.

Afterwards, Darcy held Elizabeth on his lap on the bench in the cramped carriage, her head resting against his, her body warm and relaxed. It might have been clumsy and cramped, but none of that had made it any less fulfilling or blissful. Even now, pleasure still shimmered in his body. If only he could hold her hand or caress her! But his left arm was around her, and his right would not obey. All the automatic, unthinking times he had never considered how much it meant to have two hands.

"Can you reach inside my coat?" he asked. They had been too eager to undress fully, even if there had been room for it in the cramped carriage. "There is a small pocket on the inside, near my heart."

She gave him a teasing look. "Always wanting my hands inside your clothes."

"There is something for you there. A gift I bought for you in Paris, just a small thing, but it reminded me of you."

For some reason, that sobered her. Her hand crept inside his coat, pulling out the small package wrapped in a piece of linen. She unfolded it carefully to reveal the handkerchief embroidered with violets, cowslips, and lily of the valley. She stroked it gently, and then brushed it against her cheek. "I have heard of how fine French silk is, but I have never felt anything so soft," she said with a catch in her voice. "Thank you."

"Do you remember seeing the wildflowers together as we walked to the cottage in the woods? I thought of that when I saw it. It was like having a little bit of you with me."

She kissed him tenderly. "I will treasure it." She placed it on her lap, and then reached down to touch his limp hand. "Can you feel things with it?" she asked softly.

"To a degree," he said. "It is less than it was."

She hesitated. "It does not seem to pain you when it moves."

He shook his head. "No." Only the shoulder hurt, and an occasional stabbing pain down the arm that came out of the blue.

Her hand moved over his, grasping his wrist, and then she raised it until his palm rested against her cheek. "I do not want you to forget what it feels like to touch me with it," she said with a catch in her voice.

The softness of her skin was a balm to his fingertips, a sensual pleasure and a reassurance that his injury did not disgust her. As well as a tenderness that fed a deep well in him. How fortunate he was to have her, and how he adored her!

If only they could remain in this moment forever, their eyes locked together in the darkness and love flowing between them! It was as if her essence were giving him much-needed strength. A tingle of her Talent flowed into his fingers, his hands, and down his wrist, curling around his sinews and bones. It felt heavenly.

"No," he gasped. "Do not use your Talent. It is not safe."

The tingling drained away, leaving emptiness behind. "I did not even realize I was doing it," she said tremulously. "I was only thinking of how much I wanted your hand to heal. But I will not do it again."

"I am not angry at you," he said gently. "Simply worried about being caught."

"I know. I am supposed to be watching for that, when my Talent slips out of my control." Then she smiled, and with what sounded like a deliberate attempt to lighten her voice, she said, "You would not believe the scoldings I have received on the subject! But I will save that story until we have more time."

"I want to hear all of it," he said. "Every single thing that has happened while we have been separated. And how on earth you made your way here."

"The dragons managed most of it." She brought his hand down and carefully interlaced her fingers with his. Amazingly, he was able to tighten his hand just a fraction, nothing that could qualify as a grip, but enough that she should be able feel it. "My task was only to find where you were being held prisoner and report it to Colonel Fitzwilliam, who would have handled the dangerous parts of rescuing you. I did not even know if I would see you."

"Richard? Is he here, too?"

"He wanted to come, but I thought he would draw too much attention, a foreign man of fighting age. No one has shown any concern about me. The War Office should use women who are increasing for all their missions. Men are suspected at every turn, but I have barely had my papers checked. Everyone offers to help me."

She made it sound so easy, but he knew better. "Coming to France is simpler than leaving. How will you get back?"

She nestled her cheek against his. "The dragons have a plan for that, too. We will be going home through a Gate."

The upstairs maid came down to the kitchen the next morning. "You," she said to Elizabeth rudely. "Madame wants you in the sitting room." The lazy girl. Napoleon's spy.

Elizabeth put aside the carrots she was peeling and untied the apron she had borrowed from the cook. "Right now?" she asked.

"Of course right now!" the woman snapped. "Follow me."

What could Mme. Hartung want with her? Elizabeth trailed after the maid, through the dining room and to a charming sitting room overlooking the gardens. Her eyes immediately flew to Darcy's familiar form, standing by the window.

She had to fight the urge to run to him. Instead she ignored him, making her curtsy to Mme. Hartung.

"Ah, Mme. Dubois, there you are," she said to Elizabeth. "I have had a change of plans which might prove of benefit to you. A friend of mine in Strasbourg is ill, and I will be leaving tomorrow morning to visit her, along with my children. Kapitan Kupillas will escort us."

Elizabeth swallowed. Strasbourg was near the mountains where the French Nest was located. It could not be a coincidence. But she had to be careful; the spying maid was standing beside her. "Yes, madame. I hope your friend recovers quickly."

"Thank you. Now, I do not know where you are headed, but you would be welcome to ride into town with us. I will give you fare for the diligence to your uncle's house; I hate to see a woman in your condition traveling on foot."

Definitely not a coincidence. "Madame, you are too kind! May the saints bless you for your generosity." It would make Darcy's travel much safer in a private carriage with the protection of Mme. Hartung, but why was this woman risking so much to help Darcy?

"Excellent. It is settled, then. We will leave first thing in the morning." She rubbed her arms as if she felt cold. "Colette, pray fetch me my shawl."

The maid curtsied and left, and they were alone together.

Mme. Hartung smiled at her warmly. "I am sorry I cannot offer you better accommodations, but Colette will insist on coming with us, and I could not explain taking you with us the entire way. I hope this will be helpful, though."

"Very much so," Elizabeth said fervently. "You have done so much for..." she could not bring herself to say the false name.

She gave a light laugh. "For my dear cousin Ernst? How could I do any less?"

Darcy said in a low voice, "I owe her a great deal. She taught me how to use a German accent and gave me her late father's identification papers with the birth year altered. I have been Ernst Kupillas this last month. They would have arrested me long ago without her help."

Elizabeth could not help a little surge of jealousy at the warmth in his voice. "I am very grateful to you, Mme. Hartung."

"I had hoped to do more. I wrote to the emperor requesting his permission to return to Prussia. Ernst... pardon, your husband, could have returned to England more easily from there, but it was not allowed."

"I thank you for your efforts."

Mme. Hartung smiled up at Darcy. "He has been good company, and he has been helping my children with their lessons."

Darcy gestured to his bad arm. "It was the only way I could be of use."

"The little ones will miss you." But her eyes said they were not the only ones.

How could she be angry at this brave, kind woman who had risked so much for Darcy? "I will remember you in my prayers. And should you ever find a way to England, you will always be welcome at Pemberley."

Then the maid returned with the shawl, and nothing more could be said.

Chapter 30

FREDERICA WAS OUT IN the garden, wrestling with using dragon magic to cast illusions, when Georgiana's companion, Belinda Lowrie, approached her. "Lady Frederica, may I have a moment of your time?" the young woman asked, valiantly ignoring the illusory unicorn Frederica was attempting to cast.

"Of course." Frederica blew her energy through pursed lips until the unicorn faded away. "How may I be of service?"

"Mr. Darcy expects me to report to him when Miss Georgiana does something unusual. In his absence, I would normally go to Mrs. Darcy..."

"But she is away, too," Frederica said briskly. "If you have a concern, I hope you will share it with me."

The young woman looked down at the toes of her half-boots. "Some of the lesser fae have convinced Miss Georgiana that she ought to learn to defend herself against the High Fae," she said in a low voice.

"That seems eminently sensible." Especially since no mortal could do anything to stop a High Fae bent on destruction.

Miss Lowrie's eyes widened. "But they are teaching her to use knives and daggers, and she has asked me to purchase one with iron in it. I cannot imagine Mr. Darcy would approve."

Darcy most certainly would not approve of his little sister learning to fight, so it was a good thing Frederica was here in his place. "I will take care of this. Thank you for telling me. Now, do I understand that congratulations are in order?"

Miss Lowery's cheeks grew pink. "Thank you, Lady Frederica." Her longtime suitor from a neighboring family had finally come up to scratch, and there would be wedding bells soon.

It was good news, but who could possibly replace her as Georgiana's companion, given the girl's unusual situation? That was a problem she was happy to leave for Darcy and Elizabeth. Knife fighting was much simpler.

Frederica found Georgiana and her invisible instructor – or was there more than one? – in the ballroom. A good choice, with plenty of empty space to move. Georgiana clutched a wooden dagger as if it were a stick – a particularly clumsy stick that she thrust at apparently empty air. Too low to strike a human effectively. Jasper had taught Frederica to strike high, since any assailant would likely be taller than her.

It was obvious when Georgiana spotted her in the doorway because the girl froze in place, and then awkwardly dropped her hand to her side as if to hide the dagger. "Lady Frederica," she said weakly.

Frederica strode toward her and plucked the wooden dagger from her. "Hold out your hand."

Georgiana obeyed, though her arm trembled.

Frederica set the hilt across the girl's palm in the orientation Jasper had drilled into her, and then wrapped Georgiana's fingers around it. "There. Do you feel the difference?"

The girl clutched it hesitantly. "I think so."

"No, do not tilt your hand. Relax your wrist, so that when you strike, you can put the weight of your body behind it." She demonstrated the movement. "Try it, just like that. Excellent. Now bend your knees just a little and thrust again."

Georgiana tried it once, and then several times. "That is better." She sounded surprised. "Where did you learn that?"

"Jasper's sister, remember? His victim, too, when he had exhausted all his other sparring partners."

"You do not think this is too unladylike?"

Frederica widened her eyes in mock shock. "It is absolutely unladylike, but, to quote Jasper, which do you prefer – ladylike or dead?"

Georgiana giggled. "I suppose that is a good point."

"Seriously, I am delighted that your fae friends are taking your education in hand. But you should also be trained by someone who understands the ability of the human body and can recommend weapons suited to your hands."

A deep voice rasped, "The mortal is correct. There are limits to what I can teach you while you wear that form."

"Could I truly do that?" asked Georgiana. "Have a weapons tutor?"

Frederica grinned. "Nothing easier."

"The Honorable Mr. Fitzwilliam," the butler announced.

Frederica jumped up and embraced her lanky blonde brother. "That was fast, Jasper! Thank you for coming." How good it was to see him, her baby brother, her favorite of the entire family! She loved Richard and Charles, too, but Jasper was special.

"Hullo, Freds. You did say you had an unusual weapons challenge for me." He said it as if that explained his haste, which, this being Jasper, it did.

She beamed at him. "This will be a new one even for you! Did you know that Cousin Georgiana is a changeling?"

His face showed a small measure of surprise, but very little could truly move Jasper if it did not have a sharp edge and a point. "No, truly?"

"Yes. She is trapped in a mortal body and needs to learn how to defend herself against the High Fae."

He whistled, his mind clearly whirring with possibilities. "Interesting. Can she use iron?"

Anyone else would have asked why Georgiana needed to fight a High Fae, but Jasper would never see anything beyond the weapons question. "Yes, though she has been practicing with a wooden dagger for now. Some lesser fae have been teaching her, but their techniques are not suited to her body. I have gone over the basics with her, but she needs more."

A light kindled in Jasper's eyes. "Lesser fae, too? I wonder if they would be willing to spar with me. I bet they have techniques I have never seen. Where are they? When can we begin?"

She laughed. "I will take you to Georgiana right away."

Frederica looked up from her book with profound relief when the butler came in. Studying Arabic so that she could someday read Elizabeth's books had seemed like a clever idea, but she had forgotten how difficult book learning was for her. How would she ever make sense of all those little squiggles?

"Mr. Roderick is here, Lady Frederica," Hobbes intoned.

Roderick, damn him. How dare he? Her hand itched to throw that blasted book at his head.

But she had been raised to take her place in the *ton*, so instead she told Hobbes to show him in and sank into a graceful curtsy when he entered. "Mr. Roderick, what a lovely surprise." With only the slightest bite to her words, lest he think he was truly welcome.

He looked just the same. How dare he make her heart skip a beat, after what he had done to her?

"Lady Frederica, I thank you for receiving me," he said. Of course Roderick would not pay her the automatic compliment any gentlemen of society would have given a lady, be she the plainest chit in Town.

But she already knew all too well that he did not find her attractive, and she might well have exploded if he had said she was as lovely as ever. If he could even manage to say it in face of her truth-casting.

Oh, why was this one man able to confuse her so?

"I suppose you did not know I was here, or you would have stayed away." Blast her ready tongue! She had meant to stay polite, especially with Hobbes stationed just inside the door like the well-trained butler he was, unwilling to leave Lady Frederica Fitzwilliam alone with an unmarried man. Especially a Welsh commoner.

"No, Lady Frederica, I was well aware of your presence," he said in the same gentle voice he had always used, the one that had foolishly made her think him kind. "I would have called earlier, had I thought you would welcome it. Business brings me here today."

Of course he would not have come to her of his own free will. "What is it you require?" she asked bluntly. Not her, that was for certain.

His mouth quirked. "Rowan plans to spend a few days strengthening the wards against the Wicked King. He asked me to take on the lesser bond again as his anchor for it. In the absence of the Darcys, I wished to ask your permission for the two of us to be on Pemberley grounds while he works."

Her stomach flip-flopped. Several days of his presence? Even having him nearby would hurt, that constant ache of knowing she was not enough for him, not even with her wealth, birth, and connections. "I suppose you wish to stay here, then."

"It would be convenient, but I could ride back and forth each day." How did he always sound so reasonable?

No. It would be unbearable to have him in the house at night. There had to be another way. She said, "Hobbes, Mr. Roderick will be staying at the Dower House for a few days."

Hobbes bowed. "I will make the arrangements, your ladyship."

Frederica raised her chin. "Mr. Roderick, I hope you will forgive me for sending you there, but with Mrs. Darcy away, I cannot have an unmarried gentlemen stay in the same house as Miss Darcy." It had the benefit of being true, by society standards, even if she had already made an exception for her brother Jasper.

"I understand completely." His voice was muted. "Pray forgive me for taking up so much of your time."

If she did not know better, she would have said he sounded hurt. But she did know better.

He bowed and departed, leaving her feeling more alone than ever. Alone and empty.

But she was not alone anymore. She had Quickthorn now.

She reached out through the connection that was always there, to her irritating, short-tempered, beloved dragon. *Her* dragon. She still could not believe it. *Quickthorn, are you there? Roderick is here, saying he and Rowan will be working on the Pemberley wards.*

A mental snort came in reply. *It is just an excuse. Rowan quarreled with the Eldest and now is desperate to get away from the Nest, so he has concocted this. It will do no harm, though.*

Rowan was the most even-tempered dragon she met, and the Eldest nearly so. *What happened?*

No one knows, and he will not say. The sending was flavored with Quickthorn's annoyance that Rowan did not trust her, his nearest age-mate in the Nest. *But he has been moping for days. I am glad he is leaving.*

Interesting. *Will I see you tonight?* It was the Eldest's decree; while Rana Akshaya was at Pemberley, Quickthorn must be, too. Frederica was glad of it, even if it made Quickthorn cranky. It meant being with her dragon more. With Roderick nearby she would be even more grateful.

As always. The sending cut off. So the wards were an excuse. Did Roderick know that? Or did Roderick want an excuse to be here, too?

No. Roderick had made his feelings plain that horrible night in the coaching inn before they reached London, that she was good enough for a momentary distraction, but nothing else. Daydreams were pointless and would only hurt her more. And there had been quite enough pain. She was so tired of living with this aching hollow deep inside her where once she had thought Roderick cared for her.

Foolish, foolish, foolish!

She needed a distraction, and the primer of the Arabic language would not do. Perhaps she could convince Jasper or Georgiana to spar with her. Trying to stab someone sounded just right.

Janet, the maidservant that Frederica knew from her own time at the Dower House, was out of breath when she arrived in Pemberley's breakfast room. Had she run all the way?

"What is the matter?" Frederica asked.

"It's Mr. Roderick, your ladyship. He's terrible sick."

Frederica ignored the tug of fear in her gut. Janet was prone to exaggeration. "What seems to be the matter with him?"

"Last night, he said he was tired and refused dinner, but he was that flushed, your ladyship, cheeks red as apples. This morning we could not wake him. Cook said I should run and tell you."

How had Frederica ended up on her feet, with her hand over her mouth? "What do you mean? Is he...alive?" Her lips moved in silent prayer.

"He is breathing, but burning up with fever. Tossing and turning, like in a dream."

Her throat was so tight she could barely get the words through. "Has the apothecary been called?"

"Yes, your ladyship, and we're sponging him to bring down the fever."

She swallowed hard. There was nothing she could do, and it would be totally improper for her to go to his bedside. But something was terribly, terribly wrong.

"I am coming," she whispered, as if he could hear her. Then she spun on her heel and set out for the Dower House.

Frederica's stomach churned as she held Roderick's burning hand in her own, trying to pour her strength into him. His eyes had opened briefly, but he had not recognized her, nor even his own name. Dear God, how could he have become so ill so quickly?

It was like Elizabeth's sickness after Cerridwen bonded her to the land of Pemberley. That same sudden onset, coming out of nowhere. Elizabeth had barely survived.

Could it be? She turned her gaze to the maid who was wringing out towels. "Send a runner to the main house. I need Chandrika, Mrs. Darcy's maid, here without delay." Chandrika had recognized what was happening with Elizabeth. Perhaps she would know what to do.

"Right away, your ladyship." The maid hurried out, leaving Frederica alone with Roderick and her regrets.

Why had she been so unkind to him, simply because he had made it clear he did not want her? Though he had seemed to enjoy her kisses quite well at first, before pushing her away and saying those fateful words that still echoed in her head. She could at least have had him as a friend for a little longer, had her vanity not been so terribly piqued. And her temper.

And now he lay here, unable to object to her holding his hand. She pressed her forehead to the back of it, wishing fiercely that the world could be somehow different, that he could have loved her. That he could survive this terrible fever. Somehow. Anyhow.

Because he was the only man who had ever taken her seriously, every impulsive word that poured out of her mouth. The only man who had understood her desire to be heard, to be liked despite her dratted truth-casting. The only man who had ever treated her as a person rather than the Earl of Matlock's Talented daughter. He had seen her as a person in her own right.

How she had loved that long journey from Pemberley to London with him and Granny, she, who usually despised being trapped in the carriage with nothing to busy her restless mind. How they had talked for hours about everything under the sun – well, everything except that mysterious Welsh village of theirs. When she finally had realized that he enjoyed her company, after thinking he despised everything about her, her Englishness, her aristocratic blood, her connection to the King's Mage. And then she jumped to thinking that perhaps he more than liked her, and how very wrong she had been. Oh, why could she never settle for what she had? Why did she always want more?

Tears leaked down her cheek, and she swiped them away fiercely. She never cried. Ever. Ever. Ever.

Chandrika confirmed that it indeed looked like nagapani, or dragon fever. "Where is the dragon he worked with? Perhaps he would know."

Silently Frederica reached out for Quickthorn.

Oak and ash, what is wrong with you? the dragon sent. Frederica's distress must be leaking through their bond.

Frederica pushed it all through wordlessly, the sight of Roderick before her, her misery and guilt, and the question of dragon fever.

It cannot be dragon fever if all they did was the lesser bond. There is no blood mixing for that. Unless... There was an abrupt shift in Quickthorn's aura, switching from concern to outright fury. *That thrice-cursed fool! That idiot! How dare he?*

Now Frederica was even more frightened. *What is it?*

I will find that ridiculous excuse for a dragon and bring him there if I have to drag him. Quickthorn ended the connection.

Leaving Frederica even more confused. Was she talking about Rowan? Rowan the kind, gentle, amiable dragon? What had he done to Roderick?

And more importantly – much, much more importantly – would he recover?

It was an eternity later – half an hour by the ridiculously slow mantle clock – before Quickthorn announced her arrival with an annoyed rap on the diamond-paned window.

Finally! Frederica unlatched the window and pushed it open, but it was not large enough for Quickthorn's peregrine falcon form to fit through.

With a squawk of outrage, Quickthorn transformed into a starling just long enough to get through, followed by another bird. Rowan, perhaps?

The peregrine falcon perched on the railing of the bed. "Look what you have done," Quickthron snapped, her voice tinged with the odd squeak that went with her bird form.

Rowan flew to the floor and blurred for a long moment into his human shape.

Frederica winced. By the Dark Nest standards, Rowan was considered particularly gifted at taking human form, but if that was true, dragons were truly bad at it. Except Rana Akshaya, apparently, and Napoleon, but perhaps dragons did things differently outside of Britain. Looking at the odd angles of Rowan's joints was painful, and as for his face – well, better simply not to look at it at all. It reminded her of a porcelain doll.

He bent down to touch Roderick's cheeks, his expression – if he had one – unreadable. But his aura shone with sorrow and fear.

"What did you do to him?" Frederica burst out.

Quickthorn replied in his stead. "They tried to form the companion bond – against the wishes of the Eldest. Now your friend is paying the price."

Rowan did not move his gaze from Roderick. "The Eldest only re-fused in order to keep me here in the Dark Peak. She knew Roderick must return to Wales."

As if Frederica needed any reminders of that.

"And you want to leave?" snapped Quickthorn.

"I want a companion. This companion. If that means I must leave, then yes." Now his pain was apparent. "Roderick promised we could come back to visit often."

"You risked his life by sneaking off here, pretending to work on the wards, to create the bond behind the Nest's back."

"We did work on the wards. I knew we could not lie to you or to Companion Frederica."

But Roderick had lied to her by omission. It should not hurt, but it did.

"There is a reason we do bondings at the Nest, where our healers are nearby," Quickthorn muttered.

Rowan retorted, "It was so easy when you bonded to Companion Frederica! I thought he might be a little ill, but not like this."

And it had been easy for her. For all the warnings that she might be sick for weeks, she had only suffered a mild fever and a day in bed. It had been no worse than a summer cold. "Why is it so different for him?" she asked.

"No one knows why some mortals take the bond easily and some fight it. I would have thought Roderick a likely candidate, with a history of many dragon companions in his family," said Quickthorn.

Finally Rowan looked up at his nestmate. "Have you any advice to offer? Useful advice, that is?"

"What is done is done. I will ask the healers." Quickthorn switched back to the starling form and took wing out the window.

Frederica missed her already.

Then her hand, the one entwined with Roderick's, began to tingle. "Are you using magic on him?" she asked Rowan suspiciously.

"I am giving him strength. You may be more comfortable if you do not touch him right now," he said apologetically. "Though he seems to be taking some comfort from you."

She tightened her fingers. If this was helping, she would not let go. "I suppose he wanted the companion bond." How many times had Roderick admitted to envy of dragon companions? He would have jumped at the chance, despite the risks. Just as she had.

Rowan bowed his head. "He did. He was worried about how his family would react, but then he laughed and said they would think it was fate. Because of my coloration."

How could the color of a dragon possibly matter? Admittedly, Frederica was secretly proud of Quickthorn's shimmering sea-green scales, but it would not make any difference to her if her dragon was not beautiful. Then it struck her.

A red dragon was the emblem of Wales, and Roderick was one of its disinherited princes.

It would be a potent symbol – if Roderick lived through the bonding, which seemed increasingly unlikely.

Chapter 31

D ARCY LET OUT A slow breath, one that had been trapped in his lungs for five endless days of separation, of long hours in the carriage with Mme. Hartung and the children, of worry about what might be befalling Elizabeth as she journeyed on her own half-way across France through unknown county. Even when Cerridwen had come to him that morning and told him how to find Elizabeth, he had not fully believed she was alive and unharmed. But there she was, exactly where the dragon had said, sitting beside a vineyard at the edge of the bustling town of Vieux-Thann on the eastern flank of the Vosges mountains.

Elizabeth's face lit up when she spotted him, and she hurried to his side. There were others on the road, though, so she greeted him as a stranger. "Good sir, are you walking this way? I am headed for my uncle's house in Wildenstein and would be glad to have company along the way."

He inclined his head. "Madame, I have only one strong arm, but I would be happy to offer you its defense." He had dropped his Prussian accent along with his uniform; too many people in this region spoke German and could catch him out easily.

"I thank you, and I will do my best not to slow you down." Her eyes moved from the sling he wore to past his shoulder, where a boy was leading a goat to market.

He nodded, forcing down all the words he wished to say, and they began to walk towards the cloud-shrouded mountains. Green foothills already rose on each side of the road which wound along the riverbank.

He had seen her briefly on the morning of their departure from Mme. Hartung's home, when she had clambered to sit beside the coachman, but he had not dared even to nod to her. It seemed like months since their night in the carriage shed. It was hard to hold back the many things he wished to tell her, all the questions he wanted to ask, but there was still the possibility of being overheard. Silence was the safest option. What would the highborn Prussian he claimed to be have to say to a common woman from Marseille, after all? No, they had to play their roles of chance-met strangers.

At least she was beside him, and she would stay there. It was enough to make him want to shout for joy.

He had to say something, if only to hear her voice. "Have you been traveling long, madame?"

Her smile was teasing. "Several days on a *diligence*. It was uneventful. Everyone has been very kind." She must know how much he worried.

It was true. He had fretted for her safety every inch of the way, trying not to watch for her every time his carriage stopped. Not to mention his concern about the many miles they would have to walk to reach the Nest. At least this time he was better prepared than when he had been on the run before, with a map and compass, a haversack of food, and a blanket roll large enough to share.

Finally they reached an empty stretch of road, "I am sorry we must travel so far on foot. Even the *diligence* must have been easier for you."

"Oh, I do not mind in the least! I can see so much more that way, and who knows if I will ever have a chance to visit here again?" She smiled, her dark eyes sparkling. "And traveling by stage was interesting. I had the most fascinating conversations. I will be happy never to do a scullery maid's work again, but I am glad to have tasted that slice of life."

"You are in remarkably good spirits this morning." Especially for someone facing several days of hard exertion, though he intended to protect her as much as he could.

"Have I not reason to be? You are alive, we are together, and for once, all I need to do is something I am actually good at, which is walking." She laid her hand on her stomach. "Though I am not quite as fast as I used to be."

"For the best possible reason," he said warmly. If only he could take her in his arms, or at least hold her hand! But while there was any possibility of being seen, he could not risk it. "And you have many talents, of which walking is the very least."

"Ha!" She glanced around, as if making sure they were still alone, and then continued in a low voice. "I thought my land bond to Longbourn was good, but it is nowhere near as deep as yours. I am only just learning household management. Frederica is no doubt doing a much better job of it in my absence. And she knows far more about fashion than I do; the modiste agreed with all her recommendations and almost none of mine. As for my magery, despite Frederica's lessons, my illusions are second-rate at best, and I can do almost nothing with weather magic. Sending is my only real ability. Apparently that trick where I made you almost appear in the library is something special, but I have been lectured by every dragon in the Nest that I must never, ever do it again, because it is terribly dangerous to both me and to Cerridwen. So, yes, let me be proud of my ability as a great walker, for at least it is truly mine."

He stared at her. "That was real? That day when I suddenly thought I was sitting in my chair in the library, and you were looking at me? I thought I had imagined that." Or rather, that he had been losing his mind, but better to keep to himself those moments when he had doubted his sanity.

"I could see you clearly, and it was real enough that all the dragons in the house felt it and had me dragged before the Eldest for a scolding!"

Astonishing, that she could create such a strange power! "Was this something you read about in your Arabic books?"

She shook her head. "I was just missing you so badly, and wishing you were there in your chair." She gave him a flirtatious glance. "Apparently I am not allowed to miss you quite that much!"

"Wait. You said all the dragons in the house? Not just Cerridwen, then?"

"Oh, I have so much to catch you up on! Do you remember Rana Akshaya? She is staying at Pemberley now, and she is a dragon, not a mage at all. Then there is Quickthorn, who has bonded to Frederica. Rana Akshaya keeps very much to herself when she is at the house, so I usually only see Quickthorn and Cerridwen."

Frederica was a dragon companion now, too? Good Lord. He stepped on an uneven rock, sending a sharp stab through his shoulder. He pressed his hand against it, waiting for the throbbing pain to fade to the usual dull ache.

Elizabeth asked in a quiet voice, "Is your arm troubling you?"

"Just a little jolted. It is nothing," he said stiffly.

"You were not wearing a sling before." Of course she would not allow him to pretend it was nothing. "Is it worse than it was?"

"No," he said irritably. "Jessica thought I would be less likely to re-injure it if I wore the sling. And it keeps people from wondering why I am not at the front."

"Jessica?" There was a bit of an edge to her voice.

"Mme. Hartung," he corrected. "Since I was supposedly her cousin, raised with her, it only made sense that I would use her Christian name."

"She risked a great deal for you."

Was she jealous? Surely she must know that no other woman could possibly catch his interest. "For the sake of her late husband. She loved him very much. He tried to escape a battlefield, but no one would help him, and he was executed. Since she could not save him, she decided to save me instead."

"Poor lady. I —" She broke off as the sound of cartwheels and hoofbeats came from behind them.

Hoofbeats that were slowing. The hair on the nape of Darcy's neck rose, and he had to force himself not to look back.

Elizabeth did, with a smile.

"Care for a ride?" It was a man's voice, gruff and strongly accented. "'Tis quite a weight you are carrying, madame." A humble mule-drawn cart pulled up beside them.

"You are very kind," said Elizabeth with a degree of relief that belied her earlier assertion that walking was still easy for her.

"My wife would pour salt in my beer if she knew I let a pregnant woman walk. Oh, the complaints I heard from her when she was carrying! The aching back, the swollen ankles, needing to be up five times a night." He chuckled.

How dare he speak so casually about Elizabeth's condition? In fine society, it would be the height of ill manners to even acknowledge it, but perhaps it was different among commoners. At least the French ones.

Elizabeth seemed to take it in stride. Had she grown accustomed to such things? "How well I know it!"

The driver slid across the simple plank seat to make room for her. Darcy carefully helped her up onto it with his good hand. The man eyed his more expensive clothes. "You are welcome to sit on the tail if you wish, though once the road gets steep, you will have to walk."

His first instinct was to refuse, to insist on walking alongside, but he should preserve his energy while he could. His stamina was not yet what it once was, but this was not the time for pride. When he was back at Pemberley, he would regain his strength.

"I thank you." He hopped on the back of the cart, grateful it was low enough to manage with one hand.

Elizabeth glanced at Darcy as the farmer drove his cart down a grassy track. He had taken them a good several miles, through a small town and beyond it. According to him, there was a village a short distance ahead, and after that the road would climb high into the mountains. It already seemed steep to her.

She did not want Darcy to know how tired she was, though. He would insist on slowing down, and she desperately wanted to reach the Nest as soon as possible. They might be safe enough at the moment, here on this country road, but she had noticed the sidelong glances Darcy had received. He was a young man in a land where any male his age was in the army.

So she hid her fatigue and stoutly set forth as quickly as she could manage. "How far until we leave the road?" she asked. They would be protected from suspicious eyes then, even if the walking would be much harder.

Darcy matched her pace. "Another two miles, at a guess. This should be the last village we will pass, though."

The first house came into sight as they rounded a curve. It could not be much of a village, tucked between a sharp incline and the river, but the small houses and gardens looked well-tended and welcoming.

At least until they reached the center, where a dozen French soldiers loitered outside the largest house.

Cold sweat trickled down Darcy's neck. What were soldiers doing in this tiny remote mountain village, on a road that led nowhere? They had seen him, too, and one of them, a young lieutenant with a scraggly mustache, gestured him over.

His heart pounding, Darcy muttered to Elizabeth, "Keep going. I will catch up."

Her face had gone ashen, but she said in a steady, clear voice, "Thank you for bearing me company, good sir. I will remember you in my prayers."

"Good fortune to you," he said. Would those be the last words he ever spoke to her?

No. He would not allow that to happen. He strode towards the lieutenant as if he had nothing to hide, forcing himself not to look back at Elizabeth.

The lieutenant held out his hand. "Papers," he drawled.

Darcy dug his *passeport* out and handed it over, trying to look bored by the routine.

The soldier glanced down at it. "Not in the Grand Armée?" he asked sharply.

Darcy indicated his wounded shoulder with his thumb. "Not anymore. Damned Austrians." He spat on the ground. These were lines he had rehearsed in his head over and over.

"Bastards," agreed the Frenchman. "We taught them a lesson, though."

"About time, too."

He handed back the *passeport*. "What brings you to this godforsaken place?"

Darcy glanced from side to side, trying to look crafty. "I have heard there is a healer in the mountains. The damned surgeons say there is nothing to be done for my arm, but I am not giving up. I want to get back to the front."

"Huh." The lieutenant stepped forward and said in a low voice, "A word to the wise, *mon ami*. If you are looking for dragon healing, you have chosen a bad time. We are hunting them for the emperor."

An icy chill ran up Darcy's spine. If Napoleon was seeking dragons, there was likely another massacre in the offing. Not only that, but his own route to England was at risk. "Dragons? Killers, like in Austria?" He let his voice tremble.

"Not so far, but who is to tell?"

"I heard about that battle. I never want to see a dragon. But I want to find that witch woman I was told about."

The lieutenant shook his head. "You cannot trust the stories. Well, good luck to you. But take my advice – do not linger in the mountains." He slapped Darcy's good arm.

"My thanks for the tip." Darcy pocketed his papers and headed up the street, feeling eyes on his back as he went. Up the hill, between the small houses, trying not to think of Elizabeth. He would find her eventually; Cerridwen would take care of that, with her uncanny ability to find them both. But he wanted to see her this minute, to reassure her that he was safe, to feel the comfort and delight of her presence.

He was hard pressed not to grin like a fool when he spotted her lingering in the doorway of the small church, as if she had gone in to say a prayer. She had not seen him yet. Her shoulders were slumped and her head down, no doubt terrified of what was happening to him.

He began to whistle a country tune, as if he were a farm laborer and not the well-bred gentleman he was, but it was enough to catch her attention.

She looked up, light blossoming on her face. And all was well in his world again, despite French soldiers and the menace of Napoleon's war.

Chapter 32

FREDERICA TOUCHED HER HAIR before she entered Rana Ak-shaya's room, making certain nothing was out of place after her long hours at Roderick's bedside. At least the dragon from India had agreed to see her, without Frederica having to resort to the various pleas she had planned to get past her servants. The dragon from India usually kept to herself at Pemberley, staying in her own room and interacting only with her entourage.

Whatever luck had made Rana Akshaya agree to it, Frederica was grateful for it. This was her last hope, and she needed it to go well.

She made a deep curtsy as she approached the large dragon. "Great Rana, I appreciate your generosity in seeing me."

"What is it you wish, Companion Frederica?" The dragon had not been so abrupt when pretending to be a human mage in London.

"I do not know if you have heard about Rowan, the young dragon of the Dark Peak, who recently bonded to a human against the wishes of his Nest."

Rana Akshaya stared at her with giant bronze-ringed eyes. "The young are often foolish."

Frederica took a deep breath. "I am a mere mortal, so I cannot judge Rowan's behavior, but the gentleman he bonded to is very ill. The Dark

Peak healers cannot help him because they are unable leave the Nest, and they say it would be too dangerous to bring him there."

"So you wish to avail yourself of the dragon healer who is under your own roof."

Frederica could read nothing in her aura, but she did not sound friendly. "I came to throw myself on your mercy. You owe me nothing. But Roderick has been a good friend to dragons all his life, and he is very dear to me."

"Everyone has someone whom they hold dear. Including the many thousands of people in my land who have been killed or enslaved by the English."

Definitely not friendly. Frederica's heart sank, and she bowed her head. "The British have given you many reasons to hate us. I never understood that until I met Roderick, who told me what the English have done to his people, and how even now they suffer from it. My ignorance is no excuse, though, nor does it make any difference that I am ashamed of what my government has done."

"He is not English, this man?"

"No, he is Welsh. His country has been under England's thumb for centuries. He despised me at first for being English."

"Why are you pleading for the life of one of your country's enemies?"

The image of Roderick lying so still rose before her. "He is not *my* enemy. He is a good person, one of the best I have known." Her voice shook, despite her best efforts. "We quarreled, and he thinks I despise him, and I cannot bear the idea that he will never know the truth."

The enormous dragon set back on her haunches and stared at Frederica silently, her eyes filled with light and mist. The silence went on for a minute, two minutes, three.

Was she to take this as a dismissal? Or was the dragon waiting for her to say something more? Then Frederica felt a light sensation on her skin, like the brush of a butterfly's wing. Not that she had ever been brushed by butterflies, but how she would imagine it.

Then it struck her. She was being read, without the touch required by the dragons she knew. Without being asked. But if there was any chance of convincing Rana Akshaya to heal Roderick, she would accept it. After all, she had nothing to hide, no secrets apart from the one she had already revealed, her feelings for Roderick.

Though perhaps she ought to be nervous. Had not Quickthorn said that Rana Akshaya had powers beyond those of the Nest? Frederica's mother always told her she had more courage than good sense.

"Does your dragon know you have come to me?" Rana Akshaya rumbled.

"Yes. She told me not to waste my time."

"You enjoy hopeless tasks?"

Stung, Frederica snapped, "Should I give up on trying to save my friend, simply because it is unlikely to succeed? I would rather fail while trying to do the right thing than admit defeat without even an attempt."

The dragon's chest rippled. Did that mean amusement, as it would for an English dragon? "Tell my servant where your friend is. I will do what I can."

Hours later, well into the evening, Rana Akshaya arrived at Roderick's bedside, when Frederica had all but given up on her. She swept into the room in her veiled human guise and took one glance at Roderick, who was in one of his thrashing phases. "You may go now," she said to Frederica, dismissing her as if she were a servant.

Somehow Frederica had not expected that, but she swallowed the desire to beg to stay. She retreated from the room and began to wander the old gallery, pacing from end to end as if her steps could somehow help the healing.

But Rana Akshaya did not emerge. Each time Frederica passed the doorway to Roderick's room, dragon magic tugged at her, powerful beyond her ken.

A half-hour. An hour. What kind of healing took this long? If, in fact, Rana Akshaya was trying to heal him. What if she made a terrible mistake in bringing her here?

Another half-hour. They would have expected her back at the main house long ago. But she wanted, she needed, to be here to hear the news, whether it was good or bad.

No. She would remain. She sought out the housekeeper and asked her to send a servant to Pemberley, informing them she would spend the night at the Dower House. Mrs. Reynolds would no doubt send a squad of maids to protect Frederica's reputation from a night alone with an unmarried man, even if he was unconscious.

A guttural cry of pain came from Roderick's room. Frederica clutched her arms around her, digging her fingers into her flesh until it hurt.

Another cry, this one wild and ululating. She swallowed a sob.

And ran. Ran out of the Dower House, through the moonlit walled garden, and to the old dovecote, to the only other being who would also find this as unbearable as she. Rowan.

It was pitch black in the dovecote, but as soon as she entered, a glow began at the base of the circular walls, enough that she could see the red dragon curled up against the far edge. She ran forward and threw her arms around his scaly neck, an impossible forwardness.

But it felt right, and she could sense his pain, too. "Rana Akshaya is trying to heal him," she sobbed.

I know. Rowan spoke in her head, as if mortal speech was beyond him. *She asked my permission. You were very brave to go to her.*

"But she is hurting him!"

I can feel it. But sometimes healing causes pain. His own deep distress leaked through the sending.

"The healers of the Nest, would they have hurt him too?"

I do not know, but Rana Akshaya is unusually powerful. We do not understand some of her abilities. If anyone can save him, she can.

She breathed raggedly with relief. If Rowan trusted Rana Akshaya, so would she. "Are you in trouble with the Nest?"

Very much so, but I expected that. He switched to speaking aloud. "They cannot put me under Silence right now, when they need every able-bodied young dragon to manage the visitors. If Roderick lives, I will go to his Nest, and it will not matter."

"He will live," she said fiercely. "He must."

"Did Rana Akshaya state a price for doing this healing?"

Her mouth went dry. "No. Should I have offered payment?"

"Not unless she asked it. A deep healing like this takes an enormous amount of power, so it is rarely undertaken without a reason."

If there was a price, she would find a way to pay it. As long as Roderick lived.

"Wake up, Companion Frederica!"

Frederica's bed was shaking. No, not her bed; she must have drifted off to sleep against Rowan's flank, there in the old dovecote. Then it all came back to her. "Is there news?"

"Rana Akshaya says we can see him now."

She jumped to her feet and hurried out of the dovecote, momentarily blinded as she came out of the darkness into early morning sunshine. Had Rana Akshaya been working on Roderick all night?

Blinking hard, she ran through the garden, into the house, and pounded up the stairs in the most unladylike manner.

Roderick's door stood open. Inside it, he was sitting propped up in bed, sipping something from a cup held in both his hands.

Relief flooded her. "You are awake! Do you know who I am?" Because the last two times he had opened his eyes, he had not even seen her.

The corners of his mouth twitched. "How could I ever forget you, Lady Frederica?" His voice was thin and gravelly with disuse, but it was his voice, his melodic Welsh accent.

"You terrified us," she blurted out.

"My apologies." This time he did smile. "It was most unintentionally done. And I am beyond honored that the great Rana troubled herself with my case." He nodded to the figure slumped in the armchair.

"You should be!" Then she remembered her manners, stopping herself just in time from pouring out her thanks. "Rana Akshaya, I honor you for your impressive abilities and the grace you have shown in helping us."

Even through her veils and the layers of cloth she was wrapped in, it was obvious for the first time that Rana Akshaya was not human. Her knees were bent in at an unnatural angle and her arms foreshortened. Had she exhausted her power working on Roderick, leaving little for her careful masquerade?

"He would not have lived on his own," Rana Akshaya said flatly. "His blood was not strong enough. I had to go deep into his bones to create new blood."

Hearing the words made Frederica's chest tight, even though she had known he was dying. The rest of it was nonsense, though. What did blood have to do with bones? The Indian dragons must have odd ideas of how the human body worked. "Your efforts do you great honor."

Her eyes kept darting back to Roderick, as if he were a magnet. He was alive!

Rana Akshaya stood. "Lady Frederica Fitzwilliam, I will speak to you outside." She enunciated the words with unusual care, and it was clearly a command.

And one not addressed to Companion Frederica, as Rana Akshaya had called her ever since her binding to Quickthorn. It must mean something, but what?

"Yes, great Rana." With one last glance at Roderick, Frederica followed Rana Akshaya from the room and down to the far end of the gallery.

Rana Akshaya swung around to face her. "Lady Frederica Fitzwilliam."

Definitely significant.

"Yes?"

"I may find myself in need of someone to be my spokesman to your government, to manage negotiations on my behalf. They see dragons as mere animals, and dangerous ones at that, and people from my country are only slightly better. I need someone they will listen to." Her gaze seemed to bore into Frederica, even through the thick veil.

So there was a price. The Indian dragon clearly saw the British government as her enemy, or at least that of her country. Speaking for her was likely to put Frederica at odds with a great many people, not least of all her father. She would be lucky not to be ostracized by society, much of which was perfectly content with large profits the East India Company brought home.

Still, she was fortunate the price was no higher. "As long as it is not in violation of my companion bond or my oath to the Nest, I will be happy to give you whatever assistance I may."

"You are cautious. That is good. But I will tell you this: ignorance of your country's misdeeds is indeed a valid excuse, but once you are no longer ignorant, you become complicit – unless you work to make changes."

The words hit with force. Was there magic behind them, or was it simply a very unpleasant truth? "You are correct. I would like to see my country change certain of its ways."

Rana Akshaya nodded curtly. "You will be informed when you are needed."

"Yes, great Rana." What else could she say?

The veiled form began to turn away, and then stopped. "One other matter, Companion Frederica. Love is a rare treasure, not to be squandered. Do not allow pride and vanity to starve your soul."

Frederica took an involuntary step back. What a shocking personal statement from the haughty Indian dragon! How could she possibly answer it? Instead, she bowed her head and made her deepest curtsy, the one she would use to the King himself, as Rana Akshaya walked off.

Was that what she had been doing, putting pride and vanity ahead of love?

It was not a pretty picture.

Frederica's thoughts swirled as she returned to Roderick's room. The chair where she had spent the last two days was still beside his bed, and she automatically sat in it without waiting for an invitation.

Her hand felt achingly empty after all that time holding his. She wanted to reach out and take it, but that would be beyond improper, now that he was conscious.

Rowan, in his peregrine falcon form, perched on the footboard of the bed. The dragon spoke in her mind. *So there is a price?*

I can afford it. Though it would likely cost her a great deal of her social standing. At least that might discourage her most persistent suitor, Mortimer Percy.

Roderick said, "May I beg you to set down this cup for me? I fear I will spill it if I try." He still held it in both hands.

"Of course." She reached out and took it by the handle. As her fingers brushed his, a tingle ran up her arm. Oh, that heat in her cheeks! How she hated her fair complexion that showed every blush.

"Yes, I am still as weak as a newborn kitten," he said in response to her unasked question.

"But you are alive."

"For which fact, Rowan tells me, I am indebted to you."

It embarrassed her, and that made her cross. "You can just thank me. I am not a dragon to take offense at the words. And your dragon is a busybody."

He gave a small, self-deprecating laugh. "Then I thank you. I am quite attached to my life, as it happens." He leaned his head back against the pillow, closing his eyes.

"Yet you risked it doing a blood binding so far from the Nest!" All her fear came back to her.

He opened one eye. "As if you would have hesitated for even one second, if it were your only chance to become a dragon companion."

"Well, yes, but you are always cautious," she said, flustered. "And you care about your responsibilities."

He closed the eye again. "Perhaps I have learned something from someone who throws caution to the wind when she sees something she truly wants."

The word seemed to echo between them.

Pride and vanity. Nourishing the soul. Throwing caution to the wind.

She could not help herself. She took his hand in hers and held it firmly, like an anchor in the storm.

His eyes stayed closed, but he smiled slightly. And his fingers squeezed hers, ever so gently.

Her heart just might burst.

She was still there several hours later, tired and hungry, when he woke again. But nothing would have made her leave his bedside before she was certain he was recovered.

"Is it true, then, what Rowan said, that you stayed by my bedside?" he asked huskily. "How shocking." It was a tease.

"I went back to the main house at night. Except last night, during your healing, when I fell asleep on your dragon in a dirty old dovecote. And pray do not say that I am a mess because of it," she said fiercely. She ought to have at least brushed her hair and put it back up, but that would have meant letting go of his hand. Out of the question.

That smile again, the one she had thought lost forever. "I would have said you look charmingly informal. And that Darcy would take a horse whip to me if he walked in at this moment."

"Then it is a good thing Darcy is in France." She turned to the maid. "Pray fetch some tea and food for Mr. Roderick. He needs to rebuild his strength."

The maid curtsied and left.

Roderick's expression grew serious. "You must take better care of your reputation."

Exactly what she had spent the last two hours considering. "What I do with my reputation is my business, Roderick ap Rhodri. It is not your problem."

He shook his head. "But it is. I cannot offer you a future; that has not changed. But neither will I be party to your ruination."

"You are too late for that. I took care of that matter several years ago," she informed him briskly, enjoying the sight of his dropped jaw.

"You did... You did what?"

"And why not? I was fated for a marriage of repulsion, where my husband's every touch would only bring me pain unless I was drugged to accept it. Can you blame me for wanting to know something kinder and happier before I condemned myself to that?" She never told anyone before, but she was not going to let Roderick off the hook with false excuses.

"You... I..." He heaved aside. "I have no interest in judging you. It sounds eminently sensible."

"If shocking."

"I will not deny that."

She leaned forward. "I understand that you are going back to Wales and I cannot follow you. What has changed is that I have decided to take what I can get in the meantime, rather than live with regrets over chances missed." She narrowed her eyes. "Unless you tell me that you are not interested. Then I will leave you in peace."

He chuckled, albeit weakly. "You would ask me to lie to a truth-caster?"

"I never know what you are thinking," she complained. "I thought, after that night at the coaching inn, that you despised me."

"Despised *you*? Despised myself, rather, and all the reasons why it was impossible for anything to happen between Lady Frederica Fitzwilliam and simple Roderick ap Rhodri."

"Not so simple, as I understand it." Granny had told her about Roderick's illustrious forebears. "And it seems the problem lies more in your desire to keep your Welsh village a secret than in my birth."

He sighed. "Would you have me expose my family and friends, and force the dragons who live among us into hiding, all for the sake of my own desires?"

"No," she said crossly. "But I do wish you would tell me what you are keeping from me."

He groaned. "May God protect me from truth-casters!" But he did not meet her eyes.

She waited as he fidgeted.

His shoulders slumped. "You are taking advantage of my weakness, but so be it. I have the King's Bond to the land."

It hit her like a shock. The King's Bond, far beyond a simple land Talent, an ability that ranged wide and permitted the monarch to use the land itself in its own defense. No British rulers since Queen Elizabeth had carried the King's Bond.

She swallowed, her mouth suddenly dry. "How far is your reach?"

His expression was self-deprecating, of course. "Much of northern Wales, except the far eastern part."

Good God. If the government had any clue, they would execute Roderick, and his every relation along with him.

"And you are a powerful mage on top of that, and now a dragon companion as well."

His eyes met hers. "Now you see why I cannot afford to draw the attention of English society by attaching myself to one of their well-known aristocrats."

The problem was that she did see. And it broke her heart. She raised her chin. "Then I will learn to be glad of the little time I have with you."

His eyes softened. "Though we may need to wait until I am strong enough to, say, sit up on my own."

She gave him an arch look. "For some things, perhaps." And then she stood to lean over the bed – and claimed his lips with her own.

At last.

Chapter 33

E LIZABETH HAD SLEPT FITFULLY between the demands of her growing body and the occasional twig poking through the blanket, despite
Darcy's best efforts to make a soft area of dried leaves for them behind a
boulder that would hide them from any passersby. But she had been curled
up in his arms all night, and that more than made up for it.

Darcy kissed her lingeringly, sending a rush of heat through her. "Rest
here while I fetch some water," he said.

"Thank you." She would be happy to rest for hours, if only she could.
To think they might be back at Pemberley in just a day or two, in their
own bed! Where she could stay in that bed all day and night if she wished.
It sounded like heaven. They had left the road earlier than planned the
previous day, after their encounter with the soldiers, and the terrain had
been rough and challenging. Her legs ached from carrying the extra weight
of her heavy belly as she clambered up the steep slope, but it was worth it
to get away from the soldiers.

She pulled the blanket up to her chin, watching Darcy pick up his coat
with his left hand. He sighed and set it down again. His new limitations
must frustrate him every day.

Pushing the cover aside, she rose from their makeshift bed and took the
coat. Bending down was getting harder every day. "Pray permit me to assist
you."

He grimaced, but allowed her to slide it over his weak arm. No wonder he was wearing looser clothes now; he could never have managed it with one of his usual tight coats. That must be why he had slept in his boots, too, to avoid having to ask her to help him with them.

What a blow this must be to him!

She could think of no words to make it better, but he was still her beloved William, so she caught his face between her hands and kissed him with every ounce of persuasive passion she had, tantalizing him to deepen the kiss until they were both breathing heavily.

Finally, when she broke away, he leaned his forehead against hers. "Oh, my dearest Elizabeth. When we are back at Pemberley, I am not letting you out of bed for a week."

She laughed because it was so close to her earlier thoughts – and so completely different. And even more appealing. "I will hold you to that."

"But first, water, so that we can actually make it home."

"I am completely in favor of that." She rubbed her aching back.

He sauntered out of their little hiding place, his mood clearly improved.

She turned back with a smile, her insides still warm from that kiss. No point in trying to rest now. Instead she shook out the blankets and rolled them up, tying them tightly with the leather straps. Her dress was hopelessly wrinkled, but she straightened it as well as she could before forcing her half-boots onto her swollen feet.

Perhaps they could cover some ground before breaking their fast on the nuts and dried fruits in the haversack. That way they could —

"*Arrêtez!*" The man's deep, angry voice sounded a short distance away. "Keep your hands where we can see them."

Elizabeth froze.

"What seems to be the problem, my good man?" It was Darcy, sounding completely calm.

"You are under arrest, you filthy traitor, and now you are going to lead us to the dragons."

"Dragons? How would I know where to find them?"

"Stop wasting our time with lies. The landed Talent in the village felt your power as you passed."

"This is nonsense. I have no magic, and I already told you I am looking for a witch woman."

And then Darcy's voice sounded in her head, so sweetly familiar and yet full of pain. *Stay hidden. I will lead them away. You must warn the Nest – and protect our child.*

But –

Do not send! They may be tracking your Talent. Go home, I beg you. I will follow if I can.

If he could. Her heart plummeted. He was only a few feet away from her, but it might as well have been a thousand miles.

She would never see him again.

Every inch of her cried out to run to him, to somehow save him, or just to embrace him one last time. But it would be a heedless waste. It would only lead to her imprisonment, too, if not worse, and a loss of their child's future.

"Bind his hands. Tightly."

Darcy's voice. "My right arm is useless."

A snort. "A trick, no doubt. Tie them both."

Darcy grunted in pain. Elizabeth fell to her knees, her hands clenched, biting her lip until she tasted blood.

"This is all a mistake. I can tell you nothing about dragons."

"We shall see about that. Corporal, what does the lodestone show?"

"Just a tiny wobble."

"It is him, then. Now, *mon ami*, do you wish to show us where the dragons are, or must we persuade you further?" The sound of a fist striking flesh.

Elizabeth rocked back and forth, tears burning her cheeks.

"This way," Darcy gasped.

"Ah, that is more like it!" He sounded triumphant and Elizabeth wanted to kill him.

But she had a baby to protect and dragons to warn, or this Nest would soon meet the fate of the Austrian one, scorched and empty.

Oh, it was like a knife turning in her gut, to let it happen! She could not help him. Darcy's Talent was so much stronger than hers; if he thought magery would make a difference, he would have already used it.

Or not. He could have made himself invisible, but he had not. He could not, if he wanted to keep the Frenchmen from finding her. He was deliberately sacrificing himself for her, for the child, for the dragons.

And she could do nothing but accept his sacrifice.

Tramping footsteps and the sound of breaking twigs, and then French voices fading away. Darcy must be leading them off. She strained her ears for their direction. Eastward, perhaps. The trail to the Nest lay just to the northwest.

He was giving her the best chance he could.

This was her fault. If she had never left England, Darcy would be safe at Mme. Hartung's house, not being dragged off by French soldiers.

Perhaps the Nest could help him, if she could reach it quickly enough. As the noise faded away, she began to gather what little she could carry. No point taking anything that would slow her down. The food, yes, and the tin cup for water. She took the compass in Darcy's haversack and consulted it. Towards the tall, pointy peak first.

She cast a longing look at the blankets she had shared with him, likely for the last time. There was no time for sentimentality, though. She could not afford to think of what might be happening to him at this very minute.

She peeked out of their hiding place behind the boulder. No sign of anyone, but she tiptoed anyway, lest her movements be overheard. When she was farther away, she would move faster. As fast as she could.

It was a painfully slow journey. The deer path she had taken veered off in the wrong direction, leaving her to force her way through rough underbrush to maintain the correct direction. Thorny branches scraped her hands and cheeks. She nearly sobbed with relief when she came across a dry streambed she could follow.

The sun was high in the sky. She ought to stop and eat, but it would slow her down, and her stomach cramped painfully at the very idea of food. She pushed on, wiping the perspiration from her brow.

On and on, higher and higher. At least there was no sign of the French soldiers.

Nothing mattered except getting to the Nest as quickly as possible. Not the ache in her back, not her sore feet, not the bleeding scratches, not even the worry for Darcy that sent stabs of pain through her stomach. It was nothing to what he must be suffering.

One foot after another. Check the compass. Back into the woods. Finally her breath was coming so fast she had to rest, leaning back against a rough tree trunk. Breathe in and out, and no thinking.

Another cramp assailed her, stronger than the others. She pressed her hands against her swollen abdomen as if that could stop it. Her suddenly very hard abdomen.

Horror filled her. No. It could not be. It was too early. Mrs. Sanford had said it would be another two months at the least. A child born this early would not survive.

But as the pain passed, the tightness under her skin relaxed a little. There was no mistaking it; her womb was causing the cramps.

And she was alone in the wilderness, many hours' walk from the nearest road that might lead to help. Far from the land she needed for her Talent, to give herself strength. As a last resort, she could send to Cerridwen, but that risked making things worse if the soldiers' lodestone found her dragon.

And Darcy was lost to her.

A brief sob escaped her. This was a nightmare.

There was no one to help her. If her baby was to have any chance to survive, she had to find safety. She could not lose them both, not Darcy and their child, too.

The Nest. She had to reach the Nest. Someone there would know what to do. And she might not have much time.

She straightened and set forth again, as quickly as her swollen, weary body could go. Her heart ached, even as she dreaded the next pain.

Finally, an eternity later, or perhaps only a few hours, sudden power surged into her from the land beneath her feet. It stopped her, holding her briefly in place as it tested her, and then let her stumble through unharmed.

It must be a ward. She had crossed a line of wards, like the one Rowan had built at Pemberley.

She had made it. She had reached the territory protected by the Nest.

Falling to her knees, she sought out her bond to Cerridwen, the one she had struggled so hard to silence since reaching France. But there it was, strong and pulsing, always there for her. *Cerridwen, I need help.*

As the two French Kith who had come to Elizabeth's aid helped her through the illusions and into the Nest, the familiar smell of cinnamon and hot metal brought fresh tears to her eyes. Safety, at least of a sort, but only for her. Not for her beloved husband.

Cerridwen transformed beside her, the first time she had seen her in dragon form since coming to France, her aura full of concern and desire to comfort. But even that could not help.

A mid-sized dragon awaited them in the vast chamber, "Welcome, Companion Elizabeth. We have been expecting you. But where is your mate?"

"Lost," she said with a catch in her voice. "Taken by soldiers, who are hunting for this Nest. Oh, there is so much I must tell you, to warn you, but my baby is coming and I must go through the Gate as swiftly as possible."

The dragon exchanged a glance with Cerridwen, the tingle of rapid sendings filling the air. "Will you tell me quickly?"

Another pain lanced through her, making her clutch her stomach. "There is...so much," she gasped. "Pray, could you not read me instead?"

The Kith woman put an arm around Elizabeth's shoulder. "She is in no condition to explain, not while she is in childbirth. The need for haste is great."

The dragon extended his forelegs. Elizabeth grasped them, turning her gaze up into his huge gold ringed eyes. She could not organize her thoughts, only put the memory of the day before him, all the agony and the fear, and everything she knew about Napoleon's dragon lodestone.

His presence in her mind was delicate, but his shock was palpable, as was his horror. He withdrew and said, "I must take this to the Eldest instantly."

"I beg you, may I go through the Gate first? There is no time to lose."

"Someone is coming to help you through it. We are in your debt, Companion Elizabeth, for your warning."

But none of that would stop her child from being born too soon.

Chapter 34

T HIS SHOULD HAVE BEEN a glorious moment, riding from the Dark Peak Nest to Pemberley on dragonback, even in the full dark necessary to protect the secrecy of the Nest.

But Elizabeth wept through it all. Until then, too much had been happening for her to think. The Gate, falling into the Dark Peak Nest and the brief period of disorientation afterwards, facing the many questions from the dragons while waiting for the night to fall.

Now, sitting astride Quickthorn's shoulders in a cleverly contrived harness, with no distractions, her predicament became all too real. Darcy, whom she would never see again. Their child, whose movements had been her steady companion these last months, would be the only part of Darcy she had left – but she knew all too well how often babies born early did not survive their first days.

And oh, how she wanted this child! How could she bear losing both of them?

We are almost there. Quickthorn's voice in her head. Even Quickthorn, who was always irritable and never comforting, knew how distressed she was. She could hardly miss it, though, when with each pain, Elizabeth had leaned forward on the dragon's neck and whimpered?

"You are very kind." It was all she could manage.

Then there were lights ahead of them, and the dragon glided more slowly until a thump traveled up Elizabeth's spine. They had landed in a circle of lanterns.

And among a crowd of people, far more than she would expect to come racing toward a very large dragon. Elizabeth brushed away her tears as the faces swam into focus. Mrs. Reynolds and Frederica in the lead. Mrs. Sanford, thank heavens! And was that Roderick? What was he doing here? Half a dozen footman, too.

Of course. Quickthorn must have told Frederica what was happening, and she had rallied the troops.

Elizabeth fumbled with the buckles on her harness. Then Roderick was there, pulling himself up beside her, snapping the links with an experienced touch.

He helped her down into the waiting hands of a tall golden-haired gentleman she did not recognize. She was too distraught even to care that she was being carried by an unknown man.

The stranger set her on her feet, and the power of Pemberley came up to meet her, as if recognizing her desperate need. The blessed strength of it, the depth of it, flowing into her and giving her new life.

Mrs. Reynolds commanded, "Bring the chair." Two footmen came forward and set an oddly shaped wooden chair before her. "Pray sit, Mrs. Darcy. They will carry you to your room."

"I can walk," said Elizabeth. And it was true, especially with Talent burning into her from the land, filling the places that had been empty since she left.

"You can, but you will not," snapped the housekeeper.

Elizabeth stared at her in shock, and then saw the fear in the older woman's expression. She had forgotten that other people cared about her baby, too. Chastened, she sank down in the chair and let the footmen bear her to the familiar hall and up the stairs. She was back, home at last.

But Darcy should be here, too. It was his home, and he would never see it again.

She closed her eyes and let her head sink back.

Upstairs, Chandrika, her face tight, helped her into bed. Frederica and Mrs. Reynolds hovered nearby.

Mrs. Sanford elbowed her way to the front. "Tell me what has been happening. How often are your pains? Has your water broken? Any blood? Did anything happen to bring this on?"

Had anything happened? It almost made her laugh. Elizabeth answered her questions as best she could.

"Open your mouth," the midwife said.

When Elizabeth obeyed, Mrs. Sanford pressed down her lower lip. "As I suspected. You are parched. Mrs. Reynolds, some broth with plenty of salt, watered wine, sweetened tea. Chamomile, if you have it. Right away. If she drinks enough, we may be able to stop this, or at least delay it. No lemon; that might agitate the womb."

The housekeeper gave a sharp nod. She was no sooner out of the room than Chandrika was at Elizabeth's side, holding a cup of tea. Of course Chandrika would have prepared everything as soon as she heard the news. She always did.

Elizabeth gulped it down and held out the cup for more. Why had she not realized how thirsty she was?

Mrs. Sanford said briskly, "Good. Now, tell me each time you have a pain."

"I will. Whatever you say." Had it only been that morning that she had awakened in Darcy's arms, thinking all would finally be well? "I am so very tired."

"I am hardly surprised. Climbing mountains and riding dragonback during your labors? That is a new one for me." But she said it with a smile.

"That was the easiest part of it." Her eyelids drifted closed. It was such a relief to have someone else handling the decisions.

"Stay awake, Mrs. Darcy. Resting is very important, but you must drink a great deal more before you sleep."

Chandrika began to wipe Elizabeth's face with a damp washcloth. The coolness felt good. She winced as a pain began. "It is happening."

The midwife laid her hands on Elizabeth's bulge, her mouth moving as she counted silently until it faded. "It is still weak and short. That is a good sign."

Weak? Elizabeth did not want to think of what a strong pain would feel like, but she would take it as good news.

Two days later, the midwife grudgingly announced that Elizabeth seemed to be out of imminent danger. "For now, at least. There is a good chance your labors will start again if you resume your normal activities. I strongly urge you to stay in bed for the next month."

"For a month!" Lying in bed with nothing to do was already driving her mad, when the only thing she could think of was Darcy. "What if I promise to be careful and to avoid exerting myself?"

"Do you wish to carry this baby to term or not?" Mrs. Sanford retorted.

Elizabeth sank back against the pillows. "Of course I do."

"Then you will rest. You are fortunate, compared to most women with early labor who have no choice. You have servants to do all the work and friends to bear you company." Mrs. Sanford's voice was sharp.

Frederica said in a low voice, "I beg you, Elizabeth, take no risks." There were lines of fatigue on her face.

"And this coming from someone who has never seen a risk she would not take!" Elizabeth teased in a vain effort to rally her own low spirits. "Very well, I shall obey, but I do not promise to be cheerful about it."

Not when Darcy was most likely in a French prison, suffering God knows what ill treatment..

"Good," the midwife said briskly.

"There is one thing," Elizabeth said slowly. "If I must remain abed, I want to do it in the cottage at the oak grove. I am too far from the land here. Should my husband need to draw on Pemberley's power through me, I have to be able to access it." It was the only thing she could do for him.

Mrs. Sanford rubbed her knuckles over her lips. "I do not know that it is a good idea for you to act as a conduit—"

"His life may depend on it!" Elizabeth snapped.

The midwife sighed. "I suppose moving you would do no harm, if you are willing to be carried there in a litter, and if Mrs. Reynolds can supply you with everything you need."

The housekeeper said instantly, "There will be no difficulty about that."

"It may even be beneficial to you to have more access to the land. It gives you strength. Mrs. Reynolds, may I speak to you outside about the arrangements?"

The housekeeper nodded, and the two women left the room.

"I will perish from boredom," Elizabeth said glumly.

Frederica said, "I can entertain you. Perhaps now you would like to read your letters? I know you did not want to before, but—"

"No." Frederica had tried to give her the pile of correspondence from her sister Jane earlier, but Elizabeth could not bear to read about Jane's happiness with Bingley and pleasure in the company of the neighborhood Elizabeth had lost. Their lives had diverged so far that hearing from Jane only made Elizabeth feel lonely. Perhaps someday they could meet and reconnect, but right now that seemed as hopeless as everything else. Just one more loss, on top of everything else.

"I could read them to you if you are too tired," Frederica urged.

"No!" She was much sharper this time.

"But what if something is the matter? Would you not want to know? She has been writing to you every week without fail."

Elizabeth pushed the letters away. "You can read them if you think them so important," she said irritably. But she could not help growing tense as Frederica took her at her word, cracking the seal on one of them and slowly reading it. "Well?"

Frederica refolded the paper. "No bad news. Just that she is misses you and is imagining all sorts of terrible things that could have kept you from writing."

When had she written last to Jane? Probably before her decision to go to France. No wonder Jane was fretting. "I suppose I should try to send her something," she mumbled. But she could not face it. That would mean telling her of losing Darcy and the failure of his mission, and how it might still cost her the baby.

Frederica eyed her with concern. "If it would help, I would be happy to send her a note and tell her you are well, simply very fatigued by your condition."

"That would be a kindness," Elizabeth said. Jane would not believe a word of it, but it would be better than nothing.

When Cerridwen finally made it to Pemberley the following day, Elizabeth turned her head away. The sight of her dragon made her ill with regrets.

"What is it?" Cerridwen asked. "Why are you hiding your mind from me?

"I do not want to talk about it. Go to the Nest; they will want to see you."

Hurt cascaded from Cerridwen. "And you do not?"

"I want my husband!" It was a cry of anguish, from deep in her soul. "I want him to be safe, as he was before we tried to rescue him. I convinced him to leave the house where he was safe. It is my fault he was captured."

Cerridwen seemed to fold into herself. "You blame me, then, for it."

Elizabeth waved her hand, trying to brush her words away. "I know you had no choice, that you had to follow your vision. But I did not realize the price I would pay. Did you know what would happen, that I would lose him?" She had not meant to ask that. She did not truly wish to know the answer.

The dragon lowered her head. "I cannot see the details, only the result at the end. I never meant to hurt him, or you."

"But we did! Oh, how I wish I had refused to go. Now I will never see him again, and I may lose our child, too. All because I foolishly thought I could help." She turned onto her side and buried her face in the pillow, tears cascading down her cheeks.

Silence. Only Cerridwen's aura of distress, and even that was subdued, as if the dragon was trying to hide it. And then a small voice. "As I was leaving the Nest, they were planning to try to rescue him."

Elizabeth picked up her head. "Do not give me false hope! It will only make it worse!"

"I do not know if they will succeed, but I let them think they must, that my vision would come true if they did not save Darcy." Cerridwen sounded steadier now.

"You let them think that? What do you mean?"

Wretchedness rolled off the dragon. "I told them he had to be saved. They assumed it was because he was needed to prevent the disaster I foresaw, and I did not correct them. But I have had no visions about him."

"Because you knew it was our fault, too!" It was unfair, but she could not bear to listen to this. Not when Darcy was suffering.

"I know there are no easy answers. All the futures I see contain death and suffering. In the best of them, some dragons and people will die. There will be sacrifices. And all of them will be my fault, for the choices I make!"

The door opened to reveal Mrs. Sanford. "My apologies for interrupting, but I must ask you not to upset Mrs. Darcy. It is very important that she remain calm, or she may lose this child."

Cerridwen gave a guttural cry, and then she transformed. The wind from her kestrel wings blew against Elizabeth's cheeks as she flew out the door.

Frederica settled herself beside Elizabeth's bed. "Well, you look terrible," she said.

Elizabeth groaned. "Are you not supposed to be consoling me?"

"My attempts at tact always fail. Likely you would not believe me if I told you some men would find reddened, swollen eyes appealing."

A gurgle of laughter escaped her, despite her misery. "I do not understand how you survived in society for so long."

"Neither do I, to be truthful," Frederica said without any apparent distress. "Now, what happened with Cerridwen? Quickthorn is worried. Apparently she is refusing to talk to anyone."

Elizabeth leaned her head back and closed her eyes. It was not what she wanted to hear. "We had words. I do not know how things will ever be the same for us again." She had to force out the words.

Frederica's eyes widened. "Oh, no! What happened?"

"It is my own fault," she said tiredly. "I misunderstood what it meant to be a companion. Somehow I thought it meant Cerridwen loved me and would always do what was best for me, since she had stayed with me when they told her to break the bond. But it is not true. She does what is best for the dragons, as I suppose she ought to."

"Cerridwen does love you. I am certain of it," Frederica exclaimed.

"Perhaps in her own way, she does care," Elizabeth said slowly. The dragon had tried to help Darcy, after all. "But she still insisted we had to take him through the Gate, and he might have survived if he had stayed with his initial plan of going to Prussia."

"Or he might not have. He was still being hunted, even if he was momentarily safe. Are you going to blame yourself forever for being unlucky in your choices, when you were doing your very best to help him?" Frederica asked. "Do you think Darcy would want you to do that?"

She shook her head wordlessly. Of course Darcy would not want her to blame herself, but that did not mean she was blameless.

"Did Cerridwen know what would happen to him?"

"She says not."

"Do you know why she insisted on taking him to the Nest?"

"Her far-seeing, as always. If we did not take him to the Nest, terrible things would happen."

Frederica rubbed her fingers along the edge of the counterpane covering Elizabeth. "Before he met you, Darcy was willing to sacrifice himself to prevent another dragon massacre. If Cerridwen had given him the choice, that his being captured would prevent a disaster, what do you think he would have done?"

Elizabeth did not want to listen to reason. She wanted Darcy. Tears slipped down her cheeks. "I wanted Cerridwen to save him for me."

"We all wanted that." Frederica handed her a lace-edged handkerchief. "Even Cerridwen, I daresay."

"She has to follow her vision. I know." But she said it grudgingly.

Frederica hesitated. "I always say the wrong thing, so I should probably keep my lips sealed, but I never can manage that, can I? You may not be able to forgive me for this, either. But you would not respect Cerridwen if she had let the dragons die and England go up in flames in order to save Darcy."

Bile rose in Elizabeth's mouth. "Do not ask me to like her choice."

"No, of course not. But..." Frederica took a deep breath before plunging forward. "Someone told me recently that love is a treasure and should not be squandered, and that denying love will starve your soul. And I think that applies to your love for Cerridwen, too, even if you disagree with what she did."

Elizabeth turned her head to look at her. "That does not sound like you. Did Quickthorn put you up to this?"

"No, she told me to give you a good shake and knock some sense into your head." Frederica gave a quick smile. "All this talk of love does not sound like me, does it? But it is something I have been thinking about a good deal lately."

No doubt due to Roderick's presence. Elizabeth was still puzzled by that, how he had ended up here and bonded to Rowan, but everyone was busily trying to protect her by refusing to tell her the full story.

And she did not have the energy to argue with them, or even to care.

Elizabeth might have been able to hold onto her anger at Cerridwen more than a few hours if only she could have taken a long ramble through the countryside, but how was anyone to bear being confined to bed just at the time when their thoughts were the most painful? Her grief, anger, and helplessness were inescapable.

As was the conclusion that Frederica was right. She had been unfair to Cerridwen. And she should try to do something about it.

Hesitantly Elizabeth reached out with her mind. Would her dragon even be willing to speak to her? There was only one way to find out. *Cerridwen?*

Silence for a moment, and then, *What?*

I was wrong to blame you. You did what you had to do, and you tried to protect both of us. I have been too distraught to think clearly.

Silence again, but she could tell Cerridwen was listening.

She tried again. *I miss you. It was hard not being able to send to you in France, and then you were too far away.*

I hated it. Now Cerridwen's frustration poured through their connection. *All those weeks of silence, of avoiding using my powers. It was horrid.*

Yes, it was. And then, with her own feelings open to the bond, *I wish you were here with me now.*

Then I will come. The connection faded away.

Elizabeth let her head sink back into the pillow as relief washed over her. Then she called out to Chandrika, in her little cot behind a screen. "Cerridwen is coming. Would you let the others know? I would not want them to be taken by surprise." The staff had erected a tent outside the cottage where an assortment of armed footmen and grooms took turns guarding her. Elizabeth had said it was unnecessary, but Mrs. Reynolds had enlisted the steward in her insistence that Mr. Darcy would not have it any other way. The one argument Elizabeth could not deny.

"Yes, Mrs. Darcy. It will be good to have her here again."

"Yes, it will."

Chapter 35

DARCY STOOD BY THE narrow window slit in his cell, waiting for the moment when the sun would be low enough to stream in directly. It was just a crack of an opening, and the light through it was only strong enough for him to work with for a few minutes late in the afternoon.

There it was, casting sudden shadows in the cellar room serving as his prison. Quickly he gathered the rays of sunlight to him, braiding them together to create the energy he needed. Then he focused it all on his broken rib, urging it to knit together.

He had never healed a broken bone before, only cuts and scrapes, but he had to try. Another sleepless night from pain might leave him confused enough that he would blurt out the truth. The only thing protecting him was the soldiers' belief that he was a Prussian gentleman lacking in Talent, and he needed to keep his wits together to manage that masquerade.

He kept pouring in the power he collected, little as it was, until the first tell-tale signs of giddiness appeared. Reluctantly he released the threads and sank down to sit on the dirt floor, leaning his head back against the damp wall. He took an experimental breath, first a shallow one, and then deeper. His side still ached, but the stabbing pain was much less.

It had worked, at least to a degree, and that would have to be enough.

He tore off a chunk of the stale bread they had left for him and began to chew it. Even if it was a far cry from the sugared tea and cake he was accustomed to using for magical replenishment, it was nourishment of a sort, and he could not afford to go without it. And it would give him strength to keep resisting the questioning from the soldiers. He had to keep delaying them as long as he could, to make certain Elizabeth had enough time to reach the Nest and get safely back to England.

He yawned, despite his swollen jaw. Three days in captivity, and he had plenty of bruises to show for it. A blow to his head on the second night had left him dazed and confused, thinking that the walls of his cell were talking to him in Elizabeth's voice. His thinking was still not completely clear, and he had moments when he saw two of everything.

But Elizabeth was free. He would accept those blows gladly, if that was the price.

It could have been worse. The soldiers had not been as rough with him as he would have expected. They wanted him in good enough shape to ransom if they could not get directions to the Nest from him.

Thanks to Cerridwen and her bindings, they never would. But once they learned there was no aristocratic Prussian family to pay his ransom, things would get much uglier.

But he would not let his mind go there. Instead, he remembered the sensation of his baby kicking against his hand through Elizabeth's skin. He was a real child now, not just a concept, and he desperately wanted to meet him. Or her. Somehow Darcy would find a way to freedom. And failing that, he would die a death his son could be proud of.

Thinking of that was the road to madness, though, especially since the light was fading completely away. He wrapped himself in a ragged blanket and found the least foul spot on the floor for his bed. Closing his eyes, he let the world fade away, imagining himself in the silent cottage at the heart of Pemberley with Elizabeth in his arms, and for a moment he almost felt free.

He woke to a hand shaking his shoulder. His cell was full of smoke that blurred his vision – no, not smoke, but fog. But why would there be mist indoors? Perhaps his vision was blurred from the head blow. But he could see the man leaning over him had a cloth wrapped around his face and a lantern.

"Get up," the man hissed softly in French. "Come quickly and be quiet about it."

"Who are you?" Darcy croaked.

"Your rescuer, at least if you cooperate." He sounded exasperated.

A chance to escape? Darcy pushed himself to his feet and limped after him, out of the walls that had enclosed him, into even more clouds of mist. The man paused to replace the bar on the door to his prison. Then he was off again, Darcy doing his best to keep up, out into a fog-filled corridor, up rickety steps, past a pair of slumped bodies wearing French uniforms. Dead or drugged? He did not care, as long as he was free. Out the door into a dark night, the unnatural mist continuing even here.

A chill went up his spine. His vision was not the problem. This was magic at play.

"This way," whispered his rescuer. "Time is short."

Fortunately he slowed down, or Darcy would have lost him as he pushed through the pain that came with every movement, up the cobbled street until they reached a hay wagon. Finally the haze was starting to thin, and the waxing moon cast long shadows.

Another man crawled out from underneath the wagon. "In there, and put this over you," he said, pulling a ragged blanket off the bed of it. In French, but in a voice so familiar it resonated in Darcy's very bones.

Darcy froze in place, peering at the man's face. It could not be. It was impossible. Utterly, utterly impossible.

But it was. The cleft chin, the sculpted cheekbones, the scar on his brow from a childhood tree-climbing expedition gone wrong, and above all, the lithe body that moved like a hunting tiger. A few more lines on that face he knew as well as his own, but that was all.

Darcy took two clumsy steps forward, barely able to trust his feet. "Jack?" he asked hoarsely. That damned blow to the head! Now he was seeing things that were not there. But it was worth it to catch a glimpse of his brother, even if he was not real.

An incredulous expression Darcy would have recognized anywhere spread over Jack's face. "Good God, Will, is that you under all those bruises? Damn, but they might have told me! What are you doing here?" He pulled Darcy into a hard embrace.

It was like a knife in Darcy's half-healed rib, but he did not care. "I know you are dead, but I am glad to see you, anyway. Or am I dead now, too?" Perhaps this was just a dream, and he was actually still in the cell. If only it could be real!

Jack's brow furrowed, and he reached up to snap his fingers in front of Darcy's face. "What did they do to you, Will? Wake up! I am alive and so are you."

He could feel Jack's arm around him, steadying him. That arm was definitely not his imagination. It was one thing to hear voices or even to see phantoms, but to feel them? "Are you certain?"

Jack released him, shaking his head in disbelief. "They will pay for doing this to you, I swear it."

"No time for this!" the other man snapped. "Get under that blanket if you value your life. And no English, you fools!"

"Right." Jack was suddenly all business. "In there, Will. We can speak later."

Darcy hesitated. "A hand, if you please. My right arm is weak." He could not possibly swing himself into the high wagon bed without it.

"Damn bastards!" But Jack did not hesitate. He bent down and made his hands into a stirrup for Darcy to step into, and then lifted him in.

"Lie back," said the other man urgently.

Jack tossed the blanket over him, and then something else landed on top of it – some hay, by the scent and the dust that made him want to sneeze. A moment later the cart creaked into motion.

Darcy lay there, half stunned. If this was a dream, why could he feel the bumps in the road shaking him, his half-healed rib throbbing with each jarring movement?

How could Jack possibly be alive? He had been in the midst of the battle at Salamanca, everyone agreed on that, and the few survivors had been on the very outskirts. And Jack's ring, his half-melted signet, found on an unrecognizably burned body.

It made no sense. If Jack had indeed survived, why had he never been in touch? It was difficult to get word to England with the blockade, true, but he could have sent a letter to the British consul in Prussia. And what was he doing in the wilds of Alsace?

The coincidence was too great, too preposterous. It must be a trick. Napoleon had successfully impersonated a human all these years. Could a dragon have taken on Jack's appearance?

No. He knew Jack's voice, the way his brother threw back his shoulders. It was truly him.

The cart lurched, making him stifle a cry of pain. But Jack was alive, and the wildest, most impossible good fortune had brought them back together.

He had a brother again.

Or had this been just an astonishingly lucky chance? According to Elizabeth, Cerridwen had insisted on traveling to France, and later that they must come to this Nest instead of trying to sneak across the Channel. Cerridwen, with her gift of foresight. Could she have known Jack was here?

He racked his brain for everything he had been told about Cerridwen's abilities. That she could foresee a disastrous outcome and she made decisions based on whether a particular action would lead toward or away from that end. Nothing about finding missing brothers.

Unless finding Jack was somehow important to preventing the disaster.

They turned onto a different, even bumpier surface. A track of some sort, perhaps? He was bursting with questions for his brother. If they both managed to live through this escape.

They finally rolled to a stop, but he remained motionless. Had they reached safety, or were the soldiers hunting for him? The blanket was yanked away, loose hay floating around him.

Jack's face grinned down at him. "Come along; we ride from here. You can still ride, I hope?"

"I can manage." He had never ridden with both reins in one hand, but he would make do. His rib would be a worse problem.

"Good. Let us go; no telling how long that Artifact will keep the soldiers asleep."

Another Artifact. That explained it – and that the dragons were somehow involved.

"What about him?" Darcy gestured to the other man as Jack led him to two sturdy horses, already saddled.

"He lives here and wants to be out of sight as soon as possible. We can talk once we are safely away."

He needed Jack's help to mount. All the things he had never thought about needing two hands for! But nothing could lower his spirits now, not his weak arm nor the untrained farm horse, not even the pain in his side with each step or the ache in his bruised face. He was free, and Jack was alive!

He turned the horse to follow his brother to the edge of the field and off into the woods. Or, more accurately, his horse followed its stablemate, since breaking the two-handed rein habit was harder than Darcy had anticipated. Onto a narrow path, up the hill, climbing, climbing. Past switchbacks and streams, cutting across clearings and rock fields.

Questions bubbled up in Darcy's head as he watched his brother's familiar riding stance, but there was no chance to talk.

Finally Jack reined in at the top of a steep slope that left the horses breathing hard. "We had best let them rest a bit before we tackle the last part."

Darcy managed to dismount, although it was more a matter of sliding down the side of the stolid farm horse than anything his riding instructor would recognize. An involuntary grunt escaped him when his feet hit the ground, jarring his rib.

Jack courteously ignored it, instead uncapping a flask and holding it out. "Wine?"

Darcy took a gulp, and then a second. After days of nothing but dried bread and small beer, it tasted rich and luxurious. The warmth of it spread through him.

"Take it all," Jack said. "You need it far more than I."

He could not argue that. After he had drained it, he handed it back. "You are a sight for sore eyes, brother."

Jack laughed. "The same to you, although your eyes look particularly sore! Do you remember when I blacked your eye, that time when you tried to stop me from running away from home?"

Darcy could not help smiling back. "It was unforgettable."

"And your lynx pounced on me." Jack snapped his fingers. "Your lynx! I should have known you must be the prisoner. Word is that the soldiers are afraid to leave the village after two of them were mauled by a lynx. Guess he did not like how they were treating you, eh?" He chuckled.

"They deserved it," Darcy said. "But you – we thought you died at Salamanca. Why have you sent no word?"

Jack's grin faded. "I wish I could have, but I am a prisoner here. They do not let me communicate with anyone."

Darcy eyed him with frank disbelief. "A prisoner who rides free on rescue missions?"

Jack shrugged. "I gave them my parole. My word of honor that I would not escape or try to send a message. Would you have me stay locked in a cave always? I would lose my mind." He sighed. "This is the first time they have allowed me to go so far. I begged for the opportunity."

"Who? Who is holding you captive?" He had assumed Jack was somehow allied with the Nest, but surely dragons did not take prisoners.

"The dragons, of course. Oh, not in a terrible way; they are gentle captors who treat me as an honored guest. One who simply is not allowed to depart."

"But why? What did you do?"

"That is the strange thing – they will not tell me. Only that they must keep me. They are very apologetic about it."

It made no sense. "How did you escape from Salamanca?"

Jack uttered a short bark of laughter. "The last thing I remember was lining up for the battle, ready to fight, and then I awoke here."

"Did you take an injury to your head, then?" That could explain his loss of memory.

"Not that I am aware of. The first thing I recall was being in the Nest here, with my heart pounding and naked as the day I was born. Not a scratch on me apart from a nick from shaving that morning. Halfway across Spain and most of France in an instant, though I did not know it at the time. And dragons everywhere."

They must have sent him through a Gate. Why could he not remember? Dragons had the ability to take memories away, but was there any reason they would do it to Jack? His tired brain could make no sense of it. "Sounds terrifying. It is hard enough to discover dragons are real without all of that."

"Oh, I already knew about them. I met a dragon once at Pemberley. He asked me if I wanted to be a dragon companion, something about having spilled my blood on the old Dragon Stones, but then he found out I wanted to be a soldier and said it could not work. The worst part was the binding, that I could tell no one."

Darcy could sympathize with that. "I had no idea. Well, thank God you are alive."

"What happened at Salamanca? I do not even know if we won or lost. I have heard no news."

Darcy drew in a long breath. "We lost catastrophically. It was a massacre by dragonfire."

Jack swallowed hard, his face suddenly ashen. "How many were killed?"

"All but a handful of survivors. And one of the burned bodies was wearing your signet ring." It came out almost as an accusation. "Which is why we thought you were dead."

"My ring." Jack looked stunned, and suddenly Darcy realized he just told him that everyone he once knew at Salamanca was dead. "I gave it to someone. You did lose a brother there, a half-brother. Did you know our father had a second family at Pemberley, one he hid from us? I met him in Spain and decided he deserved the ring more than I did." Bitterness dripped from his words.

"I just learned of it recently." When his half-sister had saved Elizabeth's life.

Elizabeth. In his utter shock over Jack's reappearance, he had not even asked about her. "My wife was on her way to your Nest when I was arrested. Did she make it?" He held his breath.

"A woman came a few days ago and went almost immediately through the Gate. I did not see her. Was that your wife? Good Lord, when did you marry?"

Elizabeth was safe! "Last autumn. You will be an uncle soon."

"You, a father! Astonishing." Then something changed in his face. "Why are the dragons helping you? After hiding for centuries, after keeping me prisoner, the Nest has suddenly shown their hand to rescue you. What makes you so important to them?"

He had to stop to think about that. "I have information they want, and my wife is a dragon companion." Odd, that the binding had not stopped him from saying that. Perhaps it was because Jack already knew about dragons.

Jack whistled silently, an old habit. "Interesting. The dragons say I must be a close descendent of a dragon companion, since I am immune to dragonfire." He raked his hand through his hair. "I never wondered how they could tell I would not be affected by dragonfire. I guess we know at least one thing that happened at Salamanca." A line of perspiration appeared on his brow.

Darcy had spent so many months imagining Jack dying in flames that the thought had lost its ability to shock him, but it was new to his brother. "Whatever saved you, I am grateful for it."

"And I." Jack wiped his forehead with the back of his hand, making an obvious attempt to rally from his shock. "But what brings you here? I dare not hope the war has been won and Napoleon defeated."

"Hardly. I was part of a last-ditch attempt to assassinate him. It failed, of course, and now I am trying to get home." The reality of it suddenly hit him. "By God, it is good to see you, Jack! Beyond good. It was worth everything just for this." Even worth losing the use of his arm. He would have happily given his arm in exchange for his brother.

"I cannot believe the dragons sent me to rescue you without a word!" Jack grumbled, but his color rose. "But tell me, what is the news of the war, and everyone at home?"

Chapter 36

DARCY FOLLOWED JACK THROUGH the illusions that guarded the Nest, trying not to wince at the prospect of walking straight through a stone cliff. It gave way before him, though, and suddenly he was inside a chamber decorated with glass mosaics. A large dragon sat coiled in it, her bronze scales glinting with ruby highlights, lacking the head crest that would mark a male. "You succeeded, then," she said approvingly to Jack.

Jack gave her a lazy mock salute. "And returned as promised." He seemed to have recovered from his shock over the news Darcy had given him.

"I never doubted that. But what have we here?" The dragon turned her attention to Darcy. "You do not look well, even for a mortal."

"He is my brother, astonishingly enough," Jack said. "The bastards beat him, and he is in a good deal of pain, though he would rather die than admit to it. Would you be willing to heal him?"

Darcy opened his mouth to protest that it was not so bad, but then he snapped it shut. If this dragon was willing to heal his wounds, he would be glad of it. He had no desire to appear before Elizabeth covered in bruises, with his eye nearly swollen shut.

The dragon brought her gold-circled eyes near his face. "Do you wish that, young mortal?"

"I would be grateful, but first I must deliver a warning. The soldiers are close to discovering your Nest."

The dragon ducked her head. "The woman who came before you told us. It is why I am standing guard here."

"You never mentioned any of this to me!" cried Jack.

"We do not wish to worry you, Little One. You will be kept safe, no matter what."

"I would still want to know!"

Little One? The dragon called Jack Little One? Oh, how his brother must hate that! "But there is more. Napoleon is himself a shape shifter."

A cloud of darkness seemed to fill the chamber. "So your Nest has informed us. The Eldest will wish to speak more to you of this. But first, allow me to make you well."

"You are very generous. What should I do?"

"Simply look into my eyes." Her aura shifted to one of comforting. She raised her forelegs and brought them together so that the heels of her talons rested on his cheeks, warm and heavy with magic.

He nearly staggered as a powerful presence flowed into him and spiraled down into his chest. It paused by his broken rib with a burst of heat, and suddenly the pain there was gone. Then the magic found his bullet wound. It lingered longer this time, tracing the path the bullet had taken, before traveling down his arms, first one and then the other. The purple bruises on his hands faded to yellow before disappearing entirely.

But she was not done. The power moved through his legs and then back up his body to circle through his skull. It was everywhere, his ears, his nose, even his eyeballs. Now he could open his eyes fully again. As the magic slowly withdrew, his face felt cool with the absence of her touch.

Her aura, though, was sad. "I am very sorry about the wound in your shoulder. It is better, but I could not fix it fully."

Yet the constant ache there was much lessened. And most amazing of miracles, the fingers of his right hand moved when he commanded them to. He bent his elbow, raising his forearm. It seemed as heavy as lead, but it moved. His arm worked!

"This..." He said brokenly, his voice trembling. "This is so much better. It is an amazing gift." He turned his hand over and back just because he could. Never had the prohibition against giving thanks to a dragon been harder to keep.

"I am happy that I could help, though I wish I could do more."

"This is beyond anything I ever hoped for."

Jack said gaily, "Excellent! Coquelicot is the finest healer in the Nest, and she loves doing it. We are all in disgustingly good health because of her."

"Mortals are very satisfying to heal," the dragon allowed. "You break so easily."

Darcy flexed his hand again. It did not close completely, but surely it would grow stronger with time. Even if it did not, he might be able to write again, to hold his reins properly, to carry his child. "I am forever in your debt. If there is any service, however small that I can ever do for you, I pray you to ask it."

Her aura turned to pleased embarrassment. "Go to the Eldest, then. The Little One will take you. I must remain at my post."

Yes. He needed to pass on his information, since Elizabeth did not know what the soldiers had told him. He should share the memories of the sea serpents, too. And as eager as he was to see Elizabeth again, to reassure her he was well, he would be glad of the opportunity to steal a little more time with Jack first.

At the Gate, Darcy shook Jack's hand. Two astonishments at once, that Jack was alive and so was Darcy's hand. "We will meet again," he said fiercely. "If nothing else, when the war ends, I will come back to see you."

"I will look forward to it. I would tell you to give everyone my greetings, but I know you cannot."

And it was true, because the Eldest had laid another binding on him. "It is not fair." He hated the idea of leaving Georgiana and his mother believing Jack was dead, but what choice did he have? Not that he could truthfully tell them Jack was safe, with the Nest about to come under attack.

Jack clapped his arm. "Many things in life are unfair. Now go, before Saxifrage here gets impatient." He nodded to the small green dragon by the Gate.

Darcy nodded and strode toward the ring of sparkling air that marked the Gate. What would it feel like? Determinedly he stepped over the threshold of the shimmering space. Soon he would be with Elizabeth again.

It felt like nothing at all. No resistance. Not even the air was different. The chamber looked exactly the same.

He turned to look back, and there Jack stood staring at him in shock.

"What happened? Why am I still here?" Darcy asked. Disappointment rushed through him, along with fear. How could he get home if the Gate did not work?

Jack turned up his hands and shrugged. "What is the matter?" he asked the dragon.

"Curious." The dragon carefully reached out a talon to the edge of the Gate. Sparks flew from it. He picked up a metal rod and pushed it into the shimmering air. Half of it disappeared. When he drew it back again, it became whole. "The Gate is working, but it will not take him."

"Why not?" Jack asked.

"I cannot say. He is not a companion, but he is your brother, is he not? You came through the Gate with no difficulty."

"I came through..." Jack sounded shocked. "Never mind that; how can we get Will home?"

The dragon moved his head from side to side. "That I cannot say. The Eldest might know, or Gentiane or Renoncule. They understand the Gate better than I."

"Come, Will. We need some answers."

Darcy could not agree more. It had never crossed his mind that the Gate would fail, leaving him stranded in the mountains of France to face an impending battle.

Darcy picked up a metal sculpture of a strange fae creature with a horse's forequarters and the tail of a fish. Jack's quarters had several of these, with mosaics on the wall similar to those he had seen in the Dark Peak Nest. Not the sort of thing he would have expected Jack to like. The room was bare of anything that indicated his brother's personality. Two battered books lay on the table beside the bed. Darcy flipped through them: a history of France and a tome on metallurgy, both in French. Jack's tastes usually ran more to travel guides and novels.

Had Jack been brought here with nothing but the clothes on his back? That would account for the lack of personal touches.

It had been nearly an hour since Jack had left him here while he sought information about the Gate. They had tried doing it together, but the first dragon they found flatly refused to speak in front of an unknown mortal, so his brother decided to try on his own.

Finally Jack appeared, pushing aside the blanket that hung over the entryway. Apparently dragons had little sense of privacy, so Jack must have improvised. He did not look pleased.

"What did you learn?" Darcy asked.

His brother scowled. "Nothing. They are all too busy making plans to protect the Nest. When I pressed, the Eldest suggested you travel by land instead."

"If it were that simple, I would have done so months ago!" Darcy said explosively. Dammit, if that was the best the dragons could offer, he would have been better off staying with Mme. Hartung and hoping to reach Prussia eventually.

If it were just a matter of delay, he could tolerate it for himself, but Elizabeth must be frantic. "Could I at least send a message through the Gate to reassure my wife that she is not a widow? My wife believes I am still a prisoner of the French, if not dead."

"I assume so, if your Nest will deliver it to her." Jack reached into a small desk and pulled out paper from a drawer. "You can use this. See how the dragons spoil me? They sent out one of their Kith specifically to get this for me. Not that I can write to anyone, but keeping a journal helps preserve my sanity in this place."

"Thank you." Darcy sat at the desk.

Jack winced. "I have obviously been here too long. Even hearing thanks makes me edgy. Speaking English tastes strange in my mouth. I even dream in French these days. Still, it is far better than one of Napoleon's prisoner camps, which would likely have been my fate otherwise." He looked thoughtful for a moment. "Write your letter, and I will go talk to Coquelicot, the healer you met. I doubt she knows much about the Gate, but she usually makes time for me."

Darcy nodded as he took up the well-sharpened quill and dipped it in the inkwell. "Good luck."

As the blanket swished behind Jack, Darcy wrote in a shaky but legible hand, "My dearest Elizabeth..."

Jack returned with the news that the healer dragon wished to see Darcy. When the two brothers arrived, Coquelicot asked, "How is that arm?"

"A little sore, which is hardly surprising, since I did not use it for so long. But it works, which is all I ask." Even if it was a long way from his usual strength.

"Ah, good. Now, the Little One has been telling me about your other problem. Is it true you cannot return to your home any other way?"

"Not without risking my life."

She tilted her head. "I do not know why the Gate refused you, nor why you would lack enough dragon blood when it allowed the Little One through. Still, there may be a way around it. You could attempt to create the lesser bond with one of us. Then the Gate should see you as a companion and allow you through."

His experiences to date with dragon magic did not warm him to the concept. "What is the lesser bond?" he asked with reluctance.

"It is similar to the companion bond, but temporary and with no sharing of Talent. We use it when a dragon with no companion wishes to take a short journey. With the lesser bond, they can travel away from the Nest with a human, as long as they return promptly."

Roderick had done something like that when the dragons set the wards at Pemberley, though the Welshman was far more comfortable with bonds than Darcy would ever be. But getting home to Elizabeth would be worth it. "What would I need to do?"

She stared at the floor for a long moment, her talons clicking together. Finally she said, "With a young dragon, it is a simple matter, only requiring a little of your blood. But all our youngsters are trying to bond elsewhere to escape the upcoming battle. No, I will do it myself, but with great care, for my blood is too strong for a mortal body. There are reasons why only young dragons take companions; when they are older, the blood bond would destroy a mortal's mind, if not kill him outright." Her aura settled into one of determination.

Blood. Of course it had to involve a blood bond. "Can you do that?"

"I believe so, yes." Another thoughtful pause. "I will need time to make a tincture for the lesser bond. A few days, perhaps. Are you willing?"

For any other dragon, he would have hesitated, if not outright refused, to do blood magic. But she had healed him and given him the use of his arm again. "Will it harm me?"

"No more than any other bloodletting. When you take the tincture, it may make you queasy, or perhaps give you excess energy."

It would let him return to Elizabeth. He would be with her at Pemberley when their child was born. That was worth the risk. "I am willing and grateful for your assistance."

"Come, then. Little One, will you help with bleeding him?" She produced a silver knife and a small basin from nowhere.

"Just tell me what to do," Jack said.

Chapter 37

ELIZABETH STIRRED FROM SLEEP the next morning to the sound of an argument outside.

"You cannot go in. Mrs. Darcy is still asleep," growled one of the footmen.

"She will want to be awakened for this," Roderick's Welsh-accented voice responded, broken by heavy breathing. "Immediately."

Elizabeth rubbed the sleep from her eyes. Roderick was not prone to dramatics. "Let him in," she called, pulling the counterpane up to hide her nightdress.

The door burst open to reveal the Welshman in a dressing gown. Had he not even bothered to dress before leaving the house? But his broad grin told her this was not bad news.

"Darcy is at the French Nest," he burst out. He bent over to hold his knees, clearly trying to recover from a run.

It was so unexpected she could not even take it in at first, and then joy began to radiate through her chest. Excited, she sat up. "What? Are you certain?"

"Rowan says so. The French Nest is sending their hatchlings here for safety, and one of them told him." Roderick straightened and threw back his head. "Lord, what a relief!"

Chandrika's hands pressed Elizabeth's shoulders back. "You must lie down, Mrs. Darcy. You know what the midwife said."

How could she lie back when she wanted to get up and dance, to embrace everyone in sight? Somehow she managed to obey. "What else do you know? When is he coming through the Gate? Tell me everything!"

Roderick's gaze became unfocused. "Apparently there is some problem with sending him through the Gate. The hatchlings do not know what it was, but they all agree that the rescued Englishman helped them go through the Gate."

Elizabeth clasped her hands together in front of her heart. Darcy was alive! "Is he well? Did they hurt him?"

The Welshman shook his head. "Rowan cannot tell. The hatchlings are very young and disoriented, in a new place among complete strangers, having left behind everyone they know. They likely would not be able to tell if a human was hurt... no, wait. One says he seemed to walk with no trouble, for what that is worth. Rowan will try to find out more, but first he must help the hatchlings settle."

"Thank you, thank you! And pray tell Rowan how much this news means to me." Tears of joy began to stream down her face, but she did not care who saw them. Her world was bright again, after days of darkness.

Cerridwen stirred from where she had slept by the hearth. "I will go and see if I can learn anything more." She lumbered to her feet.

"A good idea," said Roderick. "Though they may put you to work, too. Rowan says it is chaos there. They sent twenty hatchlings! It must be a huge Nest. I have no idea where we will put them all."

Elizabeth's mind finally began to work. "If they are sending all their young here, the situation there must be desperate."

"Or simply a sensible precaution," Roderick said. "They will not let anything happen to Darcy, in any case. Dragons always do their best to protect humans."

He was alive and free. She would hold onto that with all her might.

Darcy heard nothing more from the healer dragon for four days, a time of what Jack referred to as utter chaos in the Nest, dragons hurrying back and forth about urgent business. Their auras weighed on Darcy, so much worry, sadness, and anger. Who could blame them, when they faced the real possibility that their home would be left a smoking ruin like the Nests in Austria and Spain? Not to mention the terror that Napoleon would trap them into becoming killers, enslaved to the High King of Faerie. They seemed confident that they could delay the soldiers for at least several weeks, but he was not privy to their plans. And no one would tell him how they intended to protect Jack if the worst happened.

No matter how much Darcy longed to get home to Elizabeth and never set foot in France again, he could not stand by doing nothing as the dragons poured their energy into defending the Nest, so he offered his assistance. Alongside Jack and a few of the human Kith who served the dragons, he helped to build defenses for the Nest, digging traps to catch intruders and creating piles of rocks which could be tumbled down into narrow valleys.

But no defenses could last forever, so the Nest was evacuating as many dragons as possible. When Jack was sent on missions to the towns below, Darcy assisted at the Gate, herding young nestlings through, some no bigger than a puppy. They were all going to the Dark Peak Nest, since changing the destination of the Gate would take more power than the Nest could afford to dedicate to it in these circumstances. And Darcy was glad to help, for some of those nestlings were carrying the message of his presence at the Nest, after the Eldest had refused to allow anything in writing to be sent through.

He envied each nestling that disappeared through the Gate, even as he wondered how the Dark Peak Nest would handle this unexpected influx. What was Elizabeth thinking of his absence? What if Coquelicot could not manage to find a way to send him through the Gate?

At last the healer dragon sent word to meet her in the Gate chamber. She waited there, a leather satchel beside her, her aura weighed down with fatigue. "Are you ready?"

He felt a new sympathy for her. She must have worked very hard to help him yet again. "I am." Darcy glanced at Jack beside him. If only he could take his brother with him!

The dragon held out a stoppered glass vial whose contents swirled with iridescent ruby and amethyst. "First you must drink this. It may feel strange as you swallow it, but it will not harm you."

He took the tiny bottle in his hand. Magic thrummed from within it. "Should I sip it or take it all at once?"

"Whichever you prefer."

In for a penny, in for a pound. He opened the vial and swallowed it in one go.

It burned, like the intense heat of repulsion, but without pain. It tasted of the memory of free flight in open air, gliding off the mountain on giant wings, of the joy in seeing an autumn leaf bejeweled with dewdrops, of deep and abiding peace.

Warmth built in his belly, the heat of a fire on the cold night or friendship returned. It was odd, but by no means unpleasant. It made him feel strong, as if he could bend an iron bar with his bare hands.

She gave him the satchel. "This contains more of the elixir. You must drink one bottle each morning for the next fortnight without fail. This is very important. A bond like this is temporary, but it must not be taken lightly."

"I will." He could feel the bond building in him, a sudden sadness over leaving the dragon behind.

"One last thing." She brought out a silver locket, perhaps two inches wide. "Put this around your neck. We will mingle our blood inside it – not much, just a drop or two – and then you must go through the Gate immediately. Wear it until you are done with the elixir."

Like the other Artifacts he had encountered, it was heavier than he expected. He slid it over his head and hefted the satchel of elixir to his left shoulder.

Coquelicot reached out a foreleg to open the locket on his chest. Despite her size, her touch was delicate. With one talon, she nicked her opposite foreleg until her crimson blood filled the locket. "Now you."

She took his hand and made a tiny cut on his middle finger. Odd, he could barely feel it, as if her touch stopped the pain before it began. As his darker blood met hers in the locket, it hissed, and a few golden sparks flew. She snapped the locket shut. "Now go."

Darcy nodded to Jack. "Until we meet again." Without waiting for reply, he stepped into the Gate.

And into chaos. The temperature was suddenly warmer, the glowing lights brighter, and three dragons crowded the small chamber along with a pile of large crates.

He was in England, his own country! Where no one would arrest him, beat him, starve him. Where he was safe.

The smallest dragon, the currant-red one he had met before, came forward. "Ah, Darcy. From the Vosges? Pray step aside and allow us to move these through while they still have it open." The dragon slung a crate through, followed quickly by two more from the others.

It was bizarre watching the crates simply disappear. Especially as the Gate had left him a little dizzy, or perhaps it was the elixir.

The room was empty in just a few minutes. "My apologies, Darcy," said the dragon. Rowan, that was his name. "We are sending everything we can to help them protect their Nest, but they cannot afford the power to keep the Gate open for long."

"Understood." It would take far more than that to trouble him.

The dragon came a step closer and studied him. "You have the mark of another dragon."

It made him self-conscious, as if he had been caught in an infidelity. "I could not pass through the Gate on my own, so one of the dragons was kind enough to form the lesser bond with me."

"Ah, clever! The Eldest is eager to speak to you. May I take you to her?"

He ached to go straight to Elizabeth, but he could not deny that he had important information to deliver. "Indeed. Is it possible to send word to Pemberley that I am back? I do not want my wife to worry any longer than necessary."

Rowan's eyes unfocused briefly. "It is done. Roderick will tell her."

Roderick was at Pemberley again? Well, he supposed he was in for many surprises when he arrived.

Here he was, back in the chamber of the Eldest. It had only been four months, but it felt like years, as if it had been a different man who stood there then. A man who had never known hunger, the lack of a warm bed, or what it meant to be a prisoner. One who did not know what it meant to disguise himself, to run for his life, to be helpless, and the fear of losing the woman he loved.

What an innocent he had been! He, who had always had every advantage in life, yet had thought he knew everything.

The Eldest was unchanged, though. It was only Darcy who was different, as he returned the Artifact he had been given a lifetime ago. "It saved me, when all else seemed lost," he said, in lieu of thanks.

"I am glad of it," the Eldest said in her resonant voice. "I have learned something of your adventures from Companion Elizabeth, but I would appreciate hearing from you directly."

"Will you read me, then? I would not wish to miss giving you any details." And it would hurry the process along so he could go to Pemberley that much sooner. He could not wait to be in Elizabeth's arms, in his own home.

"You have changed. You used to find that uncomfortable."

"I have changed a great deal, and I spent the last fortnight in the French Nest."

"Ah, yes. I would be eager to hear any details about that as well. They have communicated little beyond the bare bones of their situation, no doubt because their time is better spent otherwise."

"I can share that, though I am under a binding about something that happened there." He suddenly realized how suspicious that must sound. "It is something personal about me, unrelated to the danger the Nest finds itself in."

The great dragon tilted her head. "How curious. Let us begin, then." She held out her forelegs.

Darcy grasped them and gazed up into her huge eyes, letting the power of her mind explore his as he replayed the events of his journey, from the sea serpents to the Vosges Nest. The painful parts still hurt, though the soothing presence of the Eldest eased the ache of the memories.

Finally the Eldest withdrew. "You have given me a great deal to think about, Friend Darcy. Your information is most valuable and may save many lives."

"I fear for the dragons of the Nest I just left." He had not intended to say that, but it was true. And he worried about Jack even more.

The nictitating membrane came down over the dragon's eyes. "It is a terrible situation. We must find a way to stop this mad dragon you call Napoleon, but it will be very difficult."

Then Rowan came scurrying in, looking tiny next to the bulk of the much larger dragon. "Forgive me, Eldest. My companion tells me Darcy must go to Pemberley immediately. Companion Elizabeth is in childbirth."

Darcy caught his breath. Already? Had she not said it would be another two months? He had to go to her this very instant. "Is there a horse I can borrow? Time is of the essence." There was no time to send to Pemberley for one.

Rowan said, "I will see what I can do."

Darcy gritted his teeth. The horse was a farm animal, more accustomed to dragging a plow or pulling a cart than being ridden. Getting him to go beyond a trot was an impossibility. Even that had to be broken by periods of walking. It would take him hours to get home at this rate.

He stopped at the first inn outside the Dark Peak to hire a faster animal, only to meet with a wholly unexpected refusal from the innkeeper who gave one look at his obviously foreign attire and French coins. "Darcy of Pemberley?" the man guffawed. "And I am King George. Take your traitor's money elsewhere."

It had made him seethe. A few months ago, he would have tried to demand the service with the assurance of a gentleman who had never been rejected, but his mission had taught him humility. He turned on his heel and left. He would have to make do with the farm horse until he reached a place where his face was known. But his stomach churned with the need to reach Elizabeth, to be beside her during this time.

And he had hoped to leave fear behind him in France.

He trotted on, the slow pace infuriating. It was not the horse's fault that they had not even gone half the distance needed.

In the distance, riders were approaching along the empty road. Ones on good horses with proper saddles. Was there any chance it would be someone who might recognize him and take pity on his situation?

The lead rider waved his arm, trying to catch his attention. As if there was anything else for him to look at! But as they drew closer, he recognized the third horse, the one without a rider. What was his own Hercules doing here?

He pushed his reluctant mount into a rough canter until he reached them. Pemberley grooms, both of them! And doing a poor job of hiding their shock at his current state.

"Mr. Darcy, sir! Mr. Roderick ordered us to bring you a fast horse," said the groom. "I hope we were right to listen."

They could not have brought him a greater prize. "Excellent work, and greatly appreciated," he said as he slid inelegantly from the ill-fitting saddle and hurried to Hercules's side. "Pray bring this one back to Pemberley until he can be returned."

"Yes, sir." The groom detached the lead he had used for Hercules. "Good to have you back, sir!"

Darcy threw himself into the saddle. As always, Hercules responded to his slightest touch, and soon they were flying like the wind.

Chapter 38

Darcy tossed the reins to a startled footman outside the cottage. Why in God's name was there a tent here? But that could wait. So could Pemberley, which was greeting him with an unprecedented surge of power, strong enough to make him stagger. He strode to the door and threw it open.

Inside was a hive of business, women everywhere. The bed had been moved to the middle of the room. But he cared about nothing but the figure lying there.

Elizabeth's hair was disheveled, coming out of a tight braid, and exhaustion lined her beloved face. Her eyes were closed, but she gripped Frederica's hand.

Darcy could do nothing but stare at her, aware that he was intruding on a scene forbidden to men, but unable to walk away. Not when his Elizabeth was there – and in pain.

Frederica leaned down. "Elizabeth, look who is here."

Her eyes flew open. "William!" Elizabeth cried, raising herself on her elbows. "Thank God!"

He was by her side in an instant, leaning down to gather her to him, cradling her beloved form. "Dearest, dearest Elizabeth!" he murmured.

"You made it," she whispered, and then she wrapped her arms around him, squeezing him tightly as if she dared not let him escape. "I thought I had lost you."

They were not alone, and she was in childbirth, so he did not cover her with kisses and pour out his heart to her as he longed to. "You cannot rid yourself of me so easily, my love. I will always come back to you." If it were up to him, he would never leave her side again.

"Good," she said softly, and then released her fervent grip on him, as if fatigued.

He laid her gently back against her pillows and took her hand in his. "But what of you, my dearest? Is there anything I can do to help?"

She gave a weak smile. "I have all the assistance I can possibly need, but having you beside me is the best gift in the world." Her eyes drifted closed, as if she were too fatigued to keep them open.

Frederica said, "This began just before midnight, so she is very tired. But I imagine she would like to hear your voice."

"How did you escape?" Elizabeth asked drowsily.

"Two men came to rescue me," he said. How he wished he could tell her about Jack! His story could not be complete without that. "They hid me in a hay cart and brought me to the Nest. And my lynx has been wreaking havoc on the soldiers, both while they held me prisoner and afterwards. Apparently he holds a grudge."

Her lips curved upwards. "Good for Fire Eyes. Did they hurt you?"

There were times when telling the truth was over-rated, but with Frederica present, he could not outright lie. "They roughed me up a little, but I am perfectly well now. There was..." The words stopped in his mouth. Was his healing by Coquelicot under a binding, too? "The dragons there took good care of me."

Elizabeth gasped suddenly and her hand tightened on his. Perspiration dotted her brow as the lines of stress deepened.

Someone touched his arm. Chandrika. He had completely forgotten everyone else's existence.

"Step back, Mr. Darcy. She is having a pain," the Indian maid said. Then, perhaps in response to his uncomprehending expression, she added, "You can still hold her hand, if you wish."

As if he would ever let go of it!

"Breathe, Mrs. Darcy." It was the midwife, Mrs. Sanford. His unknown half-sister, whose brother had died at Salamanca. "Do not push. It is not yet time."

"But I must!" It was almost a wail.

"You must not," Mrs. Sanford said firmly. "Look at your husband. Think of how far he has come to see you. He does not want you to push."

What was she talking about? What was she not supposed to push, and why should she not do it? But Frederica and the other women were nodding in agreement, so he said, "Pray do not push, my sweetest. It is very important." Whatever it was.

Elizabeth was panting. "It hurts so much," she whispered.

He could not bear to see her in pain. "Is this normal?" he asked Mrs. Sanford desperately.

"Completely normal," she said drily. "You should not be here, Mr. Darcy, but for your wife's sake, I will permit it for now – as long as you help her stay calm." It was definitely a command.

He nodded. She was the expert, after all. Then he turned back to Elizabeth. "Look at me, my love. You can do this. You crossed France in wartime all by yourself, and I am so very proud of you."

A cry escaped her, and she grabbed for his other hand, squeezing it until it hurt.

"I am here with you," he whispered.

Then suddenly she relaxed, breathing more easily. The spasm must have passed.

He leaned down to kiss her cheek. "My poor love. Thank you for working so hard for our child."

But her eyes were fixed on his hands. "Your arm. You are using it."

As if that mattered, compared to what she was going through. "It is better. As I said, the dragons took good care of me."

Darcy paced the clearing through the long afternoon shadows, back and forth, back and forth, as if his footsteps could somehow help Elizabeth. At least he was home, where the welcoming power of Pemberley flowed through him. The vitality of it was always a shock when he returned after a long absence, but this time was even more so, as if the magic in the land had deepened into a new strength. The richness of the soil and the life of it was a comfort, but it could not take his mind away from what was happening in the cottage.

He had left without complaining when the midwife told him it was time to go, since she had bent every rule to allow him to stay as long as he did. He still wanted to rip the door off its hinges for daring to stand between him and his Elizabeth.

The thick walls that had once provided a quiet refuge also silenced most of the sounds from inside. But Elizabeth's periodic cries of pain still came through faintly, making him ache that he could not relieve them.

A footman came towards him with a plate of cold meat and fruit. Darcy tried to wave him away, but the servant ignored him. "At least have something to drink, sir, to keep up your strength."

With a sigh, he accepted a glass of what looked like wine. It shocked his mouth by turning out to be port. The port he always drank at Pemberley, not the wine served everywhere in France. A taste of home. Why did it seem so strange?

He was off-balance, no question. And he needed to take better care of himself, for Elizabeth's sake. He had not eaten anything since that morning unless he counted the elixir, which might explain his odd sense of disorientation. "You are right. I should eat," he told the footman.

Immediately several more servants appeared, carrying a small table and a stool. The food was set before him, and all he needed to do was sit and eat. Just as it had always been, all his life, until he went to France and had to fend for himself. He looked at each servant in turn, met their eyes, and said, "I thank you."

They looked startled, but the footman who had brought him the port recovered first. "We are glad you are back, sir."

As soon as he tasted the first slice of venison, his hunger came roaring back. He demolished the entire plate between glances at the cottage door, as if watching it closely would make something happen.

Another pained cry, a longer one, and then more silence. He had learned that much, that the pains came and went, with an easier time in between. But this silence continued. Was Elizabeth better, or had something gone terribly wrong?

Finally Mrs. Reynolds came out of the cottage, closing the door quietly behind her. Exhaustion lined her face.

Darcy jumped to his feet, almost toppling the stool, and hurried to her. "What is happening?"

"It is a girl, sir," she said, but without any of the triumph or joy he would have expected.

"Elizabeth," he said, his heart in his throat. "Has something happened to her?"

She shook her head. "She is as well as can be expected. But the babe is small and not as strong as we would like."

Dread filled him. "What does that mean?"

"I cannot say, sir. Only time will tell."

"May I see Elizabeth? And...the baby?"

"Not yet. Once the afterbirth is delivered, if Mrs. Darcy is agreeable, you can come in."

The midwife carried a lantern as she came out of the cottage. "May I speak to you privately, sir?" she asked Darcy, gesturing towards the servants by the tent.

His heart rose in his throat. "Of course." He led her away from the others, up the slope towards the ruined keep. "What is the matter?"

She met his eyes. "The baby is still with us, but I do not expect her to live. It happens, when they are born too early. I am very sorry."

His mouth was dry. Their child, on whom they had pinned so many hopes, whose existence had let him draw on his land Talent while in France, whom he loved so fiercely even without meeting her. Dying before she had a chance to live, just like the son Anne de Bourgh had carried. "And my wife?"

"She does not appear to be in any danger." She watched him steadily.

There was one thing he had to know. "Did this happen because of her travels? Or because of the Talent we used?"

She rubbed her hands together. "We do not know what makes some babies come too soon. Oftentimes it seems to happen for no reason at all. Your wife tells me her mother lost an early child, too. It is tragic, but not uncommon."

"I thank you for helping her." The words seemed to burn in his mouth. He ought to say something more to her, now that he knew she was his half-sister, but there was nothing left in him to give.

"I have asked the others to leave to let you have some privacy. I will remain just outside if you need me."

He moistened his lips. "How long..." He could not even finish the sentence.

"Hours, perhaps, or even a day or two. It is in God's hands."

He nodded jerkily, not trusting himself to speak. Instead he headed for the cottage door.

Inside, Elizabeth sat propped up in the bed, a tiny bundle in her arms and a slow trickle of tears running down her face. She barely looked up at him as he entered, but she shifted to make room for him to sit beside her on the bed.

As he sat, he placed his arms around hers, a double ring of protection around the baby. If only it could make a difference. "I am so sorry, my love," he whispered.

"She is so tiny and so perfect." Elizabeth's voice shook. "It is my fault. I should have taken more care." A sob broke through.

"Elizabeth, listen to me. You know my first wife had a child who did not live. He was born too soon, too, and Anne was as coddled and as careful as any woman could be. It made no difference. The fault may be in me, or in my seed." He could not fix anything for their child, but he would protect Elizabeth with every ounce of his strength.

She bowed her head silently.

"May I see her?" he asked.

Elizabeth tipped back the swaddling cloth that half-covered the infant's head. "Her name is Jane. For your brother and my sister. I was going to call her Jenny."

Her face was impossibly tiny, smaller than a doll's, pale and wrinkled. He could see her fighting for each rapid breath. "She is beautiful." Because she was. The most beautiful, precious thing he had ever seen, and they were going to lose her. Their little Jenny, the child of their love.

Elizabeth raised her tear-filled eyes to him. "Will you hold her and try to give her strength from the land? I tried it and it seemed to help her a little, but Frederica made me stop. She said I was giving too much."

He would have happily opened a vein if it would have helped little Jenny. "Can you show me how to hold her?"

Shakily Elizabeth placed the baby in his arm. "Like that, so her head is supported." Her voice caught.

She weighed almost nothing, like a wren, and now that she was pressed against his chest, he could feel even through the swaddling how hard she was working to breathe. Her skin was so thin he could see the veins through it, and his heart wanted to burst with love for his tiny, doomed daughter.

He grounded his feet on the floor, letting his Talent sink into the land. As it received him eagerly, he begged it in his head to help his daughter, the flesh of his flesh, the blood of his blood. The words he would have said in the ceremony to bond her to the land.

The power wound up around his legs, tingling through him. He laid his finger on Jenny's cheek – how tiny it was in comparison! – and let the power trickle through. Just a bit at first, fearful of hurting her with too much. He could feel the weight of it entering her.

He knew nothing of the healing arts, but desperation was a powerful instructor, so he told his power to make it easier for her to breathe. He felt his own lungs expanding and contracting, as he tried to give that strength to the baby. Rocking back and forth, his entire existence focused on the slight quick flutters of her chest.

Elizabeth asked tremulously, "Is her breathing a little better, do you think?"

"Perhaps." Or it might be just his own desire speaking, and even then, he knew it was not enough. Her skin was still pale, almost blue. And Elizabeth looked so bereft, sitting there with empty arms. "Perhaps if you hold her, I could try to give her power with both hands." Not that he wanted to give up his precious burden, not for a second.

"It is worth a try." But there was no hope in her voice, and her tears flowed.

He managed to transfer little Jenny back to her, his hands wanting to linger on her tiny form. Then he put both forefingers on her face and resumed feeding her the power of the earth. He would give her everything he could. And now he could feel the subtle tang of Elizabeth's Talent underneath his.

It was so terribly unfair, that all their love and all their Talent was not enough to save one tiny baby. He wanted to howl his pain to the sky, but all he could do was to try to treasure the few moments they had.

A rap at the door interrupted them. Who would dare interrupt this moment? Then a woman in full Indian regalia and a heavy veil sailed in without waiting for an invitation. It took Darcy a moment to recognize Rana Akshaya, the Indian mage he had last seen before his wedding. No, the Indian *dragon* – Elizabeth had mentioned that in France.

Rana Akshaya ignored his glare, her gaze firmly on Elizabeth. "Chandrika informs me your infant is unwell. Do you wish me to attempt to heal her?"

Could it be possible? A normal healing Talent was rarely useful for more than injuries and infections, but his mother had mentioned Rana Akshaya's extraordinary powers.

Elizabeth's mouth dropped open in a gasp. "Would you? If you could do anything, I would be very glad of it."

"Perhaps I can help her, and perhaps not. It depends upon the problem." Her tone was completely neutral, as if she did not care one way or another, but Darcy was prepared to fall on his knees and beg if that would make a difference.

She came to the bedside, where little Jenny lay swaddled in Elizabeth's arms, her face even more blue-tinged. Without a word, she peeled back the cloth to expose her entire head, revealing her sparse black hair. She cradled her tiny head in her talons, which looked huge in comparison.

Magic thickened the air, rough and flavored with cinnamon. At first Jenny's infant face crumpled, as if she wanted to cry if only she could get enough air, the veins under her thin skin even more prominent. But she did not seem to be in pain. If anything, she seemed to relax a little.

Even if this healing only made her more comfortable, that would be something. Watching her struggle was devastating. Darcy's lips moved in silent prayer, his eyes fixed on his daughter's face.

Rana Akshaya straightened, lifting her hands from Jenny's head. So quickly? Was there nothing she could do?

"That will help," she announced. "It was a simple matter, a hole in the vessels of her heart. I repaired it and cleared her lungs. She will be very hungry and will need to sleep a great deal."

And it was true. Jenny's skin was turning pink, and suddenly she let a howl of protest, far louder than any sound that had come from her before. Elizabeth clutched her tightly, tears streaming down her face, clearly beyond the ability to speak.

Darcy did it for her. "I have no words to tell you how much this means to us. Your generosity does you great honor." He had to raise his voice to be heard over Jenny's squalling, the sweetest sound he had ever heard.

Rana Akshaya did not respond to him. Instead the mage – no, the dragon – studied Elizabeth. "Chandrika knows healings come at a price. She came to me, offering to return to my service for life if I helped your hatchling."

Elizabeth's teary eyes widened. "Chandrika did that? Oh." She turned her eyes to little Jenny. pressing her lips to her forehead. "It was...good of her."

"I refused her. I have no need of servants who wish to be elsewhere. This healing was a gift to your dragon, who helped me find your Nest, and to you, for the hospitality you have shown me." She said it almost grudgingly, as if she resented owing anything.

Elizabeth swallowed and said, "You could not have chosen a gift I would treasure more. I will always remember what you have done."

Rana Akshaya gave a curt nod and walked out without a word.

Darcy gathered Elizabeth in his arms, with little Jenny between the two of them, his heart overflowing. She sobbed in his embrace, but he could tell it was tears of happiness. They were together again, and now they were a family, too.

Then Jenny began to cry again, a good, healthy cry, and Darcy released Elizabeth.

Elizabeth's eyes were glistening with happiness. "Could you ask Mrs. Sanford to come in and help me to feed her?"

"With pleasure, my love." At that moment, Darcy would have considered it an honor to jump over the moon for Elizabeth and their Jenny.

Chapter 39

I N THE MORNING, DARCY emerged from the cottage, bleary-eyed from lack of sleep while at the same time floating on a cloud of joy. Little Jenny was in Elizabeth's arms, both sleeping peacefully.

He almost stumbled across Roderick, who rose from a stool by the tent outside. "Good to see you back, Darcy. How are they doing?" He tipped his head towards the cottage.

Darcy beamed. "Both are well. And my deepest thanks, both for sending word to the Nest that I was needed here, and for getting my horse out to meet me."

The Welshman laughed. "Easily done. Dragons do not understand why we make such a fuss about childbirth. When it is their time, they simply lay their eggs and then go on with their day." He seemed more light-hearted than Darcy remembered. "I am glad you made it in time."

"No one could be happier than I about that," Darcy said fervently.

"Rowan heard from Cerridwen that you plan to do the land bonding, and I wondered if you would like any assistance with the preparations," Roderick said. "I know the ritual, at least as we perform it in Wales."

A year ago Darcy would have refused, but he had learned hard lessons since then. "I would be glad of it. My right hand is still not strong, which will make it a challenge to dig."

Roderick nodded. "So I have heard. Dragons are terrible gossips, you know." There was something about the off-hand way he said it that raised an inkling of suspicion in Darcy.

"You and Rowan…" he prompted.

He grinned. "Yes, we bonded while you were gone. I hope you do not mind that your house is overrun with dragon companions. Soon enough I will be returning to Wales, though, once the Nest here can spare Rowan." A fleeting shadow crossed his face.

"Congratulations," Darcy said, and to his surprise, he meant it.

"He says you took on a lesser bond, too. An interesting experience, is it not?"

Darcy stiffened. In the chaos of childbirth and the aftermath, he had forgotten completely about the potion he was supposed to drink each day. "Excuse me a moment." He tiptoed back into the cottage, hardly daring to breathe lest he wake Elizabeth and Jenny, and fetched his worn satchel.

Once outside, he plucked out a vial and downed the contents. The sweet taste, redolent of wildflowers and slightly spicy, warmed him deep inside. Suddenly it felt as if the great red healer dragon was standing beside him, beaming down at him with pride. He let out a long breath as a feeling of peace grew within him.

Roderick stared at him in shock. "What is that? I can feel the power of it from here."

"The dragon I bonded to made it for me. I am supposed to drink it every day for a fortnight."

The Welshman frowned. "I have never heard of such a thing for the lesser bond. Well, no doubt they do many things differently in France. If it brought you home, that is the most important thing."

The tincture had cleared Darcy's thoughts, too. "The Nest here seems to have had a sudden change of heart about taking companions."

Roderick glanced to each side, as if making certain they were not overheard, and then he said in a low voice, "It is because of what has happened. If a Nest is attacked, a dragon with a companion can escape and find a new Nest. Suddenly it is a great advantage to bond to a mortal."

Darcy nodded slowly. It fit with what Coquelicot had said, about the young dragons in the French Nest trying to take on companions quickly.

They were all preparing for war, humans and dragons alike.

Darcy chose a spot in the center of the oak grove. His own afterbirth had been buried near the house, like his father's before him, but it seemed correct to do the rites here, in the heart of Pemberley. It would be easier for Elizabeth, too.

With Roderick behind him, Darcy placed the spade in the ground, right in the center of the oak grove, and began to dig. The shovel slid in easily as the land cooperated with him, opening itself and separating out the roots to make way for his spade. He sank into his knowledge of the earth, sensing the earthworms and the insects, the burrowing dormice preparing for winter, the squirrels with their nests almost full of nuts. The powerful roots of the majestic oaks supported it all.

How he had missed this connection when he was in France!

To think that a year ago he had also been without his land Talent at Netherfield, preparing to wed Elizabeth! How different his life was now – yet the world beneath the surface was unchanged, full of the cycle of life. Birth, death, and rebirth in the spring.

After the first two shovelfuls, he surrendered the spade to Roderick, who made short work of the rest.

Then Darcy returned to the cottage, where Elizabeth was now sitting in a rocking chair nursing little Jenny – and three dragon nestlings clustered around her. Little ones, the largest the size of a roe deer, but they were all bigger than the puppy-sized hatchlings he had helped through the Gate in the Vosges Nest. Together they crowded the small room.

"What is this?" Darcy asked.

Elizabeth turned a rueful gaze on him. "Apparently little Jenny is going to have a dragon brother or sister, at least for a time. The Eldest insists, because of her exposure to dragon magic."

"Are not all children of dragon companions exposed to it?"

She smiled, then looked down at their baby with a bewitchingly adoring expression. "She more than most. She was part of me when I made the blood bond to Pemberley with Cerridwen, when I took my final vows, and when I came through the Gate. Add in Rana Akshaya's healing, and that is a great deal of dragon magic for a very tiny mortal baby."

His stomach churned. "Do they think it may have hurt her?"

She shook her head. "More that it might cause her Talent to be unpredictable, or even to erupt very early. Hence the desire to have a dragon watching her, for her own safety."

He frowned. "No. I will not agree to a blood bond." Jenny was far too tiny, and he would not permit even the slightest danger to touch her.

"As I understand it, the bond would be only on the nestling's side. That is why they are trying to decide who is best suited for her."

"I thought a dragon cannot be away from the Nest without a companion."

The largest of the nestlings looked up. "That is only for grown dragons. We are young enough to go anywhere." He said it as if it were obvious, and Darcy a poor pupil not to have known it.

Yet another dragon in his household, which was apparently quite full of them at present. Cerridwen in Elizabeth's bedroom, Rana Akshaya in the state parlor, Frederica's dragon in the ballroom, Rowan somewhere with Roderick, and now another for the nursery.

But he no longer doubted their motives, and if it helped keep Jenny safe, that was all that mattered.

The baby seemed to be done with nursing. Elizabeth lifted her to her shoulder and tentatively patted her back.

"Mine." It was the mid-sized dragon, the one no larger than a fawn. "She is mine, I think. I can feel her." He sounded awed. Or was it a she? If there was a way to tell with a dragon too young to have developed the head crest that marked the adult males, he had not learned it. Darcy almost envied the creature; how he would love to be able to feel his daughter's presence! Perhaps this would turn out to be a good thing.

Darcy aimed a bow at the nestling. "May I have the honor of knowing your name?"

The tiny dragon did not take his eyes from Jenny, watching her as if she were the most fascinating thing in the universe, a sentiment with which Darcy wholly concurred. "I am Agate."

"You are welcome to our home, Agate." Darcy turned to Elizabeth and added, "I am about to complete Jenny's land bond. Do you wish to join me, since you have your own bond to Pemberley? But only if you feel able to walk that far, of course."

"I would not miss it, and I am eager to get my legs under me after all this time in bed," she said firmly. She stood up, handing the baby to Chandrika, and then winced at her first step.

Alarmed, Darcy said, "Perhaps you should stay here, if it hurts you."

She gave an amused, if weary, laugh, music to his ears. "It is normal to have pain after pushing a baby out, even a very small one! But walking will help me heal." That was his Elizabeth, always ready to press onward.

Now he was particularly glad that he had chosen a nearby spot for the ritual.

He collected the package Mrs. Sanford had prepared for him. His half-sister, another new beginning.

A different dragon was waiting outside the cottage, an unfamiliar one, with wings glinting in blue and bronze like Cerridwen's. Darcy stopped abruptly and stared. It *was* Cerridwen, doubled in size, if not more. No longer the size of a small stag, but an imposing figure larger than a stallion. He had not seen her in dragon form since before he had gone to France, but still, that was an astonishing rate of growth.

Cerridwen said nothing, only lowered her head in acknowledgement of the importance of the ceremony about to take place, but under his feet, her familiar dragon power swirled through the earth.

Darcy nodded back and led Elizabeth into the grove. There he gently laid the wool-wrapped afterbirth in the prepared hole. Letting his power sink deeply into the land, he covered it with the earth of Pemberley. At last all the soil he and Roderick had removed was back in place, heaped up slightly over the surrounding ground.

Darcy caught Elizabeth's gaze and held it. Then he spoke the ancient phrases his father had taught him, letting the ritual words roll off his tongue in each of the ancient languages the land had known, Celtic, Latin, Saxon, Norman French, and finally English. "Let my daughter, the flesh of my flesh, blood of my blood, become part of the land which gives us life. Let the earth be one with her, that both may gain strength through their bond."

A capricious breeze blew through the grove, lifting the curls by Elizabeth's face as she echoed the ritual language. Somehow he had not expected that, but of course her father must have taught her as well. Now they were joining together their two bloodlines in one land bond, echoing the love that brought them together and had given them little Jenny.

As she finished, Darcy stepped forward to the pile of soil and leaves, a small knife in his hand. This was the one piece of blood magic that he had always been taught was good and right. He set the sharp knife to the inside of his elbow and twisted it.

It took two tries before his blood flowed into the earth, pooling briefly until he spoke the final words. "It is done."

"It is done," Elizabeth repeated.

And the land answered, too, with a rush of power and life rising up into him, a gift of acceptance and acknowledgement. From the stunned look on Elizabeth's face, she must be feeling it, too.

His blood sank and disappeared. Then, unexpectedly, something green began to emerge from the same spot, a tiny seedling among the fallen autumn leaves. First just tendrils, then leaves, and finally a bud, growing before his very eyes. It opened into a scarlet poppy – a miniature one, only a few inches tall.

Elizabeth said shakily, "My father never mentioned this part."

"Nor mine," said Darcy, his mouth dry. "And he would have told me." Was it an omen? An illusion? Or something else entirely? He crouched down and brushed it cautiously with one fingertip. The leaves moved and bounced back against his touch. Apart from its size and being out of season, it was just an ordinary flower.

One that felt welcoming – and celebratory. The land seemed content with it, too.

Once he would have paid no attention to such unscientific notions, but he had learned better, and he was willing to hope. "I think it is a good sign. Perhaps the land recognizes all the magic that has gone into our Jenny."

Elizabeth tilted her head. "Have you given blood to Pemberley before?"

"Not unless you count when my afterbirth was buried." Darcy could not take his eyes off the bright flower.

"Before your bond to Georgiana and your lesser bond to the dragon in France, then," she said thoughtfully.

"And before our connection."

Then Cerridwen's voice came from behind them, but something was different about it. Not her usual flute-like tones, but something sonorous and ringing that raised the hairs on the back of Darcy's neck. "Just as your land has become a beacon of safety to many races, your child joins the blood of humans, royal fae, and dragons. She will become a bridge between the great powers, between the past and the future, between the mortal world and Faerie, supported by the redoubled power of Pemberley." Her words echoed off the ancient oaks surrounding them.

Darcy turned to stare at her. The dragon stood at the edge of the grove as if frozen there. Then, as if something had awoken her, she shook out her wings and stretched. In her usual voice, she said, "How odd that was! Do you think it was a prophecy? They said that might happen to me."

A prophecy. As soon as she said the word, Darcy knew deep in his bones that it was the truth. There were a few prophecies mentioned in the old dragon tales, always of deep significance. Now there was one about his daughter. A chill ran down his spine.

Elizabeth, though, seemed delighted, excitement sparkling through her fatigue. "You said she would be a bridge between the past and the future – and that means there will be a future, not merely a disaster!"

Cerridwen cocked her head. "Do you know, I think you may be right!"

Darcy said slowly, "You mentioned the redoubled magic of Pemberley. Since my return, I have felt that the land is stronger than it was before."

The dragon's chest rippled with amusement, and she made a sound that was a deeper version of her old kestrel's kee-kee-kee. "Of course it is. Pemberley has always had powerful magic because of the Dragon Stones. When I gave it my blood to help Elizabeth bond to the land, it became something even greater. The lesser fae have added uncanny magic of their own, and the presence of so many dragons has an effect, too."

Pemberley was his rock, the firm foundation he had always stood on. How could it have been altered? He himself had been transformed, both from marrying Elizabeth and his experiences in France, but at some deep level he wanted Pemberley to always be the same. But of course the land changed all the time, from season to season, with new crops or grazing animals, with cold snaps and storms. It had provided a home for ancient tribes as well as modern civilization, taking in new generations of Darcy heirs every few decades. The roots of Pemberley were solid, and they could adapt to a new age of magic, too.

Elizabeth nodded slowly, as if this explained something she had wondered about. "And your prophecy. What could it mean?"

Cerridwen sat back on her haunches. "It is a very odd feeling to have said something I do not understand," she said plaintively. "But there it is."

Just then the little nestling from the cottage waddled into the clearing. "Chandrika asked me to tell you Jenny needs to feed again."

Elizabeth smiled down at him. "I see you will be a helpful member of our household."

Agate seemed to swell with pride. "I will do what I can."

She gave Darcy a ruefully amused look. "And I have a task that cannot wait, despite prophecies, miraculous flowers, and magic redoubled. Our little Jenny may change the world someday, but for now she is a hungry baby who needs her mother." She held out her hand to Darcy. "Will you come with me, my love?"

He took it with alacrity and raised it to his lips. Whatever the future might bring, he would meet it with his beloved Elizabeth beside him.

Coming in 2025: The Guardians of Pemberley

THE THRILLING CONCLUSION TO
FITZWILLIAM DARCY, MAGE

Preorder Now!

About the author

Abigail Reynolds may be a nationally bestselling author and a physician, but she can't follow a straight line with a ruler. Originally from upstate New York, she studied Russian and theater at Bryn Mawr College and marine biology at the Marine Biological Laboratory in Woods Hole. After a stint in performing arts administration, she decided to attend medical school, and took up writing as a hobby during her years as a physician in private practice.

A life-long lover of Jane Austen's novels, Abigail began writing variations on *Pride & Prejudice* in 2001, then expanded her repertoire to include a series of novels set on her beloved Cape Cod. Her books have won multiple awards and several have been national bestsellers. Her most recent releases are *Spellbound at Pemberley*, *The Price of Pride*, *A Matter of Honor*, and *Mr. Darcy's Enchantment*. You can find her other books listed on her Author Page at Amazon. Her books have been translated into seven languages. She lives on Cape Cod with her family and a menagerie of animals. Her hobbies do not include sleeping or cleaning her house.

Visit Abigail's website at Pemberley Variations

Also by Abigail Reynolds

Spellbound at Pemberley
The Magic of Pemberley
The Price of Pride
A Matter of Honor
Mr. Darcy's Enchantment
Conceit & Concealment
Mr. Darcy's Journey
Alone with Mr. Darcy
The Darcys of Derbyshire
Mr. Darcy's Noble Connections
To Conquer Mr. Darcy
What Would Mr. Darcy Do?
By Force of Instinct
Mr. Darcy's Undoing
Mr. Fitzwilliam Darcy: The Last Man in the World
The Man Who Loved Pride & Prejudice
Morning Light
Mr. Darcy's Obsession
A Pemberley Medley
Mr. Darcy's Letter

The Darcy Brothers (co-author)
Mr. Darcy and the Enchanted Library (co-author)